Maria Luisa
bh regent of Spain

49
Pietro +
Marianne - diff. centuries

Carol

650.451.8272

fresco painter
Intermassen

Lina + Lene -
daughters of cow-man
he reads books on heraldry

Fela -
daughter of
a horsed man

Innocenza - cook

Raffaele Cuffa - valet
lodge in Bagheria - she
stays there - father leaves it to her
husband - Pietro Maria
stays in Palermo
3 girls before a boy
Marianus

The Silent Duchess

Giuseppe influenced by ideas of Signoretti's wife Domitilla

XVII. birth of Ferdinand son of Chas. III

The Silent Duchess

Dacia Maraini

Translated from the Italian by
Dick Kitto and Elspeth Spottiswood

Afterword by Anna Camaiti Hostert

The Feminist Press
at The City University of New York
New York

Published by
The Feminist Press at The City University of New York
Wingate Hall/City College
Convent Avenue at 138th Street
New York, NY 10031

First U.S. edition, 1998

Originally published in 1990 in Italian as *La lunga vita di Marianna Ucrìa* by RCS Rizzoli Libri S.p.A.,
Via Mercenate 91, 20138 Milan, Italy. Published by arrangement with RCS Rizzoli Libri.
English translation originally published in 1992 in Great Britain by Peter Owen Publishers, 73 Kenway
Road, London SW5 0OR, England. Published by arrangement with Peter Owen Publishers.

Library of Congress Cataloging-in-Publication Data
Maraini, Dacia.
    [Lunga vita di Marianna Ucrìa. English]
    The silent duchess / Dacia Maraini ; translated from the Italian by Dick Kitto and Elspeth
Spottiswood ; afterword by Anna Camaiti Hostert. — 1st U.S. ed.
        p.   cm.
    ISBN 1-55861-194-0 (hardcover : alk. paper)
    I. Kitto, Dick.   II. Spottiswood, Elspeth.   III. Title.
PQ4873.A69L8613   1998   98-22699
853'.914—dc21   CIP

The Feminist Press would like to thank Helene D. Goldfarb, Florence Howe, Joanne Markell,
Caroline Urvater, Genevieve Vaughan, Patricia Wentworth and Mark Sagan, and Marilyn Williamson
for their generosity in supporting this publication.

Special thanks to Rose Trillo Clough and Sara Clough for encouraging The Feminist Press to give
voice to *The Silent Duchess*.

Front and back matter typesetting by Dayna Navaro.
Text typeset by Action Typesetting Limited, Gloucester, England.
Printed on acid-free paper in the United States of America by McNaughton & Gunn.

*The Ucrìas
a family tree*

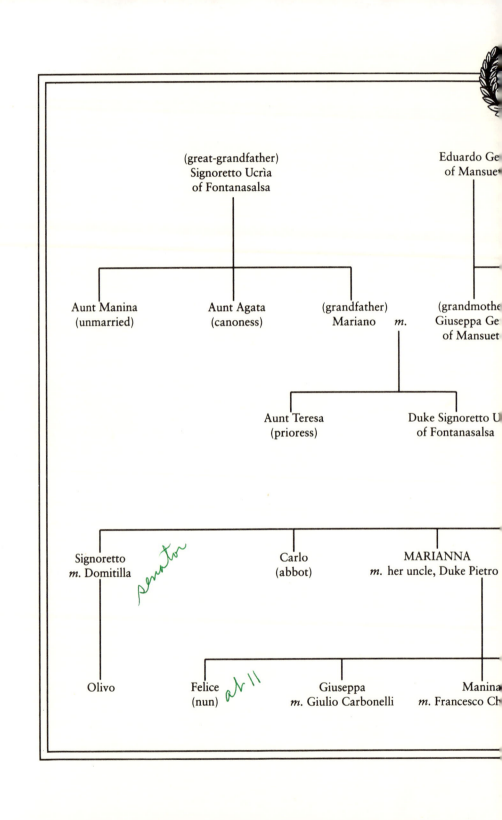

(great-grandfather)
Signoretto Ucrìa
of Fontanasalsa

Eduardo Ge
of Mansue

Aunt Manina
(unmarried)

Aunt Agata
(canoness)

(grandfather)
Mariano   *m.*

(grandmothe
Giuseppa Ge
of Mansuet

Aunt Teresa
(prioress)

Duke Signoretto U
of Fontanasalsa

Signoretto
m. Domitilla

senator

Carlo
(abbot)

MARIANNA
m. her uncle, Duke Pietro

Olivo

Felice
(nun)

at 11

Giuseppa
m. Giulio Carbonelli

Manina
m. Francesco Ch

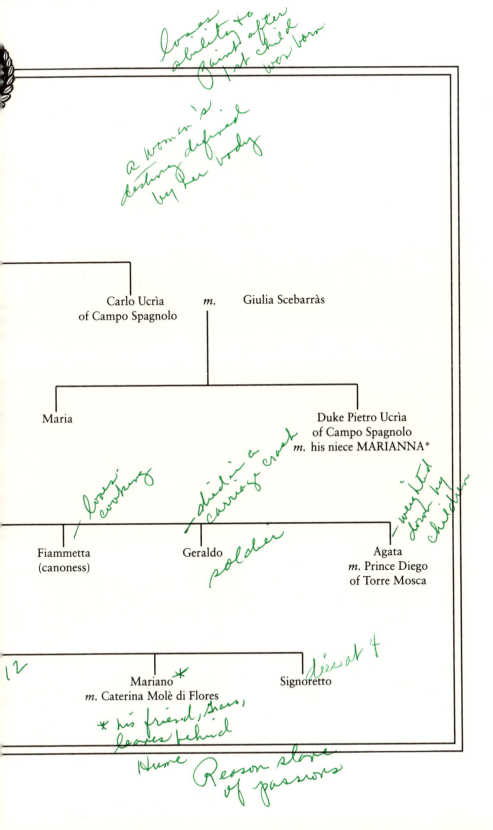

Carlo Ucrìa
of Campo Spagnolo   *m.*   Giulia Scebarràs

Maria

Duke Pietro Ucrìa
of Campo Spagnolo
m. his niece MARIANNA*

Fiammetta
(canoness)

Geraldo

Agata
m. Prince Diego
of Torre Mosca

Mariano *

m. Caterina Molè di Flores

Signoretto

The Silent Duchess

I

Here they are, a father and a daughter. The father fair, handsome, smiling; the daughter awkward, freckled, fearful. He stylish and casual, his stockings ruffled, his wig askew; she imprisoned inside a crimson bodice that highlights the wax-like pallor of her complexion.

The little girl watches her father in the mirror as he bends down to adjust his white stockings over his calves. His mouth moves but the sound of his words is lost as it reaches her ears, as if the visible distance between them were only a stumbling block: they seem to be close but they are a thousand miles apart.

The child watches her father's lips as they move more and more rapidly. Although she cannot hear him, she knows what he is saying: that she must hasten to bid goodbye to her lady mother, that she must come down into the courtyard with him, that he is in a hurry to get into his carriage because as usual they are late.

Meanwhile Raffaele Cuffa, who when he is in the hunting lodge walks with silent watchful footsteps like a fox, approaches Duke Signoretto and hands him a large wicker basket on which a white cross stands out prominently. The Duke opens the lid with a flick of his wrist, which his daughter recognises as one of his most habitual gestures, a peevish movement with which he casts to one side anything that bores him. His indolent, sensual hand plunges into the well-ironed cloth inside the basket, shivers at the icy touch of a silver crucifix, squeezes the small bag full of coins, and then slips quickly away. At a sign from him, Raffaele Cuffa hastens forward to close the basket. Now it is only a question of getting the horses to gallop full speed to Palermo.

Meanwhile Marianna has rushed to her parents' bedroom, where she finds her mother the Duchess lying supine between the sheets, her dress fluffed up with lace slipping off her shoulder, the fingers of her hand closed round the enamel snuff-box. The child stops for a moment, overcome by the honey-sweet scent of the snuff mingled with all the other odours that accompany her mother's awakening: attar of roses, coagulated sweat, stale urine and lozenges flavoured with orris root.

Her mother presses her daughter to her with lazy tenderness. Marianna sees her lips moving, but she can't be bothered to guess at her words. She knows she is telling her not to cross the road on her own; because of her deafness she could easily be crushed under the wheels of a carriage she has not been able to hear. And then dogs: no matter whether they are large dogs or small dogs she must give them a wide berth. She knows perfectly well how their tails grow so long that they wrap themselves round people's waists like chimeras do and then, hey presto, they pierce you with their forked points and then you are dead without ever realising what has happened to you.

For a moment the child fixes her gaze on her mother the Duchess's plump chin, on her beautiful mouth with its pure outline, on her soft pink cheeks, on her eyes with their look of innocence, yielding and far away. I shall never be like her, she says to herself. Never. Not even when I am dead.

Her mother the Duchess continues to talk about dogs like chimeras that can become as long as serpents, that press against you with their whiskers, that bewitch you with their cunning eyes. But the child gives her a hasty kiss and runs off.

Her father the Duke is already in the carriage, but instead of summoning her he is singing. She can see him puffing out his cheeks and arching his eyebrows. As soon as she puts a foot on the running-board she is seized from inside and pulled on to the seat. The carriage door is closed with a sharp bang. Peppino Cannarota whips the horses and off they go at a gallop.

The child relaxes, sinks back into the padded seat and shuts her eyes. Sometimes the two senses on which she relies are so alert that they come to blows, her eyes intent on possessing every image in its entirety, and her sense of smell obstinately insisting that it can make the whole world pass through these two minute tunnels of flesh at the lower end of her nose.

But now she has lowered her eyelids so as to rest her eyes

for a while, and her nostrils have begun to draw in the air, recognising the smells and meticulously noting them in her mind: the overpowering scent of lettuce water that impregnates her father's waistcoat, below that the scent of rice powder mingled with the grease on the seats, the sourness of crushed lice, the smarting from the dust on the road that blows through the joints of the doors, as well as the faint aroma of mint that floats in from the fields of the Villa Palagonia.

But an extra hard jolt makes her open her eyes. Opposite her on the front seat her father is asleep, his tricorn hat capsized over his shoulder, his wig askew on his handsome perspiring forehead, his blond eyelashes resting gracefully on his carelessly shaven cheeks. Marianna pushes aside the small wine-coloured curtain, embroidered with golden eagles. She catches a glimpse of the dusty road and of geese streaking away with outspread wings in front of the carriage wheels. Images of the countryside round Bagheria glide into the silence within her head: the contorted cork trees with their naked reddish trunks, the olive trees with branches weighed down by their little green eggs, the brambles that are struggling to invade the road, the cultivated fields, the giant cactuses with their spiny fruit, the tufts of reed, and far away in the distance the windswept hills of Aspra.

Now the carriage passes the two pillars of the gate to the Villa Butera and sets off towards Ogliastro and Villabate. Her small hand remains gripping the cloth, heedless of the heat that seeps through the coarse woollen weave. She sits straight upright and motionless to avoid accidentally making a noise that will wake her father. But how stupid! What about the noise of the wheels as they clatter over the potholes in the road; what about Peppino Cannarota shouting encouragement to the horses; and the cracking of the whip and the barking of dogs? Even if she can only imagine all these sounds, for him they are real. And yet it is she who is disturbed and not him. What tricks intelligence can play on crippled senses!

From the gentle shimmering of the reeds, hardly affected by the wind from Africa, Marianna is aware that they have arrived at the outskirts of Ficarazzi. In the distance is the big yellow barracks known as 'the sugar mill'. A pungent acidulous smell creeps through the cracks in the closed door. It is the smell of sugar cane as it is cut, soaked, stripped and transformed into molasses.

Today the horses are flying along. Her father the Duke continues sleeping in spite of the jolts. She is pleased to have him there safe in her hands. Every so often she leans forward to straighten his hat or to brush away a too insistent fly.

The child is just seven years old. In her disabled body the silence is like dead water. In this clear still water float the carriage, the balconies hung with washing, the hens scratching about, the sea glimpsed from afar, her sleeping father. The images are almost weightless and easily change their positions, but they coalesce into a liquid that blends their colours and dissolves their shapes.

Marianna turns to look out of the window and to her surprise they are right alongside the sea. The smooth calm water splashes gently on to the big grey pebbles. On the horizon a large boat with limp sails goes from right to left.

The branch of a mulberry tree snaps against the window. Purple mulberries are squashed on the glass by the impact. Marianna turns aside, but too late, the jolt has made her bang her head against the window frame. Her lady mother is right: her ears are no use as sentinels. The dogs can catch hold of her by the waist from one minute to the next. That is why her nose has become so keen and her eyes so quick to warn her of any moving object.

Her father the Duke opens his eyes for a moment and then sinks back into sleep. Suppose she were to give him a kiss? How happily she would embrace him. How happy she would be to caress that cool cheek nicked by a careless razor. But she refrains because she knows he dislikes any mawkishness. And, anyway, why wake him up when he is happily asleep, why bring him back to another day of 'turmoil', as he puts it, writing it for her on a small sheet of paper in his beautifully rounded and shapely handwriting.

From the regular jolting of the carriage the child guesses that they have arrived in Palermo. The wheels have begun to bounce over the cobblestones and it seems to her that she can almost hear their rhythmic clanking.

Soon they will be turning towards Porta Felice, then they will go into the Cassaro Morto, and then? Her father the Duke has not told her where he is taking her but from the basket Raffaele Cuffa has given him she can guess. To the Vicaria?

12

II

It is indeed the façade of the Vicaria that greets her as she gets down from the carriage, helped by her father. The expression on his face makes her laugh: he has woken with a start, feeling the pressure of his powdered wig rammed down on to his ears, slapping on his tricorn hat and jumping from the footplate, a movement he intends to appear confident and carefree but which turns out to be clumsy. He almost has a heavy fall because of the pins and needles in his legs.

The windows of the Vicaria are all similar, bristling with spiral gratings that end in menacing spikes; the great entrance gate is studded with rusty bolts; there is a door handle in the form of a wolf's head with an open mouth. With all its brutishness it looks so like a prison that people passing in front of it turn their heads away to avoid seeing it.

The Duke is about to knock on the door when it opens wide and he enters as if it were his own house. Marianna follows behind him and the guards and servants bow as they pass. One gives her a surprised smile, another frowns at her, another even tries to stop her by grabbing hold of her arm. But she breaks free and runs after her father. The child gets tired following him as he advances with giant strides towards the gangway. She skips along in her little satin shoes but she cannot manage to keep up. For a moment she thinks she has lost him, but there he is round a corner waiting for her.

Father and daughter find themselves together in a triangular room dimly lit by a single window immediately below the ceiling. A manservant helps her father the Duke remove his redingote and his tricorn hat. He relieves him of his wig and hangs it on a knob that juts out from the wall. He helps him to put on the long habit of white cloth lying in the basket together with a rosary, a cross and the purse of coins.

Now the titular head of the Chapel of the Noble Family of the White Brothers is ready. In the meantime, without the child noticing, other members of the Noble Family have arrived, also dressed in white habits. Four ghosts with cowls flopping round their necks.

Marianna stands on her own watching the attendants bustle round the White Brothers as if they were actors getting ready to come on stage: the folds of their spotless habits must be straight so that they fall modestly over their sandalled feet; the cowls must come down over the neck and the white points must be straightened so that they face upwards.

Now the five are indistinguishable: white on white, piety on piety. Only their hands peeping through the folds of their habits and that little area of blackness blinking in the two holes in the hood reveal the person underneath. The smallest of the ghosts leans towards the child, flutters his hands and turns to her father the Duke. She can see that he is angry from the way he stamps his feet on the floor. Another brother takes a step forward as if to intervene. It looks as if they are going to seize each other by the scruff of their necks but her father the Duke orders them to be quiet with a gesture of authority.

Marianna feels the cold soft cloth of her father's habit against her bare wrist. The right hand of the father clutches the fingers of the daughter. Her nose tells her that something terrible is going to happen, but what can it be? Her father the Duke leads her towards another corridor and she walks without looking where to put her feet, seized by an excited and burning curiosity.

At the end of the passage they encounter steep slippery stone steps. The noble gentlemen grab their habits with their thumbs and fingers just like ladies picking up their full skirts and raising the hems so as not to stumble. The steps exude dampness and it is difficult to see, even though a guard goes ahead with a lighted flare. There are no windows, neither high nor low. Suddenly it is night, smelling of burnt oil, rat droppings, pork fat. The head of the prison guards gives the keys of the dungeon to Duke Ucrìa, who advances till he reaches a small wooden door with reinforced bosses. There, with the help of a boy with bare feet, he unlocks the padlock and slides back a big iron bar.

The door opens. The smoky flare casts light on part of the floor, where cockroaches are running in all directions. The guard raises the flare to throw a shaft of light on several half-naked bodies lying against the wall, their ankles shackled in heavy chains.

An ironsmith appears from nowhere and bends down to release the chain from one of the prisoners, a boy with bleary eyes. He gets impatient because it takes so long and kicks out with his foot almost as if he was trying to tickle the ironsmith's nose. He laughs, showing a large toothless mouth.

The child hides behind her father. Every so often he bends down

14

and gives her a quick caress, but more to make certain that she stays there watching than to comfort her.

When the boy is finally free he stands up. Marianna recognises that he is still almost a child, more or less the same age as Cannarota's son, who died of malarial fever a few months ago at the age of thirteen. The other prisoners look on without speaking. As soon as the boy, his ankles freed, starts to walk about, they resume their unfinished game, glad to be able to make use of so much light. The game consists of louse-killing: whoever can squash between their two thumbs the greatest number in the shortest time wins. The dead lice are delicately placed on a small copper coin and the winner takes the money.

The child is absorbed in watching the three players, their mouths wide open and laughing as they shout words that she cannot hear. Fear has left her; now she thinks calmly of how her father the Duke will want to take her with him to hell; there must be a secret reason, some high-flown reason which she will only understand later on. He will take her to look at the damned wallowing in mud: some who walk burdened with heavy rocks on their shoulders, some who have been changed into trees, some who have swallowed burning coals and breathe out fiery smoke, some who crawl like snakes, some who are changed into dogs whose tails grow longer and longer until they become harpoons with which they hook passers-by and carry them to their mouths, just as her lady mother keeps telling her.

But her father the Duke is there to rescue her from these horrors. And, anyway, for living visitors like Dante hell can even be beautiful to look at. Those who are there, dead and suffering, and we who are here watching them: is this not what these white-hooded brethren, who pass the rosary from hand to hand, are offering us?

III

Rolling his eyes, the boy watches her, and Marianna returns his look, determined not to let herself be intimidated. But his eyelids are swollen and discharging pus; it is quite likely he cannot see properly, the little girl thinks to herself. Who can tell how he

15

perceives her? Perhaps as gross and fleshy, like when she looks at her reflection in Aunt Manina's distorting mirror, or maybe undersized and all skin and bone? At that moment, in response to her grimace, the boy dissolves into a dark, crooked smile.

Her father the Duke, assisted by a hooded White Brother, takes the boy by the arm and leads him towards the door. The players return to the half-darkness of their days. Two dry, slender hands lift up the child and place her gently on the bottom step of the staircase.

The procession starts up: the guard with the burning torch, Duke Ucrìa leading the prisoner on his arm, the other White Brothers, the ironsmith and two attendants dressed in dark tunics behind. Again they find themselves in the triangular room, astir with the coming and going of guards and footmen, who carry torches, arrange chairs, and bring basins of tepid water, linen towels, a basket of fresh bread and a dish of candied fruit.

Her father the Duke leans over the boy with an affectionate gesture. Marianna tells herself that she has never seen him so tender and solicitous. He takes water from the earthenware basin in his cupped hand and splashes it on the pus on the boy's cheeks; then he cleans his face with the freshly laundered towel handed to him by a footman. Next he takes a piece of soft white bread between his fingers and offers it to the prisoner as if he were his favourite son.

The boy allows himself to be looked after, cleaned and fed, without uttering a word. Every so often he smiles, at other times he weeps. Somebody places a rosary of large mother-of-pearl beads in his hands. He fingers it and then lets it fall to the ground. Her father the Duke gestures impatiently. Marianna bends down, picks up the rosary and replaces it in the boy's hands. For a moment she experiences the contact of two cold, calloused fingers.

The prisoner stretches his lips over his toothless mouth. His blood-shot eyes are bathed with a small piece of cloth steeped in lettuce water. Under the indulgent gaze of the White Brothers the prisoner reaches out towards the dish, looks round him apprehensively and then thrusts into his mouth a honey-coloured plum encrusted with sugar. The five gentlemen have knelt down and are telling the rosary. The boy, his cheeks bulging with the candied fruit, is pushed gently on to his knees, for even he is required to pray.

Thus the oppressive heat of the afternoon passes in somnolent

16

prayer. Every so often a footman approaches bearing glasses of water flavoured with aniseed. The White Brothers drink and return to their prayers. One of them mops his perspiring face, others doze off and then wake up with a start and return to telling the rosary. After swallowing three crystallised apricots the boy falls asleep too, and no one has the heart to wake him up.

Marianna watches her father praying. Is that cowled figure Duke Signoretto or can it be someone else whose head is swaying from side to side? It seems as if she can hear his voice slowly reciting Hail Mary. In the shell of her ear, long since silent, she retains a faint memory of familiar voices: the hoarse gurgling of her mother, the shrill voice of the cook Innocenza, the sonorous kindly voice of her father the Duke, which every so often used to falter and become disagreeably sharp and splintered.

Perhaps she too had learned to talk. But how old was she then? Four or five? She was a backward child, quiet and absorbed, lurking in some corner where everyone tended to forget about her before suddenly remembering her and coming to scold her for having hidden herself. One day, for no reason, she fell silent: silence took possession of her like some illness, or perhaps like a vocation. Not to hear the merry voice of her father the Duke was the most distressing part of it. But in due course she became accustomed to it. Now she experienced a sense of happiness, almost a sly satisfaction, in watching him talk without being able to grasp the words.

'You were born like this, deaf and dumb', he had once written in an exercise book, and she had tried to convince herself that she had only dreamed up those distant voices, unable to admit that her sweet gentle father, who loved her so much, could lie to her. So she had to believe it was all a delusion. She lacked neither the imagination nor the desire for speech.

> *e pì e pì e pì*
> seven women for one *tarì*
> *e pì e pì e pì*
> one *tarì* is not a lot
> seven women for an apricot. . . .

But her thoughts are interrupted by the movement of a White Brother, who goes out and returns with a big book, on the cover of which is written: ATONEMENT OF CONSCIENCE. Her father the Duke wakes up the boy with a gentle tap and they withdraw together to a corner of the room, where the wall makes a niche and a slab of stone fits into it like a seat. There the Duke Ucrìa of Fontanasalsa bends down towards the prisoner's ear and invites him to make his confession. The boy mutters a few words through his young toothless mouth. Her father is affectionately insistent. At last the boy smiles. They seem almost like a father and son talking casually about family matters.

Marianna watches them filled with dismay. What does he think he is doing? This parrot roosting next to her father, as if he has always known him, as if he has always held his impatient hands between his fingers, as if since the day he was born he has known his smell in his nostrils, as if he has been clasped round the waist a thousand times by two strong arms that have helped him to jump down from a carriage or a sedan-chair, from a cradle, from steps, with the impetuosity that only a real father of flesh and blood can feel for his own daughter. What does he think he is doing?

A compelling urge to commit murder rises up from her throat, invades the top of her mouth and burns her tongue. She could throw a big dish at his head, plunge a knife into his chest, tear the hair off his scalp. Her father does not belong to that boy, he belongs to her, to the pitiable dumb girl who has only one love in the world – her father.

These murderous thoughts are dispelled by a sudden rush of air. The door opens wide and a man with a belly shaped like a melon appears in the entrance. He is dressed like a clown, half in red, half in yellow. He is young and corpulent, with short legs, square shoulders, the arms of a wrestler and small shifty eyes. He is chewing pumpkin seeds and spitting out the husks with a cheerful leer.

When the boy sees him he blanches. The smiles that her father the Duke has wrung from him die on his face, his lips begin to tremble, his mouth starts to quiver and his eyes to run. The clown, spitting out husks of pumpkin seeds, draws closer to him. The boy slides downwards like a wet rag and the clown gestures to two servants, who raise him up beneath the armpits and drag him towards the door.

The atmosphere resonates with sombre reverberations like the beating of the gigantic wings of an unseen bird. Marianna looks around her. The White Brothers proceed towards the entrance with ceremonious footsteps. The great door opens wide at a single blow and the beating of the wings becomes close enough and loud enough to deafen her. It is the viceregal drums, together with the shouts from the crowd, everyone rejoicing and waving their arms.

The Piazza Marina, which earlier had been empty, is now seething with people: a sea of undulating heads, raised standards, stamping horses, a pandemonium of thronging bodies, struggling forward to invade the rectangular piazza.

IV

The windows are overflowing with heads. The balconies are tightly crammed with gesticulating bodies leaning out so that they can get a better view. The Ministers of Justice with their yellow robes, the Royal Guard with their gold and purple ensign, the Grenadiers armed with bayonets, are all there, restraining the impatience of the mob with some difficulty.

What is going to happen? The child guesses but does not dare to answer that question. All these bawling heads seem to be knocking at the door of her silence, asking to be allowed in.

Marianna shifts her gaze from the crowd and focuses it on the toothless boy. She sees him standing motionless, steady and upright. He is no longer trembling or keeling over. He has a glimmer of pride in his eyes: all this uproar for him! All these people dressed up in their Sunday best, these horses, these carriages, are only there for him. These banners, these uniforms with shining buttons, these plumed hats, all this gold and purple, all on his account. It is a miracle!

Two guards brutally interrupt this ecstatic contemplation of his own triumph. They fasten the rope with which they have tied his hands to another longer and stronger rope, which they secure to the tail of a mule. Bound thus, he is dragged towards the centre of the piazza.

At the far end, on the Steri Palace, a splendid blood-red flag flaunts itself; from there, from the Palazza Chiaramonte, the Noble Fathers of the Inquisition are emerging, two by two, preceded and followed by a swarm of altar boys. In the centre of the piazza is a raised platform several feet high, similar to those on which are enacted the puppet stories of Nofriu and Travaglino, of Nardo and Tiberio. But instead of black canvas there is an ominous scaffolding of wood, shaped like an inverted L, to which a rope with a noose is attached.

Marianna gets pushed behind her father, who is following the prisoner, who in his turn follows the mule. Now the procession has got under way and no one can stop it, whatever the reason. The horses of the Royal Guard in front, followed by the Noble Brothers in their hooded habits, the Ministers of Justice, the archdeacons, the priests, the barefoot friars, the drummers, the trumpeters: a long cortege that laboriously makes it way along the street between the excited crowds. The gallows are only a few yards away, yet it takes the procession, winding its way in arbitrary circles round the piazza, a long time to get there.

At length Marianna's foot bumps into a small wooden step and the procession comes to a halt. Her father the Duke ascends the steps with the condemned prisoner, preceded by the executioner and followed by the other Brothers of the Good Death.

Once more the boy has that far-away smile on his white face. And it is her father the Duke who holds him spellbound and eases him towards paradise, bewitching him with descriptions of the delights of that place of repose, leisure, unlimited food and sleep. Like a baby made drowsy by words from his mother rather than his father, the boy seems to have no other wish than to rush from this world to the next, where there are no prisoners, no sickness, no lice, no suffering but only juleps and rest.

The little girl opens her aching eyes. Now a great desire leaps down upon her: to be him, if only for an hour, to be that toothless boy with the suppurating eyes, so as to hear her father's voice, to drink in the honey of that transient sound, even if only once, even at the cost of dying, hanging from that rope dangling in the sun.

The executioner continues to chew pumpkin seeds and with a defiant look spits the husks high into the air. Everything is so like the puppet theatre: now Nardo will lift up his head and the hangman will deliver a hail of blows. Nardo will wave his arms and fall under the stage and then return more lively than ever to receive more blows and more insults.

Just as in the theatre, the crowd laughs, chatters and munches while waiting for the blows to begin. Street-vendors appear from under the scaffold to offer mugs of water and aniseed, pushing and jostling past sellers of bread and offal, of boiled squid and cactus fruit. Everyone is elbowing and shoving, trying to sell their wares. A toffee seller arrives beneath the child's nose and, almost as if he has an intuition that she is deaf, approaches her with exaggerated gestures to offer her the tray held round his neck with a greasy piece of string. She gives a sideways glance at the miniature toffee-tins. She could so easily stretch out her hand, select one, press down the catch with her finger to open the circular lid and let the little round sweets with their vanilla flavour slip out. But she doesn't want to be distracted, her attention is fixed elsewhere, above those steps of blackened wood, where her father the Duke is still talking to the condemned prisoner in a soft low voice as if he were flesh of his flesh.

The last steps are reached. The Duke bows towards the dignitaries seated in front of the scaffold, the senators, the princes, the magistrates. Then he kneels down reverently with the rosary between his fingers. For a moment the crowd falls quiet. Even the itinerant street-vendors cease bustling about and stand still with their mobile stalls, their straps, their samples of merchandise, their mouths wide open and their heads in the air.

When the prayer is ended, her father the Duke passes the crucifix to the prisoner for him to kiss. It is as if in place of Christ on the Cross, it could be he himself, naked, martyred, with his beautiful skin and a crown of thorns on his head, offering himself to the uncouth lips of a frightened boy to reassure him, to soothe him, to send him to the next world calm and tranquil. With her he has never been so tender, never so sensual, never so close. Never, never has he offered her his body to be kissed, never taken her under his wing, never cherished her with tender words of comfort.

The child's gaze shifts to the prisoner, and she watches him sink down on his knees. The seductive words of Duke Ucrìa are swept away by the feel of the cold, slippery rope that the hangman places round his neck. But the boy still manages somehow to lift himself upright, while his nose starts to run. He tries to free his hand to wipe the snot that dribbles over his lips. But his hands are firmly tied behind his back. Two or three times he lifts his shoulders and tries to twist his arm. At this moment it seems as if wiping his nose is the only thing that matters to him.

21

The air reverberates to the beat of a big drum. At a sign from the judge the hangman kicks away the box on which the boy has been forced to stand. The body jerks, stretches itself, falls downwards and starts to rotate.

But something has gone wrong. Instead of dangling inertly like a sack, the boy continues to writhe, suspended in the air, his neck swollen, his eyes starting out of their sockets.

The hangman, realising that his task has failed, heaves himself up with all the force of his arms against the gallows and jumps alongside the hanged boy; for a few seconds they are both dangling from the rope like two mating frogs, while the crowd holds its breath.

This time he is truly dead. The body has taken on all the attributes of a puppet. The hangman slides nonchalantly along the scaffold and jumps nimbly down on to the platform. People start to throw their caps in the air. A young brigand who has murdered a dozen people has met his fate. Justice has been done. But the little girl will not learn about this till later. For the moment she is asking herself what a boy not much older than herself and looking so scared and stupid could have done.

The father bends over his daughter, exhausted. He touches her mouth as if he were waiting for a miracle. He catches hold of her chin, looks into her eyes, imploring, threatening. 'You must speak,' say his lips. 'You must open that accursed fish's mouth.'

The child tries to unstick her lips but she cannot do it. Her body is seized with a violent trembling, her hands, still grasping the folds of her father's habit, are turned to stone.

The boy she wanted to kill is dead and she cannot help wondering whether it might have been her who killed him, for she had desired his death as one can desire a forbidden fruit.

V

The brothers and sisters sit in a colourful group posing for her and shuffling their feet: Signoretto looking so like his father the Duke, with the same soft hair, shapely legs and bright trusting expression; Fiammetta in her little nun's dress, her hair gathered

22

inside a lace-edged coif; Carlo with his black sparkling eyes and the short breeches that squeeze his plump thighs; Geraldo, who has recently lost his milk teeth, smiling like an old man; Agata with clear translucent skin speckled with mosquito bites.

The five watch their dumb sister bending over the palette, and it seems almost as if they are portraying her rather than she portraying them. They eye her as she looks down at her paints, mixes them with the tip of her brush, and then turns back to the canvas. All at once its whiteness becomes suffused with a soft yellow; then over the yellow she lays a cerulean blue with clear, delicate brush-strokes.

Carlo says something that makes the group burst into laughter. Marianna signs to them to stay quiet for a little longer. The charcoal drawing of their heads, necks, arms, faces, feet, is already there on the canvas, but she is finding it difficult to bring the colour to life: the paint becomes diluted and runs down towards the bottom of the canvas. Patiently they remain still for several minutes. But then it is Geraldo who creates a disturbance by giving Fiammetta a pinch. Fiammetta retaliates with a kick and suddenly they are both pushing, slapping and elbowing each other. Signoretto does not intervene to put Geraldo in his place, although as the eldest he has the right to do so.

Marianna again dips her brush first in the white paint and then in the pink, while her eyes shift from the canvas to the group. There is something disembodied about this picture she is painting, something too polished, not quite real. It seems almost like one of those official miniatures which her lady mother's friends have had painted of themselves, all stiff and formal, in which the original vision remains only a distant memory.

She says to herself she must concentrate on their personalities if she does not want them to slip through her fingers: Signoretto, who sees himself as a rival to his father, with his commanding ways and resonant laughter, and as protector of his mother who, whenever she sees father and son in conflict, watches them slyly, even with amusement. But her indulgent glances linger on her son with such intensity that it must be obvious to everybody. His father the Duke, however, is irritated: this boy not only looks astonishingly like him, but acts out his movements with more grace and assurance than he does himself. It is as if he had a mirror in front of him, a mirror that flatters him and at the same time reminds him that soon he will be painlessly replaced. Amongst other things it is Signoretto who is the eldest, and it is he who will carry on the family name. Towards his dumb sister Signoretto is usually protective, somewhat jealous of the attention their father gives her, sometimes looking down on her disabilities, sometimes using her as a pretext for demonstrating to the others his generous spirit, never quite sure where truth ends and play-acting begins.

Next to him is Fiammetta in her nun's habit, her eyebrows like a pencilled line, her eyes too close together, her teeth irregular. She is not beautiful like Agata and for this reason she is destined for the convent. Even if she found a husband there could be no certainty of a marriage contract as there would be with a real beauty. In the highly coloured, twisted little face of the child there is already a look of rebellion against this fettered future, which she accepts defiantly while wearing the long narrow habit that smothers her womanhood.

Carlo and Geraldo, fifteen and eleven, look as alike as twins. But one will end up in a monastery and the other will go into the dragoons. They are often dressed up as monk and soldier, Carlo in a miniature habit and Geraldo in a boy's uniform. Whenever they are in the garden, they amuse themselves by exchanging clothes and then rolling on the ground clasped together, ruining both the cream-coloured habit and the handsome uniform with its gold toggles. Carlo is greedy for spicy foods and sweets and has begun to grow plump. But he is also the most affectionate of the brothers towards Marianna, and often comes to look for her and hold her hand.

Agata is the youngest and also the prettiest. A marriage contract has already been arranged for her which, without costing the family anything except a dowry of thirty thousand escudos, will enable them to extend their influence, to make useful connections and establish a wealthy lineage.

When Marianna looks up to focus on her brothers and sisters she finds they have all vanished. They have taken advantage of her absorbed concentration on the canvas to slip away, counting on the fact that she will not be able to hear their giggling. She is just in time to catch a glimpse of Agata's skirt disappearing behind the lodge among the spikes of aloes.

How can she get on with the painting now? She will have to dip into her memory, since she well knows that they will never come back to pose for her as a group; even today they have only done so after much cajoling and patience.

The gap left by their bodies is now filled by jasmine, dwarf palm trees and olive trees that slope down towards the sea. Why not paint this calm, immutable landscape instead of the brothers who never stay still for a moment? It has more depth and mystery and it has obligingly posed for centuries and is always there ready to be played with.

Marianna's youthful hand reaches out towards another canvas and puts it on the easel in place of the first. She dips her brush into a soft oily green. Where should she begin? With the fresh brilliant emerald green of the dwarf palm trees or the shimmering turquoise of the grove of olive trees or the green streaked with yellow of the slopes of Monte Catalfano?

Or she could paint the lodge, which was built by her grandfather Mariano Ucrìa, with its square squat shape, its windows more suited to a tower than a hunting lodge in the country. She feels certain that one day it will be transformed into a villa and she will live there even through the winter because her roots are sunk into that soil, which she loves more than the cobblestones of Palermo.

While she remains poised irresolutely with the brush dripping paint on to her canvas, she feels herself pulled by the sleeve. She turns. It is Agata, who presents her with a piece of paper.

'Come – the puppeteer has arrived.' From the handwriting she recognises that the invitation comes from Signoretto, though as a matter of fact it sounds more like a command than an invitation.

She gets up, wipes her paintbrush, still dripping with green paint, on a small damp rag, cleans her hands by rubbing them against her striped apron and walks with her sister towards the entrance to the courtyard.

Carlo, Geraldo, Fiammetta and Signoretto are already crowding round Tutui, the puppet master. He has left his donkey by the fig tree and is about to put up his theatre. Four vertical poles intersect with three horizontal planks and between them they support about four yards of black cloth. Meanwhile, leaning from the windows are the servants, Innocenza the cook, Don Raffaele Cuffa and even her ladyship the Duchess, towards whom the puppet master directs a low bow. The Duchess throws him a ten *tarì* coin which he picks up quickly. He pockets it under his shirt, makes another theatrical bow and goes off to get his puppets from a saddle bag hanging down over the haunches of his donkey.

Marianna has already witnessed those blows, those heads that slump beneath the platform only to reappear soon after, bold and unredeemed; for every year at this time Tutui appears at the lodge in Bagheria to amuse the children. Every year the Duchess throws him a ten *tarì* piece and the puppet master wears himself out with bows and greetings so exaggerated that it seems almost as if he is pulling her leg. Meanwhile, no one knows how, the word has spread and dozens of children are crowding in from the surrounding countryside. The servants come down into the courtyard, drying their hands and tidying their hair. Among them is the cowman Don Ciccio Calò with his twin daughters Lina and Lena, the gardener Peppi Geraci with his wife Maria and their four sons, and of course the footman Don Peppino Cannarota.

Soon on comes Nardo, who starts to beat Tiberio *boom boom boom*. The show has begun, while the children are still playing around. But a moment later they are all seated on the ground, heads in the air, eyes fixed on the stage.

Marianna remains standing a little apart. The children unnerve her: she has too often been a target for their teasing. They jump on to her without letting her see them and make fun of her reaction, they bet with each other who can let off a fire cracker without her catching them.

Meanwhile from the background of black cloth a new object is unexpectedly appearing. It is a gibbet, something that has never before been seen in Tutui's theatre. At its appearance the children hold their breath expectantly, for this is an exciting novelty.

A guard with his sword on his hip pursues the irrepressible Nardo up and down the black curtain, seizes him by the scruff of the neck and slips his head through the noose. A drummer appears on the left and Nardo is made to jump on a stool. That's it! The guard kicks the stool away and Nardo falls under his own weight while the rope starts to rotate.

Marianna is shaken. She shudders. Something stirs in her memory like a fish caught on a hook, something that refuses to surface and disturb the calm still waters of her consciousness. She raises her hand to take hold of her father's rough habit but only finds the bristly hair of the donkey's tail.

Nardo hangs in space with all the suppleness of his boyish body, watery-eyed and toothless, his gaze fixed in a state of inescapable trance, still attempting spasmodically to raise his shoulder to free a hand with which to wipe his running nose.

Marianna falls backwards like a dead weight, hitting her head on the hard bare ground of the courtyard. Everyone turns. Agata runs towards her followed by Carlo, who leans over his sister and bursts into tears. Cannarota's wife fans her with her apron while a servant rushes off to call the Duchess. The puppet master emerges from beneath the black curtain, with the puppet in his hand, head downwards, while Nardo remains hanging aloft on the gallows.

VI

An hour later, Marianna wakes up in her parents' bed with a wet handkerchief pressing heavily on her forehead. Vinegar runs down through her eyelashes and stings her eyes. Her mother the Duchess bends over her. Even before she opens her eyes she recognises her from the strong smell of honey-scented snuff.

The daughter gazes up at her mother: the outline of her full lips slightly veiled by blonde down, her nostrils shadowed by the constant taking of snuff, her large dark eyes. Marianna finds it impossible to make up her mind whether she is beautiful or not, because there is something about her that is off-putting. But what is it? Perhaps it is her unshakable calm, the way she always gives in to the slightest push, the way she abandons herself to the cloying fumes of snuff, indifferent to everything else.

Marianna has always suspected that her lady mother, in the far-off past, when she was very young and full of imagination, deliberately chose to become lifeless so that she would never have to die. From there must come her remarkable ability to accept every irritation with complete resignation and a minimum of effort.

Before her death, Marianna's grandmother Giuseppa wrote to her several times about her mother in an exercise book with a fleur-de-lys on the cover.

'Your mother was a beauty. Everybody loved her. But she didn't love anyone. She was obstinate as a goat, like her mother Giulia, who came from around Granada. She did not want to marry her cousin, your father Signoretto. Everyone said, "But he's a lovely young man, he really is." Not just because he was my son, the very sight of him would dazzle your eyes. Your mother married him grudgingly, she looked as if she were going to a funeral. Then after a month of marriage she fell in love with him and she loved him so much she started taking snuff, then at night she could no longer sleep so she took laudanum as well.'

When the Duchess sees that her daughter is coming round, she goes to the writing-desk, takes a sheet of paper and writes on it. She dries the ink with ashes and hands the sheet to the young girl.

'How are you, my little one?'

As she sits up, Marianna spits out the vinegar that is still sticking to her teeth. Her lady mother laughs and removes the soaking rag from her face. Then she goes to the writing-desk again, scribbles something more and comes back to the bedside with the piece of paper.

'Now you are thirteen it's time I told you you have to get married. We have found a bridgroom for you. So there's no need for you to be a nun like Fiammetta.'

The girl reads and rereads her mother's hurried note, written regardless of spelling, mixing Sicilian dialect with Italian, her handwriting hesitant and shaky. A husband? Why on earth? She had imagined that because of her disability, marriage would be unthinkable. And, anyway, she is barely thirteen.

Her mother is waiting for a reply. She gives her an affectionate smile – but there is something a little forced about it. For her, having a deaf and dumb daughter weighs her down with unbearable pain and embarrassment that make her freeze. She's at a loss how to behave towards her or how to make herself understood. She has never much liked writing, and to have to read other people's handwriting is a real torture. But with motherly self-sacrifice she goes to the writing-desk, snatches another sheet of paper, picks up the goose quill and the little bottle of ink and takes it all to her daughter as she lies stretched out on the bed.

'A husband for a dumb girl?' Marianna writes, leaning on her elbow and, in her confusion, dripping blobs of ink on the sheet.

'Your father did everything to make you talk. He even took you with him to the Vicaria where the frite might have helped you. You never uttered a word because your head is a sieve, you don't have the will. Your sister Fiammetta is bitrothed to Christ, Agata is promised to the son of Prince Torre Mosca, and you – your duty is to axcept the bridgroom we have found for you because we love you. We don't want you wedded outside the family so we are giving you to your unkle Pietro Ucrìa di Campo Spagnolo, Lord of Scannatura, of Bosco Grande and of Fiume Mendola, Count of Sala di Paruta, Marquis of Sollazzi and of Taya. On top of all that he is my brother and your father's cousin. And he loves you. Only with him will your soul find sanktury.'

Marianna reads the note with a frown, disregarding her mother's spelling mistakes and the words in dialect thrown in by the handful. Most of all she rereads the last lines; then her betrothed is to be her uncle Pietro? That sad, grumpy man, always dressed in red and known in the family as 'the prawn'.

'I will not get married', she writes angrily on the back of the sheet of paper still wet from her mother's words.

The Duchess Maria returns patiently to the writing-desk, her forehead mottled with little globules of sweat. What a lot of effort she has to make for this dumb girl who refuses to accept that she is nothing but an encumbrance, and there's no more to be said.

'No one will even look at you, my own little Marianna. And the convent will want a dowry, you know that. We already have to pay for Fiammetta. That costs a lot. Unkle Pietro will take you for nothing because he loves you. Then all his property will be yours. Now do you understand?'

She puts the pen down and starts talking to Marianna ever so softly, just as if she could hear her, absent-mindedly caressing her hair, which is still soaked with vinegar.

Eventually she snatches the pen from her daughter's hand, just as she is on the point of writing something, and traces rapidly and proudly these words: 'In ready money that is a saving of fifteen thousand escudos.'

VII

A loose pile of tufa stones in the courtyard, buckets full of plaster, great mountains of sand. Marianna walks up and down in the sunshine with her skirt tucked up round her waist so as not to get the hem dirty.

Bootees with their buttons left undone, hair gathered on her neck with little silver pins, a gift from her husband. All round her a disorderly confusion of bits of wood, boxes, stakes, posts, wheelbarrows, mallets and axes. Her back-ache has become almost unbearable and she looks round for somewhere she can rest for a few moments in the shade. A big stone beside the pig-sty, that will do, even if to get to it she has to slither through the mud. Holding her back with her hand she slides over to the stone. She looks down at her belly: the swelling hardly shows in spite of her being already five months pregnant. It is her third pregnancy.

In front of her stands the most elegant villa. There is no longer any trace of the former lodge. In its place is a building on three floors, with a staircase winding its way gracefully upwards in a snake-like spiral. From the central bay of the building extend two colonnaded wings that widen out and then narrow until they create an almost complete circle. The windows alternate in a regular rhythm, one, two, three, one; one, two, three, one: almost a dance, a *tarascone*. Some of the windows are real, others are painted so as to maintain the regular rhythm of a fugue. In one of these windows a curtain will be painted with perhaps a woman's head looking out, maybe she herself watching from behind the window pane.

Uncle husband wanted to leave the lodge as it was, since it had been built by her grandfather Mariano, and the cousins had shared it amicably for so long. But she would not take no for an answer and was so obstinate that in the end she persuaded him to build her a villa where she could spend the winter as well as the summer, with rooms for the children and the servants, and for friends and guests. Meanwhile her father the Duke has got himself another hunting lodge near Santa Flavia.

Uncle husband was seldom to be seen on the building site. He could not bear bricks, dust, lime. He preferred to stay in the house in the Via Alloro in Palermo while she busied herself at Bagheria with the builders and the painters. Even the architect did not often appear there but left everything in the hands of the foreman builder and the young Duchess.

Already the villa has swallowed up vast sums of money. The architect alone cost sixteen hundred *onze*. The sandstone bricks were continually breaking and every week new ones had to be brought in; the foreman had fallen from the scaffolding and broken his arm, and the work was held up for two months. Then, when it was all finished except for the tiled floors, an epidemic of smallpox broke out in Bagheria: three masons were laid up and again the work had to be interrupted for months.

Uncle husband took refuge at Torre Scannatura with their daughters Giuseppa and Felice. She remained, in spite of notes from the Duke ordering her to 'come quick or you will get it. Your first duty is to the child you are carrying.'

But she had been adamant: she insisted on staying and all she asked was for Innocenza to remain with her, the others could all go off to the hills of Scannatura.

Uncle husband was upset but had not insisted. After four years of marriage he was resigned to his wife's obstinacy. He respected her wishes provided that they did not involve him personally and did not interfere with his ideas on the education of his children or affect his rights as a husband. Unlike Agata's husband he did not claim the right to keep interfering in everyday decisions. Silent and solitary, his head sunk between his shoulders like an elderly tortoise, his expression severe and discontented, her uncle husband was in reality more tolerant than many other husbands she knew.

She had never seen him smile except once when she had taken off a shoe to dip her foot into the water of the fountain. Never again. Since the first night of their marriage this cold, shy man had slept on the edge of the bed, his back turned towards her. Then one morning when she was buried in sleep, he had leapt on top of her and violated her.

The body of the thirteen-year-old wife had reacted with kicks and scratches, and very early the next day Marianna fled to her parents in Palermo. Her mother the Duchess wrote that she had acted 'like an inky squid' in leaving her place as a wife, and had made an exhibition of herself and brought discredit on all the family. 'Whoever marries and never repents, can buy Palermo for a hundred pence' and 'Marry for love and end up in pain' and 'Women and hens will go astray, if they ever lose their way' and 'A good wife makes a good husband'. They had attacked her with reproofs and proverbs. Her mother was supported by her aunt Teresa the Prioress, who wrote that by leaving the conjugal roof she had committed a mortal sin.

To say nothing of old Aunt Agata, who had taken her by the hand, ripped off her wedding ring and stuffed it forcibly between her teeth. Even her father the Duke had rebuked her and had taken her back to Bagheria in his own gig, handing her over to uncle husband with the request that he should not be too severe with her, having regard to her youth and her disability.

'Shut your eyes and think of *something else*', Aunt Teresa had written, slipping the little piece of paper into Marianna's pocket, where she found it later. 'Pray to the Lord and He will reward you.'

In the mornings uncle husband would get up early, at five o'clock. While she continued sleeping, he dressed hastily and went the rounds of his estate with Raffaele Cuffa. He returned at around half-past one to eat with her. Then he slept for an hour and afterwards went out again or else shut himself in the library with his books on heraldry.

With her he was courteous but cold. For whole days he seemed to forget that he had a wife. At times he went off to Palermo and stayed for a week. Then all of a sudden he would return and Marianna would catch him looking at her breasts with a dark insistent intensity. Instinctively she would cover her neckline.

When his young wife was sitting by the window combing her hair, Duke Pietro would sometimes spy on her from a distance. But as soon as he realised he was being watched he would slip away. However, they were not often alone together during the day because there was always a servant going round the rooms, lighting a lamp, making a bed, putting clean linen away in the cupboards, polishing the door handles, arranging freshly ironed handtowels in the linen chest next to the wash-stand.

A mosquito as large as a bluebottle settles itself on Marianna's bare arm. For an instant she looks at it with curiosity before shooing it away. Where could such a gigantic creature have come from? She had the pool next to the stable drained six months ago; the ditch that takes water to the lemon trees was cleaned out last year; the two swamps along the path going down to the olive grove were filled up with earth only a few weeks ago. There must still be some stagnant water somewhere or other, but where?

Meanwhile the shadows have lengthened. The sun is slipping behind the cowman Ciccio Calò's house, leaving the courtyard half in shadow. Another mosquito alights on Marianna's perspiring neck. She flicks at it impatiently. Fresh lime must be put down in the stables. Or perhaps it is really the water in the watering trough, where the cows from Messina drink, that is a breeding ground for these bloodsuckers. There are some days in the year when there is no net, no veil, no perfumed oil that can keep the mosquitoes at bay. Once it was Agata who was their favourite. Now that she has married and gone to live in Palermo it seems that the insects have transferred their affection to the white naked arms and the slender neck of Marianna. Tonight she will have to burn verbena leaves in the bedroom.

By now the work at the villa is almost at an end. Only the finishing touches to the interior are still to be done. For the wall-paintings she has called in the fresco painter Intermassimi, who presented himself with a roll of paper under his arm, a dirty tricorn hat on his head, and outsize boots in which were engulfed two short skinny legs. He dismounted from his horse, made a bow, and gave her a smile that was both daring and seductive. He unrolled the sheets of paper in front of her, smoothing them out with his two hands, which were so small and plump that they made her feel uneasy.

The drawings are bold and fantastic, disciplined in form, respectful of tradition, but as if driven by nocturnal flights of fancy, brilliant and mischievous. Marianna admired the chimeras, whose heads were not shaped like lions as the myth has it, but instead had the faces and necks of women. When she saw them for the second time, she was aware that in some strange way they resembled her, and she found this quite disquieting. How had he come to draw her in those weird mythical beasts when he had only seen her once, on the day of her wedding, when she was barely thirteen years old?

Beneath those blonde heads with large blue eyes stretches the body of a lion. It is covered with bizarre curls, its back waving with crests, feathers, mane. Its paws are spiky, with claws shaped like a parrot's beak; its long tail makes rings that spiral backwards and forwards with forked tips, like the dogs that so terrified her mother. Some carry half-way down their backs the small head of a goat that juts out, sharp-eyed and cheeky. Others do not, but they all look through their long eyelashes with an expression of foolish astonishment.

The painter cast admiring glances at her, not at all embarrassed by her dumbness. Indeed he had immediately begun to talk to her with his eyes, without reaching out to the small sheets of paper she kept sewn to her waist together with a wallet for pens and ink. The bright eyes of this small hirsute painter from Reggio

33

Calabria were telling her that he was all ready to knead with his dark chubby hands the milk-white body of the young Duchess as if she were dough placed there to rise for him.

She had regarded him with contempt. His bold, arrogant way of presenting himself displeased her – for Heaven's sake, what was he? A simple painter, an obscure nobody come up from some Calabrian hovel, brought into the world by parents who were probably cowmen or goatherds.

But later she laughed at herself in the darkness of her bedroom, for she recognised that her social disdain was a lie, that there had risen in her an agitation she had never before experienced, an unexpected fear that almost throttled her. Up till now no one had revealed in her presence such a visible and unrestrained desire for her body, and this seemed to her quite unheard of, but at the same time it filled her with curiosity.

The next day she had the painter informed that she did not want him, and the day after she wrote him a note to begin work. She put two boys at his disposal to mix the colours for him and clean his brushes. She would remain shut away in the library, reading.

And so it was. But twice she went out on to the landing to watch him while, perched on the scaffolding, he busied himself drawing with charcoal on the white walls. It excited her to watch the movements of his small hairy hands. His draughtsmanship was confident and graceful, demonstrating a skill so profound and delicate that it could not fail to arouse admiration.

His hands daubed with colour, he rubbed his nose, smearing it with yellow and green, grabbed a slice of bread and tripe, and lifted it to his mouth, scattering crumbs of bread and fragments of offal.

VIII

No one expected that the third child, or rather the third daughter, would be born so quickly, almost a month early, with feet foremost like a calf in a hurry. The midwife had sweated so much that her hair stuck to her head as if she'd had a bucket of water emptied over her.

Marianna had followed the movements of the midwife's hands as if she had never seen them before: put to soak in a basin of hot water, softened in lard, making the sign of the cross on her chest and then once again being immersed in water. Meanwhile Innocenza kept putting handkerchiefs soaked in essence of bergamot over her mouth and on her belly, stretched taut with pregnancy.

> Come out, come out, you little sod
> With help from our Almighty God.

Marianna knew the lines and read them on the lips of the midwife. She knew that the midwife's thoughts were on the point of reaching out to her and that she had done nothing to fend them off. Perhaps they would alleviate the pain, she said to herself, and concentrated on them with her eyes shut.

What is the little stinker up to? Why don't you get born, eh? He's taken a bad turn, the turnip. What on earth is he up to? Is he turning somersaults or something? The legs are coming out first and the arms are all squashed to one side. It's almost as if he's dancing . . . and dancing . . . and dancing, my little one . . . but why don't you get born, you naughty little snail? If you carry on like this I'll give you a good thrashing . . . but then how could I ask the Duchess for the forty *tarì* I've been promised? Ahhh, but it's a little girl, ahi ahi . . . oh oh, oh my, oh my, nothing but girls come out of this ill-starred belly, what a misfortune. She doesn't have any luck, the poor dumb creature. . . . Get born, get born, you stinking little girl. . . . Suppose I promised you a little sugar lamb – no, you're determined not to come out. . . . If this one don't get born I'll be in trouble . . . everyone will know that Titina the midwife can't manage to bring a baby into this world and lets both mother and baby die. Holy Madonna, help me . . . even though you never gave birth. . . . What do you know of birth and work? . . . Help me to get this baby girl out and I'll light a candle as big as a pillar for you, I swear to you in God's name. I'll spend all the money the Duchess has promised me, the good soul. . . .

Seeing that the midwife was about to give her up for lost she wondered whether the time hadn't come for her to prepare herself for death with the baby locked inside her. I must recite a few prayers straightaway and ask the Lord's forgiveness for my sins, Marianna thought to herself.

But just at the very moment when she was preparing for death the baby came out, the colour of ink, not yet breathing. The midwife seized her by the feet and shook her as if she was a rabbit ready for the pot, until the little baby screwed up her face like an old monkey and, stretching her toothless mouth open, began to cry.

Meanwhile Innocenza brought the scissors to the midwife, who cut off the umbilical cord and then burned it with a small candle. The smell of burning flesh rose to Marianna's nostrils as she gasped for breath. She was not going to die; the acrid smoke brought her back to life and all at once she felt very tired and contented.

Innocenza continued to busy herself: she tidied the bed, tied a clean bandage round the mother's hips, put salt on the navel of the new-born baby, sugar on her little belly still soiled with blood, and oil on her mouth. Then, after sprinkling her with rose-water, she wrapped the new-born infant in bandages, squeezing her from head to foot like a mummy.

And now who is going to break the news to the Duke that it is another girl? Someone must have bewitched this poor Duchess. . . . If it was a peasant woman the child would be given a little spoonful of poisoned water. One on the first day, two on the second and three on the third, and the unwanted baby takes off for the next world ... but these are grand folk and girls are kept even when there are already too many.

Marianna was unable to take her eyes off the midwife as she dried her sweat and gave her a *consu*: a potion consisting of a small piece of linen that had been burned and then steeped in a mixture of oil, white of egg and sugar. All this she was familiar with already: each time she'd given birth she had seen the same things, only this time she saw them with the smarting eyes and the longing of a woman who knows that after all she is not going to die. It proved an entirely new pleasure to follow the confident routine of the two women who were taking care of her body with so much solicitude.

Now the midwife used her long sharp nail to cut a small membrane that still held the new infant's tongue, so as to ensure that she wouldn't stammer when she grew up; then, in accordance with tradition, a finger dipped in honey was thrust into the crying baby's mouth to comfort her.

The last things that Marianna saw before sinking into sleep were the calloused hands of the midwife holding the afterbirth towards the window to demonstrate that it was whole and that she had not torn it or left any fragments inside the mother's belly.

When she opened her eyes after twelve hours of unconsciousness Marianna found her other two daughters, Giuseppa and Felice, standing in front of her, all dressed up, festooned in bows, lace and coral: Felice already walking, Giuseppa in her nurse's arms. All three looked at her with astonishment, almost as if she had risen from her coffin in the middle of her own funeral. Behind them stood the baby's father, her uncle husband, in his best red suit, just managing to force out something close to a smile.

Marianna's hands stretched out, searching for the new-born baby lying beside her; not finding her she was seized with panic. Had the baby died while she was asleep? But her husband's half-smile and the festive appearance of the nurse in her best clothes reassured her.

As for the baby's sex, she had known it was a girl from the first month of pregnancy. Her belly swelled smooth and round, and not pointed as happens when it is going to be a boy, or at least so her grandmother Giuseppa had taught her; and indeed on each occasion her belly had taken on the gentle curve of a melon, and each time she had given birth to a daughter. Besides, she had dreamed of a girl: a little blonde head leaning against her breast and watching her with a look of bored detachment. The strange thing was that on her back the child in the dream had a little goat's head with tousled curly hair. What would she have done with such a monster?

Instead the baby was born perfect in spite of being a month · early, rather smaller than usual but clear-skinned and beautiful, without Felice's purple pear-shaped head or the down that had covered Giuseppa when she came into the world. She immediately showed herself to be a tranquil, quiet baby who never asked for her milk but took it when she was given it. She did not cry and she slept for eight hours at a stretch in exactly the same position as when she was laid down in her cradle. If it had not been for Innocenza, who, clock in hand, would come and wake the young Duchess for the feed, mother and daughter would have gone on sleeping regardless of what all the midwives, wet-nurses and mothers say: that new-born babies must be fed every three hours or they will die of hunger and bring shame on the family.

She had borne two daughters with ease. This was the third time and once again she had given birth to a daughter. Uncle husband was not too happy even if he had been generous enough not to criticise her. Marianna knew that until she had managed to produce a son she must go on trying. She was afraid of having flung at her one of those strongly worded notes of which she already had quite a collection and which would read something like: 'A boy – when will you make up your mind?' She knew of other husbands who had refused to speak to their wives after the birth of a second girl. But Uncle Pietro was too vague for such decisive action. And then he was not in the habit of writing much to her anyway.

So here was Manina, child of her seventeenth year, born during the final phase of the building. She took the name of her old aunt Manina, the unmarried sister of Grandfather Mariano. The family tree that hangs in the rose room is full of Maninas: one born in 1420, who died of the plague in 1440; another born in 1615, who became a barefoot Carmelite and died in 1680; another born in 1650, who died two years later; and the last, born in 1651, the most elderly of the present Ucrìa family.

From her grandmother Scebarràs the child has inherited her slender wrists and her long neck. From her father Duke Pietro she has inherited a certain look of melancholy and severity, even though she has the vivacious colouring and delicate beauty of the Ucrìa di Fontanasalsa branch of the family.

Felice and Giuseppa play happily with their baby sister, putting little sugar puppets in her hand and pretending she has eaten them, which makes the cradle and the curtains all sticky. Sometimes Marianna is worried that their affection has become so aggressive and noisy that it might be dangerous for the baby, so she always has to keep an eye on them when they are near the cradle.

Since Manina was born they have even left off playing with Lina and Lena, the twin daughters of the cowman Ciccio Calò, who lives next door to the stables. The two girls remain unmarried. After the death of their mother they devoted themselves entirely to their father, the cows and the house. They have grown tall and sturdy, and it is hard to distinguish between them. They dress alike in faded pink skirts, lilac-coloured velvet bodices and little blue aprons always smeared with blood. Now that Innocenza has made up her mind to refuse to kill any more chickens, the duty of strangling them and chopping them in pieces has fallen to the girls and they do it with great determination and speed.

The gossips have it that Lina and Lena lie with their own father in the same bed where they used to sleep with their mother, that already they have both become pregnant and have aborted themselves with parsley. But these are slanders that Raffaele Cuffa once wrote on the back of a sheet of household accounts and it didn't do to pay any attention to such gossip.

When they hang out the washing the Calò twins sing, which is wonderful. This has become known in a roundabout way from one of the servants, who comes to the house to do the washing. Marianna discovered it herself one morning as she leaned against the painted balustrade of the long terrace above the stables, watching the girls hanging out the washing on the line. They bent together over the big laundry basket, standing gracefully on tiptoe, taking a sheet and twisting it with one at one end and one at the other as if they were having a tug of war. She saw they were opening their mouths but she could not be sure whether they were singing. She was overcome with a desire to hear the sound of their voices, which people said were so beautiful, and this left her with a feeling of frustration.

Their father the cowman calls them with a whistle just as he calls his cows. And they run to him with firm, resolute steps that come from doing heavy work and having strong muscles. As soon as their father has gone off, Lina and Lena whistle in their turn to the horse Miguelito. They mount him and ride round the olive grove, one of them clutching the back of the other, without worrying about the branches snapping against the flanks of the horse, or the overhanging brambles that get entangled in their long hair.

Felice and Giuseppa go to find them in the dark sunless hovel next door to the stables, between the pictures of saints and the jugs full of milk set aside for ricotta. They get them to tell stories of murdered corpses and werewolves, which they then repeat to their father, who always gets cross and forbids them to mix with the twins. But as soon as he has gone off to Palermo the two children rush over to the cowman's house, where they eat bread and ricotta surrounded by hordes of horseflies. And their father is so absent-minded that he does not even recognise the smell they bring with them when they steal back to the house after having stayed for hours crouched on the straw, listening to terrifying stories that make their flesh creep.

At night the two little girls often slip into their mother's bed because of the fear these stories have aroused. Sometimes they wake up crying and sweating. 'Your daughters are so stupid: why do they keep going over there if they get frightened?' That is her husband's logic and one cannot disagree with it — except that logic is not sufficient to explain the fascination of associating with the dead in spite of the fear and the horror. Or even perhaps because of this.

Thinking of her two eldest children forever running off, Marianna lifts the baby out of the cradle. She sinks her nose into the lacy dress that covers the tiny feet and smells the unique odour of borax, urine, curdled milk and lettuce water, which all new-born babies carry on them — and no one has any idea why that smell is the most delicious in the world. She presses the little tranquil body against her cheek and asks herself how soon she will start talking. Even with Felice and Giuseppa she was afraid that they would never speak. How anxiously she had watched their breath, touching their little throats with her finger so as to feel the sound of their first words! And in each case she was reassured, seeing their lips opening and shutting, and following the rhythms of their speech.

Yesterday uncle husband had come into the room and seated himself on the bed. He had watched her feeding the child with a bored and thoughtful expression. Then he had written a shy note: 'How is the little one?' and 'Is your breast better?' and at the end he had added kindly: 'The boy will come. Leave it to time. Do not lose heart — he will come.'

IX

The son and heir arrived in due course exactly as uncle husband had desired, and is called Mariano. He was born just two years after the birth of Manina. He is fair like his sister, though better looking, but his character is quite different — he cries easily and if he is not receiving continuous attention he flies into a tantrum. As it is, everyone holds him in the palms of their hands like a precious jewel, and at a few months old he has already learned that no matter how, his every wish will be satisfied.

This time, uncle husband has smiled openly. He has brought his wife a present of a necklace of pink pearls as large as chickpeas. He has also made her a gift of a thousand escudos because 'kings do this when queens give birth to a boy'.

The house has been invaded by numerous relations never before seen, loaded with flowers and cakes. Aunt Teresa the Prioress has brought with her a swarm of little girls from the nobility, all nuns-to-be, each one with a gift for the mother: one presented her with a silver teaspoon, another with a pincushion in the form of a heart, another with an embroidered pillow, another with a pair of slippers encrusted with stars.

Her brother Signoretto stayed for an hour, sitting by the window drinking hot chocolate with a happy smile imprinted on his lips. With him came Agata and her husband Don Diego and their children, all dressed up for a feast day. Carlo also came from the Monastery of San Martino delle Scale, bringing her a present of a Bible transcribed by hand by a monk during the previous century, embellished with miniature paintings in delicate pastel colours.

Giuseppa and Felice, mortified at being ignored, pretended not to be interested in the baby. They have gone back to visiting Lina and Lena, where they have caught lice. Innocenza has had to comb their hair first with paraffin and then with vinegar, but even though the adult lice are annihilated, those within the eggs remain alive and emerge to infest the girls' hair, once again multiplying at a terrifying rate. It is decided to shave their heads and now they go around looking like two condemned souls, with naked skulls and a shamefaced look that makes Innocenza laugh.

Marianna's father the Duke has encamped at the villa so that he can 'watch out for the colour of the little one's eyes'. He says that the pupils of new-born babies don't tell the truth, that no one knows whether they are 'turnips or beans', and every time he takes the baby in his arms he cradles him as if he were his own son.

Her mother the Duchess has come all by herself, and the upheaval cost her so much effort that she had to go to bed for three days. The journey from Palermo to Bagheria seemed to her an 'eternity', the ruts in the roads 'abysses', the sun 'uncouth' and the dust 'stupid'.

She has found Mariano 'too beautiful for a boy; what are we to do with such beauty?' she has written on light-blue paper scented with violets. Then she uncovered the baby's feet and bit them gently. 'With feet like this he'll make a dancer', she wrote. Unlike her usual self, she has really enjoyed writing. She has been laughing, she's been eating, she's even abstained from taking snuff for a few hours, and at the end of the day she withdraws to the guest room together with the Duke and they sleep till after eleven next morning.

All the dependants of the villa have wanted to hold this long-awaited baby in their arms: the cowman Ciccio Calò held him gently in his hands furrowed with cuts and black with dirt. Lina and Lena kissed the baby on his mouth and his feet with surprising tenderness. And there was Raffaele Cuffa, who put on a new redingote of damask decorated with arabesques in the Ucrìa colours, and his wife Severina, who never leaves the house because she gets headaches that almost blind her; Don Peppino Geraci the gardener, accompanied by his wife Maria and their five children, all with red hair and eyebrows, all unable to utter a word through shyness; and Peppino Cannarota the footman, with his big son who works as a gardener in the Palagonia household.

They pass the new-born baby from hand to hand as if he were the Infant Jesus, smiling like proud fathers, hindered by the long trailing folds of the lace dress, sniffing blissfully the scents that emanate from the small princely body.

Meanwhile Manina crawls round the room on all fours with only Innocenza to take care of her. She pushes herself forward on hands and knees underneath the tables, while the guests come and go, trampling over the precious rugs from Erice, spitting in the vases from Caltagirone, and fishing with both hands in the dish piled with nougat from Catania that Marianna keeps by her bed.

One morning her father the Duke came in with a surprise – an entire writing outfit for his dumb daughter: a reticule made of silver mesh, and inside it a small bottle with a screw stopper for the ink, a glass case for the pens, a little leather bag for the ash, as well as a notebook held on by a ribbon fastened with a little chain to the silver reticule. But the biggest surprise of all was a small portable table, in the lightest of wood, made so that it could hang from her belt by two gold chains.

'In honour of Maria Louisa di Savoia Orléans, the youngest and most intelligent queen of Spain ever. Let her be an example to you. Amen.' With these words her father the Duke had inaugurated the new writing outfit.

At the insistence of his daughter he was inspired to write a brief history of this unforgettable queen, who died in 1714:

A young girl of no great beauty, but full of life. Daughter of King Victor Amadeus, our king from 1713, and Princess Anna of Orléans, niece of Louis XIV. She became the wife of Philip V of Spain at the age of sixteen. Soon afterwards her husband was sent to Italy to fight and she, at the suggestion of King Louis of France, was made Regent. There was much grumbling that a girl of sixteen should be made head of state. However, it was subsequently acknowledged that it had been a choice that was fully justified. The young Maria Louisa had a talent for politics. She used to spend many hours in the Council of State, listening to everything and everyone, intervening with brief and well-aimed observations. When an orator went on speechifying for too long, the Queen would pull out her embroidery from beneath the table and concentrate on it. The message was understood! As soon as a speaker saw her reaching for her embroidery he made haste to cut short his speech. In this way the sittings of the Council were much shorter and more to the point.

She kept up a correspondence with her uncle the Sun King and listened discerningly to his advice, but when she had to say no she said it – and how forthrightly too! The elder statesmen were nonplussed in the face of her political intelligence; the people adored her.

When the defeat of the Spanish army became known, the young Maria Louisa set an example by selling all her jewels and going from the richest to the poorest to collect money to put the army back on its feet. At that time she had had her first son, the Prince of Asturia, and she announced that if she were needed she would go to the front on horseback with her small son in her arms. And everyone knew she was capable of doing just that.

When the news came of the victories of Brihuega and Villaviciosa her joy was so great that she went out into the street, mingling with the crowds, dancing and skipping with the people.

She had a second son, who, however, died after only a week.

Then she was struck by an infection of the glands in her neck. She never complained about it and tried to cover the swellings with a lace collar. She gave birth to another son, Ferdinando Pietro Gabriele, who had the good fortune to survive. However, her illness worsened. The doctors said it was a case of phthisis. Meanwhile the Dauphin, father of Philip V, died, and immediately afterwards her sister Maria Adelaide died of smallpox, together with her husband and their eldest son.

Two years later she realised that the time had come for her to die too. She confessed, took the Holy Sacrament, bade goodbye to her sons and to her husband with a serenity that filled everyone with admiration, and drew her last breath at the age of twenty-four, without having uttered a single word of complaint.

Then one day one of Peppino Geraci's sons became ill with smallpox and the whole tribe of relations took to their heels. Once more – smallpox in Bagheria! It was the second time since Marianna had begun to transform the lodge into a villa. In the first epidemic there were many deaths, among them Ciccio Calò's mother and the small son of the Cuffa family, who was their only child; since then his wife Severina has suffered from headaches that are so devastating she always has to have her temples bound with bandages soaked in herbal vinegar *dei sette ladre*, and everywhere she goes she is preceded by a pungent smell of acid.

During this second epidemic two of Peppino Geraci's four remaining sons died. A girl betrothed to Peppe Cannarota's son also died; she was a beautiful girl from Bagheria, who was a servant in the Palagonia household. Two cooks from the Butera household also died, as did the old Princess Spedalotto, who only a short time ago had moved into a new villa not far from them.

Even Aunt Manina, who had arrived all wrapped in woollen shawls and supported by two footmen and had held the little Mariano in her skeletal arms, has died. But no one knows if this was because of smallpox. The fact is, she died there in the Villa Ucrìa all on her own and nobody knew a thing about it. They only found her two days later, lying on her bed like a small bird with ruffled feathers, her head so light that Marianna's father the Duke had written that 'she weighed as much as a worm-eaten nut'.

When she was young Aunt Manina had been 'much sought-after'. She was small-featured and had the body of a siren. Her eyes were so vivacious and her hair so glossy that Great-grandfather Signoretto was forced to change his mind about making her a nun so as not to disappoint her suitors. The Prince of Cutò wanted to marry her and also the Duke of Altavilla, Baron of San Giacomo, and even the Count of Patanè, Baron of San Martino.

'But she preferred to stay single at home with her father. To remain unmarried she had to feign illness for years.' So said Marianna's father the Duke. 'So much so that she became really ill, but no one knew the cause. She used to bend double, coughing; all her hair fell out and she grew thinner and thinner and more and more fragile.'

In spite of her illness Aunt Manina lived to be nearly eighty, and everybody wanted her at their festivities because she was such an acute observer and an accomplished mimic of both old and young, men and women, much to the delight of her friends and relations. Marianna used to join in the laughter, though she could not hear what Aunt Manina was saying. It was enough to watch her, small and nimble, manipulating her conjuror's hands, assuming the contrite expression of one person, the foolish expression of another, the foppish look of a third, to be completely overcome.

She was known for her waspish tongue and everyone tried to be on good terms with her for fear of what she might say behind their backs. But just as she did not let herself be hypnotised by adulation, she would not hesitate to make fun of people when she saw them behaving foolishly. It was not gossip itself that attracted her but the excesses indulged in by various characters such as the miserly, the vain, the weak, the thoughtless. Sometimes her thrusts hit it off so well that they became proverbial, as for instance when she said of the Prince of Rau that 'he despised money, but treasured coins like sisters', or when she had said of the Prince Des Puches, who was waiting for his wife to give birth (the Prince was known for his small stature), 'he will be in a state of agitation, walking up and down nervously under the bed', or when she described the little Marquis of Palagonia as a 'stake without a stake in life'. And so on and so on, to everyone's amusement.

About Mariano she mumbled that he was a 'small mouse disguised as a lion disguised as a small mouse' and she looked round her with her eyes sparkling, anticipating the laughter. By then she was like an actress on stage: she would not have given up her audience for anything in the world.

'When I die I shall go to hell,' she once said. And then she added, 'But what's hell? Palermo without any cake shops. And, anyway, I don't like cakes all that much.' And then a moment later: 'Come to that, it will be better than that ballroom where the saints spend all their time doing tapestry – that's paradise for you!'

She died without troubling a soul, all alone. And no one wept for her. But her witticisms continued to circulate, as salty and piquant as anchovies in brine.

X

Duke Pietro Ucrìa has never discussed one iota of what his wife has been gradually planning for the villa. He only digs his toes in when a small 'coffee house', as he calls it, springs up in the garden, built of wrought iron, with a domed ceiling, white and blue tiles on the floor, and a view over the sea.

Nevertheless, it was built, or rather it will be built, because although the wrought iron is all ready, the skilled workmen who will erect it are missing. At this time in Bagheria dozens of villas are being built, and craftsmen and bricklayers are hard to come by. Uncle husband often says that the lodge was more convenient, particularly for hunting. But it's a mystery why he keeps saying this, considering that he never hunts. He hates game and he hates guns, although he has a collection of them. What he really likes most are books on heraldry, and playing whist, when he isn't walking in the countryside among the lemon trees, whose grafting he attends to himself.

He knows everything about his ancestors and the origins of the Ucrìa family of Fontanasalsa and Campo Spagnolo, their orders of precedence, their rank, their decorations. In his study he has a big copper engraving of the martyrdom of Saint Signoretto. Beneath, incised in copper plate: 'Blessed Signoretto Ucrìa of Fontanasalsa and Campo Spagnolo, born in Pisa in 1269.' In smaller writing is the life of the blessed saint, telling how he arrived in Palermo and dedicated himself to pious works, 'frequenting hospitals and succouring the many poor people who infested the city'. At the

46

age of thirty he retreated to a 'most barren desert by the edge of the sea'. But where was this 'most barren desert'? Did he end up on the North African coast? In the 'desert bordering on the sea' Signoretto was 'martyred by the Saracens' but it is not known why he was martyred, the engraving does not give us any clue. Why was he beatified? But no, how foolish, of course he was beatified much later, after he was dead. It is said that one of the Blessed Signoretto's arms is in the possession of the Dominican friars, who venerate it as a relic. Uncle husband has done all he can to recover this family relic but up to now he hasn't had any success. The Dominicans say they have ceded it to a convent of Carmelite nuns, and the Carmelites say they have passed it on as a gift to the Poor Clares, who maintain that they have never seen it.

In the picture the sea is dark – a brown boat is moored by the shore; it is empty, its sails furled. In the foreground a ray of light is slanting down from the left as if someone were holding a flaming torch just outside the picture frame. An old man – but wasn't he only thirty? – is being manhandled by two robust youths with naked torsos. At the top to the right, three flying angels are lifting up a crown of thorns.

For Duke Pietro the history of the family, however full of myth and fantasy, is more real than the tales told by the priests. For him God is 'far away and couldn't care a dried fig'. Christ, 'if he were truly the son of God, was, to put it mildly, quite stupid', and as for the Madonna 'if she had been a woman of noble birth she would never have conducted herself so thoughtlessly, carrying that poor little fellow among the wolves, leaving him to roam around the whole blessed day long, and giving him to believe he was invincible when everyone knows the end he came to'.

According to uncle husband the first of the Ucrìas was no less than a king of the sixth century BC, namely King of Lidia. From that inaccessible land, still according to him, the Ucrìas migrated to Rome, where they became senators of the Republic. Finally they became Christians under Constantine. When Marianna writes to him jokingly that some of these Ucrìas were nothing but turncoats who went along with whoever was top dog, he scowls and refuses to look at her for several days. It is not proper to joke about the family patriarchs. On the other hand, if she asks him to tell her about some of the large pictures stacked in the yellow drawing-room, waiting to be hung when the house is eventually finished, he rushes for the pen to write to her about the Bishop Ucrìa, who fought against the Turks, and that other Senator Ucrìa, who made a famous speech to defend the right of primogeniture.

What she replies is unimportant. He seldom reads what his wife writes to him, even though he admires her quick, neat handwriting. The fact that she haunts the library disconcerts him, but he dare not oppose it. He knows that for Marianna reading is a necessity. He himself avoids books because they are 'all lies' and the imagination is itself unaccountable. For Duke Pietro reality consists of a series of immutable and eternal rules, which no sensible person can fail to conform to.

Only when a visit has to be made to a mother after the birth of her child, as is the custom in Palermo, or to attend some official function, does he expect his wife to get dressed up and to fix the diamond brooch that belonged to Grandmother Ucrìa di Scannatura on her chest and accompany him into town.

If ever he decides to remain in Bagheria he always arranges to have company at the table of the Villa Ucrìa. Sometimes he might invite Raffaele Cuffa, who acts as his bailiff, caretaker and secretary, but never his wife. Or he may ask his lawyer Mangiapesce over from Palermo, or else he sends the sedan-chair for Aunt Teresa, Prioress with the Clarissa nuns, or he may send a rider on horseback with an invitation to one of his cousins, Alliata di Valguarnera.

He likes the lawyer best of all because with him he can stay silent. There is no need to stand on ceremony, for the 'young pundit', as Duke Pietro calls him, does all the talking. He is someone who revels in holding forth on subtle points of law; he is very well up on the latest affairs in city politics and he doesn't miss a jot of gossip about the important families of Palermo. When Aunt Teresa is there it is more difficult for the lawyer to hold his own, because she takes the words out of his mouth, and as far as town gossip is concerned she is far better informed than he is.

Of all his relations, Marianna's aunt Teresa, sister of her father the Duke, is the one Duke Pietro likes best. With her he sometimes even talks with enthusiasm. They exchange news of the family. They exchange presents: reliquaries, rosaries that have been blessed, and family heirlooms. From the convent she brings little pastries filled with ricotta mixed with sugar and fennel seeds, which are a great delicacy. Duke Pietro guzzles them ten at a time, twitching his nose like a greedy mole.

Marianna watches him chewing and thinks to herself that uncle husband's brain is in many ways not unlike the contents of his mouth: mixed up, chewed up, minced up, ground up, gobbled up. But he retains almost nothing of the food he gulps down, which may account for why he is so skinny. He puts so much concentration into chewing up his thoughts that nothing remains in his body but hot air. As soon as he swallows them he is consumed with haste to eliminate the dross which it seems to him is too worthless to remain in the body of a nobleman.

For many of the noblemen of his age, who grew up and lived in the previous century, logical thought has something ignoble, even vulgar about it. To confront other minds, other ideas, is considered in principle an act of perfidy. The common people, with their crowd mentality, behave like flocks of sheep; only the nobleman stands alone, and out of this aloofness come his glory and his daring.

Marianna knows he does not think of her as an equal, although he respects her as a wife. For him, his wife is the child of a new century, incomprehensible, with something trivial in her passion for change, for action, for building. All action is an aberration – dangerous, futile, false: so declare his melancholy eyes as they watch her going busily about the courtyard, still littered with bricks and bags of lime. Action is choice and choice arises out of necessity. To give shape to the unknown, to render it familiar, known, means leaving less to the freedom of chance, to the divine principle of idleness that only a true nobleman can allow himself, in imitation of the Heavenly Father.

Even though she has never heard his voice Marianna knows exactly what is fermenting inside that sullen throat: a proud, attentive passion for the infinite possibilities of day-dreaming, of aimless aspirations and unattainable desires. A persistent voice, piercing the tedium and yet fully controlled, belonging to someone who never lets himself go. There's no doubt that is what he's thinking; she can tell from the breath that reaches her, hot and sour, whenever she is close to him.

Among other things Duke Pietro considers this mania of his wife for staying at Bagheria even in the cold winter months quite idiotic when they have a large comfortable house in Palermo. And it also annoys him to have to give up his evenings at the Casino dei Nobile, where he can play whist for hours, drinking glasses of aniseed-flavoured water and listening in a bored way to the desultory conversations of his contemporaries.

For her, on the other hand, the house in the Via Alloro is too dark, too cluttered with ancestral portraits and too frequented by unwelcome visitors. As for the journey from Bagheria to Palermo, she just cannot bear all the dust and the roads so full of potholes. And too often as she passes through the village of Acqua dei Corsari she has found herself face to face with the heads of bandits impaled on pikestaffs as a warning to the populace. Heads dried by the sun, infested by flies, often with chunks of arms and legs with blackened blood sticking to the skin.

Useless to turn her head away or shut her eyes. A small whirlwind sweeps through her mind. She knows that shortly she will be passing through the two colonnades of the Porta Felice, that they will go down the Cassaro Morto and immediately come into the wide rectangle of the Piazza Marina between the Piazza della Zecca and the church of Santa Maria Caterina. Then on the right will appear the Vicaria, and the wind in her head will become a hurricane, her fingers will contract as they clutch her father's hooded habit and end up tearing the little velvet cloak she is wearing round her shoulders.

Consequently she hates going to Palermo and prefers to stay on her own at Bagheria. So she has come to the decision that apart from exceptional occasions such as funerals or births or christenings, which unfortunately occur with great frequency among her prolific relatives, she will set up her winter quarters at the Villa Ucrìa even if the cold confines her to only a few rooms surrounded by braziers of lighted charcoal.

By now this is common knowledge and people come to seek her out when the roads are not rendered impassable by the flooding of the river Eleuterio, which often inundates the countryside between Ficarazzi and Bagheria.

Recently her father the Duke came and stayed with her for a whole week. They were alone together as she had always wanted, without the presence of sons, brothers, cousins and other relations. Since her mother's death, which occurred suddenly without any warning, he often comes to look her up on her own. He sits in the yellow room beneath the portrait of Grandmother Giuseppa and he smokes or sleeps. He has always slept a great deal, but it has got worse as he has grown older: if he does not sleep for ten hours every night he feels ill. And as he finds it difficult to get so many hours of unbroken sleep he ends up by dozing off in the daytime, lolling on the armchairs or on the couches.

When he wakes he invites his daughter to play a game of piquet. Happy and smiling in spite of the rheumatism that deforms his hands and makes his back bent, he never gets worked up over trifles and is always ready to amuse himself and to entertain others. He does not have the quick tongue of Aunt Manina, he is more ponderous than her, but he has the same sense of comedy and if he were to take the trouble he too could be an excellent mimic.

Every so often he grabs the notebook that Marianna keeps tied to her waist and writes on it impulsively.

'You are a little fool, my daughter, but now I am growing older, I realise that I prefer little fools to anyone else.'

'Your husband, my brother-in-law, is a simpleton, but he loves you.'

'Dying displeases me because I shall be leaving you, but it does not worry me having to go to see if knowing Our Lord is worth the penance.'

What never ceases to surprise her is the difference between uncle husband Pietro and his sister Duchess Maria and cousin Duke Signoretto. Just as her mother the Duchess was plump and lazy, he is wizened and athletic, always needing to be active even if it is only to pace up and down through his vineyards. Not to mention her father, Duke Pietro's cousin, who is so calm and well-disposed towards others, while Pietro is hostile and suspicious towards everyone. In short, uncle husband seems to have been born of a rogue seed that fell askew into the family soil and grew up twisted, bristly and resentful.

The last time they were together, Marianna and her father the Duke played piquet, eating candied fruit and drinking perfumed wine from Málaga, while Duke Pietro went to Torre Scannatura to see to the grape harvest. In between the game and having a drink, her father the Duke wrote down all the latest gossip from Palermo, about the Viceroy's mistress, who they say sleeps between black sheets to show off the whiteness of her skin; about the last galleon arriving from Barcelona with a cargo of transparent chamber-pots which everyone gave as presents to their friends; about the fashion of the 'Adrienne' skirt, first launched at the French court in Paris, which flowed through Palermo like an unstoppable avalanche and had set the dressmakers all of a twitter. He had even confessed to her his love for a lace-maker called Esther, who worked in a house on his estate at Papireto. 'I gave her a room that overlooked the street – you should see how delighted she is.'

Yet this man, who is her father and who loves her tenderly, caused her to experience the greatest horror of her life. But he does not know that. He did it for her benefit: a renowned doctor of the school of Salerno had advised that his daughter's deafness had arisen from some experience of great fear and that to cure it an even greater fear was needed. *Timor fecit vitium timor recuperabit salutam.* It was not his fault that the experiment failed.

The last time he came to stay with her, he had brought her a present: a child of twelve, the daughter of a man sentenced to death, whom he had accompanied to the gallows. 'Her mother died of the smallpox, her father was hanged, and he entrusted her to me when he was on the point of death. The White Brothers wanted to shut her away in a convent for orphans but I thought it would be better for her to be with you, so I give her to you as a present. But love her well, she's all alone in the world. They say she has a brother but no one knows where he has hidden himself. For all I know he's dead. Her father told me he had not seen the baby since he had given him to a country woman. Promise me that you'll look after her.'

So Filomena, usually known as Fila, has come to live in the villa. She has been clothed, provided for, and cherished, but she is still very distrustful. She talks very little or not at all; most of the time she hides behind doors, and she's unable to hold a plate in her hands without letting it drop. Whenever she can she escapes to the stables and sits down on the straw beside the cows so that when she comes back she brings with her a stench of manure that can be smelled at least ten feet away.

It is a waste of time to scold her. In her terrified gaze, always on the alert, Marianna recognises something of her own childhood moods, so she lets her alone, much to the anger of Innocenza and Raffaele Cuffa, and even of her uncle husband, who endures the newcomer with great difficulty and only out of respect for his cousin and brother-in-law and his dumb wife.

XI

Marianna wakes with a start and a sensation of freezing cold. She peers into the darkness to see if her husband's back is in its customary place beneath the sheets, but however much she tries she cannot make out the usual bulge. The pillows seem untouched and the sheets flat. She is on the point of lighting a candle when she notices that the room is flooded with a pale-blue light: the moon hangs low on the horizon and scatters drops of milky white on to the black waters of the sea.

Evidently, uncle husband has stayed in Palermo for the night, which he has been doing lately more and more often. This does not worry her – indeed she looks on it with relief. Tomorrow she will at last pluck up courage to ask him to have his bed made up in another room, perhaps in the study beneath the picture of the Blessed Signoretto, between the books on heraldry and history. Recently he has taken to thrashing about in bed like a tarantula and these unexpected earthquakes keep waking her up.

When this happens she would like to get up and go out but she does not do it for fear of waking him. If she were to sleep alone she would not have to keep asking herself whether she dare light a candle; she would be able to read a book or go downstairs into the kitchen to get a glass of water.

Since her mother's death, followed a few weeks later by the sudden deaths of Lina and Lena, both of them victims of quartan fever, Marianna often wakes up with sad, disturbing thoughts, and is troubled by nightmares. Half-sleeping and half-awake, she is haunted by memories of her mother, to which she has never before paid much attention, as if she were seeing her for the first time: how she used to dangle her white swollen feet from the side of the bed, her big toes like two puff-balls, twitching as if she were playing an imaginary spinet with her feet. Her mouth with its full red lips that parted listlessly to imbibe a spoonful of broth; the finger she would dip into the little basin of hot water and then bring to her mouth to test the temperature with her tongue, as if she were about to drink it rather than wash her face; and how she would all of a sudden struggle to her feet, her face flushed with the effort of trying to lace up a silk sash behind her back. At table, after eating an orange, she used to take a pip, split it in two with her front teeth and then spit it out on to her plate; then she would take another and spit it out in the same way, until her plate was a small cemetery of pips, once white but now, gutted of their husks, green.

She departed this life unobtrusively, without bothering anyone, as she had done everything in her brief existence, fearful of attracting notice or putting herself into the limelight. Too idle to make decisions herself, she willingly left everything to others without bad feeling. What she really liked was to sit by the window with a bowl of candied fruit beside her, an occasional cup of hot chocolate, a glass of laudanum to lull her into a state of peace and a pinch of snuff to tickle the end of her nose. She was quite happy watching the world go by like a beautiful pageant so long as she was not asked to participate in it. She was generous and would clap her hands at other people's achievements, but it was as if everything had already taken place a long time ago and was now merely the inevitable repetition of a familiar tale.

Marianna could not imagine her as the slim and lively girl described by Grandmother Giuseppa. She had always thought of her mother as she saw her: her broad face with its delicate skin, her eyes ever so slightly bulging, her heavy dark eyebrows, her fair curly hair, her round shoulders, her wide hips, her legs short in relation to her body, her arms weighed down with rolls of fat. She had a delightful way of laughing, between nervousness and familiarity, almost as if she was unsure whether to let herself go and enjoy the fun, or to draw back in order to conserve her energy. Whenever she shook her head her fair curls danced on her forehead and over her ears.

It is strange how often the memory of her returns now she is dead. In fact they are not memories, they are sudden visions almost as if she were there in the flesh, sagging from so many births and miscarriages: all prepared to carry out those small daily exertions that when she was still alive were performed by a woman who seemed on the point of death, and now that she is no more, display the raw, bitter flavour of real life.

Now Marianna is fully awake. Not a hope of getting back to sleep. She sits up in bed and starts to poke her feet into her slippers, but stops midway and waves her toes as if she were playing an imaginary spinet just like her mother – oh, to the devil with her, why doesn't she leave her in peace?

Tonight her feet guide her to the back stairs that lead up to the roof. She enjoys the chill of the cold steps beneath her straw slippers. Then up ten stairs, pause, ten stairs, another pause. She continues to climb with light footsteps. The hem of her wide satin dressing-gown rubs against her heels.

On one side are the doors to the attics, on the other the servants' quarters. She has not brought a candle with her; she will rely upon her nose to lead her along corridors, through narrow passages, tunnels, store rooms, hiding-places, cubby-holes, unexpected slopes and treacherous stairs. She is guided by the various smells: dust, mouse droppings, old wax, grapes hung up to dry, rotting wood, chamber-pots, rose-water and cinders.

The low door that opens on to the roof is shut. Marianna tries to turn the doorknob but it seems to be stuck; she can't move it an inch. She leans her shoulder against it in an attempt to push it open, holding the doorknob between her fingers, and at this it suddenly yields. She loses her balance and stumbles forward into the opening, scared at having made such a clatter.

After a few minutes she decides to pick her way along the tiles. A gentle wind rumples her hair, and the moonlight hits her in the face like a great silver bucket. The surrounding country is flooded with light. The plain with its olive trees is mantled with thousands of metallic scales and beyond it Capo Zafferano sparkles in the distance like another world. The jasmine and the orange blossom send their perfume upwards like diaphanous wisps of smoke that evaporate between the roof tiles.

Far away in the distance, on the horizon, the black, motionless sea is traversed by a wide ribbon of tremulous light. Nearer, at the bottom of the sloping valley, the outlines of the olive trees, the carobs, the almonds and the lemons give the impression they are all asleep.

Out of the wood the young knight comes,
A stalwart man and proud of mien,
His very garments white as snow,
His helmet graced by plover's plume.

These lines from Ariosto came sweetly into her memory. But why on earth did they come just now?

It seems as if she can make out the beloved figure of her father the Duke. The only 'knight errant white as snow' who ever offered himself for her love. Since she was six years old the 'knight' has fascinated her, with his white plume of plover's feathers; then as soon as she began to respond to him he went off to conquer other hearts, other restless eyes.

Perhaps he grew tired of waiting for his daughter to speak, perhaps unconsciously she had disappointed him with her stubborn dumbness. The fact is that by the time she was thirteen he was already bored with her and had given her, on a generous knightly impulse, to his unfortunate brother-in-law Pietro, who was in danger of dying without a wife or children. Perhaps her father's thinking had been, They'll reach an understanding through sharing each other's misfortunes. And he had shrugged his shoulders with cheerful indifference, as only he can do.

But now – what can this smell of burning tallow be? Marianna looks around her but there are no lights to be seen. Who can be awake at this hour? Balancing on the leads, she takes a few steps forward and leans against the balustrade that encircles the roof and on which stand mythological statues: a Janus, a Neptune, a Venus and four enormous cupids armed with bows and arrows.

The light comes from a window beneath the eaves. She leans right forward so that she can see part of the room. It is Innocenza who has lighted the candle beside her bed. Strange that she should still be dressed as if she has only just come into the room.

Marianna watches her while she unlaces her high ankle boots. From her angry gestures Marianna can guess exactly what she is thinking: How I hate these laces that are always having to be threaded and unthreaded through the eyelets; but Duchess Marianna has them made for her and then passes them on to us, and how can I spit on a pair of Viennese chamois-leather boots that cost thirty *tarì*?

Now Innocenza goes to the window and looks out. Marianna is suddenly afraid: what if she sees her here spying on her from the roof-top? But Innocenza looks downwards, also spellbound by the extraordinary brilliance of the moonlight that bathes the garden with phosphorescence and lights up the distant sea.

She watches her bending her head a little as if listening to some unexpected noise. It is probably the bay horse Miguelito stamping his hoofs on the stable floor. Yes, once again Innocenza's thoughts come through to Marianna and almost attack her: He's hungry, Miguelito is, that poor horse is starving. Don Calò has been

56

stealing the hay again. Everyone knows about it but who is going to tell the Duke? I'm not one to tell tales, let them sort it out!

Her feet bare, wearing a pink bodice with channels of sweat beneath her armpits, the top of her dress unlaced and an ample brownish-red skirt billowing over her hips, Innocenza goes to the centre of the room and, kneeling down, gently raises one of the floorboards. Her hands rummage impatiently in the hole and she brings out a little leather bag tied with a thick black cord. She takes it to her bed and unties the knot with agile fingers, plunges her hand into the bag and shuts her eyes while she explores something she obviously holds dear. Then very slowly she extracts from the purse a number of large silver coins and places them one by one on the sheet, like a gardener handling with great delicacy flowers that have only just come into bud.

Up at five tomorrow morning, up to her arms in coal as usual, whiffs of smoke billowing in her face while she struggles to light the cursed fire beneath the cooking pots, and then there are the fish to be gutted and those wretched rabbits, and when she feels their poor drooping heads with her fingers she thinks of all the trouble they've had to go through to feed themselves and to grow and then *wham*, one blow on the head and their eyes go dull and they never cease to look as if they were asking, 'But why? Why?' Then tomorrow morning she will have to cope with the chickens – what a misfortune that Calò's two daughters are dead, they were so good at killing fowls. . . . There's no doubt they were virgins even if Severina claimed she'd watched them one morning in the stable and while one was milking the cow the other was milking their father. Well, that's what she said, but Lord knows whether it's true. Since her son died Severina's been not quite right in the head, she sees odd things all over the place. Still, it's true that they both missed their periods for a few months, first one and then the other. They told Maria, and she's someone you can trust . . . she's in charge of the towels hung out each month to dry and she keeps a tally. . . . But suppose it was someone else who tumbled them? Why does it have to be their own father? Yet that's what people say, and come to that Don Peppino Geraci saw all three of them in bed together one morning when he came to fetch the milk very early. . . . And then they miscarried . . . poor idiots, they must for certain sure have gone to see La Pupara. They call her that because it is she who makes and unmakes the babies. No one is quite sure how she does it, but she knows all the herbs and all the roots.... For three days you're shitting and writhing and throwing up and on the third day you let go of the little mite ... dead.... Yes, they all go to La Pupara, even the baronesses. They leave her up to three *onze* for a successful abortion ... but it always works.... Oh, she's a clever one she is, that Pupara....

Marianna draws back, satiated with another person's thoughts on that deserted roof, peopled by the ghosts that have settled there. But it is not so easy to free herself from Innocenza's voice, that silent voice that continues to pursue her, together with the sickly sweet smell of burning tallow.

And then she has to decipher the notes drawn by that crack-brained duchess, who changes her mind every five minutes about what she wants to eat, and expects her to understand those queer drawings of hers – a mouse on a spit for roast chicken, a frog in a frying-pan for sautéd duck, a potato in water for baked egg-plant ... and then that impudent hussy Giuseppa comes down and she has to watch her putting her nose and fingers into the stews and sauces. She'll carry off to the library bits of tart that are still only half-cooked, and the way she looks like a barn-owl is enough to turn the milk sour. She'd like to give her a good slap but no one does that, not even her own mother ... just imagine! But what's got into her head? There's still so much to be done ... the Duke hasn't ordered anything for tomorrow and it's Manina's birthday.... Baked sturgeon? ... It will have to stand the whole night marinading in wine. Then there's the tart with puff pastry, with every sheet of pastry having to be pounded like fury and left to rest, and when at last she gets to bed it's one o'clock in the morning and at five o'clock she has to be up and at work in the kitchen ... and all for four of those miserable bits and pieces of silver each month, and even then they make it difficult for her, having to keep on asking for it because they get out of step with what's due to her.... These dukes have estates and palaces but they never have any money, to hell with whoever invented them!

Sometimes the Duchess palms off five crowns or even two *carli* but what use is small change to her? She needs something a bit more substantial to put into her purse that's always hungry and opens its mouth like a fish gasping for air.... She can't even put them back under the floor, those silly little *carli*.... What

58

we need is a few of those golden escudos with the head of Charles III, brand new from the mint, or a good golden doubloon with an effigy of Philip V, God rest his soul.... Before he gives out that cursed money Don Raffaele keeps counting it again and again ... once he tried to palm off a coin that had been filed. What an ass! As if she can't see with her eyes shut better than a wife knows her husband's cock!

Marianna shakes her head in despair. She can't get Innocenza's thoughts off her back, thoughts which seem at that moment to come out of her own mind, drunk from the moonlight. She moves away from the balustrade, possessed by impatience and anger at the voice of the cook inside her head, still continuing to mutter ... and what can you do with all this money? You can get yourself a husband, you can even buy a husband ... but who wants a husband? Not me! ... That was what my sisters wanted and one got kicked out the first time she opened her mouth and the other was abandoned like a stupid donkey when he went off with some girl twenty years younger, leaving her without a house and without a copper coin to her name and six kids to support. The joys of the bedroom? They talk about that in songs and in those books like the Duchess reads ... but perhaps she, in spite of all those brocade and silk dresses, those carriages, those jewels ... has she ever known the joys of the bed? The poor dumb creature always stuck in books and papers ... it makes me feel sad for her.

It seems unbelievable, but that's how it is: the cook Innocenza Bordon, daughter of a mercenary soldier from the far-away Venetian countryside, unable to read or write, with her hands scarred with cuts, with no one but herself to care for in the whole world, feels pity for the great Duchess who is descended directly from Adam through the paternal line....

Again Marianna leans against the balustrade, incapable of withdrawing from Innocenza's chattering thoughts and having to accept the grievances of her cook as the only real thing in this unreal balmy night. She cannot help watching her as with fingers made supple from her work in the kitchen she lifts up the heavy silver coins one by one and arranges them in pairs in the bag as if she were pairing them off to sleep together. Her fingers can judge a coin's weight so precisely that even with her eyes shut she can tell whether there is the slightest shaving off it.

With a sigh Innocenza ties the cord round the neck of the bag.

She puts it back in the hole in the centre of the room. She replaces the floorboard first with her hands and then by stamping it down with her feet. Then she goes towards the bed and rapidly gets out of her skirt, her blouse and her bodice, while her head shakes as if she's just been bitten by a tarantula and her hairpins fly through the air together with the tortoiseshell comb that once upon a time belonged to her mistress.

Marianna closes her eyes and draws back. She does not want to have to gaze on the naked body of her cook. Now it is her turn to shake her head to free herself from intrusive thoughts, cloying like carob juice. Could it be getting worse? On previous occasions she has been aware of the ruminations of whoever was next to her, but never for so long: only small garnerings of sentences, scattered morsels of thoughts, which were always encountered casually, by chance. For instance, when she really wanted to understand what her father the Duke was thinking she did not succeed at all.

Lately she has taken to dropping inside people, attracted by a lively fluttering of their thoughts that promises all sorts of unknown surprises. But then she becomes lost in them, swallowed up, without knowing how to extricate herself. How she wishes she had never gone up on to that roof, never looked into Innocenza's room, never breathed in all that clear, poisonous air.

XII

'Papa's will is creating a real scandal.'

'Cutting out his eldest son in favour of his daughters.'

'Such a thing has never happened.'

'Poor Signoretto!'

'There'll be a rumpus with Geraldo.'

'That aunt who is a canoness disagrees.'

'He's left you his half of the Villa Ucrìa in Bagheria, so why cry, stupid?'

'Mangiapesce the lawyer says that the law prohibits a legacy like this.'

'It'll all be annulled, that's the law of primogeniture.'

Marianna shuffles the notes that her sisters and aunts have

thrown on to her plate in quick succession. Her hands are wet with tears, and the words are blurred. How can they discuss estates and houses when the pale face of her dead father still haunts their eyes?

Watching them gesticulate she can see they are exchanging insults. And Innocenza's delicious dishes are not sufficient to keep their heads stuck into their plates. The realisation that while she was on the roof gazing down at the landscape stretched out in the moonlight her father was dying in his bed at the house in the Via Alloro in Palermo, makes the very thought of food abhorrent. How is it possible she did not hear the breathless breathing of his dying, she who can so easily hear other people's chattering thoughts? Yet she did have an inkling, it was as if she had seen his lovable body amongst the dwarf palm trees, and she had thought of her 'knight errant white as snow'. But she had not interpreted it as a presentiment of death. It was seduction that had been in her thoughts, without realising that she was close to the last, most profound seduction of all.

And now the birthday party for which Duke Pietro ordered Innocenza to serve baked sturgeon and a tart of puff pastry has become transformed into a funeral feast. But of mourning there is very little sign; more important is the scandal of her father the Duke's unusual will. And no one can understand how the will came to be already opened, even before his dead body had been interred.

They are all upset, but especially Geraldo, who has taken his father's generosity towards his sisters as a personal affront, even if it is after all only a matter of small bequests. In any case the largest amount goes to Signoretto, and from the unexpected inheritance the younger sons also have a life interest. But this disregard of normal custom has taken them all by surprise and, though at the end of the day they are not displeased at getting something for themselves, they feel duty bound to make a protest.

Signoretto, like the gentleman he is, does not interfere even though he is the one most affected. It is Aunt Agata the nun, sister of Grandfather Mariano, who is most determined to defend his rights, and it is she who sticks her neck out in paroxysms of indignation.

Uncle husband is the only one not to trouble himself over these disputes. He is not involved in the inheritance of his brother-in-law and it does not matter to him where it all goes. He has enough of his own, and he already knows that the Villa Ucrìa at Bagheria, which his wife cares about so much, will be entirely theirs, so he pours out the wine and thinks of other things, while his eyes rest with some irony on the heated, angry faces of his nephews and nieces.

Sitting opposite Marianna, Signoretto is perhaps the only one who feels a duty to demonstrate some formal grief for the death of his father. When someone speaks to him, he puts on a pious expression that has something comic about it because of its studied effect. Titles are raining down on him: Duke of Ucrìa, Count of Fontanasalsa, Baron of Bosco Grande, of Pesceddi, of Lemmola, Marquis of Cuticchio and of Dogana Vecchia. He still has not found a wife. His mother the Duchess chose one for him but he did not like her. Then his mother died almost overnight from heart failure and no one else was interested in the complicated arrangements that marriage into the Uzzo di Agliano family involves. When his son, still a bachelor, had reached the age of twenty-five, his father the Duke had hastened, on an impulse of parental concern, to find him another wife, the Princess Trigona of Sant 'Elia. But even she was not to his liking and his father was too weak to enforce his obedience.

Though it probably had less to do with weakness than with doubt. His father the Duke did not entirely believe in his own authority, even though he was domineering by nature. All his decisions were undermined by a lack of confidence, by an internal weariness that brought a smile rather than a frown and led to compromise rather than firmness.

Thus Signoretto, at the age when all the youth of Palermo's noble families are already married and have sons of their own, is still a bachelor. For some time he has been deeply involved in politics. He now says he wants to become a senator, not just as a formality like other people: his ambition is to increase the export of grain from the island, so reducing the price; to open roads into the interior to facilitate transport; and to get the Senate to buy ships for the use of the farmers. Broadly speaking, this is what he has been proposing, and many young people are in agreement with his plans.

'Senators only go to the Senate once in a blue moon', Carlo wrote to her behind Signoretto's back. 'And when they do it's only to argue about questions of precedence, while they eat pistachio ices and exchange the latest town gossip. They have bartered once and for all their right to say no, for the guarantee of being left in peace on their own estates.' But Signoretto is ambitious; he says he intends to go to the courts of Savoy and Turin, where other young men from Palermo have made a name for themselves with their good manners, their intelligence and their ability to split hairs. Recently he was in Paris, where he learned to speak French fluently and studied the classics with great zeal.

The person who loves him most and protects him is Agata, sister of their grandfather Mariano, and a canoness of the Carmelite order. Wrapped in shawls with long gold tassels, thrown carelessly over her habit, she has assembled a library of biographies of marshals, heads of state, kings, princes, bishops, popes. Because of the interests they have in common you'd have thought she and Duke Pietro would get on well, but this is not so. The fact of the matter is that the Duke asserts that the Ucrìa family originated in 600 BC, whereas she swears that it first appeared in historical records in 188 BC with Quinto Ucrìa Tuberone, who became a consul at only sixteen. Because of this disagreement they have not spoken to each other for years.

Meanwhile Fiammetta, since she has become a nun, has lost the stunted, resigned look she had as a child; she has full breasts, bright eyes and a rosy complexion. Her hands have become strong with all the kneading, chopping, peeling and beating she has to do. She has found out that 'eating dry bread with spittle', as ordained by the rules of the order, is not for her, so she spends her time surrounded by copper pans, cooking all sorts of delicious dishes.

Next to her is Carlo, who looks more and more like his mother: lazy, slow, enigmatic, his arms plump, his chin already on the verge of being double or even triple, his gentle myopic eyes, his cassock stretched to bursting across his massive chest. He excels at deciphering ancient religious manuscripts. Recently he has been summoned to the monastery of San Calogero di Messina to decipher the secrets of a few books from the thirteenth century that no one understands any more. And he has made a copy of them word for word, making a few additions of his own, and as a result has been lauded with gratitude and gifts.

And then Geraldo, who is 'studying to become a general', as Aunt Manina used to say. Polished, ceremonious, frigid, wearing uniforms that appear still hot from the ironing board, he pays court to women, by whom he is much sought after; but he refuses to get married because he does not possess either large estates or titles. However, there is the possibility of a match that has Aunt Agata's blessing, a certain Domenica Rispoli, the wealthy daughter of a farming family who have made their money through the ignorance of a lazy landowner. But Geraldo is not interested. He says he will not mingle his blood with that of a farm girl, even if she is as beautiful as Helen of Troy. But now he has learned that his father has left him some land of his own at Cuticchio. So long as he is able to turn it to good account, he should reap sufficient profit to keep a carriage and have a house in town. But he aspires to something more showy. Even shopkeepers in the Piazza San Domenico have carriages!

Perched on the edge of a chair like a little girl, her arms covered in midge bites, is Agata, the beautiful Agata, given in marriage at the age of twelve to Prince Diego di Torre Mosca. Once upon a time the two sisters understood each other simply by exchanging a look, Marianna recollects. Now they have become almost like strangers. Every so often Marianna goes to the Torre Mosca Palazzo in the Via Maqueda. She admires their tapestries, their Venetian furniture, their enormous gilt-framed mirrors, but each time she has found her sister gloomy, overwhelmed by distant, dismal thoughts. Since the birth of her first-born son, Agata has begun to get smaller. That white skin, so beloved by the mosquitoes for its fragrance, has grown withered and wrinkled before her time; her features have become slack and disfigured; and her eyes have grown sunken as if the very act of seeing consumes her with pain.

Fiammetta, who was considered to be the ugly one of the family, has become something of a beauty, hoeing the kitchen garden and kneading bread in the convent; but Agata, who at fifteen 'made all the angels fall in love with her', as her father wrote, at twenty-three has taken on the look of a wizened Madonna, one of those Madonnas whose picture, painted by an unknown hand, hangs over people's beds and who are so worn out that they seem about to crumble away.

She has had six children but two of them have died. After her third son was born, she suffered from a blood infection which almost carried her away. She has recovered, but only partially. Now she suffers from sores on her breasts. Every time she feeds the baby she writhes in agony, and ends up giving her own son more blood than milk. Her husband has engaged wet-nurses for her but she persists in wanting to feed him herself. Obstinately determined to sacrifice herself until she is reduced to a shadow, continuously racked by puerperal fevers, her eyes sunk into the cavity of their sockets beneath her soft fair eyebrows, she is unwilling to accept advice or help from anyone.

An almost heroic will can be divined in this tight-lipped young mother, her forehead divided by a furrow, her chin rigid, her smile forced and her teeth yellow, decayed and prematurely chipped. Every so often her husband grasps her hand, gives her a kiss and gazes at her. Who knows what the secret of their marriage can be, Marianna says to herself. Every marriage has its secrets that are never revealed, even to a sister. Her own is distinguished by silence and coldness, interrupted by moments of nocturnal brutality, which are luckily becoming less and less frequent.

And Agata's? Her husband Don Diego seems to be in love with her in spite of the disfigurements and devastations that have resulted from too frequent confinements, which she endures like a martyrdom. And she herself? From the way she accepts his caresses and kisses it seems that she is forcing herself to restrain an impatience that borders on disgust. Don Diego's blue eyes are large and clear, but beneath an apparent love and solicitude there is something else that does not readily come to the surface: perhaps jealousy, or the anxiety of possessing something he does not feel sure of. Occasionally his innocent eyes reveal flashes of self-satisfaction at the premature fading of his wife's beauty, and his hand reaches out to her with a hint almost of joy, mingled with compassion and complacency.

But now Marianna's preoccupation is interrupted by a violent push that nearly sends her sprawling. Geraldo has suddenly jumped to his feet, slamming his own chair against the wall and sweeping the tablecloth against his deaf sister. Uncle husband hurries towards her to make sure she hasn't been hurt. Marianna smiles to reassure him, and she is astonished to find herself taking his side against her brothers: for once they are friends and accomplices.

For her the villa at Bagheria is sufficient. She has had it built exactly as she wants it and she expects to grow old there. Of course she'd have no objection to inheriting one of her father's family estates so as to have some ready money of her own and not be indebted to anyone. Even though the estate of Scannatura, owned by her husband, produces a satisfactory income, she has to account to Duke Pietro for every coin she spends and sometimes she doesn't even have the money to buy writing-paper.

Even the hazelnut orchard at Pesceddi or the olive groves at Bagheria would have come in handy. Then she could have managed them according to her own ideas and have an income that would not be controlled by anyone, and of which she would not have to render an account to others. She too, almost without realising it, is being drawn into thinking about the division of the inheritance, even she is calculating, grasping, claiming rights. Fortunately she does not have a voice that makes itself heard in this stupid argument between the brothers, otherwise she doesn't know what she might not say. Anyway, no one has consulted her. They are so taken up with the sound of their own words, which acquire, as the family row gains momentum, the vibrant tones of trumpets: a sound she has never heard, but which she imagines as a metallic clanging that sets her feet dancing.

Often they behave as if they had nothing to do with her. Silence takes possession of her like one of her mother's dogs that would have seized her round the waist and dragged her far away. And there among the relations, she is like a ghost that sees but is not seen.

She is aware that the squabble about the villa at Bagheria is still grinding away under its own steam, but no one turns round to her. Her father the Duke owned a part of what used to be his grandfather's hunting lodge, and half of the olive and lemon trees surrounding the villa. With an offhandedness that seems to the others disgraceful he has left it all to his dumb daughter. But there is already one person who thinks it would be iniquitous to contest the will: uncle husband has distanced himself from it all, and has left a note in her lap talking of 'Heaven knows what legal tangles they'll get up to, seeing that lawyers in Palermo grow like mushrooms'.

The thought that her father is lying dead on his bed in the Via Alloro while she is here eating, surrounded by her brothers, who are now on the point of coming to blows, suddenly strikes her as a very comical state of affairs. She dissolves into solitary soundless laughter that transforms itself into a silent flood of tears, a senseless deluge that shakes her like a storm.

Carlo is the only one who notices her distress, but he is too involved in the row to get up. He confines himself to looking at her compassionately, yet also quite bewildered, because her soundless sobs are like shafts of lightning without thunder, something flawed and incomplete.

XIII

Part of the yellow room has been cleared to make way for a gigantic Nativity crib. The estate carpenters have worked for two days erecting a mountain that compares with Monte Catalfano. In the distance a volcano can be seen with its outline painted in white. In the centre of the volcano is a plume of smoke made out of feathers sewn together; below it is a valley of terracotta trees with leaves of green cloth, and below that the sea made from layers of silk.

Felice and Giuseppa are sitting on the carpet, intent on using some paper plumes splattered with green paint to edge a small lake made out of mirrors. Manina stands against the wall, watching them. Mariano is busy eating a biscuit, smearing it all over his mouth and cheeks. Fila is next to him; she should be setting out the little figures of shepherds on the meadow of bottle-green wool, but she is so enraptured by this splendid Nativity crib that she has forgotten. Innocenza is standing near the stable, giving some last additional touches to the manger, out of which stick tufts of real straw. Signoretto, the baby, sleeps in Marianna's arms. She has wrapped him in her Spanish shawl and rocks him quietly to and fro against her breast.

At last the lake is finished but instead of reflecting the blue of the paper pasted behind the stable, it mirrors the cautious eyes of a chimera, peeping out from between the foliage on the ceiling. Innocenza gently places the baby Jesus with his heavy wax halo on the straw. Next to him the kneeling Virgin Mary has been draped with a turquoise mantle, covering her head and shoulders. Saint Joseph wears breeches of sheepskin and a wide-brimmed brown hat. The ox is as large as an elephant and as gnarled as a toad, and the ass with its long pink ears looks more like a rabbit.

Mariano, who has just had his seventh birthday, sets off in the direction of the flower-decked basket, in which some small figures are still lying. With his hand all sticky with sugar he pulls out one of the three kings, whose turban is studded with real precious stones. Suddenly Giuseppa jumps on top of him and snatches the figure out of his hands. He loses his balance and falls down, but he does not give up. He turns to plunge his hands into the basket again and pulls out another king, whose cloak glitters with gold. This time it is Felice who rushes towards her brother to take the precious little statue from him, but he won't let go. The two of them fall on to the carpet, he kicking and she biting. Giuseppa runs to help her sister and they both jump on top of him, pounding him with blows.

Marianna leaps up, holding the baby, and dashes across to the three of them, but Innocenza gets there first and seizes hold of them by their arms and hair. The figure of the king lies shattered on the floor.

Manina watches them. She is upset and she goes to her brother and hugs him and kisses his cheek, which is wet with tears. Then she quickly seizes her sisters by the hands and pulls them close to her to kiss them as well.

That child is a really talented peace-maker, Marianna says to herself. Even more than playing and eating, she loves creating harmony. Then, to distract her two sisters from the quarrel, she fills her cheeks and blows on to the crib so as to flutter the Madonna's cloak, lift up the Infant Christ's dress and blow Saint Joseph's beard to one side. Felice and Giuseppa burst out laughing. And Mariano, his hand still clutching half of the little statue, laughs too. Even Innocenza laughs at the breeze that ruffles the cloth palm trees and sends the shepherds' hair flying up in the air.

Giuseppa has an idea – why not dress Manina up as an angel? She already has the head of golden curls, the round gentle face, the large eyes reverently lowered, that make her fit for paradise. All she needs is a pair of wings and a long skirt the colour of the sky. Filled with enthusiasm she enlists Felice to unroll a sheet of gold paper. She cuts it up while Mariano, desperate to join them even though what they are doing is beyond him, pushes his way in.

Once she realises that becoming an angel will prevent her brother and sisters from squabbling for a while, Manina joins in. They'll dress her up in a mantle of her mother's, they'll sew wings on her bodice, they'll paint her face pink and white. Everything will be all right so long as she succeeds in making them laugh by playing the fool.

Marianna sniffs the smell of the paints, the pungent smell of turpentine, the fatty smell of linseed oil. An unexpected nostalgia clutches at her throat: a white canvas, a stick of charcoal and the dexterity of her hands could capture a part of the crib, the corner of the window, the sunlight on the stone floor, the two bent heads of Giuseppa and Felice, the patient form of Manina with one wing already stuck on her back, the other spread out on the floor, the substantial bulk of Innocenza leaning mysteriously over the little terracotta trees, Fila's eyes reflecting the lights of a gigantic silver star.

Meanwhile Signoretto has woken up and his tiny bald head pops out from his mother's shawl while he looks up at her lovingly. Bald and toothless, he looks like a 'playful spirit' with a skipping heart. 'He has no peace, this playful little person', wrote Grandmother Giuseppa in the exercise book with the fleur-de-lys on the cover. 'How he laughs at having laughed.'

A mother with her children. She knew she could fit them all into the painting, including herself, if she used a sufficiently wide canvas. She would start with the chimeras, move on to Fila's raven black hair, and then to Innocenza's calloused hands, to Manina's canary yellow curls, to Mariano's eyes the colour of night, to Giuseppa and Felice's pink and violet skirts. She would portray the mother, sitting on a cushion, as she herself is now, and the folds of her shawl would merge with those of her dress, leaving her arms and shoulders bare to reveal the naked head of her baby son.

But why does the mother of these children have such a dolorous expression in a picture that portrays a cameo of family happiness? Why this strange disquiet on her face? The imaginary painting freezes Marianna's hand as if she were guilty of trying to set herself against God's will. If it is not Him, who is it that pushes them so anxiously forward, makes them curl up, makes them grow up and then grow old, and then die in the time it takes to say 'Amen'?

A painter's hand has a thirst for thieving, it steals from heaven and makes a gift to the memories of men, it feigns eternity and it delights in this pretence almost as if it had created rules of its own, more durable and more profoundly true. But is it not a sacrilege, is it not an unforgivable affront to divine trust? Yet other hands have arrested time with sublime arrogance, have rendered the past familiar. On the canvas nothing dies but it perpetuates itself like a cuckoo with its cry of poignant melancholy. Time, Marianna tells herself, is a secret that God hides from men. And because of this secret we must always live in sorrow, from hand to mouth.

A shadow comes between her imaginary painting and the sun which spreads its radiance over the floor. Marianna raises her eyes to the window and sees uncle husband watching them from outside the glass. His small penetrating eyes seem filled with gratification at the spectacle in front of him: there, assembled on the carpet of the most luminous room in the villa, is his whole family, his progeny. Now that there are two boys, his expression has become proud and protective.

The steady gaze of uncle husband meets that of his young spouse, his niece. There is gratitude in his barely discernible smile and in response she is touched by a feeling of primeval pleasure. Will uncle husband open the door of the french windows and join them beside the crib, or won't he? Knowing him, she expects that, having reassured himself, he will not be tempted by the warmth of the heated room but will go off on his own. And in fact she sees him turn his back, dig his hands into his pockets and walk with long strides towards the coffee house. There, in the shelter of the windows, with the plants climbing up the wall, he has brought to him a cup of well-sweetened coffee, and contemplates the landscape that he knows by heart: on the right the spreading peak of the Pizzo della Tigna; opposite, thickets of acacia trees on Monte Solunto; the dark bare ridge of Monte Catalfano; and, close by, the ruffled sea that today is as green as a field in spring.

XIV

The room is in shadow. There is a brazier on the floor with a pan of boiling water on top of it. Marianna is sunk in a low chair, her legs stretched out on the floor, her head lolling on the cushion. She is asleep.

Beside her is the big wooden cot with blue ribbons that has already cradled Manina and Mariano. The ribbons are stirred by a breath of air that blows through the half-open window.

Innocenza comes in, pushing the door open with her foot. In her hands she carries a jug of boiling punch and a couple of biscuits spread with honey. She places the jug on a chair close to the Duchess and seems on the point of leaving, but thinks better of it and goes over to take a blanket from the bed to protect the sleeping mother from the cold. She has never seen her in such a bad way, so thin and pale, with dark rings under her eyes. There is something dishevelled about her appearance that is quite unlike her. She whom everyone normally thinks of as a young woman of twenty now looks years older. If only she wouldn't tire herself out reading so much! An open book lies upside down on the floor.

Innocenza lays the blanket over her legs, then goes to the big cradle to look at Signoretto, the last-born child, who sucks in his breath with a wheezing sound. This poor child won't last the night, she says to herself, and this desperate thought wakes Marianna, who comes to with a start.

She has been dreaming of flying, her eyes and nose streaming in the wind. A horse's hoofs are galloping through the clouds and she realises she is astride the bay Miguelito, sitting in front of her father, who is holding the reins and urging the animal to gallop through huge boulders of cotton wool. Beneath, there in the centre of the valley, the Villa Ucrìa can be seen in all its beauty, its elegant façade the colour of amber, the arches of its two wings fretted with windows, the statues poised like ballerinas on the cornice of the roof.

She opens her eyes to find Innocenza's plump kindly face only a finger's breadth away from her. She pulls back abruptly. Her first instinct is to push Innocenza back – what does she think she's doing, spying on her like this? But Innocenza smiles at her with such affectionate anxiety that Marianna does not have the courage to drive her away. She sits up, fastens the collar of her dress and smooths her hair with her fingers.

Once again the cook moves over to the child, restless in his cradle; she unties the ribbons and scrutinises the small shrunken face with its open mouth desperately struggling for air.

Marianna asks herself by what ominous alchemy Innocenza's thoughts should reach her so clear and lucid, as if she could hear them. She finds this unnerving, a burden that is hard to bear. At the same time she enjoys breathing in the odour of the grey skirt that smells of fried onion, tincture of rosemary, vinegar, lard, basil. It is the smell of life that incongruously intermingles with the smells of vomit, perspiration and oil of camphor that exude from the beribboned cradle.

She signs to her to sit beside her. Innocenza responds quietly and, pulling down her wide pleated skirt, settles on the floor and stretches her legs out in front of her. Marianna extends her hand towards the little glass of punch. She would really have preferred a long drink of cold water, but Innocenza had thought the hot liquid would help her withstand the icy cold of the night, and she does not want to disappoint her by asking for something different. So she gulps down the hot sickly liquid in one breath, scalding her palate in the process. But instead of feeling warmer she starts to shiver with cold.

Innocenza grasps her hand with a sympathetic gesture and rubs it in hers to warm it. Marianna stiffens: she cannot avoid thinking of the bag of money and the sensual gesture as Innocenza put the coins to rest two at a time. So as not to wound her feelings with a rejection, Marianna gets up and goes over to the bed. There, behind the screen embroidered with swans, she crouches down over the clean chamber-pot and passes a few drops of urine into it. Then she takes the chamber-pot over to the cook and hands it to her as if she were giving her a present. Innocenza takes it by the handle, covers it with a corner of her apron, and goes to the stairs to pour it down into the black cesspit. She walks cautiously, holding herself upright as if she were carrying something precious.

Now the child seems to be no longer breathing at all. Marianna watches the violet lips and, bending over him, anxiously places a finger under his nostrils. Little puffs of air are exhaled at rapid irregular intervals. The mother puts her head on her son's chest to feel the beating of his heart, which is so faint as to be barely perceptible. A powerful smell of regurgitated milk and camphorated oil rises to her nostrils. The physician has forbidden washing him and the poor little body lies wrapped in layers of cloth that are increasingly impregnated with the odours of death.

Perhaps he will make it; the others have been ill too. Manina has had two attacks of mumps and had a high fever for days. Mariano nearly died of erysipelas. But none of them has ever exuded the odour of decaying flesh that comes from Signoretto's body.

He is only just four but she sees him as he was when he was only a few months old, clinging to her breast with hands that were like small spiders. Both he and Manina were born prematurely, but while she came into the world a month before she was due, he tried to jump out two months early. He grew slowly but according to the physician Cannamela he appeared to be healthy and in a few months would catch up with his brothers and sisters. At the breast he did not seem to know how to suck; he would tug violently, gulp down the milk and then sick it up. And yet he was the first to recognise her, the first to turn to her with happy lively smiles.

No one in the world could hold him in their arms except for her. And none of the wet-nurses, nannies and French maids were able to quieten him: until he was back in his mother's arms he would not stop screaming. He was a happy and intelligent child, who seemed to have intuited his mother's deafness and there and then invented a language which she alone could understand. He communicated with her by kicking, mimicking, laughing and battering her with sticky kisses. He would press his big toothless mouth against her cheek, he would shut his eyes and lick her with his tongue, he would squeeze the lobes of her ears between his gums very gently, like a puppy that knows its strength but curbs it in play.

He grew more rapidly than the others. He became longer and longer, with two enormous feet that Innocenza would take in her hands with admiration. 'With these we'll make him into a paladin,' she said one day, and Duke Pietro hastened to write it down on a piece of paper because he knew it would make Marianna laugh.

He was not at all fat, by any stretch of the imagination. Hugging him she could feel his slender ribs like crescent moons beneath her fingers. When will this child decide to put on a little more flesh? she asked herself, and she kissed his protruding navel, which was always a little red and inflamed as if it had only just been cut off half an hour ago.

A smell of curdled milk hung around him. Even baths in the washtub brimful with soap and water could not entirely get rid of it. Even with her eyes tight shut she was able to recognise this last son of her thirtieth year. She openly preferred him; in response to his unlimited love for her, her love for him was boundless. Sometimes in the early morning she would wake up

73

with a sensation of warmth on her naked shoulder and discover that he had crept furtively into her bed, attaching his toothless mouth to her flesh and pulling at it as if it were a nipple. She would clasp him round his neck and hug him against her in the dark beneath the warmth of the blankets, and he would burst out laughing and cling to her, sniffing her night smells and kissing and clasping her as he snuggled towards her breast.

At mealtimes she would have him sitting beside her in spite of peremptory notes from uncle husband: 'Children should stay with the other children in the nursery. That's why it's there.'

'Without me he wouldn't eat, my uncle.'

'And do not call me uncle.'

'The child is too thin.'

'I shall make him thinner if you don't send him to his room.'

'If you send him away I shall go too.'

An exchange of angry notes, which made Fila and the scullery maids laugh behind her back.

In the end Marianna had permission for the child to sit next to her only at lunch, so that she could feed him little pizzas filled with minced chicken, pasta made with egg-yolk and cheese, and egg-flip with orange juice: everything that, as Innocenza said, 'makes good red blood'.

Signoretto got no fatter, but he grew taller and taller, acquiring the neck of a stork and two small thin arms like a monkey's, which were openly ridiculed by his brother. At two he was taller than Agata's three-year-old. Although he did not gain any weight he shot up like a plant in search of the sun. Neither his hair nor his teeth came through. His head was like a wooden ball and she covered it with embroidered bonnets turned up and puffed out at the edges.

At the age when other children had begun to talk he only laughed. He sang, he screamed, he spat, but he did not speak. And uncle husband had begun to write threatening notes: 'I don't want my son to be dumb like you', and again, 'It is essential he separates from you, that's what the apothecary says and so does the physician Cannamela.'

Marianna was seized by such fear that he would be taken away that she had an attack of fever and while she was delirious Duke Pietro went round and round the house in a state of vacillation, overwhelmed by a frantic dilemma: should he take advantage of his wife's delirium to remove the child and put him in Aunt Teresa's convent, where he would be taught to speak, or should he be compassionate and leave him with his mother, to whom he was so uncontrollably bound? While he was fraught with indecision her fever subsided and she made him promise to leave the child with her for at least another year. In exchange he brought a tutor into the house and forced the boy to learn the alphabet. By now he was four and his refusal to speak worried her too.

So that was the situation. Uncle husband put his worries to rest – the child was healthy, he was happy, he ate well, he grew. How could he tear him from his mother's arms? But of talking he gave not a sign.

Then, one day, as the end of the year agreed on by his father drew near, he fell ill. He vomited until his body became ashen.

Doctor Cannamela diagnosed a delirium caused by inflammation of the brain. He has had a small basin of blood drawn out by the surgeon Pozzolungo, who, in addition, has put him on a fast in an isolated room which only his mother and Innocenza are allowed to enter. Moreover the surgeon has declared that it is not inflammation of the brain at all, but an abnormal type of smallpox.

Innocenza has had smallpox, from which she emerged half-dead, but she survived. Marianna has not had it but she is not afraid of it. Did she not stay all on her own in the villa when the whole of Bagheria was seized by fever and vomiting, without getting infected? On that occasion she had washed her hands continuously in vinegar, had eaten lemons with salt, and kept her mouth covered with a handkerchief tied behind her neck like a brigand.

But since Signoretto has been ill she has not taken any of her usual precautions. She sleeps in the upholstered chair next to the wooden cradle in which her son lies panting, watching for every breath. During the night she wakes with a start and puts her hand on to his mouth to make sure he is still breathing.

When she sees him drawing in air in this tormented way, his lips livid, his little hands clinging to the edge of the cradle, she can't help wondering if the best way of helping him would be to let him die. The surgeon says he should have passed away already. But with her help, with the warmth of her closeness to him, kissing him, giving him every now and then a draught of her own breath, he holds on to life.

XV

Her father the Duke has his own special way of mounting the bay horse, catching hold of its raven black mane and talking to it persuasively. What he says Marianna has never known but it is very similar to the affectionate chatter he poured into the ear of the prisoner condemned to death on the scaffold in the Piazza Marina.

Once he is in the saddle he makes a sign to her to come close, bends down over the horse's neck and pulls her up to sit in front of him astride the horse's mane. There is no need to use a whip or spurs on the bay horse Miguelito because he starts off as soon as her father has taken up his proper position with his legs pressed tightly against the horse's flanks and his chest well forward. So they descend the slope from the entrance of the villa to the open space at the spring of San Nicola, there where the shepherds lay out the sheepskins to dry and there is always a strong smell of rotting flesh and flayed skin.

So here they are, father and daughter, riding beyond the gates of the Villa Trabia, crossing the narrow lane that passes along the edge of the garden of the Villa Palagonia, leaving the two pink stone one-eyed monsters to the left. They proceed along the dusty road bordered by a prodigious number of mulberry bushes and prickly pears, in the direction of Aspra and Mongerbino.

Father leans forward, the bay Miguelito starts to gallop and they speed on beyond the contorted carob trees, beyond a scattering of peasant huts, beyond the olive and mulberry trees, beyond the vines and the river. As soon as the damp mist from the sea rises fresh and salty into his nostrils the bay lifts his front legs, and a few seconds later, with a powerful push of his hindquarters, lifts himself off the ground. The air is thinner and clearer, the gulls sweep down in surprise. Father urges on the horse, the little girl clings to the mane, balancing herself on Miguelito's neck, which seems more like the neck of a giraffe. The wind blows through her hair and cuts the breath in her throat. A cloud advances sluggishly towards them and at one bound the bay leaps into it and begins to swim in the floating foam, kicking and whinnying. For a moment Marianna can see nothing, only a clinging white cloud that fills her eyes. Then they are out of it, in the clear blue of the welcoming sky.

There's no doubt that this time Father is taking her with him to paradise, Marianna tells herself, and she looks down with joy at the trees beneath them as they become ever smaller and darker. The fields in the distance separate into blue geometric patterns, squares and triangles that overlap each other confusedly.

But now the bay horse is no longer pointing towards the sky but to the summit of a mountain. Marianna recognises the flat bare point, a grey shape that resembles a castle: it is Monte Pellegrino. In a flash they are there. Now they descend on to those burnt rocks to rest a little before setting out for unknown happy skies.

But below them a large crowd has assembled and in the middle of the crowd she can see a black object. It is a platform, a man, a rope hanging downwards. The bay Miguelito is going round and round in circles. The air becomes warmer, the birds are left behind. Now she can see everything clearly. Her father the Duke is about to find a place for himself with his horse and his daughter in front of the gallows where a boy with discharging eyes is about to be executed.

At the very instant that Miguelito's hoofs touch the ground Marianna wakes up, her night-dress soaked with sweat, her mouth burning. Since little Signoretto died, she has been unable to sleep at night. Every two hours she wakes up gasping for air in spite of the valerian and laudanum that she swallows along with tisanes of hawthorn, orange flower and camomile.

With a restless movement she throws back the bedclothes and pushes out her bare legs. The small goatskin rug lightly tickles the soles of her feet. She reaches out for the tapers. She lights a candle on the little chest of drawers, puts on a violet-coloured chenille cloak and goes out into the passage.

Under the door of uncle husband's room she can see a fillet of light. Is he too unable to sleep? Or has he gone to sleep with a book in his hand and the candle burning, as happens to him more and more often?

Further along the passage the door of Mariano's room is half-open. Marianna pushes it with her fingers and takes a few steps towards the bed. She finds her son asleep with his mouth agape. She wonders whether they should consult the physician Cannamela once more. The boy has always had a weak throat, every time he has a cold his nose swells and gets blocked and he is shaken with violent fits of coughing. He has already been to see two well-known physicians. One has prescribed the usual blood-letting, which only made him weaker still. The other recommended opening up his nose to remove a polyp that was in the way, and then closing it again. But uncle husband refused to think of it: 'In this house the only things that are opened and closed are the doors, you son of a bitch.'

Fortunately Mariano's behaviour is improving as he grows older: he is less naughty, he no longer throws himself on the floor when he can't have his own way. He is growing rather more like her mother the Duchess, his grandmother: lazy, good-natured, prone to over-excitement but just as often to depression. From time to time he comes to kiss Marianna's hand and tell her something that has happened, and he fills sheets of paper with large confused handwriting.

Sometimes Marianna is aware of her son looking with pity at her hands, which have become prematurely old. She knows that in some way he is pleased by this, as if it were a punishment she has deserved for the indecent and uncontrolled way in which she concentrated all her care on the repellent and ugly little body of his small brother, who died at the age of four.

Duke Pietro and Aunt Teresa do everything in their power to prevail upon him to behave like a duke. His father is so much older than his mother, and on his death Mariano will inherit all the titles, if not the wealth, of the dead branch of the Scebarràs family bequeathed as a legacy to Duke Pietro. And he plays along with it: he's become big-headed and arrogant but he gets easily bored and reverts to playing hide-and-seek with his sisters under the scandalised eyes of his father. But then after all he is only thirteen.

Marianna stops in front of Giuseppa's room. She is the most worrying of her three daughters. She refuses to have music lessons, to learn embroidery or Spanish; she is greedy only for cakes and horse-riding. Before quartan fever carried off Lina and Lena, when they all used to call the bay horse with a whistle and run arm in arm through the olive groves, it was they who taught her to ride. Uncle husband did not approve. 'There are sedan-chairs for ladies, there are litters, there are carriages. I don't want Amazons here.'

But as soon as her father has gone off to Palermo, Giuseppa fetches Miguelito and rides him all the way to the sea. Marianna knows about it but has never betrayed her. She too would have liked to get on a horse and gallop along the dusty paths but it has never been allowed. Her lady mother had convinced her that because she was dumb she could do almost nothing she wanted to do without being seized 'by the dogs with long forked tails'. Only her father the Duke, after much persuasion, had secretly taken her two or three times on Miguelito's back when he was still a young, happy horse.

Duke Pietro is particularly severe with Giuseppa. If she refuses to get up early in the morning, he shuts her in her room and keeps her there all day. Innocenza secretly brings specially cooked titbits for her without the Duke suspecting anything.

'Your daughter Giuseppa is eighteen and behaves like a child of seven', he writes on a sheet of paper, putting it down with a look of irritation. Marianna recognises that her daughter is unhappy but she is unable to say why. It seems as if her only pleasure is to roll herself up in her bedclothes soaked with tears, in a landslide of breadcrumbs, her hair all over the place, determined to say no to everyone and everything.

'Growing pains', Marianna's father the Duke had written. 'Let her be.' But uncle husband does not let her be at all. 'Nonsense!' Every morning he stands in front of her at the head of her bed and addresses lengthy sermons to her that inevitably have an effect exactly opposite to that intended. Above all he scolds her for refusing to get married.

'Eighteen and still unmarried. It's a disgrace. At eighteen your mother had already given birth to three children. And you – you're like an old maid. What am I to do with an old maid, I ask you? What can I do?'

Marianna advances on tiptoe. It is a long passage and the children's rooms follow one another like the Stations of the Cross. Here Manina used to sleep before she got married when she was only twelve, as her father decreed. She was always her father's favourite, the most obedient, the most beautiful. And he had considered he was making a great sacrifice, giving her up 'for her to make a good marriage to an upright and well-to-do man'.

The fringed four-poster bed, the yellow velvet curtains, the set of combs and brushes in tortoiseshell and gold, a present from Grandfather Signoretto on her tenth birthday – everything in its place as if the girl were still living there. Marianna thinks again of the indignant letters she wrote to uncle husband to dissuade him from such an early marriage. But she was defeated by relations, friends and custom. Today she asks herself whether she did enough for her youngest daughter. She did not have sufficient courage. There's no doubt she would have fought with more energy if it had been about Signoretto. With Manina, after the first battle, she had let it go, through exhaustion, boredom, through cowardice....

Hurriedly she leaves her daughter's room, partially illuminated by a little light that burns beneath a picture of the Madonna. Next door, in the room adjacent to the staircase, is where Felice, the most cheerful of her daughters, used to sleep until a few years ago. She entered the convent when she was eleven, and she created a little kingdom for herself among the Franciscan nuns, which she rules over at her own sweet will. She comes and goes as she pleases, she gives lunches and dinners for all occasions. Her father often sends a sedan-chair for her; she comes over to Bagheria for a day or two, and no one says a word.

She too has left an empty void. She has lost her daughters too early, Marianna tells herself. Except for Giuseppa, who gulps down venom and curls up in bed without even knowing why. There is something idiotic about fussing over her children as if they were eggs, with the anxious brooding of a sitting hen. As her children's bodies changed and developed, so she identified her own body with theirs, giving it up as if she had lost it when she got married. She slips in and out of her clothes like a ghost, at the mercy of a sense of duty which she did not choose but which arose from a dark, ancient, female pride. She has put into motherhood both her flesh and her feelings, adapting them, restricting them, renouncing them. But with little Signoretto she let her feelings run away with her, she knows that now; theirs was a love that went beyond the relationship of mother and son to blossom into that of lovers. And so it could not last. He was the one to realise this before she did, with the miraculous understanding of a child, and he had chosen to leave her. But how can one live without a body, as she has done for the past thirty years, without ending up mummified?

Now her feet are taking her on, down the stone staircase covered by a flowered stair carpet, past the corner of the entrance hall, the plants that twine along the wall, the white passage, the big window overlooking the sleeping courtyard, the yellow room with a glimpse of the spinet lacquered with clear varnish, the two

* biological destiny - grand but not chosen

Roman statues guarding the tall french windows, the sharp-eyed chimera peering from between the fronds on the ceiling, the rose room with its upholstered chaise-longue, the prie-dieu in reddish wood, the dining-table on which is the white basket full to the brim with porcelain pears and grapes. The air is freezing. For days an unusual and unexpected spell of cold weather has descended on Bagheria. No one remembers such cold as this in years.

The kitchen with its smell of frying oil and dried tomatoes has a welcoming feel, though it is only a shade warmer. Through the open door she can see a sliver of pale-blue light coming in. Marianna goes to the kitchen dresser and opens the doors without thinking. She breathes in the powerful smell of bread. She remembers something she has read about Democritus in Plutarch: so that his death should not cause suffering to his sister, who was just about to get married, the philosopher prolonged his death agony by smelling newly baked bread.

Out of the corner of her eye, Marianna glimpses something black wriggling on the floor. She bends down to have a look. For the past few years she has no longer seen well over a distance. Uncle husband had a pair of strong lenses sent all the way from Florence for her, but she cannot get used to them. And then she feels stupid with all this equipment on her face. It seems that in Madrid young people wear these glasses quite needlessly, simply to display the large tortoiseshell frames. And this in itself would be a good enough reason for her not to wear them.

Looking closely she sees that it consists of ants: a monstrous file composed of thousands of tiny creatures that scurry to and from the kitchen dresser, crossing the entire kitchen and climbing up the walls, to reach the lard that fills the majolica soup tureen shaped like a duck. But where is the sugar? Marianna looks around her, searching for the enamel jars in which the precious granules have been stored ever since she was a child. She finds them at last beside the shutters, standing on top of a wooden board. What ingenuity Innocenza has brought to bear to keep the ants away! The board is balanced between two chairs, the legs of the chairs immersed in saucepans filled with water, and on top of each jar is a soup plate filled with vinegar.

Marianna takes a rough-skinned lemon from a basket on the floor and smells its fresh bitter smell. She cuts it in half with a small knife that has a handle of horn. From one of the halves she cuts a fleshy slice with a soft, spongy white rind. She sprinkles a pinch of salt on it and puts it on her tongue. It is a habit acquired from Grandmother Giuseppa, who every morning, even before washing her face, ate a lemon cut in pieces. It was her recipe for ensuring healthy teeth and a fresh mouth.

Marianna feels her teeth by putting a finger between her gums and her tongue. Certainly they are sound and healthy, even though two were extracted by the surgeon last year and as a result she now chews less well on one side. One of them was broken, the other was discoloured. Being pregnant has an effect on the teeth: when children are in the womb they are avid for bone, no one knows why. Perhaps the molar could have been saved, but it was hurting and it is an established fact that the surgeon's job is to cut, not to repair. It cost him so much effort to pull those two teeth out that he was sweating and shaking as if he had a fever. He pulled and pulled with his forceps but the tooth would not budge. Eventually he broke it with a little hammer, and then he only just succeeded in extracting the broken pieces, bracing his knee against her chest and puffing and blowing like a buffalo.

With the lemon in her hand Marianna goes over to the dresser. She levers the door open with her finger nail and takes out a jar of borax. Then, shaking out a handful of the white powder, she goes up to the line of ants and sprinkles little rivulets over the moving serpent. Immediately the ants start getting agitated, breaking line, jumping on top of each other and seeking refuge in the cracks in the wall.

Her fingers dusty with borax, Marianna goes to the closed shutters and pushes them lightly aside, letting a glimmer of moonlight into the room. The whitewashed courtyard glitters. The oleanders form dark shapes that make her think of the backs of giant tortoises asleep with their heads against the wind to protect themselves from the cold. Her eyes are watering with sleepiness, her footsteps take her automatically back to her bed. It is almost morning. A faint smell of smoke filters through the closed windows. Somebody in the hovel next to the stables has lit the first fire.

The unmade bed is no longer a prison from which to escape but a refuge to take shelter in. Her feet are frozen and her fingers numbed. Clouds of vapour come out of her mouth. Marianna plunges between the blankets and as soon as she lays her head down on the pillow she sinks into a dark and troubled sleep.

But before she has time to have her fill of sleep she is woken by a cold hand lifting up her night-gown. She jumps upright into a sitting position. Uncle husband's face is within a finger's breadth of hers. She has never looked at him so close; she feels as if she were committing a sacrilege. Before, whenever she submitted to his embraces she always shut her eyes. Now instead she observes him and sees him lose his usual look of bad temper. His eyelashes are white, but when did they become faded like this, and how has she never noticed it before? Since when? He lifts a long bony hand as if to strike her but it is only to close her eyes. His belly, armed with its sword, squeezes against her legs.

How many times has she yielded to this wolfish embrace, shutting her eyelids and gritting her teeth! A flight with no escape, the paws of the predator on her neck, the breath that grows panting and heavy, the grasping of her thighs, and then the surrender, the empty void. He has certainly never asked her whether this assault is welcome to her or not. His is the body that takes, that mounts. He does not know any other way of coming close to a woman's belly. And she has shut him outside her lowered eyelids, like an intruder. That it is possible to experience pleasure in something so mechanical and cruel has never occurred to her. Yet there were times when, smelling her mother's somnolent body with its odour of snuff, she divined the smell of a secret sensual bliss completely beyond her understanding.

Now for the first time, looking uncle husband in the face, she manages to shake her head in denial. And he is paralysed, with his member erect and stiff and his mouth open, so astounded by her refusal that he lies there stock still, at a loss what to do.

Marianna gets off the bed, puts on her cloak and, shivering with cold, completely unaware of what she is doing, goes off to her husband's bedroom. There she sits on the edge of the bed and looks round her as if she were seeing for the first time this room so near to hers and yet so distant. How wretched and unwelcoming it is: the walls white, the bed also white, covered with a torn quilt, a dirty sheepskin on the floor, a little table of olive wood on which lie a small sword, a pair of rings and a wig with flattened curls. Looking further she can make out behind the half-open door of the commode a white chamber-pot bordered with gold, half-full of clear liquid, in the middle of which float two dark turds.

It seems as if this room is trying to tell her something she has never wanted to hear: the privation of a solitary man who, through lack of self-knowledge, has become tormented by a compulsive obsession with pride. Only in the moment when she had the strength to refuse him did she experience a feeling of infinite tenderness for him, for this life of an old man made brusque and oppressive by shyness.

Returning towards her room she looks for him between the cactus plants, the chimeras that extend along the walls and ceilings, the vases of flowers with frosted petals. But he is not there, and the door leading to the corridor is shut. Then she goes to the big window that opens out on to the balcony and there she finds him crouched on the ground, his head sunk between his shoulders, his gaze turned towards the opalescent countryside.

Marianna slips down on to the floor beside him. In front of them the valley of the olive trees is growing ever more luminous. In the distance between Capo Sólanto and Porticello, the pale-blue sea, calm and still, becomes one with the sky.

In the cold of the morning in that sheltered corner Marianna is about to stretch out her hand towards uncle husband's knee, but it seems to be an act of tenderness that does not belong to their marriage, something inappropriate, something unheard of. She is conscious of the body of a man turned to stone beside her, inhabited by ragged thoughts that steal away like draughts of air from that white-haired head that is so lacking in wisdom.

XVI

In the mirror Fila's hands move quickly and jerkily, smoothing out the tangle of Marianna's hair. The Duchess watches the young servant's fingers gripping the ivory comb as if it were a plough: each tangle a wrench, each knot a jerk. There is something cruel and angry about these thumbs plunging into her hair as if Fila were ripping apart birds' nests, or cutting down thistles.

Suddenly the Duchess tears the comb out of the girl's hands, breaks it in half and flings it out of the window. The maid stands watching her with amazement. She has never seen her ladyship so furious. It is true that since the death of the little boy she often loses her temper but now she is going too far – isn't it her own fault if her hair is a thicket of thorns?

The Duchess looks at her own reflection frowning from the mirror, and alongside her the stupefied face of the servant. A gurgle rises from the bottom of her palate, and a word seems almost about to emerge from the vacuum of her atrophied memory. Her mouth opens but her tongue stays locked between her teeth; it does not vibrate, it does not utter a sound. At last from her benumbed throat comes a sharp scream that is fearful to hear. Fila shivers visibly and Marianna makes a sign telling her to go away.

Now she is alone and she raises her eyes to the mirror. Her face is bare, dry, with despairing eyes staring at her from the silvery glass. Is it possible that it is her, this woman clouded by grief, a vertical furrow like a sabre cut dividing her broad forehead? Where is the charm that so fascinated Intermassimi? Where are the soft contours of her cheeks, where is the gentle colour of her eyes, the infectious smile? Her eyes have become lighter, a faded colourless blue; they have lost that vivacious twinkle, a mingling of innocence and wonder; they have become hard and glassy. A lock of white hair slips over her forehead. Sometimes Fila used to tint it for her with extract of camomile, but now she has become fond of this brush of whitewash on her mass of fair hair, a touch of frivolity above a face slackened by impotence.

Her gaze rests on the portraits of her children: small water-colours executed in rapid delicate brush-strokes, sketches snatched while they were playing games or while they were asleep. Mariano with his perpetually swollen nose, his beautiful sensual mouth, his dreamy eyes. Manina half-buried in her fluffy hair, all fair and curly. Felice with that look of a mouse greedy for cheese, and Giuseppa, who purses her lips in a bad-tempered pout.

'A fright made her deaf and a fright will make her well again', she had found one day in a letter from her father the Duke to her mother the Duchess. But what fright were they referring to? Was it some sudden shock, an involuntary arrest of her brain when she was a child? And, anyway, what had caused it?

The gentle ghost of her father the Duke restricts itself to smiling at her from beyond the mirror with his usual cheerful look. On his finger he wears a silver ring with two dolphins, which Manina had wanted for herself when he died.

The past is a harvest of cast-off and broken objects, the future is in the faces of the children who laugh indifferently, pretending not to care, inside those gilt frames. But those pictures, too, are in the process of moving into the past, together with the aunts who have embraced the religious life, the wet-nurses, the peasants. They all are running helter-skelter towards paradise and it is impossible for them to stop even for a moment.

Only Signoretto has stopped. He is the only one of her children who is no longer running, who does not change from day to day. And he has his own corner in her thoughts, the same as he has always had, repeating his loving smiles for evermore.

She was always determined not to be eaten up by her children like her sister Agata, who at thirty looks like an old woman. She has aimed to keep them at a certain distance in preparation for losing them. However, with the last one she was incapable of this, arousing the ill-will of the others by her excessive and unforgivable affection. She had been unable to resist the siren call; she played with his love until she had tasted it down to its bitter dregs.

But a light has come stealthily into the milky greyness of the mirror. She is not aware that dusk has fallen and Fila is standing in the doorway, uncertain whether or not to come in. Marianna beckons her with a movement of her hand. Fila walks forward with small faltering footsteps, puts the candlestick on the table, and is about to leave. Marianna stops her with her arm, raises the hem of her skirt between her fingers and sees that she is not wearing shoes. The girl, aware that she has been found out, looks at her with the eyes of a mouse caught in a trap.

But the Duchess smiles; she has no wish to scold her, she knows that Fila has a passion for going barefoot inside the house. She has given her three pairs of shoes, but Fila will not wear them, confident her long skirts that reach down to the dusty floor will hide her chapped and calloused heels.

Marianna moves suddenly and sees Fila's shoulders recoil as if to avoid a slap. Considering that she has never hit her, what has she to be afraid of? When she raises her hand to touch her hair, the girl bends down further as if to make it clear she is not trying to avoid a blow, only to protect herself from the pain. Marianna slides her fingers through Fila's hair and Fila gazes at her with frightened eyes. The caress seems to disturb her more than a slap would have done. Perhaps she is afraid that she will snatch hold of her hair, roll it around her wrist and pull it like Innocenza does sometimes when she gets impatient.

Marianna tries to smile but Fila is so convinced she is going to be punished that she can only watch out for where the blow will come. Discouraged, Marianna lets Fila run away hopping on the tips of her bare toes. She decides she will teach her to read, she will suggest she puts her hair up, twisting it so as to make a large knotted chignon.

But the door opens and Innocenza comes in leading a reluctant and sullen Fila by the hand. Obviously the cook has spotted the bare feet that so irritate Duke Pietro, or perhaps she has just been suspicious of the girl's precipitate flight.

Marianna gives a little mute laugh that puts Innocenza in her place and heartens the girl. It is the only way she has to show she is not angry, that she has no intention of punishing anyone; she always has to play the part of the judge, the censor, the person who is annoyed. However, she has no wish to provoke Innocenza, who in her anxiety to be understood starts gesticulating and making strange disconnected signs. To reassure them she takes two coins from a drawer in the writing-table and puts one each into their nervous hands.

Fila makes a stiff clumsy bow and slips away. Innocenza turns the coin around between her fingers with an expert look. Watching her, Marianna is aware of an avalanche of thoughts that gravitate dangerously in her direction. She does not know why it is that only Innocenza's thoughts, among all the people close to her, should have the power to articulate themselves.

Luckily today Innocenza is in a hurry to get back to the kitchen. She quickly hands her a sheet of paper on which Marianna recognises the large shaky handwriting of Raffaele Cuffa: 'What does Your Honour want to have for dinner?' On the other side of the paper she absent-mindedly writes 'Chickpeas and cuttlefish', without remembering that uncle husband hates chickpeas and can't stand cuttlefish. She folds the sheet of paper and slips it into the pocket of Innocenza's apron. Innocenza will get Raffaele Cuffa or Geraci to read it to her. Then Marianna eases her towards the door.

XVII

'Today *auto-da-fé* in Piazza Marina. My presence is requested, as is that of Her Grace the Duchess. Advise purple dress with Maltese Cross on chest. And for once, no uncouth country behaviour, please.'

Marianna reads uncle husband's peremptory note placed beneath her jar of face powder. An *auto-da-fé* means a burning at the stake in the Piazza Marina and the massive crowds that attend such important occasions: the authorities, the guards, the street-vendors selling aniseed water, boiled squid, caramel sweets and prickly pears; the smell of sweat, of bad breath, of dirty feet, not to speak of the excitement that gets more and more physical until it becomes almost visible; everyone eating and chattering as they await that razor blow in the belly, which brings both agony and delight. She will not go.

At that moment she sees uncle husband enter, wearing a perfumed shirt adorned with lace and a pair of leather shoes so shiny that they look as if they are lacquered.

'Don't be angry but I cannot come with you to the *auto-da-fé*', Marianna writes quickly and hands him the note still wet with ink.

'And why not?'

'It sets my teeth on edge. It's like sour wine.'

'They are taking two well-known heretics to the stake, Sister Palmira Malaga and Brother Reginaldo Venezia. The whole of Palermo will be there. I have to be present. So do you, signora.'

The Duchess is about to write a reply but Duke Pietro has already gone out of the door. How can she bear to submit to this order? When uncle husband assumes this hurried and self-important air it is impossible to contradict him; he becomes as obstinate as a mule. She will have to invent an illness which will give him an excuse to be there on his own.

Sister Palmira Malaga: she remembers reading about her somewhere, perhaps in a book on the history of heresy, or in some publication on quietism, or in one of those lists put out by the Holy Inquisition, giving the names of people suspected of heresy. Sister Palmira, yes, she remembers it now, she has read a short book about her; published in Rome, it turned up somehow in the library at the villa. There was even a caricature of her with two

88

horns on her head and a long ass's tail coming out from under her habit and ending in a forked point, which reminded her of the dogs so feared by her mother the Duchess.

She sees her going up the wooden steps of the scaffold one at a time. Barefoot, hands tied behind her back, her face twisted in a bizarre grimace, almost as if this horror were the last seal to affirm her commitment to peace. Behind her Brother Reginaldo, whom Marianna imagines as bearded, with a stringy neck and hollow chest, and large dirty feet in tight Franciscan sandals.

Now the executioner ties them to the posts above a pile of chopped logs. Two assistants with lighted torches approach the pile of wood. The flame does not immediately ignite the branches of elder and the broken sugar canes that someone has cut and tied with willows so as to make it easier to light the fire. White smoke puffs out into the faces of the nearby spectators.

Sister Palmira smells the acrid smoke of the faggots; fear contracts the muscles of her belly and a stream of urine runs down her thighs. And yet her martyrdom has hardly begun — how will she endure it to the end?

The secret is breathed into her ear by a most gentle voice. The secret, Palmira, is your consent, not to stiffen and resist, but to gather up into your womb these tongues of flame as if they were flowers flying through the air, to gulp down the smoke as if it were incense, and turn towards Him whose eye is suffused with pity. It is they who suffer, not you.

Then violent hands stretch up to her head to plaster her hair with pitch, and Sister Palmira turns towards her torturers with a look of love. Now they are crowding round in solemn exultation, bringing a burning torch to her smeared hair. The woman's head lights up and bursts into flames like a resplendent crown, and everyone applauds. They want her death to be a spectacle; and since Our Lord permits it He must want it too, in the mysterious and profound way in which Our Lord wills the things of this world.

Brother Reginaldo opens his mouth as if to speak, but perhaps it is only a scream of pain. In front of him Sister Palmira's head is burning like the sun, while her mouth tries to smile as it twists and curls in the heat of the blaze.

Marianna sees uncle husband sitting on a handsome golden chair upholstered in purple velvet, next to the Holy Fathers of the Inquisition, elegant in their habits embroidered with designs

89

of bunches of grapes. The crowd around them is packed together so tightly that it is almost impossible to distinguish one face from another; it is one single body with a single eye, held in suspense, looking upwards, throbbing with exultation.

At the moment when the flames set alight Sister Palmira's hair the crowd explodes into a great roar. Marianna feels it vibrating in her belly. Uncle husband is now leaning forward, his wrinkled neck stretched tight, his face rigid with a cramp that he does not understand – is it of horror or of satisfaction?

Marianna raises her hand to the bell-rope. She pulls it several times, insistently. Soon she sees the door open and Fila's head peep round. She makes a sign for her to come in. The girl does not dare, she is afraid of the Duchess's bad temper. Marianna looks at her feet. They are bare. She smiles so as to reassure her and bends her finger to beckon her, as if she were a child.

Fila comes closer on tiptoe. Marianna makes her understand that she needs help with unbuttoning her dress at the back. With their rich embroidery of pearls, the sleeves come off by themselves, like tubes of wood. The skirt rests rigidly on the floor. It is as if the Duchess were divided in two, one half the body of a woman, moving freely in her white cotton petticoat, the other Her Excellency the Duchess of Ucrìa, confined in stiff brocade, who bows, smiles, nods, approves, with all the dignity proper to her station. It is the point at which these two bodies meet that is hard to discern: where one acknowledges the other, where one is shielded by the other, where one displays itself and the other hides itself so as to become completely lost.

Meanwhile Fila has knelt down to help her take off her shoes, but Marianna is in a hurry and to make her understand that she will take them off herself she pushes her away with a small affectionate kick. Fila lifts her head. She is put out and in her look there broods an unforgivable hurt. Marianna will think what to do about it later, she decides, now she is in too much of a hurry. She takes off her shoes, picks up her bedjacket the colour of egg-yolk, and snuggles down inside the bed that has only been made a moment ago.

Just in time! The door opens before she has even had the chance to undo her hair. The trouble with being deaf is that no one ever bothers to knock before coming in, knowing they will not be heard. So she is always finding herself unprepared for the arrival of the unexpected visitor who throws open the door and appears before her with a triumphant smile, as if to say, Here I am. You didn't hear me, but now you can see me.

This time it is Felice, her daughter and now a nun, elegant in her milk-white habit, her chestnut curls popping provocatively out of her white coif. Felice goes straight to her mother's writing-desk, picks up pen and paper and takes ink from the small silver phial. Within a few seconds she hands over the written sheet of paper: '*Auto-da-fé* today. Great festival in Palermo. What's the matter – are you feeling ill?'

Marianna reads and rereads the note. Since Felice has been in the convent her writing has improved and she has taken on a carefree, confident look that neither of her other daughters has. Marianna watches her while she talks to Fila, moving her lips with sensual grace. There's no doubt her voice must be very melodious, Marianna tells herself. How she would like to hear it! Sometimes in the internal cavity deep inside her ear she has a sensation of rhythm, which seems to form a clot of blood that shifts, disentangles itself, dissolves, flows . . . and she begins to tap her feet on the ground in time with this far-off subterranean harmony.

She has read of Corelli, Stradella and Handel as marvels of musical architecture. She has tried to imagine a taut arch of enchanting colours, but all that issues from the vaults of her childhood memory is a few sonorous gurgles, ruins of buried music. Only her eyes have the capacity to grasp pleasure, but is it possible for music to be transformed into something corporeal that can be embraced with a look?

'Do you know how to sing?' she writes to her daughter, handing her a beautiful clean sheet of paper. Felice turns round in surprise. Why singing, for Heaven's sake? Everybody is getting ready for this trip to Palermo to attend the grand spectacle of the *auto-da-fé*, and here is her mother asking silly questions that are quite irrelevant. Sometimes she thinks her mother is a bit weak in the head and simple-minded. But then, because she cannot talk, each thought has to be written down and, as everyone knows, as soon as you write anything down it acquires a stiffness, a gloss, a heaviness, it is like something that has been embalmed.

Marianna guesses her daughter's thoughts, she anticipates them and pursues each new revelation with painful relish.

Our grandmother died before she was fifty, maybe our lady mother will die soon. . . . She knows she is only thirty-seven but she could have a stroke at any time . . . after all she is already disabled. . . . If she were to die she might leave her a large life interest on her inheritance from her father – let's say three thousand *onze* or maybe even five thousand. . . . The expenses at the convent are always getting heavier . . . and then there is the new sedan-chair with golden cupids and damask hangings . . . she can't be for ever waiting for her father to send her his . . . and sugar has gone up by five *grani* a sack, lard by twenty, then wax has got impossible, seven *grani* a small candle, and where is she to get the money? . . . Not that she wishes for her mother's death . . . but sometimes she is so stupid, more like a child than any of her children . . . she thinks she understands everything just because she reads so many books but she understands absolutely nothing. . . . Come to that, why did Manina get a bigger dowry than she did? Only to marry that parrot Francesco Chiarandà of the estates of Magazzinasso. . . . Isn't it more important to be married to Christ? That everything, but everything, should go to Mariano is . . . it's an insult. . . . They say that in the Netherlands it's no longer like that. There, if they want to cut their children off without a penny and leave them quite naked – why, they can do it. . . . Wouldn't it be better to leave them in paradise among trees of manna and fountains of sweet wine? That idiot Aunt Fiammetta wants her to hoe the convent orchard like all the others. . . . 'Little one, aren't you the same as everyone else, my little girlie?' But surely an Ucrìa of Campo Spagnolo di Scannatura and di Bosco Grande can never be put to hoeing the kitchen garden like some peasant or other? Some of these abbesses have turnips instead of brains, they're filled with jealousy and envy. 'I do it, and I'm a noblewoman just as much as you,' says Aunt Fiammetta, and you should see how she rolls up her sleeves and bends over the hoe, pushing down on the metal edge with her delicate little foot . . . a madwoman! Heaven knows where she unearthed this passion for menial work . . . the beauty of it is that she doesn't do it as a penance, no, she actually loves her hoe, she loves the earth, she loves bending down under the sun and getting as brown as a peasant. . . . It's impossible to make head or tail of that silly woman.

'What pleasure is there in seeing two heretics burned?' writes Marianna to her daughter, in an attempt to shrug off all these trifling and oppressive thoughts. Even though she knows there is more ingenuousness than wickedness in Felice's broodings, she feels she is being attacked.

'The whole convent of Santa Chiara will be there, the Abbess, the Prioress, the Canonesses. Afterwards there'll be prayers and refreshments.'

'So it's the cakes, confess.'

'The Sisters give me all the cakes I want, anyway. I only have to ask', answers Felice huffily, scrawling the s's sideways as if she wanted to blow them away.

Marianna goes to kiss her, forcing herself to forget those petulant thoughts. But she finds her daughter sullen and ready to reject her: she is none too pleased at being treated like a thirteen-year-old when she is all of twenty-two; and she stands there rigid, staring frostily at her mother.

That long dress . . . and socks up to her knees, she looks so old-fashioned she's positively dowdy. She's thirty-seven and she's got grown-up daughters, what does she think she's up to? Inside that deaf, cloistered head she's older than my father, and he's seventy! With his body as long and thin as a rake, he's got one foot in the grave, but still has a look of vitality, while she's all trussed up like a Spanish infanta, with collars that look like bibs. There's something faded about her that makes her seem dated . . . those antiquated laced boots in the Hapsburg style, her stockings the colour of milk. . . . The mothers of her friends wear coloured stockings woven with gold thread, with shiny ribbons round their waists, floppy skirts quilted with beads, low-heeled slippers with pointed toes and Eastern designs. . . .

As so often happens, once she has grasped the thread of a thought, Marianna cannot let it go, she turns it over between her fingers, pulling it and knotting it to suit her own purposes.

An angry compulsion to wound her daughter on account of this internal chattering, so brutally confident, makes her hand shake. But at the same time the desire to ask her once more to sing impels her towards the writing-desk. She is sure that somehow she would be able to hear her, and already she is conscious of the mercurial fluidity of that voice on her walled-up ears.

XVIII

The understanding, when it acts alone, and according to its most general principles, entirely subverts itself, and leaves not the lowest degree of evidence in any proposition, either in philosophy or common life. We save ourselves from this total scepticism only by means of that singular and seemingly trivial property of the fancy, by which we enter with difficulty into remote views of things. . . .

Marianna reads with her chin resting on her hand. Her feet warm each other, sheltering beneath a blanket from the icy draughts that whistle through the closed windows. Goodness knows who left this notebook with its marbled cover in the library. Was it brought from London by her brother Signoretto? He returned a few months ago and has visited them twice at Bagheria with presents from England. But she has never before seen this notebook. It could have been left behind by Mariano's friend, that small dark-haired youth, born in Venice of English parents, who has footed it half-way round the world. He spent a few days at Bagheria, sleeping in Manina's room. An unusual person: he used to get up at midday, having spent the whole night reading. In the morning the bed sheets would be smeared with candle wax. He borrowed books from the library and then forgot to return them. He accumulated a pile as high as his arm. He ate like a horse and had a weakness for Sicilian food: pickled egg-plants, spaghetti with sardines, little pizzas with onion and oregano, ices flavoured with jasmine, and muscatel raisins.

Although his hair was very black he had a pale skin and it only needed a little sun for his nose to peel. But what was his name? Dick or Gilbert or Jerome? She cannot remember. However, Mariano addressed him by his surname, Grass, pronouncing it with three s's. Without doubt the little notebook belonged to this young Grass, who came from London and was on his way to Messina on a journey of 'self-discovery'. Innocenza could not stand him because of his habit of reading at night with a candle balanced on the sheets. Uncle husband just about tolerated him, though he regarded him with considerable suspicion. Duke Pietro had learned English as a boy but had always refused to speak it, so by now he had forgotten it.

Grass communicated with her on rare occasions in well-formed

94

handwriting on clean sheets of paper. Only during the last few days of his visit had they discovered that they liked the same books, and their correspondence became unexpectedly close and concentrated.

Marianna turns over the pages of the notebook and stops in amazement; at the bottom of the first page is a dedication written in ink in very small handwriting: 'To her who does not speak – may she accept with her generous mind a few thoughts that are close to me.'

But why had he hidden it among the books in the library? Grass knew she was the only person who ever actually handled the books, yet he must also have known that her husband checked them from time to time. Then it was a secret present, hidden in such a way that she would find it when she was alone after his departure.

To have the sense of virtue, is nothing but to *feel* a satisfaction of a particular kind from the contemplation of a character. The very *feeling* constitutes our praise or admiration. We go no farther; nor do we enquire into the cause of the satisfaction. We do not infer a character to be virtuous, because it pleases: But in feeling that it pleases after such a particular manner, we in effect feel that it is virtuous. The case is the same as in our judgements concerning all kinds of beauty, and tastes, and sensations. Our approbation is imply'd in the immediate pleasure they convey to us.

Underneath it the name David Hume, written in green ink in minute handwriting. This reasoning cuts through the muddled pathways in Marianna's mind, unused as she is to thinking in an ordered, precise and radical way. She has to read the paragraph twice to grasp the rhythms of this explosive intelligence, so different from the other minds that have influenced her.

We speak not strictly and philosophically when we talk of the combat of passion and of reason. Reason is, and ought only to be the slave of the passions, and can never pretend to any other office than to serve and obey them.

The exact opposite to what she has been taught. Is passion not an awkward burden from whose edges spring slivers of greed that are best kept hidden? And is reason not the sword that everyone keeps at his side to cut the heads off the spectres of desire, so as to enforce the determination to be virtuous? Uncle husband would be horrified to read any one of the sentences in this little book. Already at the time of the War of Secession he had declared, 'The world is ending up on a garbage heap.' And it is all the fault of people like Galileo, Newton and Descartes, who 'wanted to distort nature in the name of science, but in reality wanted to put her in their pockets to use in their own way. Presumptuous lunatics! Traitors!'

Marianna closes the notebook suddenly. Instinctively she hides it in the folds of her dress. Then she remembers that Duke Pietro went to Palermo yesterday, and she brings the book out again. She holds it up to her nose; it has a wholesome smell of fresh paper and good-quality ink. She opens it and among the pages discovers a coloured picture: a man of about thirty with a striped velvet turban that comes down over his forehead. A broad complacent face, his eyes looking downwards as if to assert that all knowledge comes from the earth on which we rest our feet. His lips are slightly open, his eyebrows thick and dark, suggesting a capacity for concentration that is almost painful. His double chin gives the impression of a gentleman who never goes short of a good meal. His neck, delicately encircled by a soft collar of white silk, emerges from a flowered waistcoat beneath a long jacket strewn with big bone buttons.

Here Grass's very small handwriting has attributed a name: 'David Hume, a friend and a philosopher, too disturbing to inspire love except from his friends, among whom I take the liberty of including the friend who cannot speak.'

Really strange, this young man Grass. Why had he not given it to her personally, instead of leaving her to find it hidden between travel books a month after his departure?

Such is our disappointment when we learn that the connections between our ideas, the links, the efficacy are merely in ourselves and none other than a disposition of the mind.

Devil take that Mr Hume! How can he say that God is a 'disposition of the mind'? Marianna is overcome by apprehension and again hides the notebook in her skirt. Even thinking such a thought, let alone saying it out loud, she could end up being burned at the stake on a word of command from the Holy Fathers of the Inquisition, who occupy the great Steri Palace in the Piazza Marina. 'A disposition of the mind acquired through habit. . . .' She has read something similar in her father's handwriting; he was for the most part a man bound by tradition, but he sometimes allowed himself to play havoc with those traditions, merely for amusement, curling his lips in a charming and incredulous smile.

'"Every ant loves its own hole" and one puts one's worldly goods and one's morality in that same hole and they suddenly become one, morality and daily bread, fatherland and sons. . . .'

Her mother the Duchess had glanced over the words written by her husband in her daughter's exercise book, had taken a pinch of snuff, cleared her throat, and poured half a bottle of orange-flower water over herself to take away the cloying smell of the snuff. Who knew what went on in her sweet mother's head, always languidly bent down over her shoulder. Is it possible that she slipped in by one door and slipped out by another, without a pause? Was she also prey to 'a disposition of the mind acquired by habit', with that tendency to slump lazily into an unmade bed, into an easy chair, or into a dress, her soft flesh pressing against the whalebones, the hooks, even against the button-holes? A laziness deeper than a well in the tufa stone, a torpor that enfolded her as a carob pod enfolds its seed, hard and yet so soft, the colour of night. Below the dark surface her lady mother was soft just like a carob seed, forever surrendering to the small world of her family. She loved her husband to the point of forgetting herself. She stood poised on the edge of the void and so as to avoid feeling she would sit and gaze fascinated at the desert in front of her.

Her mother's voice, what was it like? In her imagination it comes over as having a deep, dark, husky resonance. It is difficult to love someone whose voice one does not know. Yet she loved her father without ever having heard him speak. A slightly bitter taste tinges her tongue and spreads over her palate; could it be the pangs of regret?

Now as we call everything custom, which proceeds from a past repetition, without any new reasoning or conclusion, we may establish it as a certain truth, that all the belief, which follows upon any present impression, is deriv'd solely from that origin.

As if to say that certainty, every certainty gets flung to the winds, and that habit holds us in submission while pretending to educate us. The pleasures of habit, the bliss of repetition – are these the glories we are talking about?

She would like to get to know this Mr Hume, with his light-green turban, his thick black eyebrows, his smiling expression, his double chin and his flowered waistcoat.

> Thus it appears, that the *belief* or *assent*, which always attends the memory and senses is nothing but the vivacity of those perceptions they present; and that this alone distinguishes them from the imagination. To believe is in this case to feel an immediate impression of the senses, or a repetition of that impression in the memory.

What logic! What an obstinate and petulant rascal he is! She can't help smiling in admiration. To be lashed by a thought like this that has floated carelessly among stories of adventures, books on love, history books, poetry, almanacs, fables! A thought abandoned to the emptiness of ancient beliefs; yes, beliefs that have the flavour of egg-plants in a sour-sweet sauce. Or has it been the continuous self-questioning of her wounded destiny which has diverted her from other deeper and more fruitful ideas?

> But as 'tis certain there is a great difference betwixt the simple conception of the existence of an object, and the belief of it, and as this difference lies not in the parts or composition of the idea, which we conceive; it follows, that it must lie in the *manner*, in which we conceive it.

To think thoughts – here is something daring that tempts her as an exercise she can secretly indulge in. Mr Grass, with an impertinence worthy of a young student, has started to trample on the meadows inside her head. If that were not enough he has brought a friend with him: Mr David Hume with his ridiculous turban. And now they want to leave her in confusion. But they will not succeed.

But – what is this skirt brushing against the door? Someone has come into the library without her being aware of it. She thinks she had better hide the notebook with the marbled cover, but she realises it is too late.

Fila comes forward with a glass and a jug balanced on a tray. She makes a small curtsy, puts the tray on top of a table covered with papers, and with a teasing gesture lifts the heavy folds of her dress to show she is wearing shoes. Then she leans against the doorpost waiting for an order.

Marianna contemplates her full round face, her slender body. Fila is nearly thirty yet she always seems like a child. 'I give her to you as a gift. She is yours', her father the Duke had written. But where does it say that people can be given, taken, thrown away like dogs or little birds? 'What nonsense!' uncle husband would have written. 'Are you suggesting that God has not created noblemen and peasants, horses and sheep?' Does this not pinpoint for her the question of equality? Is it one of those indigestible seeds wafted from the pages of Grass's little notebook to confuse the opaque brain of a dumb woman? Can she then retain something of her own that does not originate in other minds, other constellations of thoughts, other wills, other interests? A repetition in her memory of images that appear real because they dart like lizards, squirming beneath the sun of everyday experience?

Marianna returns to her notebook, or rather to the hand that holds it, so prematurely withered, with broken nails, roughened knuckles, protruding veins. Yet it is a hand unused to scrubbing with soapy water, a hand used to giving orders. But also to obedience, with a chain of obligations and duties which she has always seen as necessary. What would Mr Hume in his seraphic oriental turban say about a hand so eager to be daring and so resigned to playing safe?

XIX

Rummaging through ancient trunks and demijohns of olive oil Marianna came upon an old canvas, dark and covered with dust, that appeared from nowhere. She pulled it out, dusted it with the sleeve of her dress, and found it was none other than the portrait of her brothers and sisters that she had painted when she was thirteen. She had been painting it the morning she was interrupted by being called to see Tutui the puppet master, in the

99

courtyard of the lodge, the same day her mother the Duchess told her she would have to marry her uncle Pietro.

The black shadow that covers the canvas dissolves, revealing the bright faces, now a little faded: Signoretto, Geraldo, Carlo, Fiammetta, Agata, the beautiful Agata, who seemed then to be destined for a future as a queen.

Twenty-five years have passed since then. Geraldo died in an accident: a carriage crashed into a wall, his body was flung through the air on to the ground, and a wheel ran over his chest – and all to do with a question of precedence. 'Let me pass, I have right of way.' 'What right? I am a grandee of Spain, remember that!' They brought him back to the house without a drop of blood on his clothes, but with a broken neck.

Signoretto has become a senator, just as he had planned. After years of being a bachelor he has married a marchioness, already widowed, who is ten years older than him. The scandal threw the family into turmoil. But he is heir to the Ucrìas of Fontanasalsa and he can do as he pleases.

Marianna likes this open-minded sister-in-law, who could not care less about scandal, and who quotes Voltaire and Madame de Sévigné, gets her dresses from Paris, and keeps a music master in her household who is also, so everyone whispers, her gallant. He is a young man who speaks Greek fluently as well as French and English, and has a quick wit. She has sometimes seen the two of them together at balls in Palermo on those rare occasions when she has been dragged there by uncle husband: the Marchioness in a hooped skirt of damask edged with frills, he tightly buttoned up in a blue redingote with silver buckles, which he has cunningly tarnished.

Signoretto is not at all upset by this relationship. He even boasts that his wife has a private escort, and lets it be understood that he is no more than a protector installed by him at her side, so much does he resemble a 'singer in the style of the seventeenth century', that is to say a castrato. This may be so, but many have their doubts.

Fiammetta has become Canoness of the Carmelite Convent of Santa Teresa. She wears her thick chestnut hair imprisoned inside a wimple that she sometimes tears off, especially when she is doing the cooking. Her hands have become big and strong, used as they are to transforming liquids into solids, raw into cooked, cold into

100

hot. Her buck teeth give an air of cheerful disorder to a mouth that is always on the brink of laughter.

Agata has continued to wither. She does not even know how many children she has had, what with the ones that are alive and those that have died, having given birth to her first when she was twelve, and still going strong. Each year she becomes pregnant and if it were not for the fact that many of them die before they see the light of day, she would have had an army by now.

The taste of colours on her tongue ... Marianna moves the painting over to the window and starts once more to brush the canvas with her sleeve to remove the opaque patina that makes it hard to see. What a pity she has lost the skill of using colours; it left her for no obvious reason when her first child was born. A reproving look from uncle husband, an ironical word from her mother, the crying of the baby.... She had put the brushes and the small tubes of paint back in the enamelled box that had been a present from her father, and did not take them out again for many years, by which time her hand had lost its skill.

Gentian blue, what taste does gentian blue have? Beneath the smell of turpentine, of linseed oil and oily rags, another absolutely unique smell filters through; closing her eyes she can feel it float into her mouth and linger on her tongue, depositing a curious flavour of ground almonds, of April rain, of salt-sea wind.

And the white, sometimes clear, sometimes more or less stippled; the whiteness of the eyes inside the dark picture; maybe the shameless insolent eyes of Geraldo; the white of Agata's delicate hands; the forgotten whites that have become encrusted on that dirty canvas and now, after being rubbed with her sleeve, peer out shyly with the unconscious daring of witnesses from the past.

When she painted that picture the villa was not yet here. In its place was the hunting lodge built by her grandfather almost a century ago. Then it was possible to go all the way from the garden to the grove of olive trees by following a goat track, and Bagheria did not yet exist as a village, but consisted of the servants' quarters attached to the Villa Butera, of stables, of store rooms, of little churches which the Prince had built. Every year were added new stables, new store rooms, new churches and new villas belonging to friends and relations from Palermo.

'Bagheria was born out of betrayal', her grandmother Giuseppa had written when she got it into her head to teach her small deaf-mute grandchild the history of Sicily. 'During the time of Philip IV – indeed, at the time of his death – there was a quarrel in Spain over the succession; Philip did not have any sons and no one knew which, amongst all the little nephews, would inherit the throne.'

Her handwriting was minute, contracted, distorted. Like so many women amongst the nobility of that time, she was somewhat illiterate. It could be said that she had learned to write to 'get inside her grandchild's pumpkin head'.

'Bread became dearer and dearer, my little one, you don't know what that hunger was like, when people ate earth to fill their bellies, they ate chaff and acorns like pigs, they ate their nails just like you do, you thoughtless little monkey. We aren't suffering from famine now, so leave your nails alone.'

Sometimes she would open Marianna's mouth with her fingers, look at her teeth and then write, 'Little one, my little girlie, why don't you talk? Why? You've got a beautiful pink palate, you've got beautiful strong teeth, two lovely lips, so why do you never utter a word?'

However, Marianna enjoyed her grandmother's stories. So old Giuseppa, if only to make sure she did not run away, got ready to write in her granddaughter's notebook, struggling with pen and ink.

'At that time when you walked on the pavements in Palermo you would stumble so that you didn't know whether you were sleeping or dreaming or dying from the effort. There were public penances ordered by the Archbishop. People were kneeling on broken glass and whipping themselves in the piazza. And some princesses as a penance took registered prostitutes into their houses and fed them with what little bread they had.

'My father and mother fled to the estate at Fiumefreddo, where they caught a stomach fever. To prevent me from catching it they sent me back with the nurse. In any case they said I was a "little girl, and what harm could I come to?" So I found myself alone in Palermo in the empty palace when the bread riots broke out. A certain La Pilosa went round shouting that it was a war of the poor against the rich, and they set about burning all the palaces.

'They burned and they burned so that everybody's faces were blackened by smoke, and La Pilosa, whose face was blackest of all, as black as a Spanish bull, charged head down against the barons and the princes. The nurse told me she was very afraid they would come to the Palazzo Gerbi Mansueto, and so they did. Ciccio Rasone the porter told them there was no one there. "So much the better," they said. "There's no need for us to raise our hats to Their Excellencies!" and with their hats on their heads they invaded the upper floors and took away carpets, silver, enamelled clocks, paintings, clothes, books, and they made a bonfire and burned the lot, every single thing.'

Marianna saw the flames rising from the house and imagined that her grandmother must have been swept away by them, but she did not dare to ask in writing. Suppose it turned out that she had died and that the person who was talking to her was none other than one of the ghosts who peopled the placid nights of her mother the Duchess?

But Grandmother Giuseppa, as if guessing the thoughts of her granddaughter, exploded into one of her joyful laughs and began to write impetuously: 'At one time my nurse fled in panic. However, I wasn't aware of this, I was sleeping peacefully when they threw open the door and marched over to my bed. "And who are you?" they asked. "I am Princess Giuseppa Gerbi di Mansueto," I told them. I was a little monkey then, even worse than you. I had been taught this and I flaunted it proudly like a silver dress that everyone had to admire. Some of them looked at me and said, "Ah ha, we cut off the heads of princesses, and carry them aloft in triumph." Even more of a little fool, I said, "If you don't go away, you rabble, I shall call my father's dragoons." As luck would have it, they began to laugh. "Here is a little nothing who thinks she's a paladin," they said and laughed and spat everywhere. Even now you can still see the marks of their spit on the tapestries in the Palazzo Gerbi in the Cassaro.'

At this point she threw back her head and began to laugh too. Then she returned to worrying about her granddaughter's deafness and wrote, 'There are earholes in your pretty little ears. Suppose I try blowing into them, do you hear anything?'

The little granddaughter shook her head and laughed, infected by her grandmother's cheerfulness. 'You laugh, but it doesn't make a squeak. You should try blowing. Open your mouth . . . force a sound out of your throat . . . like this – ah ah ah ah. . . . Oh, my little one, you're a disaster, you'll never learn!'

Her grandmother wrote everything with infinite patience,

although by nature she was far from being patient. She enjoyed running and dancing, she slept little and she used to spend hours in the kitchen, watching the cooks at work, sometimes lending them a hand. She amused herself gossiping with the maidservants, getting them to tell her about their love affairs. She could play the violin and even the flute a little. Yes, she was a marvel was Grandmother Giuseppa. . . .

But she had her 'but' times, as everyone in the family well knew. There were dark days when she would shut herself in her room and refuse to see anyone. She would stay incommunicado with a handkerchief over her head, refusing to eat or drink. When she eventually emerged, leaning on Grandfather's arm, she would behave as if she were drunk.

Marianna tried hard to put these two people together: for her they were quite different women, one a friend and the other an enemy. When she went through her 'but' times Grandmother Giuseppa was withdrawn and hostile. Mostly she would refuse to write or talk, and if she became aware of the child pulling at her sleeve she would grab the pen with an angry gesture and write, jumbling up the words: 'Dumb and stupid, better dead than Marianna', or 'You'll end up like La Pilosa, a menace, you tiresome dumb-wit', or 'Wherever you came from, you've stirred my pity, except that I don't have any', and she would throw the sheet of paper in her face with a scowl.

Now Marianna regrets that she never kept these ill-tempered notes. Only after her death did she really comprehend how these two very different women were one and the same, because she missed them both, with a similar sense of loss.

She knew how it ended with La Pilosa because her grandmother had written an account of it several times with a certain sense of mischief: 'Torn to pieces with red-hot tongs.' She continued, 'Papa and Mamma returned with pockmarks all over them and I became a heroine', and she threw her head back and laughed exultantly just like a woman of the people.

'And out of that betrayal Bagheria was born, Grandmother Giuseppa?'

'Considering you've no ears and no tongue, you're still very inquisitive. . . . What do you want to know, little cuckoo? The betrayal of Bagheria? That's a long story, I'll tell it you tomorrow.'

Tomorrow was always tomorrow. And in the meantime her 'but'

times arrived and Grandmother shut herself away in a darkened room for days and days on end without showing even the tip of her nose. Finally one morning when the sun had only just risen, all new like the yolk of an egg emerging out of broken shells of clouds, brightening the palace on the Via Alloro, her grandmother seated herself at her writing-bureau and wrote in her quick, minute handwriting the story of the famous betrayal.

She was breathing with difficulty as if her chest was desperate for more air and she was trying to free herself of the bodice that gripped underneath her armpits. Though her skin was blotchy, her 'but' times had gone away together with the dust-blown wind that came across from Africa, and she was once again ready to laugh and tell stories.

'Excise duty, do you know what that is? No matter. And the toll? Not even that, you're only a silly little girlie. Well, the Viceroy Los Veles was beside himself with fear because in May there'd been La Pilosa and in August a watchmaker who had the gift of the gab was in charge of all the beggars and did all the talking, and they were demanding bread and staging a revolution for it. But the watchmaker was loyal to the King of Spain and also to the Inquisition. Alesi – that was the watchmaker's name – knew how to control the populace, who were looting, eating, burning; he did not have a black face, that rascal, and the princesses were leaning over backwards to give him presents: silver glove-boxes lined with silk, diamond rings. Until it all went to his head and he believed himself as handsome and important as the King of all Austria: he got himself made Mayor for life, Captain-General, most illustrious Praetor. He demanded complete subservience and he had himself borne through Palermo on a horse, carrying a gun in each hand and wearing a crown of roses on his head.

'The Viceroy returned from Spain and said, "What does this fool want?"

'"Bring down the price of grain, Your Excellency."

'"We will do just that," he replied, "but this buffoon must be got rid of."

'So they took the watchmaker and cut his throat and then threw his body into the sea, except for his head, which they paraded on a pikestaff right through the city.

'Two years later another revolt broke out, on the second of December in the year 1649, and that time the nobility got involved.

They wanted the island to be independent so that they could be masters of the Royal Kingdom. There was also a lawyer by the name of Antonio Del Giudice, who wanted independence. Several priests and very respectable nobles with a score of carriages took part in this rebellion. Even my father, your great-grandfather, became inflamed by the prospect of a new, free Sicily. They met in secret at the house of the lawyer Antonio and made brave speeches about liberty. But almost immediately they split into two factions, those who wanted Prince Don Giuseppe Branciforti as Viceroy and those who backed Don Luigi Moncada Aragona di Montalto.

'Prince Branciforti, who was a very touchy person, thought he had been betrayed by certain people who were always around the place, so in his turn he betrayed them, denouncing the plot to the Jesuit Father Giuseppe Des Puches. Without a moment's delay the Father blurted it all out to the Holy Office, who passed it on to the Chief Justice in Palermo, and he told the Viceroy.

'In the twinkling of an eye they took them all prisoner and tortured them with red-hot irons. They beheaded the lawyer Lo Giudice and hung his head up in the Quattro Canti in the centre of town. They also beheaded Count Recalmuto and the Abbot Giovanni Caetani, who was only twenty-two years old. My father spent two days in prison and he had to pay out a large sum of money to keep his head on his shoulders.

'As for Don Giuseppe Branciforti Mazzarino, well, they pardoned him for having denounced Moncada. But he was disillusioned by politics and he retired to Bagheria, where he had his estates. He built himself a sumptuous villa and all along the cornice was written:

> *Ya la speranza es perdida*
> *Y un sol bien me consuela*
> *Que el tiempo que pasa y buela*
> *Llevará presto la vida.*[*]

'Thus, my dear little Marianna, my dumb baby, was Bagheria

---

[*]Here all hope is gone/Only the sun consoles me/Time passes and flies/My life will soon be done.

born through the betrayal of an ambitious plot. However, it was a princely betrayal, the Lord did not punish it with destruction like He punished Sodom and Gomorrah. Instead He made it so beautiful and sought after that all the world wanted this land set like a jewel between the ancient mountains of Catalfano, Giancaldo and Consuono, the coast of Aspra and the wonderful headland of Capo Zafferano.'

XX

'I don't want my uncle, Mother, I'm telling you.' The note is crumpled between Marianna's fingers.

'But your mother married her uncle', Duke Pietro replies to his daughter.

'But she was dumb and who else would have her?' While writing this, Giuseppa looks at her mother as if to say, Forgive me but for the moment I have to use what weapons I can to get my own way.

'Your mother may be dumb but she's more cultivated than you. You're nothing but a bunch of wild chives, you don't seem to have an ounce of common sense. Also your mother was a sight more attractive than you, she was a beauty, a queen.'

It is the first time Marianna has read a compliment from uncle husband and she is so dumbfounded that she is at a loss for words to defend her daughter.

Unexpectedly Signoretto comes to the rescue of the two women. Since he married the Venetian he has become more easy-going. He has taken to using ironic expressions that recall those of his father.

Marianna watches him opening and closing his arms, arguing with his uncle, who will certainly not fail to point out that Giuseppa is now twenty-three and it is inconceivable that at this age she should still be unmarried. Marianna seems to recognise the word 'spinster' coming several times from the lips of the Duke. And has Signoretto brought up the argument about freedom which he has lately held in such high esteem? Will he remember that their great-grandfather Edoardo Gerbi di Mansueto went to prison 'in defence of his liberty and indeed of ours'?

Signoretto is very proud of this ancestral glory, but it only irritates his brother-in-law all the more. To be consistent with his idea of 'independence' her brother has adopted a supportive attitude towards the women of his family. He allows the girls to study together with their brothers, something that would have been simply unthinkable twenty years ago.

Uncle husband argues scornfully that Signoretto 'with his foolishness has wasted all his own money and will have nothing to leave his sons except learning and tears. . . .'

Giuseppa seems happy to be caught between her uncle and her father, who are quarrelling with each other. Perhaps in the end she won't have to marry her uncle Gerbi after all. At this point her mother intercedes for her and for Giulio Carbonelli, a childhood friend of the same age as Giuseppa and secretly betrothed to her for years.

A moment later the three of them disappear into the yellow drawing-room. As usual they have forgotten about Marianna. Though maybe the idea of continuing their discussion in front of a dumb woman who might read their lips makes them feel uncomfortable. In fact they shut the door, leaving her on her own as if the affair was no concern of hers.

Later Giuseppa comes back and embraces her: 'I've done it, Mamma, I'm marrying Giulio.'

'And your father?'

'It's Signoretto who convinced him. He accepts Giulio rather than have me left a spinster.'

'Even though he has no money, and a reputation for idleness?'

'Yes, he said yes.'

'So now we start preparing for the wedding.'

'No preparations. We shall get married in Naples, without any festivities. They don't have such antiquated rubbish there any more. . . . Just think, a wedding feast with all those bigwigs who are friends of my father. . . . We'll get married in Naples, then we'll set off at once for London.'

The next moment Giuseppa has flown away through the door, leaving behind her a delicate smell of sweat mingled with lavender.

Marianna remembers that in her pocket there is a short note from her daughter Manina that she has not yet read. It only says, 'Expecting you this evening for the Ave Maria.' But the idea of going to Palermo does not attract her. . . . Manina has called her last child Signoretto after her grandfather. He looks very like the little Signoretto who died of smallpox at the age of four. Every so often Marianna goes to the Casa Chiarandà in Palermo to hold this small, fragile and voracious-looking grandchild in her arms. The sensation of holding little Signoretto close to her is so strong that sometimes she puts him down and rushes away with her heart overflowing.

If only Felice would go with her. But Felice, after having been a novice for so many years, has taken her final vows with ceremonies that lasted for ten days: ten days of festivities, alms-giving, masses, dinners and sumptuous suppers.

For the admission of his daughter into the convent uncle husband has spent over ten thousand escudos, what with dowry, food, wine and candles. A celebration that everyone in the city will remember for its magnificence, especially as the Viceroy Count Giuseppe Griman, President of the Kingdom, took offence and promulgated a notice to warn the nobility that they were spending too much and getting into debt, and forbidding monastic festivals that lasted more than two days. A notice that everyone in Palermo completely disregarded.

For who was there to listen to him? The greatness of the nobility lies in scorning accounts and bills, whatever they may be. A nobleman never calculates, cannot add or subtract and does not know arithmetic. For this there are administrators, major-domos, secretaries, servants. A nobleman does not sell and he does not buy. If ever he offers something, it is the best that can be found on the market, to be given to whomever he considers worthy of his generosity. It might be a son or a nephew, but it is equally likely to be a beggar, a swindler, an adversary at cards, a singer, a washerwoman, according to the vagaries of the moment. Seeing that everything that grows and multiplies in the beautiful Sicilian earth belongs to them by birth, by blood, by divine grace, what sense is there in calculating profit and loss? That is a matter for tradespeople and the rising bourgeoisie: those same tradespeople and bourgeoisie who, in the words of Duke Pietro, 'will one day swallow up everything', as is already happening. They are gnawing like rats at one morsel after another, olive trees, cork trees, mulberry trees, corn, carobs, lemons, and so on and so on. 'In future the world will belong to speculators, thieves, profiteers, sharks, assassins', according to the apocalyptic vision of uncle husband, and everything will go to ruin because 'with the nobility something incalculable will be lost: the spontaneous sense of the absolute, the glorious impossibility of hoarding or putting on one side, the self-exposure, the laying of oneself open with divine courage to the nothingness that devours everything without leaving a trace. The art of saving will be invented and mankind will succumb to vulgarity of the spirit.'

What will remain after we have gone? ask the restless eyes of Duke Pietro. Only a few crumbling vestiges, a few sticks and stones of a villa inhabited by chimeras with a long dreamy gaze, some patch of a garden where a few stone musicians are playing stone music among the skeletons of lemon and olive trees.

The feast at which Felice took the veil could not have been more splendid, with the entire aristocratic throng dressed with great elegance: the women swinging their trains, their hooped skirts, their dresses from Paris, their muslins light as a butterfly's wings, their heads arrayed in gold and silver nets, wearing ribbons of velveteen, and lace and silk that floated down from painted girdles. Amidst feathers, dress swords, gloves, muffs, bonnets, artificial flowers, slippers with pearl-studded buckles, tricorns covered with plush, tricorns gleaming in the light, suppers of thirty courses were served. And between one course and the next, crystal goblets were filled with lemon sorbets perfumed with bergamot. Snow was brought down from the mountains wrapped in straw on the backs of donkeys, having been kept underground for months: Palermo had never lacked its prodigious ices.

When, in the centre of the oratory, flanked by two rows of guests, Sister Maria Felice Immaculata had prostrated herself on the floor with her arms spread out like a corpse, and the Sisters had covered her with a black pall and had lighted two candles at her feet and two at her head, uncle husband had started to sob, leaning on the arm of his dumb wife – something that filled her with astonishment. Not once during their marriage had she seen him weep, not even when little Signoretto died. And now this daughter who was to become a bride of Christ was breaking his heart.

When the festival was over Duke Pietro sent his cloistered daughter a maid to help her dress and keep her things in order. He also lent her his sedan-chair upholstered in velvet with gold cherubs on the roof. And today he still makes sure she does not lack money to favour her confessor, whom it is the custom to indulge with choice fruits, silks and embroidery.

Each month fifty *tarì* is needed for the candle wax, another fifty for the altar offerings, seventy for new tablecloths and thirty for sugar and almond paste. A thousand escudos has gone in reconstructing the convent garden, which is now most certainly a wonderful sight, embellished by artificial lakes, stone fountains, paths, porticos, groves of trees and fake grottos where the Sisters can rest and eat sweets and tell their rosaries.

The fact is that Duke Pietro is not at all resigned to having his daughter so far away, and whenever he can he sends a carriage for her so that she can come to the house for a day or two. For Aunt Fiammetta the convent is a kitchen garden where hoeing should be part of prayer. Her niece has made her cell into a luxurious oasis where she can retire from the ugliness of the world, where her gaze can rest only on pleasant and beautiful things. For Fiammetta the garden is a place of meditation, of inward concentration, for Felice it is a centre of conversation, where she can be comfortably seated in the shade of a fig tree, exchanging news and gossip. Fiammetta accuses Felice of 'corruption', her young niece accuses her aunt of 'bigotry'. One of them reads only the Gospels, which she takes with her to the kitchen as often as she does to the orchard, so that they are reduced to a mass of greasy pages, while the other reads romanticised lives of the saints in small white books bound in leather. Between the pages are images of saints, their bodies covered with sores, reclining in sensual poses and wrapped in robes heavy with scrolls and flourishes.

When Aunt Teresa the Prioress was alive there were two of them to criticise Felice. Now that Aunt Teresa has passed away, an event which occurred on almost the same day as Aunt Agata the Canoness died, only Fiammetta remains to offer recriminations. There are times when it seems that she is no longer quite rational and as a result has become much harsher and harder. But Felice is not worried: she knows she is in a strong position because she has her father on her side. As for her deaf and dumb mother she has never given her much thought; she reads too many books and this makes her seem cut off and 'a little bit mad', as she says to her friends to excuse her.

Mariano in his turn regards his sister as 'pretentious' and doesn't share her taste for exhibitionism and novelty. He is preparing to inherit all his father's wealth and every day he grows more handsome and more arrogant. He is patient with his mother even though his patience is somewhat affected. Whenever he sees her he bows and kisses her hand, and then takes possession of her pen and paper and writes a few well-turned phrases in large looped handwriting.

He has fallen in love with a beautiful girl, Caterina Molè di Flores e Pozzogrande, who will bring him a dowry of twenty estates. The wedding will be in September and already Marianna is thinking of the work involved in preparing for the celebrations, which will last for no fewer than eight days, ending with a night of fireworks.

XXI

Outside it is dark. Silence envelops Marianna: absolute, barren. In her hands a love story. Words, writes the author, are harvested by the eyes like bunches of grapes hanging from a vine, ground out of thought like the turning of a millstone and then spreading like liquid and coursing freely through the veins. Is this the divine grape harvest of literature?

To suffer with the characters who run through the pages, to drink the essence of other people's thoughts, to taste the repeated excitement of other people's emotions, to feel one's own sensations heightened by the never-ending spectacle of the drama of love, is this not itself love? How much does it matter that this love has never been actually lived face to face? To participate in embracing the bodies of strangers who have become close and intimate through the printed page, is this not as good as experiencing that embrace, with one additional advantage: that of being able to remain in control of oneself?

But a suspicion crosses her mind: that this could merely be spying on the life-breath of others. Is to pursue in the pages of a book the making and unmaking of other people's love affairs similar to watching the person beside her and trying to interpret the rhythm of the words on their lips? Is this not a painful caricature? She has spent so many hours in the library learning to extract gold from stones, sifting and cleaning for days and days, her eyes moist in the misty currents of literature. What has she been able to get out of it? Some convoluted grain of knowledge? From one book to another, from one page to another. Hundreds of stories of love, of happiness, despair, death, joy, murders, encounters, farewells. And she always there, seated in her armchair with the worn embroidered antimacassar behind her head.

The lowest bookshelves, which are within a child's reach, contain mostly lives of saints: *Events in the Life of Saint Eulalia*, *The Life of Saint Leodegario*, a few books in French, the *Jeu de Saint Nicolas*, the *Cymbalum Mundi*, a few books in Spanish like the *Rimado de Palacio*, or the *Lazarillo de Tormes*. A mountain of almanacs: of the *New Moon*, of *Love under Mars*, of the *Harvest*, of the *Winds*; even stories about the French paladins and a few romances for young ladies that speak of love with hypocritical licence. Further up on the shelves, at the height of a man, are the classics, from the *Vita Nuova* to *Orlando Furioso*, from *De Rerum Natura* to Plato's *Dialogues*, even a few fashionable romances like *The Faithful Colloandro* and *The Legends of the Virgins*.

All these were in the library of the Villa Ucrìa when Marianna inherited it. But since then she has frequented it so industriously that the number of books has doubled. To start with she made the study of French and English the pretext, and procured dictionaries, grammars and books of exercises. Then a few books of travel to far-distant countries, and last of all with growing enthusiasm some modern romances and books on history and philosophy.

Since her children have left home she has had more time, and there are never enough books for her. She orders them by the dozen but they often take months to arrive. For example, the parcel that contained *Paradise Lost* was held up for five months at the port of Palermo without anyone knowing where it had got to. Or like the *Histoire Comique de Francion*, which was lost at sea between Naples and Sicily when the boat sank off Capri. Other books she has loaned to someone but she cannot remember whom, like the *Lays of Mary, Queen of Scots*, which was never returned. Or *The Romance of Brut*, which must still be in the possession of her brother Carlo in the monastery of San Martino delle Scale.

This reading continues far into the night. It exhausts her but also fills her with delight. Marianna never seems to be able to bring herself to accept that it is time to go to bed and if it were not for the thirst that almost tears her away from her reading she would probably go on till daybreak. To leave a book is like leaving the better part of oneself. To pass from the soft and airy arcades of the mind to the demands of a graceless body always grasping for one thing or another is in any case a surrender: a renunciation of characters one has studied and cared for in favour of a self one does not love, confined within a stupid succession of days, each day indistinguishable from the last.

A thirst has put its fist into this sensuous quietness, taking away the scent of flowers, darkening the shadows. The silence of the night is suffocating. Back in the library, with its guttering candles, Marianna asks herself why the nights are closing in on her, why everything is rushing into her head as if it were a well of dark water in which from time to time there is a heavy resounding splash; something has fallen – but what?

Her footsteps slip lightly and silently over the carpet in the corridor; they reach the dining-room, they cross the yellow room and the rose room and stop at the entrance to the kitchen. The black curtain that hides the big jar in which the drinking water is kept is drawn back – someone has already been down for a drink. For a moment she is seized by panic at the prospect of a nocturnal encounter with uncle husband. He has not come to find her since the night she refused him. She has an intuition that he is involved with Cuffa's wife. Not the elderly Severina, who died a while ago, but his new wife Rosalia, who has thick black plaits that swing down her back. She is about thirty, with a forceful temperament and a lot of energy. But with her master she knows how to be gentle and to satisfy his need for someone who welcomes his assaults without turning to ice. Marianna recalls their own hurried couplings in the dark, he armed and relentless, she distant, turned to stone. They must have looked comical, as foolish as those people who repeat without the least glimmer of understanding a duty which has no meaning for them and for which they are not cut out.

Yet they have had five children, and three who died before birth, making eight in all: eight times they have encountered each other beneath the sheets without a kiss or a caress. An assault, a bearing down of cold knees against her legs, and then a fast and furious explosion. Sometimes she would close her eyes while doing her duty

114

and distance herself, thinking of the couplings of Zeus and Io, and Zeus and Leda, as described by Pausanias and Plutarch. The divine body selects the terrestrial image, a fox, a swan, an eagle or a bull. And then, after prolonged ambushes among the cork trees and the oaks, a sudden apparition. No time to say a word. The creature curves its claws, nails the woman's neck with its bill and steals her for itself and its own pleasure. A beating of wings, a panting breath on her neck, teeth biting into her shoulder, and it is over. The lover departs, leaving her suffering and humiliated.

She would like to ask Rosalia whether uncle husband is transformed into a wolf who tears her to pieces and then runs off. But she knows she will never bring herself to do so, through timidity, but also perhaps because of a fear of those long black plaits. When Rosalia is in a bad mood they seem to rise up and spit like dancing serpents.

There are no lights in the downstairs rooms and Marianna knows for certain that her husband never walks around in the dark like she does; as a result of her deafness her sight has become particularly acute, as if she had the eyes of a cat.

The pitcher seeps moisture. It feels cold and porous to the touch, and exudes a good smell of earthenware. Marianna dips a small metal scoop attached to a stick into the pitcher and drinks avidly, letting the water run down her embroidered bodice.

Out of the corner of her eye she sees a faint light filtering through one of the doors to the servants' quarters. It is Fila's room and her door is half-open. Marianna has no idea what time it is, but it is certainly past midnight or even one o'clock, perhaps nearer to three. She seems to sense a slight rippling of the night air, set in motion by the bell of the chapel of the Casa Butera striking two.

Almost without realising it her feet take her in the direction of the light, and she peers through the gap in the door, trying to distinguish something by the flickering of a small smoky candle. She sees a naked arm dangling over the edge of the bed, a foot with a shoe on it going up and down. She draws back feeling ashamed. Spying is unworthy of her. But then she smiles at herself: shame can be left to noble souls, curiosity lies at the root of a thirst for knowledge, as Mr David Hume of London would say, and it is similar to that other curiosity which drives her to burrow her way into books with great passion. So why be so hypocritical? With a daring that surprises her, she returns to spy through the open crack, holding her breath as if her future depends on what she is going to see, as if her glance was already being attacked before she had even looked.

Fila is not alone. Beside her is a good-looking youth who is crying pitifully. His dark, curly hair is tied behind his neck in a small tight plait. Marianna fancies that she has already seen this young lad, but where? His limbs are delicate and smooth, his skin is the colour of well-baked bread. She sees Fila take out a handkerchief and with it wipe the nose of the crying boy.

Now Fila seems to be pressing the boy with questions which he is unwilling to answer. Swinging backwards and forwards moodily, alternately laughing and weeping, he sits on the edge of the bed and looks down with amazement at the buckskin leather shoes lying on the floor, their laces all untied.

Fila goes on talking. She seems irritated but she has put the wet handkerchief back in her pocket and is bending over him, insistent and maternal. He stops crying, grabs one of her shoes and holds it up to his nose. Then Fila throws herself on top of him and hits him vigorously, slapping him with the palm of her hand, on the nape of his neck and then on his cheek, finally battering his head with a storm of blows. He lets himself be hit without moving. Then, with all the commotion, the candle goes out and the room is plunged into darkness. Marianna moves a few steps backwards, but Fila must have relit the candle because the light returns flickering in the doorway.

It is time to go back, Marianna tells herself, but a new uncontrollable curiosity, which her inner self judges to be almost indecent, pulls her once more towards the forbidden vision. Now Fila is sitting on the bed with the boy and he is nestling close to her and leaning his head on her breast. Gently she kisses his bruised forehead and brushes her tongue over the scratch she has made under his left eye.

This time Marianna forces herself to go back to the pitcher of fresh water. The idea of witnessing a scene of seduction between Fila and the boy sickens her; she is sufficiently surprised and upset by what she has seen already. Once again she plunges the cane with its little metal scoop into the water, brings it up to her mouth and drinks in big gulps with her eyes closed.

She does not notice that the door has opened and Fila is standing on the threshold looking at her. She stands there, her bodice unlaced, her plaits undone, frozen with astonishment, unable to do anything except gaze open-mouthed. Meanwhile the boy too has come forward and stops beside her, his little pigtail hanging down beneath his reddened ear.

Marianna stares at them but without looking cross; perhaps there is even laughter in her eyes because eventually Fila frees herself from her paralysis and starts to lace up her bodice with hurried fingers. The boy does not seem afraid. He comes nearer, naked to the waist, focusing his bold eyes on the Duchess like one who has seen her only at a distance through half-closed doors, perhaps spying on her just as a few moments ago she was spying on him, standing by himself, hidden and motionless beyond half-drawn curtains, in ambush. As if he had heard much talk about her, and now wants to see what this great lady with the throat of stone is made of.

But Fila has something to say. She comes close to Marianna, takes her by the wrist and speaks into her deaf ears, making signs with her fingers immediately in front of her eyes. Marianna watches her getting all worked up while her hair slips out of the plaits and slides down on to her cheeks in black rivulets.

For once Marianna is protected by her deafness without feeling disabled. The thought of punishing them makes her cheeks flush. She knows very well that to do so would make no sense – and that, anyway, she is the guilty one for going round the house in the dead of night. But at that moment what she needs to do is to establish the proper distance between them, which has been dangerously undermined. She goes over to Fila with her arm raised, like a mistress who has discovered her servant with a stranger beneath her own roof. Uncle husband would approve of this; indeed he would provide her with a whip.

But Fila quickly takes her hand and drags her to the middle of the room, towards the mirror lit by the gleam of the lighted candle. With her other hand she takes the boy by his hair and pulls him beside her cheek to cheek. Marianna stares at these two heads in the mirror, the glass darkened by smoke, and in a flash she understands what Fila is trying to tell her: two mouths shaped by the same hand, two prominent noses out of the same mould, narrow at the top and bottom, grey eyes slightly too far apart, wide cheekbones: they are brother and sister.

Fila realises that the force of her images has got her message across. She nods and sucks in her lips with joy. But how has she

117

managed to hide the boy all this time so that even her father the Duke did not know of his existence? Now Fila, with all the authority of an elder sister, tells the boy to kneel down in front of the Duchess and to kiss the hem of her precious amber-coloured dress. And he dutifully looks up and down with a contrite yet theatrical expression and brushes the hem of her skirt with his lips. A flash of childlike cunning, a seductive guile which only someone who feels excluded from this glittering world is able to display.

Marianna gazes tenderly at the crescent moons that make a pair on his bent back. Quickly she gives a sign for him to rise. Fila laughs and claps her hands. The boy stands up straight in front of her. There is something shameless about him that displeases her but at the same time excites her. Their eyes meet in a brief moment of attraction.

XXII

Saro and Raffaele Cuffa are at the oars. The boat slips over the dark water with a regular rhythmic motion. Beneath a garland of paper lanterns there are gilded seats. Duchess Marianna, looking like a sphinx, is wrapped in a bottle-green cloak, her face turned towards the port.

On the seats, sitting across the boat, are Giuseppa with her husband Giulio Carbonelli and their two-year-old son, and Manina with her young daughter Giacinta. In the bows, on two coils of rope, sit Fila and Innocenza.

A boat comes close, a few lengths distant. Another festoon, another gilded seat, on which Duke Pietro is seated. Next to him is his daughter Felice the nun; here too is his son Mariano with his wife Caterina Molè di Flores, and Cuffa's young wife Rosalia, who has wrapped her black plaits on top of her head like a turban.

All over the water in the Bay of Palermo are hundreds of boats: *gozzi*, caiques, feluccas, each festooned with its array of lights, each with its seating for the nobility and places for the oarsmen. The sea is calm, the moon hidden behind small ragged clouds edged with violet, the boundaries between sky and water invisible in the dense blackness of a calm, still August night.

Soon the firework scaffold that rises imposingly on the shore will explode with Catherine wheels, rockets and fountains of light that will rain down over the sea. In the background Porta Felice seems like a Christmas crib all strewn with oil lights. To the right the Cassaro Morto, the dark outline of the Vicaria, the low houses of the Kalsa, the massive façade of the Steri Palace, the grey domes of Santa Maria della Catena, the square wall of the Castello by the sea, the long stark building of San Giovanni de' Leprosi. Suddenly from a maze of dark crooked lanes thousands of people are pouring out towards the sea.

Marianna reads a small crumpled note which she holds in her lap. In a graceful copperplate is written, 'Scaffold constructed by grace of the Master Weavers, the Master Grooms, and the Master Cheese Vendors. Amen.'

Now the men have stopped rowing. The boat oscillates gently on the waves with its cargo of lights, bodies dressed up for a festival, slices of water-melon, bottles of aniseed water. Marianna turns her head towards this throng of boats which, in the stillness of the night, rock to and fro like feathers floating suspended in the void.

'Long live Ferdinand, the new-born son of Charles III, King of Sicily. Amen' says another note that has fallen on to her shoe. The first rocket streaks upwards. It explodes far up in the sky, almost hidden by the clouds. A rain of silver threads plummets down on to the roofs of Palermo, on to the façades of the princely palaces, the streets with their grey cobblestones, the sea walls around the port, the boats laden with spectators, and is extinguished sizzling in the black water.

The day before yesterday a festival for the coronation of Victor Amadeus of Savoy, yesterday illuminations for the ascent to the throne of Charles VI of Hapsburg, today the birth of a son to the Bourbon Charles III ... the same merry-making, the same pot-pourri: on the first day a solemn mass in the cathedral, on the second a fight between a lion and a horse, on the third musicians in the Marble Theatre, then a ball at the palace of the Senate, horse races, processions and fireworks at the Marina ... what endless boredom....

For Marianna a look from uncle husband is sufficient for her to know what he is brooding over. Of late he has become transparent to her: neither his faded eyes nor his balding forehead can any longer hide the thoughts that until now have been closely guarded. It is as if he has lost the patience to dissimulate. For years he has prided himself on it. No one could penetrate beyond those eyebrows, beyond that bare, stern forehead. Now it seems that this skill has become too easy and consequently is no longer of interest.

It's we who are always bowing and scraping . . . that Victor Amadeus, let him be, he wanted to turn Palermo into another Turin. God help us! The waste of time, the duties, the garrisons . . . . Does Your Majesty want to put a tax on illness, on hunger? Our jasmine-scented sores, my Emperor, it is only we who understand them, thanks be to God. The Treaty of Utrecht, another wretched business: the morsels have all been divided up, one to me, one to you . . . and that harlot Elizabetta Farnese displays herself all over the island, she wants a throne for that son of hers . . . and Cardinal Alberoni is her accomplice, and Philip V, he lends a hand as well. . . . At Capo Passero the English forced that big fool Philip to drink vinegar but Elizabetta doesn't give a cuss, she's a mother who's prepared to be patient. . . . Then the Austrians are defeated in Poland and they turn their backs on Naples and Sicily, so her son got the best deal in the end. . . . They're on our backs and God knows when they'll leave. . . .

That silent voice refuses to stop. The Lord has given her this gift, to be able to enter into other people's heads. But once the door is shut she starts breathing in stale air, where words take on a musty smell.

Two hands come down on the Duchess's shoulders, lifting the shawl on her neck, arranging her hair. Marianna turns to thank Fila and finds herself face to face with the free and easy countenance of Saro.

Later, while she is admiring the rise and fall of the green and yellow lights flowering against the sky, she is again aware of the presence of the boy at her shoulders. Gentle fingers have moved the shawl aside and brush against the line of her hair. Marianna is about to push them away but an exhaustion, a dumb weariness, keeps her glued to her seat. Now the youth goes with feline grace to the prow and raises his arm to the sky. It is clear he has gone there to be admired. He stands upright on the convex triangle, precariously balanced to show off his tall slim body, his handsome face suddenly lighted up by flying sparks.

Everyone is looking upwards, following the explosions of the fireworks. He is the only one looking elsewhere, in the direction of the ducal seat placed in the centre of the boat. In the flashes of light that flood the sky with colour Marianna sees the young man's eyes fixed on her. His eyes are happy, amorous, tinged with arrogance, but there is no slyness in them. Marianna regards them for a second time and then abruptly withdraws her glance. Yet a moment later she can only return to admiring him: that neck, those legs, that mouth seem to exist only to attract and disquiet her.

XXIII

Whether she is in the garden reading a book, in the yellow room doing the accounts with Raffaele Cuffa, or in the library studying English, she is always coming across Saro, springing up from nowhere and a moment later disappearing back to nowhere – always there to stare at her with soft bright eyes that beg for a response. Marianna is amazed at his persistence; he becomes more ardent and pressing with every passing day.

Uncle husband has taken him under his wing and has had a livery made to measure for him in the ducal colours, blue and gold. The pigtail no longer dances about behind his ears, shrivelled up like a rat's tail. A lock of dark gleaming hair clings to his forehead and he smooths it back with a seductive, carefree sweep of his hand.

There is only one place he may not enter and that is the principal bedchamber; it is there she takes refuge more and more often with her books, beneath the enigmatic eyes of the chimeras asking themselves whether he will dare to continue pursuing her. But every so often she finds herself looking down into the courtyard, waiting for his appearance. It is enough for her to see him pass with his relaxed walk to put her in a good humour.

So as to avoid encountering him she has even decided to go and stay for a while in Palermo in the house in the Via Alloro. But one morning she sees him arrive on her husband's carriage, standing on the small running-board at the back, his face beaming. He is smartly dressed with a tricorn hat on top of his black curls and a pair of brilliantly polished shoes ornamented with brass buckles. Fila says he has begun to study. She has told Innocenza, who has blurted it out to Sister Felice, who has written a note to her mother: 'He is learning to write so he can talk to your ladyship.' It is not clear whether this was said out of spite or in admiration.

Today it is raining and the landscape is veiled. Each bush, each tree is drenched with water. The silence imprisons her: it seems harder to bear than her isolation. A profound longing for sounds that match this view of sparkling branches, this countryside teeming with life, catches her throat. How does the song of the nightingale sound? She has read of it so often in books, how it is so unimaginably sweet, how it resonates in the heart. But how?

The door opens just as it does in certain nightmares, as if pushed by an unknown hand. Marianna watches it slowly moving, ignorant of what is going to emerge: will it be joy or pain, the face of a friend or the face of a foe?

It is Fila. She comes in holding a lighted candelabra. As usual she is barefoot and Marianna realises that this reflects her wilful rebelliousness, a sign of revolt against the demands of her master and mistress. But at the same time she relies on Marianna's forbearance, which she thinks is due not so much to tolerance as to some uneasy secret that binds them together beyond the difference in their ages, fortunes and social position.

What does she want of her? Why does she plant her naked dirty feet on the precious rugs with such relish? Why does she walk in such an offhand manner, not caring that her skirt lifts up to reveal her blotched calloused heels? Marianna knows that the only way to re-establish a proper distance between them would be to raise her hand in a slap. Just a light one. That is what she is accustomed to. But it is enough for Marianna to look at her face with its gentle features, so like that other, masculine face with features a little more sharply delineated, for any desire to hit her to vanish.

Marianna lifts her hand to the collar of her dress, where it chafes at her throat. Her fleecy bodice is rough against her sweating back; it feels as if it were made of thorns. Making a sign with her finger she dismisses Fila. The girl goes out swinging her full skirt of red cloth. Near the door she bows stiffly and distorts her face in a simpering expression.

Left alone Marianna kneels in front of a small ivory crucifix that Felice gave her. She tries to pray: 'Oh Lord, grant that I do not betray myself in my own eyes, grant that I know how to be loyal to the integrity of my heart.' Her eyes rest on the crucifix: it seems to her that Christ too has a derisive expression. Like Fila He seems to be laughing at her. Marianna rises. She goes and lies down on the bed, putting an arm over her eyes.

She turns on her side. She reaches out for the Bible her brother the Abbot Carlo gave her when Mariano was born. She opens it and reads:

> My spirit is consumed, my days are extinct,
> surely there are mockers with me,
> and mine eyes abideth in their provocation.
> Give me now a pledge, a surety for me with thyself.

It is as if the words of Job are there to remind her of some crime. But what crime? Thinking the sort of thoughts provoked by Mr Hume? Or allowing herself to be tempted by dangerous hidden desires? Without doubt her days too are failing. Little by little the lights of her body are going out, but who will save her from the mockers?

The door starts to move again, swinging open, throwing a square shadow on to the floor. What will follow? What body, what expression? Perhaps that of a youth who looks about twelve but is actually nineteen.

This time it is Giuseppa with her little boy who has come to see her. How fat she has become! Her clothes strain to throttle her flesh, her face is pale, her expression lifeless. She enters with a resolute step and sits on the edge of the bed; she takes off her shoes, which are cramping her feet, and, stretching her legs out on the floor, looks at her mother and bursts into tears.

Marianna moves over to her affectionately and holds her close, but her daughter, far from calming down, abandons herself to sobbing while the little boy crawls on all fours underneath the bed.

'For Heaven's sake, what on earth is the matter?' writes Marianna on her notepad. She thrusts it under her daughter's nose.

Giuseppa wipes her tears with the back of her hand, unable to restrain her sobs. She turns to embrace her mother and then seizes the edge of her cloak and blows her nose noisily. Only after much cajoling does Marianna succeed in putting the pen in her hand and getting her to write.

'Giulio is maltreating me. I want to leave him.'

'What has he been doing, my little one?'

'He's brought a bonnet-maker into our bed with the excuse that she is ill. Then, as she had no clothes, he gave her mine as well as all the French fans I had put away.'

'I will tell your father.'

'No, Mamma, I beg you, leave him out of it.'

'But what can I do about it?'

'I want you to have him beaten up.'

'What on earth good would that do? We aren't still living in the time of your great-grandfather.'

'I want revenge, a vendetta.'

'What do you want with a vendetta?'

'It's what I'd like. I've been hurt and I want to feel better.'

'But why has he put this girl in your bed? I don't understand', Marianna writes quickly. Giuseppa's replies are taking longer and the writing is all over the place.

'To dishonour me.'

'But why should your husband want to dishonour you?'

'He knows why.'

A strange, incredible story. If her husband Giulio Carbonelli wants to have a bit of fun, surely he does not have to shove the bonnet-maker into his wife's bed? What can be behind this nonsensical action?

And now, little by little, with halting words and dialect phrases, more revelations emerge. Giuseppa has made friends with her aunt Domitilla, Signoretto's wife, who has introduced her to forbidden books of French philosophy, full of sacrilegious ideas and demands for freedom. Don Giulio Carbonelli hates these new ideas that are circulating among young people even more than Duke Pietro does, and has tried to prevent her taking a direction 'absolutely unsuitable for a Carbonelli of the baronial estates of Scarapullè'. But his wife completely ignored him and so he found a devious and brutal way of showing her without wasting words that he was master of the house.

Now it is a question of convincing her daughter that vendettas only lead to more vendettas and that such a quarrel between husband and wife is unthinkable. Nor can she think of separating from him: she has a small son and cannot leave him without a father. What's more, a woman without a husband can only take refuge in a convent if she is not to be branded as a prostitute. She must find a way of making him respect her without either vendettas or reprisals. What can be done?

While she is reflecting Marianna writes, 'But what are these French fans?'

'They have bedroom scenes painted between the spokes', her daughter writes impatiently. Marianna nods, embarrassed.

'You must win his respect', she insists, but she is finding it difficult to keep her handwriting composed and firm.

'We fight like cat and dog.'

'It was you who were so determined to have him. If you had married your uncle Antonio as your father proposed....'

'I'd rather be dead. Uncle Antonio is an old stick-in-the-mud with the eyes of a hen. I'd rather have Giulio with his bonnet-maker. It was only because of your wretched dumbness that you had to marry your uncle, my boorish father.... If I told Mariano, do you think he'd know how to avenge me?'

'Get that idea right out of your head, Giuseppa.'

'They could wait for him outside the door and beat him up.... That's what I want, Mamma.'

Marianna turns towards her daughter with a dark look. The girl makes an angry face and bites her lip. But her mother still has some power over her, and confronted with the severe expression in her eyes, Giuseppa withdraws and gives up the idea of a vendetta.

XXIV

The curtains are drawn. The velvet hangs in wide folds. The vaulted ceiling gathers up the shadows. A few gleams of light penetrate the curtains and dissolve on to the floor, forming bright pools of dust.

There is a smell of camphor in the stale air. Water is boiling in a saucepan placed on top of the stove. The bed is so big that it takes up one whole wall of the room. At the corners above it rest four columns of carved wood and between them hang embroidered curtains with silken cords.

Beneath the crumpled sheet is Manina's sweating body. For days and days she has lain still with her eyes closed. No one can tell whether she is going to survive. The same smells as when Signoretto was dying, the same gelatinous consistency, the same fevered heat with its cloying sickly taste.

Marianna stretches out her hand towards her daughter's. She is lying with her palms turned upwards on the blanket, and cautiously Marianna strokes the damp palm with her fingers. How many times did her daughter's hand clutch hold of her skirt just as she, in her time, had clutched at her father's habit, demanding attention, a series of demands that could be coalesced into a single plea: can I trust you? But perhaps she has also discovered it is not possible to trust anyone, even someone you love blindly. In the end they will remain distant, incomprehensible.

Manina's hands, the whiteness of which is often blemished by the red bites of mosquitoes, are just like those of Agata. The aunt and niece are alike in many ways, each very beautiful, and each with a nature that tends to be cruelly self-sacrificing. Alienated from all philandering, all care, all feeling for themselves, both are entirely dedicated to maternal love, obsessed by an adoration of their children that is close to idolatry.

The only difference lies in Manina's sense of humour, with which she tries to keep the peace by making people laugh while staying deadly serious herself. Agata sacrifices herself to motherhood without ever asking for anything in return, and regards women who have not made the same choice with some contempt. She already has eight children and her pregnancies continue in spite of the fact that she is thirty-nine. She is never tired, always wrestling with wet-nurses, nannies, surgeons, leeches and midwives.

Manina likes a quiet life too much to disparage anybody. Her dream is to weave together with one thread husband, children, parents and relatives and to hold them firmly to her. At twenty-five she has had six children and, since she was married at twelve, her sons seem more like brothers while they are growing up.

Marianna remembers her stumbling on her plump legs, dressed in a full-skirted dress patterned with red flowers she had copied from a painting by Velázquez, of which she had a reproduction in

126

water-colours. A rosy child, calm, with eyes of aquamarine. She had not yet emerged from that painting when she stepped into another on the arm of her husband, her enormous belly borne before her like a trophy offered without shame to the admiration of passers-by.

Two miscarriages and one baby stillborn. But she has survived it all without too much damage. 'My body is a waiting-room, there is always an infant coming in or going out', she wrote about herself to her mother, and these entrances and exits do not in any way disconcert her, indeed she has thrived on them: the confusion of children, forever running, eating, shitting, sleeping, screaming, fills her with happiness.

But now the latest birth may kill her. The baby was well positioned, at least according to the midwife. Her breasts had begun to secrete milk and Manina amused herself by letting the smallest ones taste it. They climbed on to her lap and attached themselves to the nipple, squeezing and pulling at the hard-worked flesh.

The baby was born dead and she went on losing blood till she became grey. The midwife, by continuing to plug her with bandages, managed to staunch the bleeding, but by nightfall the mother had become delirious. Now she hangs on by a thread, her face as white as chalk, her eyes dimmed.

Marianna takes a piece of cloth, dips it in water and lemon juice and puts it close to her daughter's lips. For a moment she sees her eyes open, but they are blind; she does not recognise her. A smile of satisfaction passes across her bloodless face, a glimmer of sublime indifference to herself, a radiance of self-sacrifice. Who can have implanted this mania for maternal abnegation, this fervour for deliberate self-immolation? Aunt Teresa the Prioress? Or the white-haired nurse with the hair shirt underneath her bodice, who compelled her to pray for hours, kneeling beside the bed? Or perhaps Don Ligustro, who is also Aunt Fiammetta's confessor and who has been close to her for years, teaching her the catechism and the doctrines of the Church? And yet Don Ligustro is not at all fanatical, indeed at one time he seemed to be much taken with the great Cornelius Jansen, known as Giansenio. Somewhere there is a note from Father Ligustro that begins with a quote from Aristotle: 'God is too perfect to think of other than Himself.'

Neither Agata nor Manina expects anything from her husband:

127

neither love nor friendship. And perhaps it is because of this that they are loved. Don Diego di Torre Mosca never leaves his wife's side for a moment and is obsessed with jealousy because of her.

Manina's husband, Don Francesco Chiarandà di Magazzinasso, is also very attached to his wife although this does not prevent him from pursuing housekeepers and servants about the place, especially when they are from the 'Continent' of Italy. As happened with a girl called Rosina, who came from Benevento: a fine-looking haughty girl who waited at table. She got herself pregnant by his lordship and everybody was very upset. Manina's mother-in-law, the Baroness Chiarandà di Magazzinasso, removed her from her son's house and sent her off to Messina to the house of some friends who were in need of an elegant-looking servant. Fiammetta came from the convent to reprimand her nephew. Aunts, in-laws and cousins scurried to the big drawing-room of the Palazzo Chiarandà in the Via Toledo to sympathise with the poor wife.

But the one person who took no thought for herself in the whole business was Manina, who volunteered to bring up the illegitimate child, keeping both him and his mother in the house. And she said wittily of the resemblance between father and son that they both sported the same little prick of a nose. But her mother-in-law remained obdurate and Manina gave in with her usual submissiveness, inclining her beautiful head, which she has taken to decorating with a string of pink pearls.

Now the pearls are there on the chest of drawers and they gleam with mauve light in the shadows of the room. Next to them are four rings: the ruby ring of Grandmother Maria, which is still stained with dirt and from which still emanate whiffs of snuff from Trieste; a cameo ring with the head of Venus that belonged to Great-grandmother Giuseppa and before her to Great-great-grandmother Agata Ucrìa; a heavy gold wedding ring and a silver ring with dolphins, which Grandfather Signoretto used to wear. Beside them is a tortoiseshell comb studded with diamonds that has been passed down from the raven-black hair of the mother-in-law to the fair hair of the daughter-in-law.

The ring with the dolphins had once been lost by Marianna's father, which created a great to-do throughout the whole family. Finally it was found by Innocenza near the water-lily pond. As a result, from then on she rested on her laurels, as they say, and became for everyone 'honest Innocenza'. Later the dolphin ring got lost once again: this time her father the Duke had left it at the house of an opera singer of whom he was enamoured.

'Out of respect I took off the ring and put it on the bedside table', he wrote confidentially to his daughter.

'Respect for whom, Father?'

'For your mother, for the family.' But as he wrote it a smile flitted across his face, something plausible and at the same time implausible. He took pleasure in familiar situations, family evenings, but also in recitals, spectacles or parades, and the daring of an occasional night's jaunt in the town. He did not want to upset convention or hurt anyone's feelings, but at the same time he was interested in new ideas, in every unexpected emotion, tolerant of the contradictions within himself and intolerant of other people's.

'But did you find the ring?'

'I was in the wrong. I thought Clementina had stolen it. Instead she had me find it a couple of days later on the pillow. She was a good little girl.'

She has a box full of notes from her father and she keeps it locked in the chest of drawers by the bed. She has thrown her own notes away but those of her father, a few of her mother's, and a few of the children's she has kept. Every so often she takes them out and reads them. The free and easy handwriting of her father, the laboured, cramped hand of her mother, the narrow, sloping o's of her son Mariano, the flying s's and l's of her daughter Felice, the distorted signature, all blotted with ink, of her daughter Giuseppa. She has not even one note of Manina's. Perhaps because she has not written much or perhaps because whenever she does write on her mother's notepad the message has been too insignificant to be worth keeping. She has never enjoyed writing, this daughter with her lush, casual beauty. She loves music more than she loves the written word. Her witticisms, which are always aimed at diverting people from their dark thoughts, quarrels and bad temper, only reach Marianna when they are written down; and it is never Manina who writes them.

During the early years of their marriage Manina and Francesco were in the habit of inviting friends to their big house in the Via Toledo every evening. They had a French cook with a pockmarked face who used to prepare exquisite *foie gras* and delicious *coquilles aux herbes*. After the customary sorbet of pomegranate and lemon they would go into the drawing-room with its frescos by Intermassimi. Marianna remembers that there were also chimeras with the body of a lioness and the face of a woman. Manina used to sit at the harpsichord and let her fingers glide over the keys, at first timidly, cautiously, and then with more confidence until her mouth took on a bitter, almost ferocious expression.

After the death of their second child and the two miscarriages that followed it, the Chiarandàs had ceased entertaining. Only on Sundays did they sometimes ask relations to dinner and then Manina would play the harpsichord with great energy. But her face no longer became distorted, it remained as smooth and calm as she looks in the portrait by Intermassimi that hangs in the dining-room amidst a cloud of angels, birds of paradise and serpents with fishes' heads. Later she gave up music altogether. Now her seven-year-old daughter Giacinta sits at the harpsichord beside a music teacher from Switzerland, who beats time on the lid with a baton made from olive wood.

Marianna has become drowsy as she holds her daughter's feverish hand. The emptiness inside her head resounds with the drumming of the bay horse Miguelito's hoofs. Heaven knows where he is galloping now, that old horse originally given to her father the Duke by a distant cousin, Pipino Ondes, who in his turn had bought him from a gipsy.

For years Miguelito lived in the stables behind the Villa Ucrìa, next to the sunless house of the Calò family, together with the other Arab horses. Then her father had taken a liking to him because of his gentle and courageous nature, and rode him when going to the Villa Butera or the Villa Palagonia, and sometimes even as far as Palermo. In old age he ended up with the Calòs, being urged up and down precipitous slopes by the twins Lina and Lena. Eventually he became blind in one eye and then he used to carry old Calò behind the cows, on the plain of Bagheria. When the twins died he could still be seen wandering round the olive grove, very thin but ready to take off at a gallop, hardly touching the dusty slope that led down from the villa.

In a little while I will jump on his back, Marianna tells herself, and we'll go to find my father. But where is the old horse now? Worn and blind, his teeth yellow and broken with age, he has not lost his look of daring or the thick coffee-coloured mane for which he was famous. But his tail has something strange about it. It has got longer, twisted, swollen. And now it stretches, wriggles and pushes out a sharp point. It seems as if it wants to grab her round the waist and throw her against a rock. Is he being transformed into one of those dogs that used to people her mother's dreams?

Marianna opens her eyes just in time to glimpse through the half-open door a quivering lock of hair and two soft dark eyes watching her.

XXV

From far off they look like three large tortoises moving slowly along the narrow path among tall grass and stones. Three tortoises: three litters, each preceded and followed by two mules. In Indian file, one behind the other, between the woods and the steep precipices, following an inaccessible path that goes from Bagheria towards the Serre mountains, passing through Misilmeri, Villafrati, until it reaches the heights of the Portella del Coniglio. Four armed men follow behind the procession, four others precede it with muskets on their shoulders.

Marianna sits suspended, enclosed in a narrow swinging seat, her heavy skirt raised a little over her sweating ankles, her hair drawn back and coiled up on her neck for coolness. Every now and then she lifts her hand to chase away a fly. In front of her, on a seat lined with brocade, in a white dress of Indian voile, with a blue scarf across her knees, Giuseppa lies asleep, oblivious to the jolting and lurching of the litter.

Now the path becomes narrower and steeper, on one side hovering on the edge of a precipice strewn with pinkish-grey rocks, on the other overhung by a steep wall of black earth and a tangle of bushes. Now and again the hoofs of the mules skid on the rocks, making the litter lurch to one side, but then they recover and climb on, struggling to avoid the potholes in the path.

The muleteer guides them by going a few yards ahead, carrying a staff to test the muddy ground. At times the legs of the mules sink into the clay and, weighed down by clods of mud, can only be got out with a great struggle and much use of the whip. At other times the tall needle-like grasses become tangled round their fetlocks, hindering their movement.

Marianna holds on to the wooden handle, her stomach churning, wondering if she will end up being sick. Leaning her head out of the door, she can see the litter suspended over a precipice. Why don't they stop, why does this infuriating swaying that turns her stomach upside down never end? The fact is that to stop would be even more dangerous than to go on, and the mules, as if they understood this, are pushing forward with lowered heads, puffing and blowing, keeping the shafts balanced by instinctively controlling their muscles.

The flies come and go from the faces of the animals to the inside of the little carriage: the movement excites them. They fly over the Duchess's tied-up hair and over Giuseppa's open lips. Marianna realises that it is better to look into the distance and try to forget that she is a prisoner suspended between two wooden poles balanced over the void. Looking out she can see, beyond the stony precipices, beyond a wood of cork trees, in the middle of a gradual slope of fields scorched by the sun, the valley of Sciara, its wide stretch of land cultivated with wheat: an expanse covered by a yellow down of feathers barely shaken by the wind. Between the fields of grain, as alive and sinuous as a snake with shiny scales, the river San Leonardo flows down into the gulf of Termini Imerese. To Marianna's wide-open eyes, the great metallic river, the groves of cork trees with their reddish streaks, the stretches of sugar cane, are enclosed within a solid block of glassy heat scarcely shaken by an internal shimmering that is only just perceptible.

The magnificent landscape has made her forget the flies and the travel-sickness. She is about to stretch her hand out towards her daughter, who is sleeping with her head bent over her shoulder, but then she stops with her hand in mid-air. She is undecided whether to wake her and show her the view, or to let her sleep, remembering that they were up at four in the morning and that the swaying motion does not make it easy to stay awake.

Trying not to endanger the balance of this fragile domed shell, Marianna leans forward to see if the other litters are following them. In one is Manina, thin and beautiful after her recovery, and Felice, who fans herself with a big fan of yellow silk. In the other litter travel Innocenza and Fila.

Among the armed men are Raffaele Cuffa, his cousin Calogero

Usura, Peppino Geraci the gardener at the Villa Ucrìa, old Ciccio Calò, his nephew Totò, and Saro. Since uncle husband died and left him a hundred escudos and all his clothes, Saro has assumed a posture of studied nonchalance, which makes him look a little ridiculous but also gives him a new resplendence. The moon crescents of his ribs have gone from his chest. His black lock of hair no longer waves audaciously over his forehead but is now firmly contained within a small white-curled wig that Duke Pietro had when he was a young man. It is a little too large for him and has a tendency to slide down over his ears.

He is still very handsome even though he looks different, less juvenile, more knowledgeable and composed. But above all he has changed his ways, which are now almost those of a gentleman born between linen sheets in a large palace in Palermo. He has learned to move gracefully but without affectation. He rides a horse like a prince, putting the point of his boot into the stirrup and lifting himself up on it with a light, self-possessed spring. He has learned how to bow in front of ladies, advancing one leg and making a broad sweep with his arm, not forgetting to reverse his wrist and toss the feathers of his tricorn hat at the last moment.

He has scaled one by one the steps that lead to glory, this determined orphan, discovered half-naked one night in Fila's room, with his mouse's tail and his penitent smirk. But he is still not satisfied: it is his ambition to learn to write and to do sums. So great is the diligence with which he applies himself, so great his patience, that even uncle husband realised his worth and helped by giving him lessons in heraldry, good manners and chivalry.

Now there remain only a few crowning steps to climb, and among these is the conquest of his lady, the beautiful dumb woman who rejects his advances with such arrogance. Is this what makes him so bold or is there something else? It is hard to say – the young man has also learned the art of dissimulation. At her uncle husband's funeral he was the most grief-stricken, as if it were his own father who had died. And when he was told that the Duke had left him a small bequest in gold, money, clothes, shoes and wigs, he went white with astonishment and has continued to proclaim that he is 'not worthy of it'.

The funeral reduced Marianna to a state of total exhaustion: nine days of ceremonies, masses, suppers with relations, the preparation of mourning clothes for the entire family, the floral decorations, the hundreds of wax candles for the church, the wailing women who wept for two days and two nights beside the corpse. At last the body was taken to the catacombs of the Capuchins to be embalmed. She would have preferred him to lie in peace beneath the earth, but Mariano and her brother Signoretto had been adamant. Duke Pietro Ucrìa of Campo Spagnolo, Lord of Scannatura, Count of Sala di Paruta, Marquis of Sollazzi, must be embalmed and preserved in the crypts of the Capuchins like his ancestors.

They had crowded down into the catacombs, stumbling over their trains, their torches in danger of setting fire to the bier, in a mêlée of hands, shoes, cushions, flowers, swords, liveries and candlesticks. Then they had all vanished, and she was left alone with the naked body of her dead husband, while the monks prepared the embalming table and the bath of saltpetre.

At the beginning she had refused to look at him; to do so seemed indecent. Her eyes were gazing further up to three old men with tarred leathery skin that stuck to their bones and fastened them to the walls, to which they were also hooked by the neck, their skeletal hands fixed across their chests with a thong. On top of polished wooden shelves lay other corpses: elegant ladies dressed in their best clothes, their arms crossed on their breasts, their bonnets yellowing at the edges, their lips stretched over their teeth. Some had been lying there for only a few weeks and emitted a strong acid smell. Others had been there for fifty or a hundred years and had become quite odourless.

A barbarous custom, Marianna told herself, and tried to remember what Mr Hume had said about death, but her mind was blank. It would be better to be burned and thrown into the Ganges like the Indians rather than remain immured in these underground passages, gathered together with all one's relations and friends with exalted names and skin crumbling like paper.

Her gaze settled on a body under a glass cover that had been perfectly preserved: a little girl with long eyelashes, fair hair, eyes like minute shells lying on an embroidered pillow, a bare exposed forehead on which glistened two drops of sweat. And suddenly she saw who it was: the sister of Grandmother Giuseppa, who died from the plague when she was six years old. A great-aunt who never grew up and seemed to be engaged in proclaiming the miraculous eternity of the flesh. Of all the bodies piled there only

134

that of the little girl had remained in a state everyone could hope for after death: without blemish, tender, rapt in a tranquil tedium. Instead, the embalming carried out by the monks so famous for their use of natural saltpetre had become after some time flaked and hardened, accentuating the outlines of the skeletons that remained scarcely veiled by a film of dark flesh.

Marianna brought her eyes back to the naked body of uncle husband stretched out before her. But why had they left her there on her own? Perhaps so that she could give him a last farewell, or possibly to reflect on the frailty of the mortal body? Oddly enough the sight of his forsaken limbs reassured her: he was so different from the other bodies surrounding her, so fresh and tranquil, distinguished by the veins, eyelashes, hair and full lips that characterise the living. Those waves of grey hair preserved intact the memory of sunlit countryside; the cheeks still retained a few gleams of pink candlelight.

Just above him a small slab incised in copper said 'Memento mori'; but the corpse of uncle husband seemed to be saying 'Memento vivere', so great was the force of his numbed flesh in comparison with the make-believe papier mâché of all the other embalmed bodies. She had never seen him like this, so naked and yet still composed and dignified, with his flaccid muscles and the severe folds of his stony countenance. A body that had never inspired her with love because of the austere, cold and violent behaviour that went with it. Of late something had altered in his way of approaching her: always furtive as if he intended to steal something from her, but accompanied by a new uncertainty, a doubt that came from her sudden inexplicable refusal of him so many years ago. This hesitancy, a little studied and clumsy, was born of a silent, confused respect and had made him less of a stranger to her. If she was ever aware of herself wanting to hold his hand she knew that even the thought of a caress was foreign to him. From his ancestors he had inherited the idea that love is predatory: to take aim, to assault, to lacerate, to devour – then to go away satisfied, leaving behind a carcass, a skin, empty of life.

This naked body lying abandoned on the stone flags, all ready to be cut, emptied and filled up with saltpetre, inspired her now with a sudden feeling of sympathy; or perhaps something more, with compassion. She stretched out her hand and with her fingers

135

she stroked his temple, while unexpected tears started to trickle without warning down her cheeks. Scrutinising this drawn, pallid face, following the fleeting curve of the lips, the jutting cheekbones, the minute, dark wings of the nose, she tried to fathom the secret of his body.

She had never imagined uncle husband as a child. It was impossible. He had always been old ever since she had known him, attired in those red garments that reminded her of seventeenth-century finery rather than the elegance of the new century, his head eternally encased in fantastic wigs, his movements cautious and stiff. Yet once she had seen a portrait of him as a child, which had later become lost. In front of a garland of flowers and fruit the heads of the two Ucrìa children stood out: the fair, dreamy Maria already getting a little plump, Pietro with even fairer hair, tow-coloured, tall and stringy, with a look of proud melancholy in his eyes. Behind, as in a showcase, the heads of his parents were visible, Carlo Ucrìa of Campo Spagnolo and Giulia Scebarràs of Avila: she robust and dark-haired, with a look of zealous authority, he delicate and elusive, shrouded in a long tunic composed of pale lifeless colours. It was from that side of the Ucrìa family that the softness of Maria's features came, while Pietro had taken after the old Scebarràs, a race of warriors and rapacious despots.

Grandmother Giulia recounted that Pietro as a little boy was choosy and touchy: he picked quarrels about nothing and amused himself having fights with all and sundry. He was always the victor, it seemed, because in spite of looking poorly he had muscles of iron. In the family he was considered odd. He spoke little, and he was morbidly attached to his clothes, which he pretended were of silk and damask, edged with gold. Yet he had generous impulses that surprised those close to him. One day he gathered together the children of the cowherds in Bagheria and made them presents of all his toys. Another time he took some jewels from his mother and gave them to a poor woman who was begging for alms.

He liked betting games but knew how to control himself. He wouldn't spend whole nights at the gaming tables playing cards, as many of his friends did. He didn't keep seamstresses or ironing women, he drank only small quantities of wine from his father's vineyards. Only fighting attracted him, even with people of lower rank, and for this Grandmother Giulia punished him with the whip. However, he never rebelled against his parents, he even venerated

136

them, and each time he was punished he accepted it with cold contrition. Throughout his adolescence and youth he loved no one except his sister Maria, with whom he played interminable games of cards.

When his little sister got married he shut himself in the house and didn't go out for almost a year. His only companion was a kid goat that used to lie on his bed and at mealtimes creep under the table with the dogs. In the family this was tolerated as long as the animal remained a kid with a delicate head and light hoofs. But as it grew older it developed twisted horns and was transformed into a full-sized nanny-goat that butted against the furniture. Grandmother Giulia ordered it to be taken into the fields and left there.

Pietro obeyed but at night he used to go out in secret to sleep in the stables with the goat. Grandmother Giulia got to know of it and ordered the beast to be killed; then in front of the whole family she whipped her son on his bare buttocks just as old Great-grandfather Scebarràs had done to her and her brothers when they were children.

From that day on Pietro became strange and unpredictable. He would disappear for weeks and no one would know where he had got to. Or he would shut himself in his room without letting anyone in, not even the servant who came to bring him food. He never spoke to his mother, although if he saw her he would bow, as was his duty.

By the age of forty he was still unmarried and, apart from the brothel he would sometimes resort to, he did not seem to know what love was. The only person he felt at ease with was his sister Maria. He often went to visit her in her husband's house and speak a few words with her. His father had died shortly after the death of the goat, but no one mourned for him; he was a man so lifeless as to seem dead even while he was still alive. When his niece Marianna was born Pietro became even more assiduous in his visits to the Via Alloro although he did not have much feeling for his cousin and brother-in-law Signoretto. He grew very affectionate towards the little girl, whom he used to take in his arms and cuddle as he had cuddled the goat years before.

No one thought of trying to find a wife for him until the death of a bachelor uncle of the Scebarràs branch of the family, who had accumulated a fortune in land and money and left it all to his only nephew. Then Grandmother Giulia decided to give him in marriage to an influential lady of Palermo, who had recently become a widow: the Marchioness Milo delle Saline di Trapani, a woman of great determination, who could have restrained the strange eccentricities of her son. But Pietro was opposed to it and declared he would never sleep in the same bed as a woman unless she were one of the daughters of his sister Maria. And since one of these three daughters had been promised as a nun, there remained only two, Agata and Marianna. Agata was too young; Marianna was a deaf-mute, but had reached the age of thirteen, when it was acceptable for girls to get married.

Moreover, as her mother Maria and her father pointed out, it would have been a waste to give Agata to her uncle, when with all her beauty she had a chance of making a splendid marriage. Therefore it was right that it should be Marianna who should marry the eccentric Pietro. He had already shown himself to be very affectionate towards her. Besides, there was an urgent need for money to pay off old and new debts, to renovate the palace in the Via Alloro, which was falling into ruin, to buy new carriages and horses and to renew the livery of the house. Marianna would lose nothing; if she did not get married, she would be incarcerated in a convent. Instead this would open up a new dynasty: the Ucrìas of Campo Spagnolo, Lords of Scannatura, Counts of Sala di Paruta, Marquises of Sollazzi and of Taya, not to mention Lords of Scebarràs and of Avila.

Before her death Grandmother Giulia had called for her son and asked him to forgive her for having whipped him in front of the servants over the business of the goat. Her son Pietro looked at her without uttering a word and then, just before she expired, said in a loud voice: 'I hope you will have the good fortune to meet your Scebarràs relations in hell.' And this while the priest was blurting out 'Glory be to the Father' and the hired mourning women were preparing to weep for three days and three nights.

So Pietro had his niece. But once they got married he became incapable of recapturing the endearments he had bestowed on her while she was a child. It was as if marriage, in consecrating her, had frozen his fatherly tenderness.

XXVI

'And Don Mariano?'
'Is your son not coming, Your Excellency?'
'What is he doing, is he afraid?'
'We are waiting for him, our new master.'
'With the death of Don Pietro we were expecting him.'

Marianna crumples the notes she holds in her lap with restless fingers. How to account for the non-appearance of Mariano, who has suddenly become head of the family, inheritor and owner of the estates of Campo Spagnolo, of Scannatura, of Taya, of Sala di Paruta, of Sollazzi and Fiumefreddo. How to say to these peasant guards and rent collectors – known as *gabelloti* – who have come to see him, that the young Ucrìa has remained in Palermo with his wife because, quite simply, he does not wish to stir himself.

'You go, Mamma, I have things to do', he had written, suddenly appearing in front of her in a new redingote of English brocade studded with incrustations of gold.

It is true that twelve hours in a litter along mountain paths is a punishing experience, and indeed few of the barons from Palermo submit themselves to such an ordeal to visit their estates in the interior. But today is one of those rare occasions regarded as imperative, as much by relations and friends as by his tenants. The new landlord must go the rounds of his estates, he must make himself known, he must talk, he must see to the renovation of old houses, he must get to know what has been going on during his long absences in the city, he must endeavour to inspire some respect, some liking, or at the very least some curiosity.

Perhaps she was wrong not to have insisted, Marianna tells herself, but he did not give her a chance. He had kissed her hand, and off he had gone as swiftly as he had arrived, leaving in the air a strong perfume of roses. The same scent as her father the Duke had used, except that he only moistened the lace of his shirt while her son uses it indiscriminately, pouring a whole bottle all over himself.

Towards Marianna, the dumb woman, the guards and the *gabelloti* react with an uneasiness that is close to fear. They see her as a kind of saint, someone who does not belong to the exclusive breed of nobles, but to that poor and in some way sacred group of the crippled, the sick and the mutilated.

They feel pity but are also disconcerted by her inquisitive and penetrating gaze. And then they are mostly illiterate, and she with her notes, her pens, her hands stained with ink, puts them in a state of unbearable apprehension.

As is usual they entrust the priest, Don Pericle, with the task of writing on their behalf, but not even his intercession satisfies them. And then she is a woman and, even if she owns the land, what can a woman understand about property, grain, the sowing of fields, about debts, toll dues, et cetera? And so, to begin with, they regard her with disappointment, and go on and on about Don Mariano even though they have never seen him. Duke Pietro came to them a year before he died. He arrived as usual on horseback, refusing the satin-lined seat of the litter, with his gun, his watchman, his rolls of paper and his saddle bags.

Now they are confronted by the Duchess Marianna and they don't know where to begin. Don Pericle sits in the middle of them on a large seat of smooth leather, and slides a rosary through his chubby fingers. He's waiting for them to start talking. As the men turn their heads towards the veranda Marianna realises that her daughters are passing by and laughing beneath the porticos, perhaps brushing their hair in the shade of the stone arches. She longs to shut herself in her room and go to sleep. Her back is hurting, her eyes are burning, her legs are stiff from having to remain still and bent in the litter for hours on end. But she knows that however she confronts these people she must make amends for the absence of her son and try to convince them that he was indeed unable to come. Consequently she pulls herself together and with a gesture invites them to speak. Don Pericle transcribes in his incisive language.

'Thirteen *onze* to refurbish the well. Result – well is dry. Will need another 10 *onze*.'

'At Sollazzi shortage of labour. Smallpox takes ten men.'

'A prisoner because of bankruptcy. A peasant from Campo Spagnolo estate. In chains for last twenty days.'

'Big sale: 120 carcasses. Supplement bills of sale. No liquid money. Cash sale 0.27 *onze*, 110 *tarì*.'

'Cheese from your sheep, 900 equal to 30 *rottoli* and 10 of ricotta.'

'Wool. Four *rottoli*.'

Marianna reads meticulously all the notes that Don Pericle passes to her one by one as the men talk. She nods her head, she watches the faces of her *gabelloti* and her guards: Carlo Santangelo, known as U Zoppu, 'the lame one', even though he does not limp at all; she met him when she came with uncle husband soon after their marriage. Strong features, sparse hair on a sunburnt cranium, a mouth with parched lips cracked by the sun. He holds in his hand a grey hat with a wide soft brim that he knocks impatiently against his thigh.

There is Ciccio Panella, who has insisted that Don Pericle should write his name for the 'Duchessa' in large letters on a clean sheet of paper. He is a new peasant guard, about twenty-two years old. Thin and sharp as a rake, with bright eyes and a large mouth with two teeth missing on the right-hand side, he seems to be the most curious about her, the least concerned at the prospect of a woman as landlord instead of a man. He gazes intently at the neckline of her dress, obviously fascinated by the whiteness of her skin.

Then there is Nino Settani, a veteran of the estate: an old man, standing firmly upright with eyes that seem as black as if they were painted, edged with black and hidden beneath the arch of thick black eyebrows. In contrast his hair is white and falls in untidy locks on to his shoulders.

Don Pericle continues handing her sheets of paper filled with his large looped handwriting and she collects them on the upturned palm of her hand, intending to read them at her leisure. In fact she does not really understand what to make of these notes or what to reply to these men who have come to account for the entries and debits, and still less how to respond to the many questions on matters that are part of the life of the peasant.

But is it true about the prisoner held in the house? Has she understood it properly? And where have they put him?

'Where is the prisoner?'

'He is underneath us, in the cellar, Your Excellency.'

'Tell the *gabelloti* and the guards to come back tomorrow.'

Don Pericle never gets upset for any reason; he makes a gesture with his head and the *gabelloti* and the guards go towards the door after having bowed to kiss the hand of the dumb Duchess. At the door they meet Fila, who comes in carrying a tray laden with glasses with long thin stems. Marianna makes a sign to her to go back, but it is too late. She gestures to invite the men to retrace their steps and accept the refreshment which has appeared at the wrong moment.

141

Hands reach out uncertainly towards the silver tray and close gently round the stems, as if a single touch of their rough fingers might make the glass explode; cautiously they bring the chalices to their mouths. Then they form another queue to kiss her hand but she sends them away to spare them this tedious obligation, and they go past her, holding their hats, bowing with eyes lowered.

'Take me down to the condemned prisoner, Don Pericle', writes Marianna impatiently, and Don Pericle, imperturbable as ever, gives her an arm draped in black perfumed cloth.

A long passage, a dark cupboard, a store room, the kitchen, a drying room, another passage, the gun room with shotguns stacked in their racks, large baskets scattered round the floor, two wooden ducks leaning against a chair. A strong smell of badly cured leather, of dust from gun-shot, of mutton fat . . . then a small room where the flags and banners are kept: the standard of the House of Savoy rolled up clumsily in a corner, the white flag of the Inquisition, the sky-blue one of Philip V, the red, white and silver one of Elizabetta Farnese, the one with the Hapsburg eagle and the blue one with the gold fleur-de-lys of the Bourbons.

Marianna stops for a moment in the middle of the room, calling Don Pericle's attention to the rolled-up flags. She wants to tell him that all these bits of cloth, so carefully stitched, are useless and should be thrown away. All they reveal is the indifference to politics of her husband the Duke, who, doubting the stability of the reigning houses, kept them there, all at the ready. In 1713, like everyone else, he hoisted the flag of Savoy on the tower of Scannatura; in 1720 he put up the Austrian flag of Charles VII of the Hapsburgs; in 1735, quite dispassionately, he hoisted that of Charles III, King of the Two Sicilies, without ever putting away the preceding ones, ready to bring them out as new in the event of a change of loyalty, as happened in the case of the Spaniards, who were thrown out of the island and came back thirty-five years later after a terrible war that caused more deaths than an epidemic of smallpox.

It was not just opportunism on the part of Duke Pietro, it was contempt for 'those dogs who come and lord it over us'. It would never have occurred to him to join with other malcontents in laying down conditions or resisting the high-handedness of foreigners. His wolf's footsteps led him to go where there was nothing to assault but a few solitary sheep. Politics were incomprehensible to him.

Problems should be resolved on their own, face to face with one's own God, in that desolate and heroic place which was for him the conscience of a Sicilian nobleman.

Don Pericle, after having stood waiting for her to decide whether to continue the walk, becomes as restless as a mouse and gives an almost imperceptible tug at her sleeve. And she moves on ahead, proceeding down to the cellar faster than he does. It is probable that he is hungry: she suspects this from a slightly too insistent pressure of the hand that is guiding her.

XXVII

The steps disappear into the darkness. The damp makes her dress cling to her. Where does it come from, this heat that smells of rats and straw, and where do they lead to, these steep steps of discoloured stone?

Marianna's feet refuse to budge, her face becomes distorted. She turns to Don Pericle, who looks at her uncomprehendingly. A sudden memory has come down like a storm-cloud: her father wearing a cassock with the hood raised, a boy with discharging eyes, the hangman who spits out pumpkin seeds. It is all there, dense and solid, and it only needs a finger to set in motion the mill-wheel that draws up the dirty water of the past.

Don Pericle is worried. He looks for something to hold on to in case the Duchess swoons into his arms; he weighs her up with his eyes and holds out his hands ready in front of him, planting his feet firmly on the ground. The priest's worried face makes Marianna smile, and now that the vision has disappeared she can balance herself again. She thanks Don Pericle with a nod and starts to go down the stairs. In the meantime someone else has come, also carrying a lighted torch. He holds it with his arm stretched upwards so as to light the steps.

From the shadow outlined on the wall, Marianna guesses that it is Saro. Her breathing becomes faster. Now she can see in front of them a heavy door of light oak tortured with great nails and bolts. Saro inserts the torch into an iron ring that juts out from the

143

wall, puts out his hand for the key and moves gracefully towards the heavy padlock. With a few quick movements he opens the door, takes back the torch and makes way for the Duchess and the priest to enter the cell.

Sitting on a small heap of straw is a man with white hair, so dirty that it seems yellow, a worn doublet of wool on his naked chest, a pair of patched breeches, his bare feet scarred and swollen. Saro lifts the torch above the prisoner, who looks at them with astonishment, blinking his eyes. He smiles and nods respectfully at the sight of the Duchess's sumptuous clothes.

'Ask him why he is shut up in here', writes Marianna, resting the sheet of paper on her knee. In her haste she has forgotten to bring the little table.

'The guard has already said, for insolvency.'

'I want to hear it from him.'

Don Pericle patiently goes over to the man and talks to him. The man thinks it over for a little while and then answers. Don Pericle writes down the man's words, leaning the paper against the wall, holding himself well away from it so as not to spill ink on himself, and bending down every few seconds or so to dip the pen in the little bottle placed on the floor.

'Debts with the *gabelloto* not paid for a year. They took away the three mules he had. Waited till the next year for their 25 per cent. The following year debt had risen to 30 *onze* and he defaulted, so they put him in prison.'

'But why was he in debt to the *gabelloto*?'

'Harvest insufficient for him to pay.'

'If the *gabelloto* knew he was unable to pay why ask again?'

'There wasn't enough to eat.'

'Idiot, how on earth could the *gabelloto* have enough when this man didn't?'

There is no reply. The man looks thoughtfully at the great lady who traces mysterious black signs so rapidly on small sheets of white paper, using a pen that looks just as if it had been plucked from a hen's backside.

Marianna insists, tapping her fingers on the paper and thrusting it under the priest's nose. He starts to question the peasant once more. Finally he answers and Don Pericle writes, this time resting the page against Saro's back. He is considerate enough to bend forward, turning himself into a writing-table.

'*Gabelloto* leases Your Excellency's land from you. Then rents it out under an agricultural tenancy to the peasant who cultivates it and takes a quarter of crop. Out of this he has to pay the *gabelloto* a quantity of seed better than the *gabelloto* provided. He must also pay protection money, and if harvest poor and there are implements to be repaired he has to go back to *gabelloto* for help. At this point guard arrives on horseback with gun and takes him to prison for insolvency. Does Your Excellency understand?'

'And how much longer does he have to stay down here?'

'Another year.'

'Let him out', writes Marianna and puts her signature beneath it almost like a state judge. And in effect, so far as this house and this estate are concerned, the landowner does have sovereign powers. This man, like Fila in her turn, has been 'given' to Mariano by uncle husband, who had in his turn been made a present of him by his uncle Antonio Scebarràs, who in his turn. . . .

It is not anywhere written down that this old man with yellowing hair 'belongs' to the Ucrìa family, but in fact they can do whatever they want with him, keep him in a cellar until he rots or send him home and just have him whipped. No one would find it anything to make a fuss about. He is a debtor who cannot pay and therefore he must to all intents and purposes answer for his debt with his body.

'From the time of Philip II the Sicilian barons obtained sovereign rights over their lands in exchange for their acquiescence and inaction in the Senate. Thus they themselves became the sole administrators of justice.' Where had she read this? Her father the Duke had called it 'justified injustice' and his own magnanimity always prevented him from profiting by it.

The peasant guards have simply done whatever the Ucrìas with their own white unsullied hands needed doing but would not dare to do themselves: lining up those devilish peasants, inflicting blows, threatening them with thrashings and incarcerating them in dungeons. It is not hard to understand: it is all written down in these sheets of paper in Don Pericle's sprawling handwriting. From honesty or from laziness he has reported the old man's words as he would have reported those of a monsignor or a father of the Holy Office. Now he is here watching, his hands folded over his prominent belly, which protrudes from under his cassock, trying to understand what this crazy duchess is all about. She has arrived here out of the blue and wants to know things that people of her sort generally pretend not to know and which it is certainly not appropriate for a well-brought-up lady to know.

A load of foolish fantasies and silly whims . . . a wavering of the spirit. . . . Marianna is aware of the priest's thoughts going round and round as he stands next to her. Whims of a great lady who today uses her intelligence to be compassionate, but tomorrow the very same intelligence will be theorising about the use of whips or hatpins.

Marianna turns towards Don Pericle with her eyes blazing, but he sits there in a respectful attitude, quiet and discreet – for what reason could he be reprimanded?

This poor dumb woman, forty years old, with such soft white flesh . . . Heaven knows what state of confusion there is inside her head . . . forever reading books . . . always skulking behind the written word. There's something quite ridiculous in this obsession with having to understand everything, always asking questions about the point of a fork, the tip of a nose, the meaning of a chair. . . . These present-day aristocrats don't know how to enjoy life . . . they meddle in everything . . . they have no conception of humility, they'd rather have libraries than litanies. . . . A dumb duchess, just imagine it! Yet there is something that shines in her face . . . poor soul . . . she needs sympathy . . . she's in a sad state . . . all head and no body. . . . If only she read books that were edifying. But I've seen what she carries about with her . . . books in English, in French, filthy rubbish . . . all modern stuff. If only she'd make up her mind to go back upstairs . . . the heat down here is suffocating, and then the pangs of hunger are beginning to gnaw. . . . At least today there'll be something good to eat . . . when their lordships arrive titbits arrive with them. As for the old man, all this sentimentality is right out of place . . . the law is the law and everyone is entitled to his own. . . .

'Curb your thoughts!' writes Marianna to Don Pericle. He reads it with amazement, at a loss how to make sense of the reproof. He raises conciliatory eyes to the Duchess, who nods to him with a little mischievous smile and goes up the stairs in front of him. Saro rushes forward to light the way. She hastens along the dusty carpets and reaches the dining-room, laughing at the priest and at herself. Her daughters are already seated at the table, Felice wearing an elegant habit and a shining sapphire cross, Manina in black and yellow, Giuseppa in white with a blue silk scarf thrown over her shoulders. They are waiting for her and Don Pericle before they begin to eat.

Marianna kisses her daughters but does not sit down at the table. The idea of being at the mercy of Don Pericle's thoughts daunts her. Better to eat alone in her room. At least she can read in peace there. Meanwhile she writes a note to ensure that the old prisoner will be set free immediately and that his debt will be paid out of her own money.

On the stairs she is joined by Saro, who gallantly offers her his arm. But she refuses and hurries in front of him, leaping up the stairs two at a time. When she reaches her room she shuts the door in his face. She has hardly turned the key in the lock when she regrets not having leaned on his arm, not having at least signalled her thanks. She goes to the window to watch him cross the courtyard with his buoyant stride. Indeed, here he is, coming out of the door at the foot of the stairs. She sees him stop by the stables, raise his head and look for her window.

Marianna is about to try to conceal herself behind the curtain, but realises that if she did this she would be seen to be playing a game, so she stays in front of the window, her eyes staring at him, severe and thoughtful. Saro's face dissolves into a smile of such seductive sweetness that for a moment she is caught by it and finds herself smiling without meaning to.

XXVIII

The hair-brush, dampened with a little orange-flower water, slides into her smooth hair, lightly scenting it with the fragrance of orange peel and brushing out the dust. Marianna tucks her hair behind her aching neck. The orange-flower water is finished; she must have another jug of it prepared for her. Her pot of rice powder is almost empty too, she must order some from her usual Venetian perfumer. Only in Venice do they prepare face powders that are almost transparent, light and scented like flowers. The essence of bergamot, however, comes from Mazara and she has it sent to her from the perfumer Mastro Turrisi in boxes with Chinese motifs that she will later use to hold the notes she receives from her family.

In the mirror something odd happens: a shadow comes into the right-hand top corner and then dissolves. In the wink of an eye a hand spreads out against the closed window. Marianna stops, her arms raised, the brush between her fingers, her eyebrows wrinkled in a frown. That hand is pressed against the window as if the intensity of its desire could miraculously fling it wide open. Marianna is on the point of getting up from her seat; her body is already there at the window, her hands sliding towards the shutters. But an inert will keeps her nailed to the chair. Now you will get up, says a silent voice within her, you will go to the window and draw the curtains. Then you will put out the candle and go to sleep.

Her legs obey this wise tyrannical voice, her feet move heavily, dragging her bedroom slippers across the floor. Once she reaches the curtains her arm lifts mechanically and with a brusque move-ment of her wrist she pulls them so as completely to obscure the window, which looks out on to the terrace of the tower. She has not dared to raise her eyes but she has felt with her skin, with her nails, with her hair, the anger of the boy she has repulsed.

Now like a somnambulist she returns to bed, puts out the candles one by one with a weak puff of breath that leaves her hollow, and slips between the sheets, making the sign of the cross with freezing fingers.

'May Christ have mercy on me.' But instead of the blood-streaked face of Our Lord on the Cross, the compassionate and ironic face of Mr David Hume dances in front of her with his turban of light-coloured velvet, his serene eyes, his mouth half-open and mocking.

'Reason can never of itself be the motive of any action of the will,' she repeats to herself thoughtfully, and her lips stretch in a sad smile. No doubt Mr David Hume is an inspired soul but what does he know of Sicily? 'Reason is, and ought only to be, the slave of the passions, and can never pretend to any other office than to serve and obey them.' And that's that! What a clown Mr Hume is inside his Indian turban, with his insolent far-away eyes, with the double chin of somebody who knows how to eat and sleep well. What does he know of a crippled woman tortured by pride and doubt?

If only my soul could embrace thee
for one blink of an eye,
then could I die.

The words of Paolo Maura, the poet from Catania, copied into her little damask-covered notebook, come gently into her memory and distract her momentarily from the pain that she is creating for herself.

Her head refuses to lie on the pillow, knowing that he is still there behind the window pane, waiting for her to change her mind. Even though she cannot see him she has no doubt that he is there; it would take so little to have him beside her, so little that she asks herself how long her cruel self-denial can hold out.

To stifle temptation she decides to get up and light a candle, put on her slippers and go out through the door. The corridor is dark and it has a smell of old carpets and worm-eaten furniture. Marianna leans against the walls, feeling her legs giving way beneath her. The smell reminds her of another long-past visit to Torre Scannatura. She was then about eight and the passage was covered in the same worn carpet. Only her mother was with her. It must have been August then, as it is now. In the tower it was hot and from the surrounding countryside rose the smell of carcasses left out to rot in the sun.

Her mother was unhappy. Her husband had disappeared with one of his mistresses and after waiting for him to return, drinking laudanum and taking snuff, she had suddenly decided to leave with her deaf-mute daughter for the estate of the Scebarràs uncles. They had a dreary time, she playing alone beneath the portico, and her mother asleep, drugged, in the small bedroom in the tower which is now hers. The only consolations were the smell of new wine inside the wooden barrels and the smell of newly picked tomatoes, which was so strong that it made her nostrils smart.

Marianna puts her hand on her chest to calm the spinning of her heart in the void. At that moment she sees Fila coming towards her wearing a brown cloak over her long white night-dress. The girl stands there looking at her as if she wants to say something important. Her soft grey eyes are hardened with resentment. Marianna lifts her arm and her hand goes of its own volition to slap that distraught face. She does not know why she does it, but she knows that the girl is expecting it and that it is her duty at that moment to comply with the compulsive pressures of a stupid servant–mistress relationship.

Fila does not react: she lets herself slide slowly to the ground. Marianna helps her to get up, tenderly wipes the tears from her cheeks, and hugs her with such vehemence that Fila is scared. Now it is clear why she came and why that slap has already expunged the crime of a sister who was furtively spying on her brother's movements. Now Fila can go back to bed.

Marianna climbs a staircase and stops in front of Giuseppa's room, from which emerges a streak of light. She knocks. She enters. Giuseppa, still dressed, is sitting at the writing-table, her pen in her hand, the little bottle of ink uncovered. As soon as she sees her mother she makes as if to hide the sheet of paper, but then thinks better of it, looks at her with an expression of defiance, seizes another piece of paper and writes: 'I refuse to have him as my husband any more. I want him off my back. We must separate.'

The mother recognises in the eyes of her daughter her own dangerously impulsive pride. 'Father is dead, the seventeenth century is long since past, Mamma. People's attitudes have changed. In Paris, who bothers about marriage any more? Oh yes, they're married, but without being slaves to duty, it's everyone for themselves. Instead of which he insists that I have to do whatever he wants.'

Marianna sits down beside her daughter. She takes the pen from her hands.

'And how did it end with the bonnet-maker?'

'It ended with her going off on her own. She's much more sensible than Giulio, for sure. I got to sympathise with her. Sleeping together a friendship sprang up between us and I really felt sorry for her, Mamma.'

'Then you no longer want to beat him up?' writes Marianna, recognising that her fingers are gripping the pen unsteadily, as if she'd intended to write something quite different. The bone nib creaks on the paper.

'For me he's a complete stranger. Dead.'

'Then who are you writing to now?'

'A friend, Mamma, Cousin Olivo, who understands me and talks to me affectionately, while Giulio just avoids me.'

'You must break it off, Giuseppa. Cousin Olivo is married and you shouldn't be writing to him.'

150

Marianna catches a glimpse of her head reflected next to that of her daughter in the mirror behind the writing-bureau, and realises that they are so alike that it is almost as if they were sisters.

'But I love him.'

Marianna is about to write another prohibition but she restrains herself. How arrogant her refusal sounds: to break off, chop off, cut off. . . . With a shiver she thinks of the hands of the Capuchin friars cutting into uncle husband to rip out his guts, to clean, to strip off the flesh, to scrape, to preserve. Those who want to preserve always use sharp knives. How apprehensive a mother she is, all out to amputate the feelings of her daughter. Giuseppa is only twenty-seven. From her young body arise tender odours of hair damp with sweat, of skin reddened by the sun. Why not give in to her desires, even if they are forbidden?

'Write your letter by all means, I shall not be watching you.' Her hands write the note by themselves, and she sees her daughter smile with relief.

Marianna pulls the young woman's head on to her breast and holds her in her arms, once again too impetuously, seized by an overwhelming impulse that throws her off balance and leaves her feeling empty and exhausted.

XXIX

A morning in August. Beneath the shadows of the portico four women are seated round a table of woven cane. Hands move daintily from the crystal sugar bowl to the earthenware cups filled to the brim with milk, from peach jam to buttered rolls, from foaming coffee to sweet fritters filled with ricotta and candied pumpkin.

Marianna chases a wasp from the edge of her cup and watches it alight a moment later, undeterred, on the slice of bread that Manina is lifting to her mouth. She is about to shoo it away from there too but her daughter stops her hand, looks at her with a gentle smile and continues to bite at her bread with the wasp still on it. At this point Giuseppa, her mouth full of fritters, waves a hand to chase off the intrusive wasp; she stops in mid-air when Manina all of a sudden starts to buzz like the insect, much to the sisters' amusement. Felice, dressed in her white habit, the sapphire crucifix on her breast, laughs, upsetting her milk as she follows the flight of another wasp that seems undecided whether to alight on Manina's hair or on the open sugar bowl. Others are arriving, attracted by such an abundance of sweet things.

They have been at Torre Scannatura for three weeks. Marianna has learned to distinguish fields of wheat from fields of oats, fields of clover from those left to pasture. She knows the market price of a cheese and how much goes to the shepherd and how much to the Ucrìa family. The structure of rents and share-cropping is clear to her. She has learned who are the peasant guards and what their function is: to act as intermediaries between negligent proprietors and quarrelsome peasants, stealing surreptitiously from both sides, armed custodians of a miraculously maintained peace. The *gabelloti*, who in their turn are lease-holders of the land, twist the neck of anyone who works it, and in two generations, if they are shrewd, put enough money on one side to buy it.

She has spent hours with the accountant Don Nunzio, who patiently explains what needs to be done. On the account books Don Nunzio traces spiky signs that are hard to decipher, but he takes care to make concessions to the dumb Duchess's intellect since he regards it as being somewhat childlike.

Don Pericle is busy in the parish, he only comes in the evening for supper, and afterwards he stops to play piquet or faro with the girls. Marianna does not like him and whenever she can leaves him with her daughters. But she likes Don Nunzio; his thoughts are well boxed-in; there is no risk of them gushing out from that calm head, always kept closed and padlocked. Don Nunzio's hands run over the Duchess's sheets of paper; as well as explaining in detail the system of prices and taxes he also quotes Dante and Ariosto. Even though it is hard deciphering the old man's handwriting, Marianna prefers it to the florid, backward-sloping script of Don Pericle, which seems to weave words with spittle like a greedy spider.

Her daughters have reverted to being children. When she watches them strolling in the garden with their white lace-trimmed sun-shades, when she observes them sitting on the wicker seats, as they are now, stuffing their mouths with bread and butter, it seems as if she has gone back twenty years to when, at the Villa Ucrìa, from her bedroom window, she used to watch them running wild, and she almost seems to hear their voices and laughter in the days before they went off to get married.

Far away from husbands and children they pass their time sleeping, going for walks, playing. They gobble up stuffed macaroni and little tartlets filled with egg-plant; and they are very greedy for the sweet made from chopped citrons cooked with honey, called *petrafennula*, which Innocenza cooks to perfection. It hardly seems possible, looking at them now, that a few months ago Manina nearly died from puerperal fever; that Giuseppa was weeping desperately over her husband's infidelity; or that Felice was clinging to her father's corpse as if she wanted to be incarcerated with him in the cave of saltpetre.

Yesterday evening they danced. Felice played the spinet; looking blissful, Don Pericle turned the pages on the music stand. They had invited Cousin Olivo, the son of Signoretto, and his friend Sebastiano, who were staying for a few weeks in the old Villa di Dogana Vecchia a mile or so away, and they had danced far into the night. At one point they had even invited Saro, who had been standing on one leg like a stork, watching. Fila, also asked, did not want to join in the dancing; perhaps because she had never learned to dance the minuet and also because she was wearing shoes and her feet moved awkwardly. To persuade her they improvised a *tarascone* but she did not let herself be tempted.

Saro, however, has taken lessons from Manina's dancing master and now dances like an expert. Each day he leaves more and more of his past behind him: his dialect, his callouses, his tousled curls, his shrill voice, his clumsy, diffident way of walking; at the same time he is leaving behind him his sister Fila, who does not want to learn like he does, perhaps out of scorn or perhaps out of a deeper feeling for her own integrity.

One morning when Marianna mounted the mule to go and look at the grape harvest in the domain of the Mendola river, she found the handsome Saro standing in front of her, holding a sheet of paper. Stealthily he handed it to her, with an expression of pride that set his eyes alight.

I LOVE YOU he had written in ostentatious, laboured, but also decisive letters. She pushed it angrily into her bodice. She did not have a chance to throw the note away as she'd hoped to do while she was riding the mule in the direction of the wine press, so she hid it in the tin box with Chinese designs underneath a heap of notes from her father.

While Don Nunzio was showing her the vats of blood-red must, it seemed as if she could feel the tremor of horse's hoofs beneath her feet; she hoped it might be Saro even though she knew she should not be waiting for him.

Don Nunzio took hold of her sleeve shyly. A moment later they were enveloped in a cloud of acidic, intoxicating fumes, in front of a platform of earth raised almost two feet from the ground. In the vat, men dressed only in short breeches were treading and retreading the grapes, their bare feet sinking into the must, spurting the light-red liquid all round them. Through a hole in the sloping floor the unfermented wine ran down into wide tubs, foaming and gurgling, leaving behind it bits of grape stalks and blades of grass. Marianna peered into this bubbling liquid and was overtaken by a strong desire to throw herself in and be swallowed up in the sludge. She was continually testing her will-power and finding it strong, barricaded within itself like a soldier in armour.

To compensate for her severity in the face of her own desires, Marianna has begun to be more indulgent towards her daughters. Giuseppa dallies with Olivo, who has left his young wife in Palermo to pursue his cousin in the country. Manina is openly courted by Sebastiano, the shy elegant young man from Naples.

Since Felice as a nun can neither dance nor dally she has given herself over to cooking. She disappears for hours down among the kitchen ranges and comes back with dishes of rice cooked with chicken livers, which are rapidly devoured by her sisters and friends. She has taken to sharing her room with Fila at night. She has had a wooden bed put at the far end of the room; she says that there are ghosts in the tower and she is unable to sleep by herself. But the twinkle in her eyes makes it clear that this is an excuse to gossip with Fila far into the night.

Sometimes in the morning Marianna finds them in the same bed with their arms round each other, the head of one on the shoulder of the other, Felice's fair hair intertwined with Fila's dark hair, their full night-dresses tied at their perspiring necks. Such a chaste embrace belongs to childhood and Marianna has never ventured to reprove her.

XXX

When Marianna comes down into the gun room she finds her three daughters all ready: light dresses and long aprons, ankle boots to protect against thorns, with sunshades, bundles, baskets and tablecloths. Today is the day of the wine harvest on the estate of Bosco Grande and the girls have decided to go to the vineyard, taking their lunch with them.

The litters carry them beyond the hills of Scannatura, to the foot of Rocca Cavaleri. Each one has brought with her a silk sunshade and a cambric handkerchief; they have been getting ready since early morning, running from the kitchen to their bedrooms, and have decided to take with them a gateau of egg-plants, an almond cake, and dates stuffed with nuts.

Marianna leads the way, sitting opposite Felice in the first litter; next come Manina and Giuseppa, and behind them Fila and Saro with the provisions. At the vineyard they will be joined by their cousin Olivo and his friend Sebastiano. The air is still fresh, the grass has not had time to dry out, the birds are flying low.

The silence around her body is dense and transparent, Marianna tells herself; yet her eyes see the magpies perching on the cactuses, the crows hopping on the bare dry earth, the coats of the mules twitching as their big tails swish away the whirling mass of gadflies. The silence is both mother and sister: Holy Mother of all silence, have pity on me. . . . The words come from her throat without a sound; they would like to become palpable, to make themselves heard, but her mouth stays dumb and her tongue is a small corpse shut within the coffin of her teeth.

This time the journey does not last long and they are there within an hour. The mules stop in a clearing. Carlo Santangelo, U Zoppu the lame one, and Ciccio Panella, who have come with them, their rifles on their shoulders, get off their horses and come over to the litters to help the ladies dismount. Don Ciccio has a strange watchful expression, Marianna notices, with his head lowered as if he were about to charge like a bull. And Saro is on the alert, already hating and despising him from the heights of his new standing. But Ciccio does not look at him at all; he does not consider him as a man but as a servant and, as is well known, servants do not count for anything. Ciccio is a *gabelloto* and a guard, something quite else. He does not carry a stack of gold hanging from his waist, he does not adorn himself with powdered wigs, he does not flaunt a tricorn on his head, his jacket of brown worsted was bought from a travelling salesman and even has patches on the sleeves; but his prestige as seen by the peasants is equal to that of a landowner. He is accumulating money so that even if he himself doesn't manage it, there's no doubt that his sons and grandsons will end up being able to buy some of the land he now leases. Already he is building himself a house that looks more like the tower of the Ucrìas, with all its outbuildings, than the broken-down hovels of his fellow peasants.

'He grabs any woman he wants', Don Nunzio had written to her in the account book. 'Last year he got a girl of thirteen into trouble. Her brother wanted to cut his throat but he was scared off because Panella threatened him with two armed guards.' So here he is, the handsome Ciccio, standing there with a brooding smile, his eyes deep black, ready to plunder the whole world.

Saro cannot put up with the effrontery of this scoundrel. He finds it unbearable. But at the same time he is afraid of it. He has to admit that he cannot make up his mind whether to confront or flatter it. In this state of indecision he limits himself to protecting the woman he loves in the style of a true gentleman.

Meanwhile they have arrived at the vineyard known as 'the vineyard of the black grapes'. The men, who were bent down picking the bunches, stand up and look with open mouths at the small group of ladies in their coloured diaphanous dresses. Never before have they seen a gathering so gay with muslins, straw hats, sunshades, bonnets, little bootees, handkerchiefs, bows and fichus.

The gentlemen and, even more so, the ladies look with astonishment at these beings, who seem to have come out of the mountains like so many Vulcans blackened by smoke, bent with exhaustion, blinded by the dark, ready to fling themselves on these daughters of Demeter and carry them off into the bowels of the earth.

The day labourers know everything about the Ucrìa Scebarràs family, the owners of these estates, vines, olives, woods and of all the game as well as all the sheep, the cattle, and the mules of Heaven knows how many generations. They know the Duchess is deaf and dumb and they have prayed for her with Don Pericle in church on Sundays. They know that Pietro Ucrìa died a short while ago and that he was opened up and had his guts removed

156

to be filled with salt and acid, which will preserve him whole and sweet-smelling for centuries, like a saint. They also know that there are three beautiful daughters, who lounge on the veranda laughing and combing their hair, one a nun and two married with children. And it is whispered that the husbands are cuckolded because that is the way in families of the nobility and God shuts His eyes.

But they have never seen them so close. Yes, years ago, when they were children and all assembled in a chapel of the parish church, the labourers had peeped at them, counting the rings on their fingers, commenting on their grand clothes. But they never expected to see them descend upon their place of work, where there are no balustrades or chapels set apart or seats specially reserved for them, but only air and sun and swarms of flies that settle indiscriminately on the black sticky hands of the peasants who are running with sweat, and on the ladies' hands as white and transparent as plucked chickens.

And then in church the men are to some extent protected by their best clothes: patched but clean, inherited from their fathers, lengths of cotton wound round their hairy legs and corn-stricken feet. Here, however, they are exposed, almost naked, with scars, goitres, missing teeth, dirty legs, greasy rags that fall over their hips, their heads covered by ancient hats hardened by sun and rain.

Marianna is upset. She turns round and lets her eyes sink into the valleys that are an unreal yellow, almost white. The sun climbs high in the sky and with it there waft strong smells of mint, wild fennel and crushed grapes. Manina and Giuseppa are like two silly girls, staring at these half-naked bodies and not knowing what to do. In these parts it is not the custom for women to work in the fields far from home and these ladies who have rained down from heaven create the impression that they are transgressing a custom of thousands of years with the ignorance of fools, as if they had entered a monastery and started to pry into the cells of the monks at prayer. It is something that is just not done.

It is Manina who puts an end to the awkwardness both groups are feeling with one of her witty remarks that sets the men laughing. Then she picks up a flask and starts to pour wine into the glasses and to distribute them among the labourers; they stretch out their hands hesitantly, keeping one eye on the *gabelloto*, one on the peasant guard, one on the Duchess and one on heaven.

But the laughter provoked by Manina is enough to break the

157

silence between the two groups. The peasants decide to accept the ladies as an eccentric and welcome novelty which has come as a break in the exhaustion of a hot, hard day. They decide to approve the whims of the Duchess as something characteristic of great ladies who do not understand anything but who at least brighten the eyes with their delicate movements, their fluttering dresses and their beringed fingers.

Now Ciccio Panella urges them back to work in a rough but easy-going manner, as if he were a bluff father concerned with the well-being of his sons. Playing his part in a mocking, exaggerated way he approaches the Princess Manina and eggs her on to throw a bunch of grapes into the basket, treating her like a rather stupid child and applauding the way she does it as if she were an unheard-of prodigy.

Among the men bent down over the vines dozens of small barefooted boys run carrying baskets, taking them back to the shade of the elm trees, cutting with small pairs of shears the mass of spreading brambles that hinder the work of the men, pouring out fresh water from the pitcher for whoever asks for it, recklessly chasing after the flies and shooing them away from the eyes of their fathers, uncles and brothers.

Cousin Olivo sits next to Giuseppa beneath the elm tree and whispers into her ear. Marianna looks at them and gives a start: they have all the appearance of knowing each other intimately. But her look of alarm is quickly transformed into admiration, observing how much they resemble each other and how handsome they are. He is so fair, like all the Ucrìas, tall and slim, his forehead balding slightly at the temples, his blue eyes wide open. He does not possess the regular features of his father but he has something of the charm of his grandfather. She can understand why Giuseppa has fallen in love with him.

She has become plumper since the birth of her latest child, her arms and her breasts are squeezed into the flimsy material of her dress. Her mouth with its well-formed lips has taken on a hard look that Marianna has never seen before. But her eyes are merry, lit up, and her hair falls over her shoulders like a wave of honey.

She should separate them, she knows that, but her feet refuse to obey her. Why disturb their happiness, why interfere with their loving chatter?

Meanwhile Manina has gone out into the middle of the vineyard, hemmed in by the low stems of the vines, pursued by Sebastiano. That boy is odd: very polite, very shy, but altogether lacking in discretion. Manina does not take to him very much, she finds him intrusive, inexcusably attentive and somewhat artificial, but he persists in courting her with a mixture of boldness and timidity.

Manina writes long letters to her husband every day. She has taken advantage of her convalescence to suspend for a while her need to sacrifice herself as a mother. But not for much longer. As soon as she feels fitter she will return to the dark house in the Via Toledo, shrouded in purple curtains, and will resume looking after her children with the same obsessive dedication as before, and may even start another child at once.

Yet during this holiday, which is not a holiday but a taking possession of the feudal domains of their father on Mariano's behalf, something has shaken her. The return to the ways of adolescence, games with her sisters that would never be acceptable in Palermo, the proximity of Marianna, from whom she has been separated since she was twelve, have all brought into her mind the fact that as well as being a mother she is also a daughter, a daughter who is wounded most of all by herself.

Looking at her now it seems as if she is sinking her teeth into the flesh of a ripe peach. In fact, it is only that she is absorbed in the fun of playing with her sisters. There is no sensuality in her as there is in Giuseppa, who has already devoured her peach and is getting ready to bite into another, and yet another. There is possibly more sensuality in Felice, shut inside her white habit, than there is in Manina, even though Manina displays her bare arms and her dresses open to her breasts. Her transcendent beauty, restored after her illness with all the recuperative powers of her twenty-five years, contrasts with the deep-seated natural chastity that possesses her.

Felice dishes out from the serving-table complicated main courses pungent with spices. She spends hours and hours at the kitchen ranges, preparing baskets of strained ricotta, *nucatelli*, almond cakes, little ice-creams, morello cherries, lemonade flavoured with tarragon.

A sacrilegious idea flashes through Marianna's mind: why not

159

direct Saro's infatuation towards the beautiful Manina? They are almost the same age and they would be well matched. She looks round for him and sees him asleep, his head leaning on his elbow, his legs stretched out among the dry twigs: how he is enjoying the shade of the elm tree alongside the baskets full of grapes! Does she really want this? A sharp pain in the roots of her eyes tells her no, she doesn't. However much she rejects his love because it seems so unrealistic, she knows she broods over him and eyes him with a bitter-sweet fascination. So why the wish to act the procuress on behalf of her youngest daughter? What makes her so certain that a love affair with Saro would bring her happiness? Would it not originate in incest: the idea that this male body could be a knot to join the heart of a mother to the heart of a daughter?

At midday the overseer gives the order to stop work. Since dawn men have been bent over the low-growing vines, pulling at the bunches of grapes that swarm with wasps, and throwing them into the baskets among a tangle of curling tendrils. Now they will have an hour to eat a slice of bread, a few olives, an onion, and to drink a glass of wine.

Saro and Fila are busy laying the tablecloth under the leafy branches of the elm tree. The eyes of the peasants are focused on the food baskets, hinged with brass, from which emerge, like one of Santa Ninfa's miracles, marvels never before seen: porcelain plates as light as feathers, glasses of crystal with silvery reflections, tiny knives and forks that sparkle in the sun.

The ladies sit on the big stones beneath the elm tree that Ciccio Panella has arranged for them in the shape of a bench. But their pretty skirts of muslin and cambric are already covered with dust and are bristling with grape stalks and prickles caught up in the hems.

The men, seated on the far side under the shelter of the two olive trees that give very little shade, eat and drink in silence, not daring to take it as easy as usual, letting the flies crawl all over their faces as if they were the muzzles of the mules; and the fact that no one ventures to chase them off as the animals do, makes a lump come in Marianna's throat. To eat this choice food in front of their envious yet discreetly lowered eyes suddenly strikes her as intolerable arrogance. She gets up followed by the anxious gaze of Saro and goes over to U

Zoppu, the oldest of her guards, to ask him for information about the grape harvest. She leaves her portion of gateau uneaten on her plate.

U Zoppu hastily swallows an enormous mouthful of bread and omelette that he has only just thrust into his mouth, wipes his lips on the back of a hand streaked with black earth, and bows bashfully over the sheet of paper that the Duchess hands him. But not knowing how to read, he gives her an absent look and then, pretending to have understood, starts to talk to her as if she were able to hear his words. Through embarrassment each has overlooked the defect of the other.

Saro, who has followed their gestures, comes to the help of the guard, pulls the sheet of paper out of his hands, reads it in a loud voice and is on the point of transcribing U Zoppu's reply on the complicated contraption that his mistress carries with her – the little folding table, the ink-pot with the screw top hanging by a silver chain, the goose-quill pen and the ashes.

But Ciccio Panella is infuriated by such presumption: how can a servant be allowed to come face to face with his mistress? How can he be allowed to show off his learning in front of a peasant who knows much more than he ever will, but who does not choose to reveal it by means of such a ridiculous and obscure activity as handwriting?

All at once Marianna sees Saro change position; the muscles in his legs stiffen, his arms stretch out in front of him with his fists closed, his eyes narrow until they become two slits. Panella must have said something insulting to him and Saro has suddenly put his aristocratic pretensions to one side to get ready for a fight. Marianna looks towards Ciccio Panella just in time to see him draw a knife with a short sharp blade. Saro goes pale but does not flinch and, seizing a block of wood from the ground, is about to attack him.

Marianna runs forward but the two are already laying into each other. A blow from the wooden cudgel has sent the knife flying out of Ciccio's hand and now the two are going for each other with fists, kicks and bites. U Zoppu gives an order and five men rush to separate them, which they succeed in doing after a struggle. Saro has a wound in his hand, which is bleeding, and Ciccio has a black eye.

Marianna makes a sign to her daughters to get back into the litters. Then she pours some wine over Saro's bleeding hand while U Zoppu makes a bandage out of vine leaves and grass stalks. Meanwhile Ciccio Panella, on the orders of the older men, has gone down on his knees to offer his apology to the Duchess and has kissed her hand.

In the litter Marianna finds herself seated facing Saro; the young man has taken advantage of the confusion to slip into the seat opposite her and now there he is, sitting with his eyes shut, his head smeared with earth, his shirt ripped open, all calculated to excite her admiration.

He seems like an angel, Marianna says, smiling to herself. It is as if while trying to reveal his angelic grace he has lost his balance and fallen from the sky and now lies battered and breathless, waiting to be taken care of. It is all a bit theatrical . . . yet only a short time ago the 'angel' was fighting a man armed with a knife with a courage and generous spirit she had not recognised in him.

Marianna turns her eyes away from that angelic face that offers itself to her with such docile effrontery. She looks out at the sunlit landscape, a land of ploughed-up furrows, a tangle of brash yellow broom, a pool of lead-coloured water that reflects the violet of the sky; but something brings her gaze back to the inside of the litter. Saro is watching her with gentle searching eyes: eyes that speak shamelessly of an aching will to become a son, without sacrificing any of his pride and independence, with all the passion of an ambitious and intelligent youth.

What does she want, Marianna asks herself? Is she not just as impatient to become a mother and to clasp this boy to her and take him into her arms? A look can sometimes become flesh, uniting two people more closely than an embrace. Thus Marianna and Saro, inside this narrow carriage suspended between two mules, swaying over an empty void, let themselves be rocked by the motion, glued to their seats, while their gaze, tender and fervent, shifts from one to the other. Neither the flies nor the heat nor the swaying of the litter can divert them from the intense pleasure of this bitter-sweet exchange.

XXXI

Coming into that strange house she is nailed to the threshold by the clammy darkness, heavy with odours. The damp air brushes against her face like a wet cloth; she can only see black shadows submerged in the dark of the room.

Then little by little her eyes become accustomed to the blackness: at the far end of the room she makes out a kneading trough with broken legs, a dented iron bowl, a high bed surrounded by a closely woven mosquito net, and a stove from which burning wood emits an acrid smoke. The heels of the Duchess's shoes sink into the floor of beaten earth scored with the marks of a besom. Next to the door a donkey is eating a small pile of hay. Squatting hens are sleeping with their heads under their wings.

A tiny woman dressed in red and white pops out from nowhere with a baby in her arms, and gives the visitor a wry smile, wrinkling her pockmarked face. Marianna cannot avoid screwing up her mouth at the impact of these brazen smells: excrement, dried urine, curdled milk, charcoal ash, dried figs, chickpea soup. She has a fit of coughing as the smoke penetrates her eyes and mouth.

The woman with the child looks at her and her smile becomes more open, almost mocking. It is the first time that Marianna has entered the house of a peasant woman on her estates, the wife of one of her tenants. For all that she has read about them in books, she has never imagined such poverty.

She is accompanied by Don Pericle, who fans his face with a calendar to keep himself from sweating. Marianna gives him a questioning look: does he know these houses, does he visit them? But fortunately today Don Pericle is impenetrable, he keeps his eyes fixed on the distance, leaning over his protuberant stomach like pregnant women who do not know whether they are there to support their bellies or if it is their bellies that support them.

Marianna gestures to Fila, who has remained outside in the road with a large basket full of provisions. The girl comes in, makes the sign of the cross and curls up her nose in disgust. Very probably she was born in a house just like this one but has done all she can to wipe it out of her memory. Now she has become accustomed to the sweet-scented fragrance of lavender in large sun-drenched rooms, and to be here fills her with resentment.

The woman with the baby gives a kick to drive away the hens that are starting to flutter and flap their wings inside the room, shifts the few poor bits of crockery on the table and waits for her share of the bounty.

Marianna takes some sausage from the basket, some bags of rice and some sugar, and puts them all down on the table with brusque gestures. With every gift she offers she feels more ridiculous, more indecent: the indecency of a benefactor who claims immediate gratitude from the other; the indecency of a conscience that is satisfied with its own generosity and can ask the Lord for a place in paradise.

Meanwhile the baby has started to cry. Marianna watches its mouth grow bigger and bigger, its eyes squeezing shut, its hands with raised clenched fists. And this crying seems to communicate itself little by little to everything in the vicinity, making them cry too: from the hens to the donkey, from the bed to the kneading trough, from the tattered skirt of the woman to the irretrievably burnt and dented cooking pans.

As she goes outside, Marianna puts her hands to her sweating neck and opens her mouth to breathe in great gulps of fresh air. But the smells stagnating in the narrow lane are not much better than those inside the house: excrement, rotting vegetables, frying oil, dust. Now many more women are crowding in their doorways for their share of alms. Some sit in front of their houses delousing their children and chattering cheerfully to each other.

Is not this act of charity the root of corruption that seduces the receiver? The landowner encourages the avidity of his dependants, flattering and satiating them not only to make himself look good with the guardians of heaven but also because he well knows that the recipients will be lowered in their own eyes by accepting these gifts that enjoin gratitude and loyalty.

'I am suffocating here. I am going back to the tower', Marianna writes on her little table and passes the note to Don Pericle. 'You carry on.'

Fila gives an ill-tempered frown at the basket supported against her hips and still piled with food. Now she'll have to carry on by herself because she cannot count on Felice, who has stopped on the paved road so as not to get her shoes dirty. As for the other two girls, Heaven knows when they'll turn up. They were playing cards till late into the night and this morning they did not appear for breakfast under the portico.

Meanwhile Marianna strides off in the direction of Torre Scannatura, which she thinks she can catch a glimpse of beyond this desolation of roofs on which anything and everything grows, from chives to fennel, from capers to nettles. Turning down a narrow alleyway she stumbles over a chamber-pot that someone has left upside down in the middle of the road. Even in Bagheria the same sort of thing happens and, for that matter, in the poorer quarters of Palermo. In the morning the housewives empty the contents of their chamber-pots in the middle of the street, then come out with a bucket of water and sluice everything further down the road, at which point they lose all interest in what happens to it. But since there is always someone upstream in the process of carrying out exactly the same operation, the narrow street is permanently overrun by an evil-smelling open drain, humming with flies. The same flies settle in clouds on the faces of the small boys who sit playing along the sides of the alleys, and cling to their eyelids as if they were an exquisite dish for them to suck. The children, with these clusters of flies hanging from their eyelids, end up looking as if they were wearing monstrous masks.

Marianna walks quickly, trying to avoid the filth, followed by a swarm of hopping creatures; she can only guess at how many by the fluttering of wings that surrounds her. She walks as fast as she can, swallowing mouthfuls of pungent air, and aims towards the end of the village with her head down. But each time she thinks she has reached the road to the tower she finds herself blocked by a low wall topped with fragments of broken crockery, or a sharp turning, or a chicken-run. The tower seems within reach but the village for all its smallness has a labyrinthine layout that is difficult to disentangle.

Walking this way and that, turning round to retrace her footsteps, Marianna suddenly finds herself in a small square piazza dominated by a gigantic statue of the Madonna. She stops for a moment to recover her breath, and leans against the base of grey stone. In whichever direction she looks it is the same: low houses jammed on top of each other, often with a single entrance that serves as both window and door. Inside she can glimpse dark rooms inhabited by both people and animals in easy promiscuity; outside are rivulets of dirty water, a few shops with grain exhibited in large baskets, a blacksmith who works in his doorway spitting out sparks, a tailor who cuts, sews and irons by the light of his open stable door, a fruit seller who displays his wares in wooden boxes with a label on each different product – FIGS: 2 GRANI A BAG; ONIONS: 4 GRANI A BAG; LAMP OIL: 5 GRANI A CAN; EGGS: HALF A GRANO EACH. Her eyes alight on the labels with their prices like buoys in a sea at high tide; the numbers reassure her and make sense of the mysterious layout of this dusty and hostile village.

But here now, under her feet, she becomes aware of the familiar thud of hoofs, a rhythmic beat that makes her look up: and there, appearing from nowhere, she sees Saro coming towards her, riding on the back of a young Arab horse that uncle husband gave him before his death and which he has ostentatiously called Malagigi.

At last she will be able to get out of this maze, and she is about to go forward to meet him when both horse and rider disappear, swallowed up behind a low wall carpeted with caper plants. Marianna goes towards this wall but turning round finds herself confronted by a crowd of women and children who look at her in amazement as if she were a supernatural being. Two cripples drag themselves along the paving stones, leaning on their crutches, and start to limp behind her in the hope of getting some money out of her. They surmise that a smartly dressed woman like her must be carrying a purse full of real gold. So they come right up to her, touch her hair, pull at her sleeves, snatch at the ribbons knotted round her waist that hold her writing-board with the ink and pens.

Once more Marianna thinks she can see Malagigi caracoling at the end of a lane and Sarino raising his hat very high and saluting her from a distance. She gestures so that he can see her signalling him to come and rescue her. In the meantime someone has grabbed her bag with the pens, thinking it must have money inside it, and is pulling hard, unable to detach it from her belt. To extricate herself, Marianna pulls at the buckle, rips it off with a tug and, leaving everything for the cripples and the children, starts running. Her feet take wings and leap over drain holes, rush up steep steps, run through potholes filled with sludge, sink into the heaps of refuse and excrement with which the road is littered.

Suddenly, when she least expects it, she finds herself outside at last, alone in the middle of a little path through tall grass. Ahead of her, silhouetted against a sky of glazed china, is the figure of Saro playing at circus tricks. Malagigi rears up on his hind legs, thrashes his front legs in the air, then lowers them on to the ground only to rise up once again, bucking and kicking as if he had been bitten by a tarantula.

Marianna watches with amusement and alarm: that boy will fall off and break his collar-bone. She signals him from a distance but he does not come to her. Indeed he draws her on towards the hills like a snake-charmer. Hitching up her mud-stained skirt, her hair escaping from its pins, damp with sweat and short of breath, she follows, happier than she ever remembers. He'll lose his balance, he'll hurt himself, how on earth can she stop him? she asks herself. Nevertheless, the thought is a happy one because she knows it is a game, and in games risk is part of the pleasure.

Horse and rider, still caracoling, have reached a coppice of hazel trees but they show no sign of stopping. They are dancing and cantering around in front of her but always keeping their distance. It is as if the entire life of Saro has been given over to horse-riding, like a gipsy. Now he is through the nut trees, and ahead there are only fields of clover, tall hedges of castor-oil plants and expanses of stony ground.

All at once Marianna sees the youth flying through the air like a rag doll and falling head down into the tall grass. She starts running again, jumping, tripping over the tangled brambles, holding her skirt up with both hands. When did she last run like this? Her heart is in her throat and feels as if it and her tongue want to jump out together.

Now at last she reaches him. He is lying on his back half-buried in the grass, his eyes shut, his face drained of blood. Gently she bends over him and tries to ease his neck and move first his arm and then his leg. But his body does not respond. It lies abandoned and deprived of all sensation. With shaking hands Marianna unbuttons his shirt at the neck. He has only fainted, she tells herself, he will soon come to. Meanwhile she cannot take her eyes off him: he seems at that moment to have been born for her in all the beauty of his young body. If she gave him a kiss he would never know it. Why not once and once only give rein to her desires, held in check by her inimical will?

With a gentle movement she bends over the boy lying on his

back, and her mouth lightly brushes against his cheek. For an instant she seems to feel his long eyelashes flutter. She draws back and looks at him again. He is a body stranded and lost in unconsciousness. Again she bends gingerly over him with the lightness of a butterfly, and places her lips against his. She seems to feel him tremble. Suppose it were a sign of delirium, the first intimation of death? She rises on to her knees and starts to stroke his cheek with her fingers until she sees him open his grey eyes, such beautiful grey eyes. They are laughing at her. They are telling her that it was all an act, a trap to steal a kiss from her. It has worked perfectly. Only the tapping of her fingers on his cheek had not been foreseen, and perhaps forced him to give away the game sooner than he had intended.

What a fool I am, what a fool! Marianna thinks while she tries to do up her hair. She knows that he will not move a finger without her consent, she knows that he is waiting, and for a moment she is tempted to disclose what was at first only a secret thought: to press him against her in an embrace that overflows with years of waiting and renunciation.

What an idiot, what an idiot!... This trap will be her joy of joys. Why does she not let herself be caught in its noose? But there is a faint whiff of sugared almonds that does not please her, a suspicion that she is being taken for granted. Her knees press into the grass, her back straightens, her feet are already moving. Before Saro can guess her intention, she is off, running in the direction of the tower.

XXXII

The two lighted candlesticks are burning with green flames. Marianna watches those little tongues of fire with some apprehension: since when has a small candle of virgin wax burned with such a green light, rising in slender columns towards the ceiling and falling back as a frothy liquid? Even the bodies next to her are different from usual, swelling with menace: the belly of Don Pericle is contorting itself into sudden protuberances as if it were inhabited by a frightened child. On the table Manina's plump dimpled fingers are opening and closing quickly, shuffling the cards as if they were acting on their own, detached from her arms, grasping and turning the court cards while her wrists remain buried inside her sleeves.

Don Nunzio's white hair falls in ringlets on to the table. Snow in the middle of August? Immediately afterwards she sees him taking an enormous handkerchief out of his waistcoat pocket, rolling it into a ball and burying his nose in it. It is evident that as well as blowing his nose he is expelling his bad temper. If he carries on like this Don Nunzio will blow his whole life into his handkerchief and expire on the card table. Marianna takes hold of his wrist and presses it.

The daughters burst out laughing at their mother's gesture of dismay. Don Pericle laughs too; Felice laughs and her sapphire cross dances on her breast. Sarino laughs, putting his hand in front of his mouth; even Fila laughs. She is standing next to Giuseppa holding a saucepan full of macaroni in tomato sauce.

Felice stretches out her hand to touch her mother's forehead. On the lips of her daughter Marianna reads the word 'fever'. All their faces look serious and she sees other hands stretching out to feel her forehead.

She'll never know how she managed to get upstairs: perhaps they carried her. She does not know how she got undressed, how she was able to hide beneath the sheets. The aching of her feverish head keeps her awake, but at last she is alone and thinking once more with disgust about her gullibility that morning, first her performance as a good Samaritan and then that childish rush over heaps of stones and through nut bushes, the submissiveness of a body possessed by ghosts, the ingenuousness of a kiss that she was going to steal and that has indeed been stolen. And now this malignant fever that brings echoes of an internal babble she cannot make sense of.

Can a woman of forty, a mother and a grandmother, wake up like a late-flowering rose from a torpor that has lasted for decades, and lay claim to a share of the honey? What is to stop her? Is it no more than her own will-power? Or perhaps the memory of a violation repeated so many times as to render deaf and mute the whole of her body?

At some time during the night somebody must have come in to see her. Was it Felice? Or Fila? Somebody who raised her head and forced her to swallow a sweet drink. Leave me in peace, she wanted to scream, but her mouth stayed shut with an expression of bitterness and pain.

> He brought me to the banqueting house. . . .
> and his fruit was sweet to my taste.
> Comfort me with apples for I am sick of love. . . .

What blasphemy: to mix in her confused memory fragments of past happiness with the brilliant words of the Song of Songs. How can she be on the verge of forgetting her own disability?

> My beloved is like a roe or a young hart.

These are words that should not be spoken, they sound ridiculous on tight-lipped mouths, they cannot belong to them. Yet they are there, these words of love, and they have become fused with the anguish of her fever.

> Take us the foxes,
> the little foxes that spoil our vineyards.

Now the room is flooded with daylight. Someone must have opened the shutters while she slept. Her eyes are stinging as if she had grains of salt beneath her eyelids. She lifts a hand to her forehead and sees an owl on the arm of the chair. It seems to be looking at her tenderly. She tries to move her hand on the sheet but discovers that there is a large coiled-up serpent calmly sleeping on the embroidered border. Perhaps the owl will eat up the serpent. Perhaps not. If only Fila would come with some water. . . . From the way her hands are crossed on her chest she concludes that she must already be dead. But her eyes are open and they see the door swinging back by itself, slowly, just as in life. Who is it?

Uncle husband, quite naked, with a great scar running down his chest and belly. The hair on his head is sparse like that of people infected with ringworm, and he exudes a strange smell of cinnamon and rancid butter. She sees him bend over her, armed as if to crucify her. A sort of dead egg-plant pulsates out of his belly, obscenely stiff with desire. I will make love out of pity for him, she tells herself. Love is above all merciful.

'I am dying,' she says to him behind closed lips. And he smiles mysteriously like an accomplice. 'I am going to die,' she insists. He nods. He yawns and nods. Strange because the dead cannot feel the need for sleep. A sensation of freezing cold makes her raise her eyes towards the unshuttered window. A crescent moon hangs in the topmost window pane. Each gust of wind sets it swinging gently. It is like a piece of candied pumpkin with the sugar grains crystallised and stuck to the rind. 'I will make love out of pity,' her dumb mouth repeats, but uncle husband does not want her consent, pity is not what he wants. Now his white body is on top of her, pressing down on her freezing belly. The dead flesh smells of dried flowers and saltpetre. The fleshy egg-plant insists on forcing its way into her womb.

At dawn the house resounds with a terrible drawn-out scream. Felice leaps from her bed. Surely it cannot be her dumb mother? Yet the scream comes from the direction of her room. She runs to wake her sister Giuseppa, who in turn pulls Manina out of bed. The three young sisters still in their night-dresses rush to their mother's bed, where she appears to be gasping for a few last desperate gulps of air.

Since there are no doctors at Torre Scannatura the local 'leech' is hurriedly summoned. He is called Mino Pappalardo and he arrives attired in egg-yolk yellow. He takes the sick woman's pulse, examines her tongue, lifts her eyelids and buries his nose in the chamber-pot.

'Fever with congestion of the lungs,' is his verdict. There is an urgent need to draw blood from the inflamed veins. For this he will require a high stool, a basin of luke-warm water, a big cup, a clean sheet and an assistant.

Felice offers to help while Giuseppa and Manina huddle in a corner of the room. The leech takes a pouch made of rolled-up canvas out of a small suitcase of light-coloured wood. Inside it, tied together by thin laces, are small sharp scalpels, small saws, pincers and a minute pair of scissors.

Moving confidently, Pappalardo bares the invalid's arm, feels the vein at the elbow, ties a tourniquet round the upper part of the arm, and then with a precise cut makes an incision, reaches the vein with the knife blade and starts to bleed her. Felice, kneeling beside the bed, collects the blood in a cup as it drops, without any sign of squeamishness.

Marianna opens her eyes. She sees the unshaven face of a man with two dark furrows on his cheeks. The man gives her a bruised distracted smile. But the snake which was curled up on the sheet must have woken because she can feel it plunging its sharp fangs into her arm. She wants to warn Felice but she is unable to move even her eyes.

But who is this man on top of her who has a strange disagreeable smell? Somebody in disguise? Uncle husband? Her father the Duke? He would be quite capable of putting on a disguise, just for fun. At that moment a revelation transfixes her from head to foot, like an arrow: for the first time in her life she comprehends with a diamond clarity that it was him, her father, who was the one responsible for her disablement. From love or from carelessness she can't say. But it is he who cut her tongue and it is he who has filled up her ears with molten lead so that she can hear no sound and circles perpetually in the kingdoms of silence and fear.

XXXIII

A carriage with a drawn hood, the horse caparisoned with gold trappings. It must be that eccentric character Agonia, Prince of Palagonia. But no, there alights a lady attired in a veil thrown in the Spanish manner over her high tower of hair. Why, it is the Princess of Santa Riverdita, who has had two husbands both of whom died of poisoning. Behind her comes an elegant small gig drawn by a young spirited horse; this must be the Baron Pallavicine, who a short time ago won a lawsuit against his brother, a case concerning a disputed inheritance that lasted for over fifteen years. The brother has been left in sackcloth and ashes, and can now only become a monk or marry a rich woman. But in Palermo a rich woman doesn't marry a pauper, even if he does have a grand title, unless she is forced to, in which case the price is very high. Moreover, the 'betrothed' has to be exceedingly beautiful and at the very least she must know how to play the spinet with grace.

A parade of carriages like this is something that has not been seen for years. The courtyard of the Villa Ucrìa is completely obstructed: calashes, palanquins, fiacres, litters, sedan-chairs pass beneath the lights of the great archway of flowers that links the access road to the courtyard.

It is the first time since uncle husband's death that there has been a big party at the villa. Marianna has decided on it to celebrate her recovery from pleurisy. Her hair has begun to grow again and the colour has regained its natural fairness.

The curtain in the blue room on the first floor has been drawn aside and she is standing behind it, watching the comings and goings of footmen, grooms, lackeys, porters and waiters in plush breeches. During the evening a new theatre will be inaugurated, built by her for the performance of music she cannot hear, for the enjoyment of plays she will be unable to enjoy. To compensate for her deafness she has made the stage large and high, with splendid decorations by Intermassimi. She has had the boxes lined with yellow damask with borders of blue velvet, she has planned a wide vaulted ceiling painted with designs showing birds of paradise, unicorns and chimeras with enigmatic expressions.

Intermassimi arrived from Naples all spruced up, accompanied by a young wife called Elena, with tiny ears, and fingers weighed down with rings. They stayed in the house for three months, eating dainty little titbits and fondling each other everywhere: in the garden, in the corridors, on the scaffolding, among the bowls of paint. He is forty-five and she is fifteen.

Whenever Marianna came across the two of them by chance in some part of the villa, clasped in each other's arms, short of breath, their clothes unfastened, he used to smile at her mischievously as if to say, Now you see what you've missed. Marianna would turn her back on him in annoyance. Latterly she avoided going through the villa when she suspected she might meet them. But in spite of her precautions she would often come across them, almost as if they had put themselves in her path on purpose.

So she went to Palermo to the palazzo in the Via Alloro, wandering ill-humouredly through the dark rooms crammed with pictures, tapestries and rugs. She took Fila with her, leaving Innocenza at Bagheria. She left Saro at the villa too. For some time he has been in charge of the cellars and the wine, swooshing

173

it from one cheek to the other with his eyes shut, and then spitting it out a long way with a sharp smack of his tongue. By now he can also make a guess at the wine's vintage.

By the time she returned in May the work was finished and she found the frescos so beautiful that she forgave the painter his exhibitionism and his boasting. He and his child wife had left on the very day that Ciccio Calò died; towards the end Calò had become quite senile, going round the courtyard half-naked, looking for his daughters, with his eyes starting out of his head.

Today is a day of celebration. In the drawing-room lit by chandeliers of Murano glass are all the great ladies of Palermo. Their enormous dresses have skirts stretched out on hoops of wood and whalebone, and tight-fitting, low-necked bodices in delicately coloured silks; beside them are the courtly gentlemen, dressed up for the occasion in long redingotes, red, violet and green, embroidered in silver and gold thread, with shirts puffed out with ruffles and lace, and wearing powdered and perfumed wigs.

Marianna looks around her with satisfaction. For days and days she has been preparing these festivities and she is confident she has arranged it all so that the evening will run on well-oiled wheels. The hors-d'œuvres are to be served on the terrace decorated with geraniums and succulent African plants. Some of the glasses have had to be borrowed from the house at Torre Mosca because after the death of uncle husband she no longer replaced those that gradually got broken. Into these glasses, lent by Agata, is being poured a light spiced drink, lemonade, or a sparkling wine.

Supper, however, will be served in the gardens, between the dwarf palm trees and the jasmine bushes, on linen tablecloths, using the dinner service known as 'the regal' in white and blue with the black eagle. The meal will consist of macaroni *di zitu*, red mullet, hare in a sour sauce, boar with chocolate, turkey stuffed with ricotta, fish cooked in wine, roast suckling pig, sweet rice, conserve of scorzonera, ice-cream, sweetmeats, almond biscuits, water ices and wines from Casa Ucrìa with the strong pungent flavour of the grapes from Torre Scannatura.

After supper there will be a theatrical entertainment: Olivo, Sebastiano, Manina and Mariano will sing the *Artaserse* of Metastasio with music by Vincenzo Ciampi, played by an orchestra of the nobility, consisting of the Duke of Carrera Lo Bianco, the Prince Crescimanno, Lord of Gabelle del Biscotto, the Baroness Spitaleri, the Count della Cattolica, the Prince Des Puches di Caccamo and the Princess Mirabella.

Luckily the sky is clear, strewn with small luminous buds of light. The moon is not yet visible but, to compensate, the fountain of the Triton, lit from the inside by candles placed in niches hollowed out of the rock, creates a dazzling spectacle. Everything moves according to a predetermined rhythm, following a choreography orchestrated in advance, so that the guests, with their precious attire, their shoes studded with jewels, are unknowingly taking part in an intricate game of charades.

Marianna has decided not to wear a ceremonial dress so that she can move more easily among the guests, go quickly to the kitchen, run to the theatre, go and see the players in the orchestra, who are tuning up their instruments in the yellow room, attend to the lighted tapers, keep an eye on her daughters and her nieces, and signal with her head to the cook and to Saro to get him to fetch more wine from the cellars.

A few of the women are unable to sit down because their skirts are so elaborate and wide, supported by a rigid framework that resembles a dome with a little clock-tower at the summit. This year the hooped skirt is in fashion at the French court, forming a canopy so wide that it could shelter a crouching couple. It is made out of plaited osiers covered by a long full skirt and surmounted by a shiny pleated bodice ornamented with bows and frills, and stiffened up the back with two quills that stretch from the nape of the neck to the waist.

At eleven o'clock there will be a ball and at midnight there are to be fireworks. A frame has been specially constructed and placed in the lemon grove next to the theatre in such a way that the bangs will only occur above the heads of the guests and the flashes will be extinguished in the carp pond or among the roses and pansies in the flower beds.

A warm soft night, pungent with scents. A light salt breeze comes in gusts from the sea, cooling the air. Marianna, in all the confusion, has not had time to eat even a vol-au-vent. The cooks have been hired for the evening; the head chef is French, or at least so he claims, and insists on being called Monsieur Trebbianó, but she suspects that he has only been in France for a brief visit. He cooks well à la française, but his best dishes are the Sicilian ones. Under the most recondite names it is possible to recognise the familiar flavours that everyone likes. For years the great families of Palermo have competed for him for supper and dinner parties with throngs of guests. And 'Monsù' Trebbianó is happy to earn his living going from one house to another, accompanied by his troop of helpers, assistants and faithful *petites mains*, to say nothing of an avalanche of saucepans, knives and moulds of his own.

For a moment Marianna sits down and under her long gown slips off her small pointed shoes. It is years since she has seen all the family together at the villa. There is Signoretto, whose affairs are not going well; he has had to mortgage the feudal estate of Fontanasalsa to pay his debts. However, he doesn't look any the worse for it. The slow descent of the family towards ruin he regards as part of the common destiny: a destiny which it is useless to oppose because, anyway, it will overtake them.

Carlo has become famous for his learning and now he is called in from all parts of Europe to decipher ancient manuscripts. He is just back from Salamanca, where he was invited by the Universidad Real, who, at the end of his stay, offered him a teaching post; but he preferred to return to his gardens at San Martino delle Scale, surrounded by his books, his students, his woods, his food. 'I invent dreams and fables', he has written on a little sheet of paper which she thrust into her pocket as if it were wiser to keep it hidden. '"All is lies, in delirium I live", as the poet Metastasio puts it.'

Marianna rereads the crumpled note, which has remained in her pocket. Her eyes search for her brother: he has sunk into a deep chair, his hair thinning, his eyes pig-like. It requires the most careful observation to perceive a vestige of spirituality in this body, which is now getting right out of control and overflowing on all sides. I must see him more often, Marianna tells herself, noting the unhealthy pallor of her brother's face, which seems to recall her mother's; even at a distance she thinks she catches the smell of laudanum and snuff.

Agata too is much changed. Signs of her beauty remain: her large limpid eyes in which the white and the blue are clearly separated. Everything else about her looks as if it has been immersed in the laundry water, soaked and washed for too long, and then spread with ashes and beaten on stones, like sheets in the river.

Beside her, Agata's daughter Maria looks like a portrait of Agata as a girl, with the sharp shoulders of a sixteen-year-old that slip like fresh almonds out of her lace-covered dress festooned with lilac bows. Fortunately Agata has succeeded in saving her from being forced to marry at twelve as her husband wanted. She keeps her close to her and dresses her like a little girl so that she will seem younger, which vexes her daughter, who would like to appear grown-up. Giuseppa and Giulio sit close together, continually looking at each other and laughing at every trifle. Her cousin Olivo watches them sullenly from another table. His wife, sitting next to him, looks less disagreeable than she has been described to Marianna: small, stiff, but capable of bursting out in sensuous rippling laughter. She does not seem upset by the expression on her young husband's face, possibly because she has no suspicion of the love affair between the two cousins. Or perhaps she does and that is why when she is serious she looks as if she had swallowed a broomstick. Her laughter could certainly be a way of enabling herself to face the situation with courage.

Mariano grows ever more handsome and majestic. Sometimes he looks arrogant and frowning, bringing to mind his father, but his colouring is that of his grandfather Signoretto, the colour of bread just taken out of the oven. His wife Caterina Molè di Flores has had several miscarriages but no children; this has created feelings of resentment between the two of them which are obvious to the naked eye. He always talks to her crossly and reprovingly, and she answers him back in a dull tone of voice as if she was always having to expiate her guilt at being childless. She talks to him about the new freedom, spellbound by the ideas of her aunt Domitilla, but never with quite her conviction. He does not even pretend to listen to her any more. His eyes are constantly on guard lest anyone invades the charmed circle in which he shuts himself to dream. From being passionately interested in having a good time, always going from one house to another for balls and card games, over the past few years he has grown lazy and self-absorbed. His wife drags him through the salons and he lets himself be led but does not join in the conversations, refuses to play cards, eats little, hardly drinks at all. He enjoys looking at other people without being looked at, sunk in his own misty clouds of thought.

What does Mariano dream about? It is hard to say. Sometimes when she has been standing close to him Marianna has been able to guess: dreams of great military adventures among foreign people, of swords held at the ready, of sweating horses, of the smells of battle and gunpowder. Like his father, he possesses a collection of arms, and every time he invites her for a family meal he shows it to her in the minutest detail: the sword of Philip II, an arquebus that belonged to the Duke of Anjou, a musket from the guards of Louis XIV, an enamelled box used by the Infanta of Spain for black gunpowder, and other marvels of a similar kind. Some he has inherited from his father, others he has bought himself. Yet he would not move from his palace in the Via Alloro even if he had the guarantee of a striking victory on the battlefield. He has abandoned himself to dreams of military strategy, which in some way have taken on a second life more real and tangible than reality.

Marianna watches her son as he gets up from the table where he dined with Francesco Gravina, son of that other Gravina of Palagonia nicknamed Agonia. The young man has been refurbishing the villa built by his grandfather, filling it with weird statues: men with the heads of goats, women who are half monkeys, elephants playing the violin, serpents that twist round flutes, dragons dressed as gnomes and gnomes with the tails of dragons, not to mention a collection of hunchbacks, Punchinellos, Moors, beggars, Spanish soldiers and travelling musicians. The people of Bagheria regard him as crazy; his relations have tried to have him put under an interdict. But his friends love him for a certain open and bashful way he has of laughing at himself. It also seems that he has transformed the Villa Palagonia into a place of enchantment: rooms lined with mirrors that break up and multiply the reflected images so as to render them unrecognisable; busts of marble that project from the walls with arms held out towards the dancers; glass eyes rotating in their eye-sockets; the bedrooms populated with embalmed animals – donkeys, sparrow-hawks, foxes, together with snakes, scorpions, lizards, worms, creatures that no one has ever before thought of preserving.

Evil-minded gossips say that his grandfather Ignazio Sebastiano collected up to his death – that is to say, to the end of last year – a local tax on coitus in exchange for giving up his claims to the feudal *jus primae noctis*. The young Palagonia is as ugly as sin: a receding chin, eyes too close together and a nose like a beak, but those who know him well say he is kind, merry, incapable of hurting a fly, courteous to those beneath him, tolerant, thoughtful and dedicated to reading romances of adventure and travel. Strange how they are friends, he and Mariano; they are so different, but perhaps it is just this that brings them together. Mariano would not read a book even if he were forced to do so. His fantasies are nourished by the spoken rather than the written word and he certainly prefers a ballad singer from the streets to a book from his mother's library.

Now she suddenly realises she has lost him in the crowd; where has Mariano, the dreamer, gone? She finds him a little later walking by himself in the direction of the bright lights of the coffee house. She watches him sip a coffee, burn his tongue and angrily stamp his foot just like he did when he was little. She watches him sit down on a straight-backed chair with the cup in his hand while his gaze rests greedily on the exposed bodies of the women guests. The pupils of his eyes grow dark, his lips tighten, his penetrating look reminds her of uncle husband. She recognises in it the sudden secret lust for rape.

Marianna shuts her eyes. She opens them again. Mariano is no longer in the coffee house, and Caterina is looking for him. Now the gazebo is full of guests, everyone with a small cup of coffee in their hands. She has known them all her life, even if she does not see much of them. Usually she meets them at weddings, when someone enters a religious order, at visits following childbirth, and at confirmations.

They are always the same, these women whose minds have been left to grow lazy in the cloisters inside their heads, so delicately coiffured in the Parisian style. From mother to daughter, from daughter to niece they are forever circling round and round the problems of their sons, husbands, lovers, servants, friends, and inventing new wiles so as not to be crushed. Their men are busy with other problems, other enjoyments, different yet parallel: the administration of their distant estates, the future of their big houses, hunting, gaming, carriages, courtship and questions of prestige and precedence. There are a very few who once in a while are able to leap on to the roof-tops and look around them to see where the city is burning, or where the waters are flooding the land, where the earth still nurtures the ripening of the corn and the vines, and how their island will be ravished by fecklessness and plunder.

The weakness of these families is also hers. She knows the secret infamies which women talk about behind their fans, such as the initiation of young boys with servant girls who, when they become pregnant, are passed on to open-minded friends or sent into religious houses as being in 'moral danger' or to hospices for 'fallen women'. Then there are the astronomical debts, the usury, the secret illnesses, the suspect births, the evenings spent at the club playing for castles and estates, the escapades in brothels, the singers competed for to the chink of money, the furious quarrels between brothers, the secret love affairs, the terrible vendettas.

But she knows the dreams too: the enchanting rhythms of the battles between Orlando, Artù, Ricciardetto, Malagigi, Ruggero, Angelica, Gano di Maganza and Rodomonte that articulate everyone's fantasies; their willingness to live on bread and turnips so as to maintain a carriage emblazoned with gold. She knows their monstrous pride, their capricious intelligence that prides itself on remaining idle as a duty to their rank, the secret biting wit that is often united with a sensual desire for decay and effacement.

Is she not like this too? Flesh of their flesh, idle, watchful, secretive and suffocated by foolish dreams of grandeur? The only difference is the disability that has given her more insight into herself and others, to the extent of sometimes being able to enter into the thoughts of someone beside her. But she has not known how to elevate this talent into an art as Mr David Hume has suggested; she has let it flower at random, suffering it rather than being guided by it, without drawing any profit from it.

In her silence, inhabited only by written words, she has elaborated theories and left them half-developed, she has pursued fragments of thought without methodically cultivating them, allowing herself to fall into the laziness typical of her kind, of those secure in their immunity, even before God, since 'to him that hath shall be given and from him that hath not shall be taken even that he hath'. And by 'having' it is not estates, land, houses, gardens, that is meant, but refinement, reflection, intellectual complexity, all those things that need abundant leisure and that favour their lordships, who then amuse themselves throwing out crumbs to those who are poor both in money and in spirit.

The water ice has melted in the long-stemmed crystal glass. The spoon has slid to the floor. A puff of air, a breath of dried figs tickles her ear. Saro is bending over her, and his lips brush against her neck. Marianna gives a start, gets up, staggering comically with her shoes slipped off underneath her skirt, and stares angrily at the youth. How dare he come so stealthily to tempt her while she is lost in her own thoughts!

With a firm hand she takes hold of the notebook and pen, and without looking at him writes, 'I have decided you must get married.' Then she hands the sheet of paper to the boy, who holds it under the flares to read it better.

Marianna watches him with fascination. None of the other young men who have been invited have the grace of his body, over which flicker the undulating light and shade of the festivities. He is full of trepidation and uncertainty that lighten the way he moves, giving him a fragility as if he were suspended in air. How she would like to take him by the waist and pull him down to the floor!

But as soon as she sees his bewildered gaze settling on her, Marianna goes hastily to mingle with the throng of guests. Now it is time for the music, and she has to lead the guests along the garden paths between the hedges of elderflower and jasmine towards the newly varnished doors of the theatre.

XXXIV

Her brother Abbot Carlo offers her a cup of chocolate and smiles at her with a questioning look. Marianna fixes her gaze beyond the tall lilies and the trunks of pomegranate trees, to the city of Palermo stretched out like a pink and green Chinese rug, in a dust-cloud of dove-grey houses. The chocolate has a bitter-scented taste on her tongue. Now her brother taps his foot on the wooden floor of the veranda. Is he impatient to get rid of her? Yet she has only just arrived, after two hours in a litter along the rocky paths that lead up to San Martino delle Scale.

'I want to find a wife for a member of my household. I would like your advice about a good honest girl', writes Marianna, using her complicated writing implements, the little folding table that hangs from her belt, the goose-quill pen with a detachable nib just arrived from London, the ink bottle fixed to a little chain and a small exercise book with detachable pages.

The sister watches the brother's face as he reads her words. It is not haste that makes him wrinkle his forehead, she realises, it is embarrassment. This sister, locked as she is in her enforced silence, has always seemed remote, strange, except perhaps when Grandmother Giuseppa was still alive and both of them used to get into her bed. Then he would hug and kiss her so fervently that it took her breath away. Since then, he does not know why, they have drifted apart. Now, it seems, he is wondering what lies behind this request for advice from his deaf-mute sister: a pretext for an alliance against their elder brother, who has been plunging himself into debt? Or curiosity about his solitary abbot's life? Or a request for money?

Clusters of discordant thoughts slip unintentionally out of his eyes, out of his nostrils. Marianna watches him tormenting the pointed leaf of a lily between his plump fingers and knows she cannot escape from the wave of his reflections, which are reaching her from the depths of his indolent, caustic mind.

His sister the Duchess is anxious. Is she afraid of getting old? It's strange how well she's worn ... not a shred of fat, no disfigurement, slim as when she was twenty, a fresh, clear complexion ... her hair still fair and curly ... only one white lock over her left temple ... does she rinse it in camomile?... Though, come to think of it, our father the Duke stayed as fair as an angel until he was quite old. But all he himself has left are a few sparse threads. A waste of time looking at himself in the mirror, he's never managed to grow any hair, he remains covered with down like a baby, and that only grows because of the tincture of herb Gerard mixed with nettles that his niece Felice told him about.... This dumb sister still has the face of a young girl ... while his has swollen up with lumps and bumps all over the place.... What if it were her dumbness that has preserved her from the ruins of growing old?... There is something virginal in her wide-open eyes ... when she looks at him like that she makes him feel uneasy.... Heaven knows what sort of a beanpole his uncle was ... he used to see Duke Pietro walking like an old crock, all jerks and twists, as if he were made of wood ... and she has kept the purity of a young wife ... behind that lace, those cloaks, those bows the colour of night, there is a body that has never tasted what pleasure is.... It must be like that ... pleasure devours, broadens, crumbles ... yes, pleasure ... he has been in it up to his neck, first of all women with thin backs and flat breasts, entwined body to body, leaving them both exhausted ... then changing over the years into a father's sensual taste for the deformed and emaciated bodies of sullen-faced little boys, whom he now loves only with his eyes and in his imagination. . . . He would never give up the joy of having around him those small beings with legs crippled from undernourishment, those small black glittering eyes, those fingers that are unable to reach for anything in spite of wanting to reach for the world. . . . He would never give up one of these protégés not even to regain that same body he had as a youth, with thick hair and a slender neck. . . . It is she who by losing her voice has lost everything . . . she is afraid . . . you can read it in her eyes . . . it's there underneath . . . it is fear that stops her from living and throws her into the grave intact and still a virgin, but already suffocated, pulled to pieces, dead like a badly chiselled block of wood. Why is she so obstinate? Where did it come from? Certainly not from her father, who was always generous and heedless, even less from her mother, who camouflaged herself under the blankets to the point where she couldn't recognise her own legs . . . snuff and laudanum kept her in a limbo from which it became more and more nauseating for her to escape.

Marianna cannot take her eyes off his mind. Her brother's thoughts slip effortlessly from his head into hers, as if the expert hand of a gardener were trying out some dangerous grafting operation. She would like to stop him, to tear out this alien branch, from which flows such an icy bitter sap, but how to do it when one is at the receiving end of other people's thoughts and is unable to stifle them? She is taken over by a harsh desire to touch the bottom of this horror, giving substance to the most secret and fugitive words, the most despicable, the most nihilistic.

Her brother seems to be aware of her apprehension, and soothes it with a twinkle in his eyes and a kind smile. Then he gets hold of the pen and writes, filling the page with minute sloping letters, beautiful to look at.

'How old is the bridegroom?'

'Twenty-four.'

'What is his occupation?'

'Cellarman.'

'Does he have any money?'

'None of his own. I will give him a thousand escudos. He has served me loyally. His sister is a servant in my house. Our father the Duke gave her to me as a present years ago.'

'And how much do you pay him a month?'

'Twenty-five *tarì*.'

Abbot Carlo Ucrìa makes a face as if to say that it's not a bad wage, and that any peasant girl would be glad of him for a husband.

I could arrange something with the sister of Totuccio the stone-breaker. They are so poor in that family that if they could sell her in the market.... They'd be free of the burden ... and there's the others too. Five sisters and a brother, a real misfortune for a fisherman without a boat who fishes from other people's old tubs and feeds off the remains which the bosses leave him in exchange for his work. He goes barefoot even on Sundays and all he's got for a house is a cave black with smoke.... The first time he went there to please that little snail Totuccio, the mother was squashing lice on the youngest of the daughters while the others stood round in a circle and laughed shamelessly, with those hungry mouths, their eyes popping out, their necks as stringy as a chicken's ... small, crooked. No one ever thinks of them as wives, they aren't even good for work, they've suffered too much hunger, who would take them on? The oldest has got a hump, the second goitre, the third is a mouse, the fourth a spider and the fifth a scorpion fish....

And yet the father is crazy about these deformed creatures, that big stupid man, you should see how he pets them. And their mother too, with her hands all scratched and filthy: she tickles them, cleans them, smooths their plaits with fish-oil ... and what laughs they all have together! Totuccio started to do odd jobs when he was nine to bring some money into the family ... but what could he earn? A *tarì* once a fortnight, not even enough to get them a bread roll. You should have seen him the day he arrived at the monastery, half-naked, carrying a basket of stones on his head, all filthy with mortar dust and mud. And how seriously he lined up the stones next to the bed with the lilies. They were so heavy he could hardly manage to shove them into the ground. He had to thank Father Domenico, who has a mania for walls. Without him that boy would never have known how to start. Now all eight of them live off what he earns ... not much, only a few *carlini*, but it's just enough ... they make soup out of fish bones, bread out of chaff ... but they are a cheerful lot and they've got a bit fatter and cleaner.... He didn't do it for their good, he hasn't got the soul of a Samaritan . . . all the same, good has come out of it . . . is this a vice?

This eternal carping of the moralists . . . these Fathers make one laugh with the stink they create under their own noses . . . my sister too with her pained frowns. Who does she think she is, Santa Genoveffa? Why doesn't she open her arms, put a foot wrong, take the bandages off her eyes? . . . Everything we do is done out of our need for pleasure. Whether it is a refined pleasure like ministering to the poor, or a coarse pleasure like enjoying the sight of a little boy with a slender waist and a bottom like a little round loaf . . . one doesn't become a saint through will-power but through pleasure. There are some who make love with the devil, some who make it with the wounded body of our Lord Jesus, some who make it with themselves, some who make it with little boys – but without abusing them, without seizing them or tearing them or violating them in any way . . . pleasure is an art that knows its own limits . . . the greatest pleasure lies in respecting these limits and making out of them a framework for one's own harmony. Excesses are not a part of how he is . . . excesses would cast him straight into a cauldron of strains and swindles, scandals and lies, and he loves books too much to believe in the searing temptations of the flesh. The eye knows how to caress better than the hand, and his eyes have had their fill, but with such gentleness, such unspoken tenderness. . . .

That's enough, says Marianna to herself, now I must write to him to stop showing me his thoughts. But her hand stays resting quietly on her lap, her eyes half-shut in the shadow of the pomegranate leaves that send out a delicate bitter perfume.

'I have a girl for you, she is called Peppinedda. She is a good girl, she is sixteen and she is very poor but so long as you encourage her . . .'

Marianna nods. It seems pointless to begin another sheet of paper. Her mind is exhausted by the thoughts that have travelled up and down her head like a gang of mice having a party. Now she only wants to rest. She already knows all about Peppina and it does not worry her that her brother has chosen her for his own eccentric reasons; one reason is as good as another. If she had asked her daughters they would have been all at sixes and sevens, and no help at all. Carlo, with his epicurean philosophy, his intelligent piggy eyes, is capable of resolving other people's

185

difficulties delicately, combining their interests with what lies close to his heart. His motive is not to do good, and that is the very reason why he sometimes does it. His truffle-hound nose can find the treasure and flush it out for her as he has done now, with generosity. It only remains for her to thank him and leave. But something holds her back, a question that prods her hand; she takes up the pen, nibbles the point and then writes as quickly as usual: 'Carlo, do you remember whether I have ever talked?'

'No, Marianna.' No hesitation. A 'no' that closes the discussion. An exclamation mark, a flourish.

'Yet I can remember hearing sounds that I've since lost.'

'I know nothing of it, sister.' And with that the conversation is ended. He prepares to get up and say goodbye, but his sister shows no sign of moving. Her fingers still twist round the pen, becoming stained with ink. 'Is there anything else?' he writes, bending over his sister's notebook.

'Our lady mother once told me that I had not always been deaf and dumb.'

Now what's got into her head? Isn't it enough for her to come and disturb him about one of her household, someone she is perhaps in love with . . . of course, why did he not think of that before . . . are they not both of the same flesh? Lecherous and indulgent towards their own desires, ready to snatch, to withhold, to pay, because everything is allowed them by right of birth. . . . Lord forgive me! . . . Perhaps it is only an evil thought . . . the Ucrìas have been good hunters, insatiable profiteers . . . even if they then stopped half-way, because they did not have the stamina for excesses like the Scebarràs. . . . Look at her ladyship his sister, with that milky pallor, that soft mouth . . . something tells him that everything is yet to be revealed in her . . . a fine game, sister, at your age . . . madness! And no one has taught her the rudiments of love . . . it's easy to see she will lose all her feathers . . . he could teach her something but they are not experiences that can be exchanged between brothers and sisters. . . . What a leveret she was when she was little . . . both happy and fearful . . . but it's true, she talked when she was four years old, maybe five . . . he remembers that very well and he recollects all the whisperings in the family, the closing up of terrified lips . . . but why? What was the awful thing that took place in the labyrinths of the Via Alloro? One evening they heard screams to make the flesh creep and Marianna with her legs all bloodstained being dragged away between their father and Raffaele Cuffa. Strange the absence of the women . . . the fact is that, yes, now he remembers, Uncle Pietro, that damned old billy-goat, had assaulted her and left her half-dead . . . yes, Uncle Pietro, now it comes back to him, how could he have forgotten? 'Out of love,' Uncle Pietro had said, 'out of a most sacred love.' He just adored that little girl and 'if only he hadn't gone crazy. . . .' How could he have lost the memory of that tragedy?

And then, afterwards, yes afterwards, when Marianna was healed it was realised that she could no longer speak as if *zap*, he had cut out her tongue. . . . Our father the Duke, with his superstitious ideas, his obsessive love for his daughter . . . seeking to make her better, made her worse . . . a little girl at an execution, how could a half-witted action like that have come into his head? Then when she was thirteen to give her to the same uncle who had violated her when she was five. . . . What a fool their father Duke Signoretto was . . . seeing that the wrong done was his brother-in-law's, he thought he might just as well give her to him in marriage. . . . Her little head has erased everything . . . no one knows . . . perhaps it's better like that, let's leave her in ignorance, poor dumb thing . . . she would be better taking a glass of laudanum and putting herself to sleep . . . he has no patience with deaf people nor with those who tie themselves in knots with their own hands, nor with those who give themselves to God with so much gullibility. . . . But it will not be him who awakens her crippled memory . . . after all, it is a family secret . . . a secret that not even our mother knew . . . an affair between men, a crime perhaps but by now expiated, buried . . . what is served by getting in a rage about it?

The Abbot Carlo, still pursuing his secret thoughts, has forgotten his sister, who by now has left and has almost reached the garden gate. From behind it looks as if she is weeping. But why should she be weeping? Has he perhaps written something? Suppose she had heard his thoughts, the little darling? Who knows if behind that deafness there might not be some more subtle hearing, a diabolical ear capable of unveiling the secrets of the mind? Quick, I'll catch her up, he says to himself. I'll take her by the shoulders, I'll clasp her to my breast, I'll kiss her cheek . . . I'll do it, even if the heavens should fall.

'Marianna,' he shouts, on the point of following her.

But she cannot hear him. And while he is getting out of the chair into which he has sunk she has already opened the gate, jumped into the hired litter and started to descend the slope that leads down to Palermo.

XXXV

'Oh Lord, I long for what I cannot will. . . .' The books emit a good smell of tanned leather, pressed paper, dried ink. This little book of poetry is as heavy in her hand as a small block of crystal. The words of Michelangelo compose themselves in her mind with the precision, the purity of a drawing in Chinese ink. A perfect little geometry of words:

> Sweet is my sleep, but sweeter to be stone;
> So long as pain and ill-repute endure
> Neither to see nor feel is my cure.
> Then do not wake me; speak in an undertone.

Marianna looks up at the window. Darkness has already fallen and it is scarcely half-past four. It is cold in the library in spite of the coal burning in the brazier. She lifts her hand to pull the bell-rope but at that very moment she sees the door slide open by itself, preceded by a halo of light. In the doorway a candlestick appears followed by Fila holding the candlestick in her hands. Her face is almost entirely obscured by a bonnet of coarse cloth that covers up her ears, comes down all askew over her cheeks and fastens beneath her chin with a little cord that inhibits her breathing. She is white as a sheet and her eyes are red as if she has been crying.

Marianna signals her to come close, but Fila pretends not to understand, makes a quick curtsy, puts the candlestick on the table and goes towards the door. Marianna gets up out of the chair into which she has sunk, and goes after her, takes her by the arm and feels it tremble. Her skin is ice-cold, covered with a veil of sweat. 'What's the matter?' she asks with her eyes. She feels her forehead, and sniffs her. From beneath her bonnet emerges an acid smell, greasy and nauseating. Then she notices a black liquid running down from her ears to her neck. What is it? Marianna shakes her and questions her with gestures, but the girl bends her head obstinately and does not reply.

Marianna pulls the bell to summon Innocenza and meanwhile continues to sniff at the girl. Innocenza cannot write but when she wants she knows how to make herself understood better than Fila. As soon as the cook comes into the room Marianna shows her Fila's head, the cloth bonnet spotted with dark stains, the black liquid that runs stinking and glistening down her neck. Innocenza bursts out laughing and slowly forms the syllables of the word 'ringworm' so that the Duchess can read it on her lips.

Marianna remembers having read in a pamphlet by the skin specialists of the School of Salerno that ringworm is sometimes cured amongst the common people by a folk remedy that uses burning pitch. But it is a dangerous and drastic method of cure; it involves burning the scalp and stripping it bare. If the unfortunate victim manages to hold out they will be cured, if they do not die ravaged by the burns. Marianna pulls the bonnet from Fila's head, but she sees that the damage has already been done. Her poor head, completely without hair, is torn open by large patches of burnt and bleeding skin.

Apparently this all took place at the home of some relations at Ficarazzi when she last visited them. She had stayed for ten days in one of those dark caves surrounded by donkeys, fowls and black beetles; and now, without saying a word to her, she is trying to get rid of the parasites by burning her head to death.

Fila had started to behave strangely after Saro's marriage to Peppinedda. She had taken to sleepwalking, wandering about in the middle of the night in her night-gown. One morning she was discovered half-drowned, having fainted and fallen into the lily pond. And now this business of the ringworm. A month ago she had asked permission to go and visit distant cousins at Ficarazzi. An enormous man with goatskin leggings had come to fetch her in a cart painted with the most beautiful pictures of paladins, trees and horses. Fila got in between a dog and a sack of grain. She went off swinging her legs and looking happy. Marianna remembers waving to her from the window, following with her eyes the minute figure on the cart with its gaudy colours, going off towards Bagheria.

For Saro's wedding Marianna had given a big party with wine from her cellars and many different kinds of fish: from mackerel and amberjack roasted over the embers to small boiled squid, from stuffed sardines to baked sole. Peppina had eaten so much that she felt quite ill. Saro seemed satisfied: the wife the Duchess had chosen for him was to his liking – small as a child, olive-skinned, her arms covered with hair, a fresh mouth with strong white teeth, large dark eyes melting like two coffee ices.

She has soon shown herself to be an intelligent and strong-willed girl, even though she is as wild as a goat. Used to suffering hunger and to working like a slave at home, mending other people's nets beneath the sun, making do with a piece of bread spread with garlic, she demonstrates her contentment by eating anything and everything, running everywhere and singing at the top of her voice. She laughs a lot and is as stubborn as a mule, but she obeys her husband because she knows it is her duty. However, she has a way of obeying him that has nothing servile about it: as if each time it is she who has made the decision about what has to be done, according to her own wishes, like a powerful queen. Saro treats her like a pet animal that belongs to him. Sometimes he plays with her on the carpet in the yellow room, throwing her to the ground, tickling her, laughing until they cry. At other times he forgets about her for days on end.

If uncle husband were alive he would chase both of them out, Marianna tells herself, but instead she tolerates them, even taking pleasure in watching them as they play. Since Saro has been married she feels much calmer. She does not walk on tiptoe any more to avoid the snares set for her throughout the day. She is no longer in terror of being left alone with him, she does not wait to see him pass beneath her window in the morning, with his freshly laundered shirt open at his delicate throat, a lock of hair sliding over his temple. She has given Peppinedda the task of helping Innocenza in the kitchen and the girl has shown herself to be very good at gutting fish, at scraping off the scales without splattering them around, and at preparing a sauce of garlic and oil, marjoram and rosemary for grilling them.

Like Fila, Peppinedda refused to wear shoes at first. Although she has been given two pairs, one of leather and one of embroidered silk, she has always gone around barefoot, leaving small damp footprints on the polished floors of the rooms. Now she is five months pregnant, she has stopped playing with Sarino and carries her belly around like a trophy. She ties her black hair lightly behind her neck with a brilliant red bow. She walks with her legs apart as if she might ladle the child out then and there in the middle of the kitchen or the yellow room, but she has not lost any of her skills. She wields the kitchen knife like a hefty soldier, she talks little or not at all, and having at first stuffed herself with food, she now pecks at it like a young sparrow.

On the other hand, she steals. Not money or precious objects, but sugar and biscuits and coffee and lard. She hides the food under the roof and then, as soon as she can, makes her way to Palermo and gives everything to her sisters. Another of her obsessions is buttons. At the beginning she only used to take ones that had fallen off. But then she started to pull them off by twisting them in her fingers with a dreamy look. Recently she has got into the habit of cutting them with her teeth and if someone surprises her doing this she keeps the buttons in her mouth until she can put them in a safe place in her room, where she piles them up in an old box.

Saro, who has learned how to write reasonably well, tells Marianna everything about his young wife. It seems as if he especially enjoys telling her about these little dishonesties of his 'woman' Peppinedda, implying that if these things are going on the fault is entirely Marianna's because it was she who forced her on to him. But Marianna is entertained by Peppinedda's extravagances. She feels happy about this girl who is somewhat round-shouldered, strong as a bull-calf, wild as a buffalo, silent as a fish. Saro is rather ashamed of her but has learned to keep quiet about it. He has committed to memory the precepts of the nobility and learned them well: never to show his real feelings, never to be serious, to make good use of his eyes and tongue but without calling attention to himself.

'Peppinedda has stolen once more. What should I do?'

'Thrash her!' writes Marianna and hands him the sheet of paper with a look of amusement.

'She is expecting a baby. And then she bites me.'

'Then let her alone.'

'Suppose she steals again?'

'Thrash her twice.'

'Why don't you thrash her?'

'She is your wife. It's your business.'

But she knows full well that Saro will never beat her. Because
at bottom he is afraid of her, he fears her in the same way as one
fears a stray dog which if disturbed can sink its teeth into one's
leg without a moment's hesitation.

But now Fila has fainted in the middle of the library. Innocenza,
rather than taking care of her, is using her apron to clean up the
pitch where it has run on to the carpet.

Marianna bends over the girl. She holds her open palm against
her chest and feels her heart beating slowly, sluggishly. She presses
her finger on the vein that runs down her neck; it is pulsating
regularly. Yet she is icy cold as if she were dead. She must be
lifted up; she makes a sign to Innocenza, who takes hold of her
feet. Marianna herself lifts her shoulders and together they lay her
on the couch. Innocenza unties her apron and spreads it over the
cushions so that they will not get dirty. From the expression on
her face it is evident that she very much disapproves of a little
servant like Fila lying down on the couch lined with the white
and gold of the house of Ucrìa, even if she has fainted, even if
it is with the permission of the Duchess.

She is altogether too odd, this duchess, she lacks a sense of
proportion. . . . Everyone has their place and if they didn't the
world would become like a circus. . . . Today Fila, tomorrow Saro
and even that little thief Peppinedda. Between her and a bitch the
only difference is the paws. . . . How the Duchess manages to put
up with her she can't imagine. But that fat Abbot Carlo found
the girl for her and she took her on. . . . In the time it takes
to turn round every drop of oil has disappeared, once a week
she clings behind the Duchess's little carriage or the gig drawn
by the little black horse that belongs to her daughter Felice the
nun, with her bodice stuffed with all her pickings. . . . That
blockhead of a husband knows all about it but what does he
do? . . . Nothing . . . God knows where his head is . . . he seems
to be smitten with love . . . and the Duchess protects him . . . she
has lost all authority . . . all restraint. If Duke Pietro were here
he would lash everyone really hard . . . that poor Duke hanging
from a nail in the catacombs of the Capuchins, and his skin has
got like a leather armchair, it hangs from his bones like a used

glove pulled over his teeth, it's as if he were laughing, but it's not a laugh it's a sneer. . . . He must have known of her passion for gold because when he died he left four hundred Roman *grani* with a papal eagle and *ut commonius* engraved on the back, and three gold coins with the face of Charles II, King of Spain.

Marianna bends over Fila, buries her face in the full cotton sleeves smelling of basil, and tries to forget Innocenza; but she is still there flooding her with words. There are some people who make a present of their thoughts with a bitter, defiant malignity, even if they are entirely unconscious of doing so. One of these is Innocenza, who, along with her affection, unloads a stream of senseless chatter on her.

She must find a husband for Fila, she says to herself. She will give her a good dowry. Yet she is not aware of her ever having fallen in love; not with one of the footmen, nor with an innkeeper, nor a shoemaker, nor a cowman, as happens continually with the living-out servants. She always follows her brother around and when she cannot be with him she stays by herself with her head slightly to one side, her eyes lost in space, her mouth shut tight in a pained expression.

It will be best for her to get married as soon as possible and to have a child immediately, Marianna repeats to herself, and smiles to find that she is coming out with the very same proposals her mother would have made, or her grandmother, or even her great-grandmother, who lived through the plague in Palermo in 1624. 'Santa Ninfa could not help them, nor Santa Agata, who was the protector of the city. Another very beautiful saint of noble birth from the ancient family of the Sinibaldi della Quisquina, little Santa Rosalia, was the only one who knew how to say to the plague "Enough, be off!"' Grandmother Giuseppa had written in one of her exercise books; Marianna has kept the sheet of paper among the notes from her father.

To marry, to have children, to marry off the daughters, for them to have children, so that their daughters marry and have children, who in their turn marry and have children. . . . Voices of the family tradition, low sugary voices that have rolled down the centuries, feathering the nest in which to keep the precious egg that is the Ucrìa dynasty related through the female line to the greatest families of Palermo. They are the confident voices that sustain with their noble life-blood the sap of the family tree weighed down with its branches and leaves. Every leaf with a name and a date. Signoretto, Prince of Fontanasalsa, 1179, next to several very small dead leaves: Agata, Marianna, Giuseppa, Maria, Teresa. Carlo Ucrìa, 1315, another leaf; and alongside Fiammetta, Manina, Marianna. Some became nuns, others married, all have sacrificed themselves and all their possessions, together with their younger brothers, to preserve the integrity of the family lineage.

The family name is an orc, a monster from the sea, a jealous Hercules, which devours everything with the voracity of a swine: fields of grain, vineyards, hens, sheep, rounds of cheese, houses, furniture, rings, pictures, statues, carriages, silver candlesticks, all put into circulation under this name that repeats itself on the tongue like an incantation.

Marianna's leaf is still alive only because Uncle Pietro unexpectedly inherited an estate and someone had to be found to marry such an eccentric character. 'Marianna' is inscribed in letters of gold in the centre of a small offshoot between the two branches of the Ucrìa family; one of these was on the point of extinction through the eccentricity of the only son Pietro, while the other was more prolific but also more dangerously unbalanced and on the edge of bankruptcy.

Marianna has found herself drawn into an age-old family stratagem: up to her neck in a scheme to unite the two branches of the family. But also completely unconnected with it because of her impairment, which has resulted in her being an observer, free from the malign spell of her own kind. 'Corrupted by books,' as Aunt Teresa the Prioress used to say; everyone knows that books are harmful and that what the Lord wants is a virgin soul who perpetuates over the centuries the customs of the dead with a blind passion of love, without reservations, without questioning, without doubts.

It is because of this that she is overwhelmed, kneeling on the carpet beside the servant with the wounded head, who writhes like a worm. Bewildered by the ancestral voices that ask for her respect and loyalty, she finds other petulant voices like that of Mr David Hume with his green turban asking her to be daring and to send to the devil that mountain of inherited superstition.

194

XXXVI

Hurried breathing, the smell of camphor and cabbage-leaf poultices: every time she comes into the room it seems to her as if she were reliving her son Signoretto's illness, the distress of laboured breathing, the foetid smell of sweat sticking to the skin, restless sleep, bitter tastes and mouths dry with fever.

Events have happened so quickly that she has not had time to think about them. Peppinedda was delivered of a little boy, round as a ball and covered with black hair. Fila helped the midwife to cut the cord, to clean the new-born baby with soap and water, and dry him with warm towels. She seemed pleased with this nephew fortune had presented to her. Then one night while the mother slept with the baby in her arms, Fila dressed herself up as if she were going to mass, went down into the kitchen, armed herself with the knife used for gutting fish and in the half-light approached the bed and began to stab the two bodies lying there, that of the mother and that of the baby. She did not realise that Saro was with them, his head on Peppinedda's shoulder. He suffered the fiercest blows, one on his thigh, one on his chest and one on his ear.

The baby died. No one knows if he was crushed beneath his father or his mother; what is certain is that he died of suffocation, without any marks from the knife. Peppinedda came out of it with one cut on her arm and a few surface scratches on her neck.

By the time Marianna came down to the ground floor, propelled along on Innocenza's arm, it was already morning and four men from the Vicaria were taking Fila away bound like a sausage. After a trial lasting three days she was sentenced to be hanged. And Marianna, not knowing who else to turn to, went to Giacomo Camalèo, the city Praetor and first among the senators, in the hope of interceding for her. The child was dead, but not from his aunt's stabs. Saro had survived and so had Peppinedda.

'A wrong that goes unpunished only breeds further crime', Camalèo wrote on the small piece of paper she held out for him.

'She will be punished anyway if she is sent to prison', she replied, trying to control the trembling of her fingers. She was longing to run home to Saro. She had left him in the hands of the leech Pozzolungo, in whom she had little trust. At the same time she was desperate to save Fila from the gallows. But Don Camalèo was in no hurry, he watched her with glistening eyes that occasionally lit up with a flash of interest.

And she had written again, steadying her wrist, recalling Hippocrates, quoting Saint Augustine. After half an hour he softened a little and offered her a glass of Cyprus wine, which he kept on a chest of drawers. And she, hiding her anxiety, made an effort to drink it, smiling graciously, humbly.

In his turn Don Camalèo quoted at length from Saint-Simon and Pascal, filling sheets of paper with a queer handwriting full of dots and flourishes, stopping every three words to blow on his goose quill dripping with ink.

'Each life is a microcosm, my dear Duchess, a living thought that is struggling to emerge from its own shadowy regions.'

Playing the same game, she answered him demurely, perfectly in control. The Praetor assumed a pompous look, entertained and amused by this exchange of erudition. A woman who has read Saint Augustine and Socrates, Saint-Simon and Pascal is not an everyday occurrence, his eyes were saying, and he must make the most of it. With her he could marry gallantry with scholarship, he could display all his learning without arousing boredom and uneasiness as was usually the case with the women he paid court to.

Marianna was obliged to swallow her haste, to forget it. She remained there discussing philosophy and drinking Cyprus wine in the hope that in the end she would extract a promise from him. The Praetor did not seem in the least worried by the disablement of his lady interlocutor. He even seemed pleased that she was unable to talk, since it allowed him to show off his knowledge in writing, omitting the usual intervals of chit-chat that obviously bored him. By the end he had made her a promise to intercede with the Court of Justice to rescue Fila from the gallows, suggesting that she should be detained as a madwoman in San Giovanni de' Leprosi.

'From what you tell me the girl acted out of love, and the madness of love is the bread of so much literature: was not Orlando mad? And did not Don Quixote bow down before a laundry maid and address her as "Princess"? Madness then, what is it if not an excess of wisdom, a wisdom without those contradictions that make it imperfect and therefore human? Reason, taken in its crystal integrity, in its dogma of caution, comes very nigh to perdition. If we apply to the letter the rules of rational knowledge, without either speculating or doubting, we fall into the hell of madness.'

The next morning a small carriage arrived in the Via Alloro, laden with flowers, two huge bunches of pink gladioli and one of yellow lilies, as well as a box of sweets. A little black boy had delivered it all to the kitchen and had gone away without waiting even to be thanked.

When Marianna went back to find out what had been decided by the Court of Justice, Don Camalèo seemed so delighted to see her that she felt quite alarmed. What if he expected something in return? The enthusiasm he demonstrated was excessive, and vaguely menacing. He gave her the best chair in the room, offered her the usual wine from Cyprus, and almost snatched out of her hand the sheet of paper that she passed to him to write down two lines from Boiardo:

Whoever greets her, speaks with her, whoever touches her,
Whoever sits with her, for him all past time will be forgot.

Eventually after two hours of literary bravura he had written that Fila was already at the Leprosi in her own interest, and that she could remain there in peace because they were not going to hang her.

Marianna had raised her blue eyes uncertainly to the Praetor, but she was immediately reassured. His face expressed a pleasure that went beyond that of a normal exchange of favours. But with his studies at the University of Salerno, his apprenticeship at the bar of Reggio Calabria, his long sojourn spent studying in Tübingen, the senator regarded blackmail as too crude a weapon for a true man of power.

He gave her permission to send every day to the Leprosi a footman with fresh bread, cheese and fruit, without however warning her that there was no guarantee the provisions would reach her protégée. In the mornings Marianna would from time to time see the Praetor arrive in a little carriage drawn by a dappled horse. She would rush to tidy her hair which had fallen on to her shoulders, and receive him severely dressed with all her writing paraphernalia to hand.

He awaited her in the yellow room, standing in front of one of Intermassimi's chimeras, which seemed to be always pining for the love of whoever was looking at them. But it was sufficient for the observer to turn his back for the same look to transform itself into a mocking grimace. When she entered, the Praetor bowed down almost to the ground, diffusing a subtle scent of gardenias. He fixed her with metallic eyes made soft by honey of a flavour that pleased him above all else. He came to talk to her about the 'poor madwoman', as he called Fila, shut away in the Leprosi under his 'gracious' protection. Always kind and polite, always preceded by armfuls of flowers and sweets, he was perfectly happy to come all the way to Bagheria to visit her. He would seat himself on the edge of the chair and hold the pen with great elegance as he wrote.

Marianna served him with hot chocolate flavoured with cinnamon, or raisin wine from Málaga with its sweet scent of dried figs. The first notes were of courteous formality: 'How is Her Grace the Duchess this morning?' 'Has her sleep been propitious?' Having swallowed two cups of hot, well-sugared chocolate and stuffed his mouth with little cakes filled with fresh ricotta, Camalèo began to send his pen darting over the sheet of white paper like a small lizard. His eyes lit up, his mouth took on a firm fold of satisfaction and he would go on for hours, talking or rather writing about Thucydides and Seneca, but also about Voltaire, Machiavelli, Locke and Boileau. Marianna began to think that at bottom she was merely an innocent pretext for a firework display of learning, and he fell in with this, always bringing new pens, little bottles of Indian ink just arrived from Venice, paper edged with a blue border, ashes to dry the words as soon as they were written.

By this time she no longer experienced fear but only curiosity about this kaleidoscopic intelligence and also – why not? – a certain liking, especially when he wrote with his head down, holding the paper in his open hand. His hands were the most beautiful things in a disproportionate body, its long elegant torso in striking contrast to its two short stumpy legs.

It is strange how the awkward body of the Praetor should insinuate itself into her anxieties about Saro's wounds. Now I am here next to him, Marianna says to herself, and I do not want to, must not, think of anything except that his life is in danger. Saro spends his time sleeping, but it seems that it is something more deep-seated and more dangerous than sleep that numbs him and keeps him a prisoner. His wounds have not healed.

Fila struck him with such violence that even though the surgeon Ciullo came at once from Palermo and sewed him up with great skill, his blood is no longer circulating with the joy it used to have, and his wounds are tending to suppurate.

Peppinedda, after the knife attack, has gone back to her father. So it falls to Marianna to take care of his wounds, alternating with Innocenza, who, however, does it with great reluctance, especially at night. For the first few days the unfortunate Saro tossed about as if he were battling against enemies trying to tie him up or gag him or imprison him inside a sack. Now, exhausted, he seems to have given up the attempt to escape from his sack and passes his time sleeping, though now and again he is overcome by a painful restlessness and convulsed by tearless sobbing. Marianna keeps him company, sitting in an armchair by his bedside. She cleans his wounds, renews the bandages and moistens his lips with a little lemon and water.

Several physicians have been to see him. Not Cannamela, who is now old and half-blind, but other younger ones: among them one by the name of Pace, who has a great reputation for his skill. He arrived one morning on horseback, wrapped in the kind of large hooded cloak that in Palermo is called a *giucche*. He felt the invalid's pulse, smelled his urine and made a face. It was hard to be sure whether he was expressing uncertainty or simply wished to put on an air of enquiry and speculation befitting a scientist faced with a sick body that is anyway destined to decay. Finally he decreed that it was necessary to apply leeches.

'He has already lost a lot of blood, Doctor Pace', Marianna had written in haste, resting her sheet of paper on the bedside table. But the physician was not prepared to discuss the matter. He regarded her note as an insult and was deeply offended. He pulled down the collar of his cloak and went off, not however without having first collected his fee, including the additional expense of the journey, with hay and new horseshoes for his horse.

In the end Marianna sent for help from her daughter Felice, who arrived with her herbs, her decoctions, her poultices of nettles and mallow. She cured his wounds with cabbage leaves and herbal vinegar *dei sette ladre*.

In less than a week Saro has begun to improve very slightly, although he is still enveloped in the sweetish smell of his dressings. He remains motionless between the sheets, white on white, his chest bandaged, his ear packed round with cotton, his leg bound up like a mummy. Every so often he opens his grey eyes, unable to decide whether to withdraw to the restful shadows of the beyond or to return to a life consisting of knives and bowls of soup that have somehow to be swallowed.

Marianna presses his hand: as she pressed Manina's hand when she was nearly dying of a blood infection after childbirth; as she pressed the hand of her father the Duke, except that when she took it he was already dead and there was an icy smell of mortal flesh about him. A litany of illnesses and deaths which have taken the splendour from the scaffolding of her thoughts; each death a rubbing in of grains of salt; her head marred by bruises and scars from which there is no recovery.

Now here she is, like a patient dove brooding over its egg, hoping to see the emergence of a beautiful young dove with a will to live. She could send for Peppinedda. Indeed, she knows that this is what she ought to do, but she has no wish to do it: she puts it off from day to day. Peppinedda will come back when she feels the need to stuff herself with food, to steal buttons and to roll around on the carpets.

XXXVII

Will it be compromising for her to go to San Giovanni de' Leprosi with Senator Giacomo Camalèo, Praetor of Palermo? Could it be seen as an act of folly that will put her brothers and her children against her?

These questions course through Marianna's head at the very moment she puts her foot on the footboard of the two-horse carriage that awaits her in the courtyard of the Villa Ucrìa. A gloved hand helps her to pull herself up. As she enters the carriage she is met by a strong scent of gardenia. Don Camalèo is dressed in dark clothes, with breeches and redingote in chestnut brown threaded with gold, a black and chestnut tricorn slipping over his powdered curls, his pointed shoes illumined by silver rosettes studded with diamonds.

Marianna sits down facing him and immediately takes out of her bag of silver mesh the wooden holder with pen and ink and the little table very like the one given her by her father the Duke and later stolen from her at Torre Scannatura.

The senator smiles in tribute to the Duchess's skill: he will be obliged to lead off with a stream of letters stuffed with quotations from Hobbes and Plato, and thus intimacy will be avoided. But he hazards a guess that one of the letters he intends to write will be preserved in the box with Chinese designs: the letter in which he reveals himself most, telling her about his studies at Tübingen when he was thirty years younger.

'I used to live in a tower with three floors that looked out over the river Neckar. I would spend the afternoons there with my books beside one of those big blue and white majolica stoves. If I looked up I could see the poplars along the river, the swans always waiting for someone to throw them bread out of a window. They made deep throaty sounds and they used to have terrible fights with each other during the mating season. I hated that river, I hated those houses with their steep roofs, I hated those swans with the voices of pigs, I hated the snow that threw a blanket of silence over the entire city, I even hated the beautiful girls with fringed shawls as they went to and fro along the island. The garden in front of the tower was actually part of a long gloomy island where the students used to walk between one class and the next. But now I would give ten years of my life to return to that yellow tower on the banks of the Neckar and hear the guttural cries of the swans. I would even be happy to eat their greasy sausages, I would even admire those fair girls whose shoulders were draped with coloured shawls. Is it not an aberration of the memory to love only what it has lost? Just why do we lose these things, only to languish with nostalgia for the same places and the same people that earlier bored us to extinction? Is not all this predictable, vulgar folly?'

Only once during the journey from Bagheria to Palermo does Don Giacomo Camalèo grasp Marianna's hand and press it for a moment in his, as if to reaffirm his thoughts, letting go of it immediately with a regretful and respectful expression.

Marianna, who is not very used to being courted, does not know how to react. She holds herself a little stiffly and looks out of the window at the countryside she knows so well. Bending slightly over the little writing-table she slowly writes out sentences, careful not to spill the ink, and drying the words with ashes while they are still damp.

Fortunately, Don Camalèo's courtship consists principally of writing sophisticated sentences and learned discourses that aim to excite admiration more than attraction, in spite of the fact that he is certainly not a man to despise the pleasures of the flesh. But so far, his eyes seem to be saying, the bonds between them have yielded unripe fruit, extracting a juice that sets the teeth on edge as they force out the pulp. Haste is for the young, who do not know the delights of waiting, the desire to protract a surrender so as to enhance it with more intense and delicate flavours.

Thoughtfully Marianna watches the prudent gestures of his fine hands, so used to seizing the world by the scruff of the neck, but careful not to cause it any harm so that he can enjoy it in a state of quiet contemplation. So different from the men, possessed by haste and greed, she has known up to now: compared with Camalèo, uncle husband was a rhinoceros. On the other hand he was as transparent as the waters of Fondachello. Her father too was of another mould: erudite and witty but without ambition. It had never occurred to him to plan a strategy for his life; he had never seen the future as an opportunity to sum up and preserve his victories and defeats; it would never have entered his mind to defer a pleasure so as to make it in the end more enjoyable.

When they arrive at San Giovanni de' Leprosi Don Camalèo jumps down from the carriage, displaying the agility of his fifty-five years without an ounce of excess fat, and delicately offers her his hand. But Marianna does not take it. She too jumps down and with a merry silent laugh meets him boldly in the eye. He is left a little off balance; he knows that women, when they are being courted, like to make themselves appear weaker and more fragile than they are. But then he laughs with her and takes her by the arm as if she were a fellow student.

A minute later they are both facing a massive iron door. Keys turn in the lock; a heavy hand stretches out and makes incomprehensible signs with its fingers. There are bows, a running of guards, a glitter of swords. . . .

Now a warder with broad shoulders precedes the Duchess down a bare passage while the Praetor shuts himself inside a room with two tall gentlemen, who from the style of their hats are Spaniards. Along the passage there are alternate doors, one of iron, one of wood, one of wood, one of iron, one polished, one unpolished, one unpolished, one polished. On each door a rectangular grill, and behind the grill curious faces, suspicious eyes, tousled heads, mouths that open over broken and blackened teeth.

A bolt slides, a door is pushed. Marianna finds herself inside a cold room with a floor of broken and dusty bricks. The windows are too high to be reached. The light drifts down from the ceiling like rain, the walls are bare and dirty, stained with black marks and sinister red blotches. On the ground are heaps of straw and iron buckets. A fearsome stench of caged humanity catches her by the throat. The warder makes a sign to her to sit down on a straw-bottomed chair that is so worn, with the ends of the straw curling up in the air, that it seems to have been eaten by rats.

Behind a grating the courtyard can be seen, with its bare stone paving softened by a single fig tree. Against the end wall a half-naked woman is asleep, curled up on the ground. Nearer, tied to a bench, another woman, with white hair that slips out beneath a patched bonnet, endlessly repeats the same gesture of spitting into the distance. Her bare arms show weals from a cane. Beneath the fig tree a little girl of about eleven years old knits with a slow precise action.

Meanwhile a finger brushes against Marianna's cheek; she draws back with a start. It is Fila, her head wrapped in a turban of dirty bandages that makes her features seem smaller and her eyes larger. She smiles happily. Her hands hardly tremble. She has got so much thinner that from behind Marianna would never have recognised her. A long dress of sackcloth comes down in tatters to her ankles. It has no belt round the waist and no collar, and her arms are bare and covered with bruises.

Marianna gets up and embraces her. The animal smell that fills the room penetrates right inside her nostrils: it is horrifying. In a few months Fila has become an old woman, her face wizened; she has lost a front tooth, her hands shake, her legs are so withered that they can hardly support her weight, her eyes are glazed even when they are stretched into a smile of recognition.

When Marianna caresses her cheek, Fila dissolves into a timid weeping that creases up her mouth. Marianna, to overcome her embarrassment, brings a little purse of money from her pocket and encloses it between the girl's fingers. She tries to hide it and, feeling in vain for pockets in the asylum uniform, ends up clutching the little purse in her hand, looking round her in terror. Marianna then takes the scarf of green silk from her neck and puts it round Fila's shoulders. Fila strokes it with fingers trembling like those of a drunkard. She has stopped crying and is smiling seraphically. Then she suddenly lowers her head as if to avoid a blow, and her face darkens.

A guard with powerful arms catches her round the waist and lifts her up as if she were a child. Marianna is about to intervene but recognises the tenderness in the man's action. While he holds up the girl he talks to her gently, cradling her in his arms. Marianna tries to catch the sense of what he is saying by reading his lips, but she does not succeed. It is a language only they understand, that they have refined over months of enforced cohabitation. And she watches Fila, who contentedly stretches up her shaking hands and encircles the neck of the giant as if she were drunk, resting her head affectionately against his chest.

The two vanish behind the door before Marianna can say goodbye to Fila. It is better like this; the guard has achieved, if not affection, at least an intimacy with the poor girl, Marianna tells herself. Even though the way the man looked at the little purse of money makes her wonder whether this intimacy is entirely disinterested.

XXXVIII

It is two days now since Saro started to eat again. His eyes seem to have grown larger inside the hollow sockets. His white cheeks become flushed with red whenever Marianna approaches his bed. He is still bandaged like a mummy, but the bandages tend to slip and unwind. His body tosses about, his muscles are returning to life and he cannot rest his head quietly on the pillow. His black quiff of hair has been washed and slides like the wing of a crow over his thin boy's face.

This morning Marianna has paid another visit to Fila and is bathing herself in bergamot water to take away the nauseous smells of the asylum. Inside the copper bath-tub that comes from France and that, seen from outside, looks like an ankle boot, she is as comfortable as if she were in bed, with the water coming right up to her shoulders and staying hot for longer than it would in an open bath-tub. It is quite the fashion for well-to-do ladies to hold conversations, receive their women friends or give orders to the servants, seated in the new French baths that are sometimes shielded by a transparent screen out of modesty. Even though Marianna enjoys wallowing in the heat while Innocenza pours saucepans of steaming water over her, she does not stay long in it because she cannot write or read there without getting the pages wet.

Winter has arrived suddenly, almost without being preceded by autumn. Yesterday she was going round with bare arms, now the stove has to be lit, and she has to wrap herself in shawls and cloaks. There is an icy wind whipping up the waves on the sea and tearing the leaves off the trees.

Manina has just given birth to another baby, and has called her Marianna. Giuseppa came to see her only yesterday. She is the only one who confides in her. Talking about her husband she says that sometimes he loves her and at others hates her, and that her cousin Olivo is continually pressing her to run away with him to France.

On Sundays Felice comes to lunch. She is struck by the down-to-earth account her mother gives her of Fila and the asylum at the Leprosi. She too has sought permission to go and see her and has returned determined to found a network of 'helpers' for derelict women. The fact is, she has changed a great deal lately, having discovered that she has a gift for healing, and has dedicated herself to exploring ways of combining herbs, roots and minerals. After some early cures people have begun to ask for her in difficult cases of illness, especially for skin diseases. And she, faced with responsibility towards the wounded bodies that are entrusted to her, has taken to studying and experimenting. On her forehead has grown a furrow as straight and deep as a sabre cut. She is no longer so preoccupied with the immaculate state of her habit, and she leaves gossip to the younger nuns. She has acquired the busy and preoccupied look of a professional healer.

Her son Mariano, however, never comes. Lost as he is in day-dreams, he never finds time to go visiting his mother. But he has sent his uncle Signoretto to find out discreetly about the frequent visitor to the Villa Ucrìa, whom the relatives are talking about with such shocked outrage.

'It is not right that at your age you should put yourself in a position where everyone is talking about you', Signoretto has written with a wary hand on a page pulled out from a book of prayers. 'You are a widow and I hope you are not planning to make yourself look ridiculous by getting married at the age of forty-five to a libertine bachelor of fifty-five.'

'Don't worry, I have no intention of getting married.'

'Then you should not allow the senator Camalèo to come and visit you. It is not right to make people talk.'

'There is no physical relationship between us. It is purely a friendship.'

'At your age, my lady sister, you should think of preparing your soul for the beyond rather than looking for new friendships.'

'You are older than I, my lord brother, but it doesn't seem to me you are thinking of the beyond.'

'You are a woman, Marianna. Nature has destined you for a serene chastity. You have four children to think of. Mariano, who will inherit from you, is worried that you could convey your property elsewhere by a rash act that would be truly regrettable.'

'Even if I did remarry, I would not take away a crumb.'

'Perhaps you are ignorant of the fact that Camalèo, before becoming Praetor of Palermo, was for a long time paid by the French to spy on the Spaniards, and they say that he then went over to the Spaniards, having had a more advantageous offer from them. In short, you are dealing with an adventurer whose trustworthiness no one would dare to guarantee. An unknown traveller who has enriched himself through secret dealings, he is not a man an Ucrìa should associate with. It is the family's decision that you should not see him any more.'

'So the family decides. By what right?'

'Do not start talking nonsense to me like my wife Domitilla. I am sick to death of Voltaire.'

'Once upon a time even you used to quote from Voltaire.'

'The stupidity of youth.'

'I am a widow and I believe that I am perfectly capable of looking after my own affairs according to my own beliefs.'

'What nonsense, sister. Still the same old worthless rigmarole! You know very well that you are not alone but are part of a family, and that you cannot, not even with permission from Monsieur Voltaire and the support of all the saints in paradise, allow yourself to take any liberties. You must get rid of that man.'

'Camalèo is a kindly person. He has helped me to save a servant from the gallows.'

'Do not allow questions that have to do with servants to dictate your life. Certainly Camalèo is aiming to marry you. To become related to the Ucrìas would be part of a secret strategy. Believe me, this individual has no real interest in you. Do not trust him, I beg you.'

'I shall not trust him.'

Somewhat, even if not entirely, reassured, Signoretto left her after graciously kissing her hand. Everyone knows that her brother has had more lovers since he got married than he ever had before. Lately he has spent ridiculous sums of money on a singer who performs at the Santa Lucia theatre, who they say has also been the Viceroy's mistress. In spite of his authoritarian manner, she was pleased to see him, with that fair head of his, in which tenderness becomes clotted beneath the skin in the form of large inflamed wens. His way of looking slightly askance, questioning, reminds her of her father the Duke when he was young. But he lacks their father's ability to laugh at himself. He has developed a subtle insidious brutality that weighs on his swollen eyelids. And the more his habit of taking command grows, the more evident his own self-indulgence becomes, to such an extent that he can no longer distinguish a chair from a chamber-pot.

Heaven knows when he began to get these new bones that have hollowed out his eyes, broadened his pelvis and flattened the soles of his feet. Perhaps sitting in the Senate or going out to attend executions with the other White Brothers and accompanying the condemned prisoners to the gallows. Or perhaps night after night, lying in the big four-poster beside his wife, who, though she is still beautiful, has become so boring to him that he cannot bear to look at her.

In recent years the memory of uncle husband has suddenly jumped to the fore when she finds herself face to face with other men of the family. That anxious, lugubrious individual, always brooding resentfully on the shortcomings of others, was at bottom more truthful and direct, certainly more faithful to himself, than any of them. With their smiles and their politeness they have holed themselves up in their homes, scared of every novelty, of being reduced to accepting ideas and beliefs which they have laughed at for years. It could be a question of perspective: as Camalèo says, time has mellowed the fading memories. Her husband Pietro's belongings that are still around the house retain something of his morose, lonely melancholy. And yet that man had violated her when she was not yet six, and she asks whether she will ever be able to forgive him for that.

Nowadays it is Abbot Carlo who is closest to her, immersed like her in books. He alone is capable of making a judgement that is not vitiated by his own immediate interests. Carlo is true to his own self: a libertine in love with books. He does not pretend, he does not flatter, he does not pride himself on meddling in the intrigues of others.

As for her son Mariano, after the euphoria of growing up, the great hunt for love, the journeys round the world, now at thirty he has settled down and has become intolerant of any behaviour that he regards as a threat to his own peace of mind. Towards his sisters he adopts a dry, ill-natured tone; towards his mother he is respectful on the surface, but she realises that he is impatient of the liberties she takes in spite of her disablement. The fact that he has sent his uncle Signoretto to see her instead of coming himself highlights the character of his fears: suppose a freak of nature like his mother brought another son into the world while he has failed to have even one, and suppose this child attracted the interest of a widowed aunt of the Scebarràs line, whose inheritance he hopes for? And suppose the nonsense of a marriage outside the accepted rules recoiled on him who more than anyone else carries the weighty name of the Ucrìas of Campo Spagnolo and Scannatura?

Mariano is fond of luxuries: he buys his shirts from Paris, as if there were not perfectly good shirt-makers here in Palermo. He has his hair arranged by Monsieur Crème, who presents himself at the palace accompanied by four assistants who carry *le nécessaire pour le travail*: large and small boxes of soap, scissors, razors, combs, cream scented with lily of the valley and powders perfumed with carnations. For the care of the feet and hands there is Signor

Enrico Aragujo Calisto Barrés, who comes from Barcelona and has a shop in the Via Cala Vecchia. For ten *carlini* he also visits ladies in their homes and pares the corns of both young and old, who all have problems with the little Parisian shoes with points like a hen's neck and heels like the beak of a swan.

Marianna rouses herself from her thoughts when Saro grasps her hand with a new vigour. He seems to be getting better, he really seems to be getting better. He opens his eyes. A fresh look, naked, emerging from the embrace of a pod like a bean, still soft from sleep. Marianna draws close to him and lays a finger on his cracked lips. His light breath, moist and regular, caresses her hollow palm. A feeling of happiness holds her immobile in that gesture of tenderness as she inhales his acid breath.

Now Saro's mouth presses on her fingers and he kisses her hand anxiously on the inside of her palm. For the first time Marianna does not repulse him. Instead she shuts her eyes as if better to savour his touch. They are kisses that come from a long way back, from that first evening when they saw each other by the wavering light of the candle in the stained mirror in Fila's room.

But the effort seems to have exhausted him. He continues to hold Marianna's fingers against his mouth but he does not kiss them any more. His breath has become irregular, hurried, spasmodic. Gently Marianna takes her hand away. From sitting in the armchair, she kneels down on the floor beside the bed and leans forward on top of the blankets. She rests her forehead on his chest, something she has often imagined but has never brought herself to do. Beneath her ear she can feel the thickness of the bandages impregnated with camphor, and below them the half-moon of his ribs, and below that the tempestuous throbbing of his blood.

Saro lies quite still, anxious lest any movement on his part might interrupt Marianna's timid advances towards him, afraid that she might at any moment retreat, as she has always done before. So he waits for her to decide, holding his breath and keeping his eyes closed, hoping, desperately hoping that she will hold him close to her.

Marianna's fingers glide across his forehead, his ears, his neck as if she can no longer put her trust in her eyes. Passing over his hair, sticky with sweat, she pauses on the bulge of the bandage that conceals his left ear, then continues along the outline of his lips, moving down towards the chin, bristly with a convalescent's beard, returning to the nose as if the knowledge of this body could only pass through the tips of her fingers, as curious and exploratory as her gaze is faint-hearted and uncertain. Her forefinger pursues the long road that leads from one temple to the other, descends along the wings of the nostril, climbs up the hills of the cheeks, brushing the thickets of the eyebrows, finds itself almost by chance at the point where the lips come close together, forces a way between the teeth and reaches the tip of the tongue.

Only now does Saro risk an imperceptible movement: he closes his teeth, but with the lightest of pressure, across the finger that remains imprisoned between palate and tongue, enveloped in the feverish warmth of his saliva. Marianna smiles. And with the thumb and first finger of her other hand she pinches his nostrils until he lets her go and opens his mouth to breathe. Then she withdraws her wet finger and begins to explore all over again. He looks at her blissfully, his eyes tell her that his blood is quickening.

Now the hands of the Duchess grasp the quilt and slide it off the bed. The same with the sheet: it is thrown to one side and falls to the floor in disordered folds. And here in front of her eyes, startled by their own daring, is the naked body of the young man, with only the bandages around his hips, on his chest and head. His ribs are there, protruding crescent moons like a map of the planets in their phases of progression, one following the other, one above the other.

Marianna's hands rest ever so gently on his barely healed wounds, still red and painful. The wound on the thigh reminds her of Ulysses attacked by the wild boar as he must have appeared to the stupefied nurse who was the first to recognise her lord and master returning after so many years of war, when everyone else still took him for a beggar. Marianna strokes him lightly with her fingers while Saro's breathing becomes quicker. From between his closed lips minute drops of saliva emerge that suggest pain but also an unimaginable savage joy, a blissful surrender.

How she came to find herself undressed beside Saro's naked body Marianna was unable to say. She knows it was very simple and that she felt no shame. She knows they were in each other's arms like two friendly bodies in harmony and that welcoming him inside her was like finding once more a part of her own body she had believed lost for ever. She knows she had never thought of enfolding in her own belly a man's flesh that was not either a child or an invading enemy.

Children find themselves in the body of a woman without her having summoned them, just as the flesh of uncle husband stayed warm inside her without her having ever invited or desired him. But she has desired and willed this body as she desired and willed her own joy. It would not pain and lacerate her as her children did every time she gave birth, but would slip away with the joyful promise of return once the spasm of love had been shared. For so many years of marriage she had thought the body of a man existed only to torment her. And she had yielded to this torment as one yields to the curse of God, a duty that no woman of refinement could accept without having to swallow gall. Had not Our Lord also swallowed gall in the garden of Gethsemane? Did He not die on the Cross without one word of recrimination? What was her trifling pain suffered in her own bed, compared to the sufferings of Christ?

And instead here is a body that is not alien to her, that does not assault her, does not steal from her, does not ask for sacrifice and renunciation, but goes to her confidently and gently. Here is a body that knows how to wait, that takes and knows how to be taken without any kind of force. How will she ever again do without it?

XXXIX

Peppina Malaga has come back to the house, two small black pigtails tied behind her ears with a piece of string, her feet bare as usual, her legs heavy and swollen, her protruding belly raising her skirt over her shin-bones. Marianna watches her through the window while she gets down from the cart and runs towards Saro. He looks up at the window as if to ask, What am I to do?

'Use not your scythe in the grain of others', says the austere Gaspara Stampa. It is her duty to leave husband and wife together for their own happiness. She will let them have a larger room where they can bring up the new baby.

And then:

> In my repose an inward doubt assails me
> That ever holds my heart 'twixt life and death.

Is it jealousy, that little fool, the 'green-eyed monster', as Shakespeare called it, 'that doth mock the meat it feeds on'? The Duchess Marianna Ucrìa di Campo Spagnolo, Countess of Paruta, Baroness of Bosco Grande, of Fiame Mendola and of Sollazzi, how can she ever be jealous of a scullery maid, of a fledgling fallen from the nest?

But that's exactly how it is: this dark ugly little girl seems to gather up in herself all the joys of paradise. She has the innocence of a pumpkin flower, the freshness of a grape stalk. Marianna tells herself that she would willingly give away all her estates and all her houses just to enter into that young determined little body that jumps down from the cart with the tiny baby curled up in her womb, to go and meet Saro.

Her hand releases its hold on the curtain, which falls back to cover the window. The courtyard vanishes and with it the cart pulled by a donkey adorned with plumes, and Peppinedda, who propels her belly towards her husband as if it were a box of jewels. Saro too disappears while clasping his wife close to him and raising his eyes towards Marianna with a look of theatrical resignation. But one can see that he is gratified by this double love. From this moment will begin a life of subterfuges, deceptions, escapes, clandestine meetings. There will be a need to corrupt, to keep others quiet, to erase all traces of every embrace. A sudden resentment clouds Marianna's eyes. She has no intention of falling into such traps, she tells herself. She has provided him with a wife so as to keep him at a distance and not to serve as a cover-up. So then? So then she has to break it off.

There is something arrogant about her thoughts, she knows that. She is not taking into account the pleasures of her body, which has woken for the first time to its own fulfilment, nor has she given a thought to Saro's wishes, she does not even consider consulting him. She will decide for or against him, but above all against herself. The long practice of renunciation has made her a vigilant custodian of herself. So many years spent keeping her own needs at arm's length have strengthened her will. Marianna looks at her wrinkled hands, which are wet from having been pressed against her cheeks. She raises them to her mouth. She tastes some of the salt that contains the bitterness of her renunciation.

She could marry Giacomo Camalèo: although she is not in love with him, she finds him attractive. And it is the second time he has asked her. But if she doesn't have the courage to seize hold of a love made of precious stones, will she ever be satisfied with one of glass? What is she to do with herself? At her age many of her acquaintances are already dead and buried, or have become hunchbacked and shrivelled and go about in closed carriages with a thousand precautions, surrounded by cushions and embroidered covers, reduced to a state of half-blindness by a veil that hangs down over their eyes, driven mad by too much suffering, made cruel and frustrated from waiting too long. She sees them shaking their plump fingers festooned with rings that can no longer be removed from their enlarged knuckles, but which, once they are dead, will be surreptitiously cut off by heirs and heiresses impatient to grab possession of those magnificent Chinese pearls, Egyptian rubies, and turquoises from the Dead Sea. Hands that have never held a book for longer than two minutes, hands that have had to learn the art of embroidery or how to play the spinet, but even then have never been permitted to dedicate themselves with any real seriousness: the hands of noblewomen, fated to be idle. They are hands that, although they have held gold and silver, have never known how it came to them. Hands that have never experienced the weight of a saucepan, or of a jug, or of a bowl, or even a duster. Possibly familiar with the beads of a rosary, mother-of-pearl or silver filigree, but entirely ignorant about the shape of their own bodies buried beneath a vast array of kerchiefs and camisoles and bodices and undervests and petticoats, considered by priests and pedagogues as sinful by nature. They have caressed, those hands, the heads of new-born babies, but they have never been immersed in their own ordure. They may have some time lingered over the wounds of Christ on the Cross, but they have never explored the naked body of a man, knowing that it would be considered as indecent by him as it would be by themselves. They have rested inert in their own laps, not knowing where to hide or what to

213

do, because any movement, any action was considered risky and undesirable for a girl of noble family.

With them, Marianna has eaten the same food and drunk the same soothing herbal teas. Since her hands have touched a lover's body, have explored its length and its breadth, she accepts them as friends and accomplices. But now she must cut them off and throw them on to the rubbish tip, Marianna tells herself, as she stands stiffly by the shuttered window. But a draught of air warns her that someone is approaching behind her.

It is Innocenza, carrying a candlestick with two branches. Looking up, Marianna sees the face of the cook very close to hers. She draws back in irritation but Innocenza continues to scrutinise her thoughtfully. She is aware that the Duchess is not well, and is trying to guess what is the matter. She places her plump hand, with its wholesome smell of rosemary mixed with soap, on her ladyship's shoulders and shakes her gently as if to liberate her from her prickly thoughts. Fortunately Innocenza does not know how to read so there is no necessity to write lies to her: a gesture is sufficient to reassure her.

The smell of fish that rises from Innocenza's apron helps Marianna to come out of her state of frozen torpor. The cook shakes her mistress with a rough impulse that is also full of good sense. They have known each other for years and believe they know everything about one another. Marianna believes she knows Innocenza through the intuitive sorcery that enables her to read other people's thoughts as if she could see them written on paper. In her turn Innocenza, having served her for so many years and listened to what others say about her, believes that Marianna does not have any secrets from her.

Now they look at each other, both curious about the other's curiosity. Again and again Innocenza wipes her oily hands on her cloth apron with red and white stripes. Marianna plays mechanically with her writing implements: the little folding table, the little silver ink bottle, the goose quill with its nib stained black. Innocenza takes her by the hand and leads her as if she were a small child who has been shut away as a punishment for too long and is now being taken back to be comforted and to join the others at the table. Marianna lets herself be led down the stone staircase, through the big yellow room, brushing past the spinet with its open keyboard, passing by the Roman dioscuri of streaked marble, beneath the secretive winking eyes of the chimeras.

In the kitchen Innocenza pushes her down into a chair in front of the lighted stove; she puts a glass in her hand, takes a bottle of sweet wine down from the shelf and pours out two measures. Then, taking advantage of the deafness and distracted state of mind of her mistress, she lifts the bottle to her mouth. Marianna pretends not to notice so that she does not have to rebuke her. But then she thinks again: why should she rebuke her anyway? With the impulsiveness of a little girl she takes the bottle from the cook's hands and presses it to her mouth. Servant and mistress smile at each other. They pass the bottle between them, one seated, her fair hair arranged over a broad perspiring forehead, her light-blue eyes growing wider and wider, the other standing up, her large belly hidden under her stained apron, her strong arms, her handsome round face rippling into a beatific smile.

Now it is easier for Marianna to come to a decision, even if it is a cruel one. Innocenza will help her, without knowing it, by keeping her a prisoner in the safe, everyday world. She can already feel on her neck Innocenza's two hands, stained by smoke, scarred with cuts, burns and deep wrinkles.

She must get away on tiptoe and she needs a push that only a hand used to counting money can give her. Meanwhile the kitchen door has opened in the mysterious way in which doors do open in Marianna's eyes, without warning, with a slow movement, heavy with surprises. It is Felice who stands on the threshold, the little sapphire cross on her chest. Beside her is Cousin Olivo, in his redingote the colour of a turtle-dove, his long face looking greatly upset.

'Your sister-in-law Donna Domitilla has broken her foot. I spent the morning with her', reads Marianna on a curled piece of paper her daughter hands her.

'Don Vincenzino Alagna has shot himself to escape his debts but his wife is not putting on mourning. No one could stand that blockhead, that prickly pear. Their little daughter had erysipelas last year and I cured her myself.'

'I've brought Olivo. He is begging me for a remedy that will cure him of being in love. What do you say, Mamma, should I give it to him?'

'At the Leprosi they won't let me in any more. They say I bring

215

disruption there. All because I cured a woman with sores when the doctor had given her up for dead. But Mamma, what's wrong with you?' . . .

XL

The brigantine moves along, scarcely swaying on the green water. In front, like a fan, is the city of Palermo, a line of grey- and ochre-coloured palaces, grey and white churches, hovels painted pink, shops with green striped awnings, streets of cobblestones cut in half by rivulets of dirty water. Behind the city, beneath the continuous gusting of dense cloud, lie the craggy rocks of Monte Cuccio, the green woods of Mezzo Monreale and of San Martino delle Scale, the gradual descent of steep cliffs shifting from dark to less dark, between which nestles the violet light of the sunset.

Marianna's eyes focus on the high windows of the Vicaria. To the left of the prison, behind a small terrace of houses, the irregular rectangle of the Piazza Marina widens out. In the middle of the empty piazza is the dark platform of the gallows. A sign that someone will be strung up tomorrow. Like that gallows to which her father the Duke dragged her out of love in an attempt to cure her dumbness. She would never have imagined that her father the Duke and uncle husband shared the same secret concerning her; and that they were in alliance to keep quiet about the wound inflicted on her child's body.

Now the brigantine is shaken by slow nervous jolts. The sails have been hoisted; the prow steers directly for the open sea. Marianna leans with both hands against the painted railings while Palermo fades into the distance with its afternoon lights, its palm trees, its refuse blown about by the wind, its gallows, its carriages. A part of her will remain there in those streets splashed with mud, in that warmth smelling of sugar-sweet jasmine and horse dung.

Her thoughts veer to Saro and the times she held him close,

216

even though she has made the decision not to see him any more. A hand grasped beneath the table, an arm held out behind a door, a kiss snatched in the kitchen during the hours of sleep. They were delights to which she abandoned herself with her heart turning somersaults. And it did not matter to her that Innocenza had guessed and looked at her with displeasure, and that the children gossiped about her, her brothers threatened to kill that 'boorish upstart', and Peppinedda spied on her with hostile eyes.

Meanwhile Camalèo was assiduous. He came to visit her almost every day in his gig drawn by the dappled grey, and talked to her of love and books. He told her she was becoming luminous like the lights on a fishing boat. And the mirror told her it was true: her skin had become clear and firm, her eyes shone, her hair fluffed up round her neck as if it had been leavened with yeast. No bonnet or ribbon could contain it, it exploded and fell back, scintillating and unruly about her happy face.

When she told Mariano she was leaving, he wrinkled his forehead with a comical grimace that was intended to show his disapproval, but which enabled her to guess his relief and satisfaction. He was not as good at dissimulating as his uncle Signoretto.

'But where are you going?'

'To Naples first of all; after that I don't know.'

'You will be alone?'

'I shall be taking Fila with me.'

'Fila is mad. You can't trust her.'

'I shall take her with me. She is well now.'

'A mad murderess and a disabled woman travelling together, really! What an idea! Do you want to make a laughing-stock of yourself?'

'No one will care.'

'I presume that Don Camalèo will be joining you. Is it your intention to bring discredit on the family?'

'Don Camalèo will not be following me. I am going alone.'

'And when do you return?'

'I do not know.'

'And who will take care of your daughters?'

'They are perfectly capable of looking after themselves. They are grown-up.'

'It will cost you a fortune.'

Marianna had rested her eyes on her son's head, still so

handsome in spite of incipient baldness, while he bent over the paper, tightening his grip on the pen. His white knuckles spoke of an unbearable rancour; he could not stand being torn away from his world of fantasy to face questions he did not understand and which did not interest him. His only anxieties were: What will people in his circle say about such an irresponsible mother? Will she end up spending too much? Will she get into debt? Will she have to ask for help over money, maybe from Naples, forcing him to withdraw God knows what sum?

'I shall not spend anything of yours', Marianna had written light-heartedly on the white paper. 'I shall only spend my own money. Rest assured I will not bring dishonour to the family.'

'You already have brought dishonour with your eccentricities. Since our father died you have continually brought nothing but scandal.'

'What scandals are you referring to, may I ask?'

'You only wore mourning for a year instead of for ever, as is decreed by custom. Do you not remember? Three years for the death of a father, ten years for the death of a son and thirty for the death of a husband, that is to say for ever. And then you do not go to church when there is a solemn mass. And you go around with low-class people, that servant, that upstart, you have made him master here. You have brought into the house not only his wife, but his sister and his son.'

'Actually, it was his sister who brought him. As for his wife, I myself gave her to him.'

'Precisely. You put too much trust in people who are not of your rank. I do not recognise you, lady mother. Once you were gentle and acquiescent. Do you know that you risk an interdict?'

Marianna shakes her head. Why think about these disagreeable things? Yet there is something in what her son has written that she does not understand: a rancour that goes far beyond the alleged scandals, the preoccupation with money. He has always been generous, why should he now be in such a state about his mother spending anything? Could it still be his childhood jealousy, from which he does not want and doesn't know how to detach himself? Has he still not forgiven her for having so blatantly preferred her younger son Signoretto?

Marianna looks at Fila's bald head, which is right beside her on the bridge of the ship, and stares at the city as it recedes towards the horizon. Now they are surrounded by waves of curling water while the figure-head thrusts its naked breast through the sea.

It was Saro's look that made her decide to leave. An involuntary early-morning look when, the light already broadening on the bedroom floor, she had prised her mouth from his shoulder and pushed him to get up. A look of love, satiated and apprehensive. The fear that this joy could be suddenly snatched from him for some unforeseeable reason which he was unable to control. Not just her body, but the elegant clothes, the whiteness of the linen, the essences of rose and myrrh, the pheasants cooked in wine, the lemon sorbets, the *gremolate* of strawberry grapes, the orange-flower water, the kindnesses, the silent tenderness, everything that was hers she found in Sarino's grey eyes, reflected splendours like those cities that can be seen in the noonday hours, turned upside down in the sea through the effect of a mirage, wet and shimmering with gauzy lights. Such mirages promised abundance, unending delights, only to vanish in the pale colourless glow of a summer sunset from across the sea. And she wanted to sweep away from the eyes of her lover the image of that happy city before it dissolved by itself in a shattering of broken mirrors.

So here she is on a heaving floor, the smell of the sea mixed with the sharp tang of tar and varnish, in the sole company of Fila.

XLI

It is evening. At the Captain's table, in the little saloon with a barrel roof, are seated an assortment of travellers who do not know each other from Adam: a deaf-mute duchess from Palermo, dressed in an elegant light coat with blue and white stripes, reminiscent of a Watteau painting; an English traveller with an unpronounceable name, who comes from Messina and wears a curious wig of pink curls; a nobleman from Ragusa, dressed all in black, who never allows himself to be separated from his small silver sword.

The sea is rough. From the two windows that open along the

side of the boat can be seen a yellowish sky streaked with lilac. The moon is full but obscured by shawls of stormy clouds that alternately conceal and reveal it. Fila has stayed in the dark cabin, lying down with a handkerchief soaked in vinegar over her mouth to guard against sea-sickness. She has been vomiting all day and Marianna has been holding her head as long as possible, but then she had to go out or she too would have started retching.

Now the Captain hands her a helping of boiled meat. The Englishman with the pink curls deposits a spoonful of fruit pickle on to his plate. The three men talk amongst themselves but every now and then turn towards Marianna and give her a polite smile. Then they continue chattering, perhaps in English, perhaps in Italian, Marianna cannot be sure which from the movements of their lips, and anyway it does not matter to her very much. After a first tentative effort to involve her in the conversation with the help of gestures, they have left her to her own thoughts. And she is relieved that they are occupied elsewhere; she feels clumsy and awkward. Astonishment at her new situation hampers her movements: it seems impossible for her to hold her fork steady between her fingers, and the lace edges of her sleeves keep falling on to her plate.

Remnants of thoughts float through her weary head. An impatient hand has buffeted those calm limpid waters that were there to drift in, and caused waves of memories, half-dissolved and scattered, to be thrown to the surface. The tender body of her son Signoretto, clinging to her breast like a breathless little monkey; the pain she had endured without being able to satisfy him. The pinched face of uncle husband when she had plucked up courage to look at him closely for the first time, and realised that his eyelashes had become white. The defiant eyes of her daughter Felice, a nun without a vocation, who has nevertheless found through herbal medicine her own kind of self-respect and now has no need of money because people pay her so well.

The little group of brothers and sisters as she painted them on that day in May when she had fainted in front of Tutui in the courtyard of the lodge; Agata's arms devoured by midges; Geraldo's pointed shoes, the same shoes that were later put on his feet inside his coffin, to be a testimonial for paradise, with the hope that he would go for long walks among the hills peopled with angels. The malicious laugh of her sister Fiammetta, who has become a little dotty with age: on the one hand she flagellates herself and wears a hair shirt, and on the other she never stops meddling in the love affairs of the entire family. The puzzled eyes of Carlo, who to preserve himself from desperation has assumed an ill-natured, irritable look. And Giuseppa, still anxious and unsatisfied, the only one who reads books and is able to laugh, the only one who has not disapproved of her eccentric behaviour and who came to see her off, in spite of her husband having forbidden her to do so. The walls of the villa at Bagheria with its soft sandstone bricks that, seen close to, look like sponges pierced by many tunnels, with holes inhabited by sea snails and minute translucent shells. In the whole world there is no softer colour than that of the sandstone of Bagheria, which receives light and holds it within like so many Chinese lanterns.

Her mother's face sagging from sleep, her nostrils darkened by snuff, her big blonde plaits flaking off her round shoulders. On the bedside table there were always three or four little bottles of laudanum. When she was grown-up Marianna discovered that this was composed of opium, saffron, cinnamon, cloves and alcohol. But in the recipes of the pharmacy in the Piazza San Domenico, the amount of opium had been increased at the expense of the cinnamon and saffron. Because of this she would sometimes find her unfortunate mother in the morning lying on the blankets, her eyes half-shut, an expression of rapture on her face, her skin with the pallor of a waxen statue.

And there, in the bedroom where Marianna had brought into the light of day all her five children, under the bored gaze of the chimeras, had come Saro with his slender legs and his gentle smile. On that bed of births and miscarriages they had come together, while Peppinedda wandered anxiously through the house, holding in her belly a son of ten months who could not make up his mind to be born: until the midwife had to force him out, by jumping on her as if she were a mattress full of straw. And just when it seemed she might die from loss of blood, an enormous baby came out, with the same colouring as Sarino, black and white and pink, the umbilical cord wound three times round his neck.

It was also on Peppinedda's account that she had made the decision to leave: because of those looks of feminine complicity and acceptance she gave her, almost saying that she was willing to share her husband in exchange for a house, clothes, abundant food, and turning a blind eye to her thefts for her sisters. It had become a family understanding, an 'arrangement' between three people, in which Saro took refuge, torn between apprehension and happiness: happiness that would soon have turned into satiety. But perhaps not, perhaps she was mistaken: caught between a mother lover and a child wife he might have carried on devotedly and tenderly for ever. He could have transformed himself, as he was already doing, into an image of himself: a satisfied young man about to lose his innocence and his happiness in exchange for an equal combination of fatherly indulgence and responsibility for the future of his family. She had heaped gold on them before she went away. Probably not from generosity, but to make them forgive her for abandoning them and to feel herself loved for a little while, even at a distance.

The English traveller with fine brown eyes has disappeared, leaving the food on his plate half-eaten. The Baron from Ragusa leans out of the tall window, gasping, while the Captain rushes two at a time up the narrow stairs that lead to the deck. What is going on?

Through the door there comes a strong smell of salt and wind. The waves seem to have turned into great horses. Enclosed in her egg of silence Marianna does not hear the cries from the bridge, the orders of the Captain to haul in the sails, the voices of the passengers sheltering under cover. She continues to put food into her mouth as if nothing were happening. No sign of the sea-sickness that has turned over the stomachs of her travelling companions. However, all at once the oil lamp slides dangerously across the table. Finally the Duchess realises that it is perhaps more than a slightly choppy sea. Drops of burning oil have fallen on to the tablecloth and have set fire to a napkin. If she does not take some immediate action about the linen the flames will spread to the table and from the table to the floor, which are both of dry seasoned wood.

Suddenly Marianna's chair begins to slide and crashes against the deckhead, its back cracking the glass of a picture frame. To die like this, sitting in her striped travelling cloak with the lapis-lazuli brooch her father the Duke gave her pinned to the collar, a taffeta rose in her hair: that would indeed be a theatrical exit. Perhaps one of her mother's dogs is about to seize her round the waist and drag her into the black water. She seems to see

222

eyelashes blinking sweetly: are they the eyes of the chimeras in the Villa Ucrìa laughing at her?

A moment later Marianna gathers the strength to get to her feet. She pours a jug of water over the burning tablecloth. With the wet napkin she covers the lamp, which goes out sizzling. Now the saloon is in darkness. Marianna tries to remember where the door is. The silence suggests flight, but nothing more. Which way? The sound of the sea is growing louder; she can only imagine the noise of its howling by the lurching of the floor that twists, rises and suddenly sinks down under her shoes. Only the thought of Fila in danger stirs her into finding the door. She opens it with difficulty and an avalanche of salt water pours on top of her. How will she climb down the rungs of the ladder in this commotion? Yet she must try, hanging on with both hands to the wooden hand-rail and feeling for each rung with her feet.

As she goes down into the hold of the ship a stench of salted sardines clutches at her throat. Some casks must have shattered, spilling their load of fish. In the darkness, trying to grope her way to the cabin, Marianna feels herself fall against something heavy. It is Fila, her body wet through and trembling. She puts her arms round her and kisses her freezing cheeks. The shapeless thoughts of her companion filter through nostrils soaked with the bitter smell of vomit.

May cancer strike you down, you head of a half-bitch, curse you, why did you make me leave? . . . That duchess, she dragged me with her, she'll be the death of me, donkey head, boiled head, let cancer strike her, curse her, curse her. . . .

In a word, she is swearing at her and at the same time clinging to her with all her strength. It seems certain that they are about to go down with the ship; all they'd like to know is how long it will be before they are swallowed up. Marianna starts reciting a prayer, but she does not manage to reach the end, there is something grotesque in this stupid preparation for death. Yet she does not have any idea what can be done to survive in a sea of this force: she does not even know how to swim. Shutting her eyes she can only hope it will not last long.

But the brigantine miraculously holds its own. Battered as it is by the waves, it withstands the storm, bending and twisting, through the elasticity of its timbers of cedar and chestnut. Mistress and servant remain on their feet with their arms twined round each other, expecting death at any moment. They are so tired that they are overtaken by sleep without realising it, while the salt water pounds their backs with pieces of wood, shoes, sardines, uncoiled ropes and bits of cork.

When the two women wake up it is already morning and they are still in each other's arms, stretched out on the deck right beneath the ladder. An inquisitive seagull watches them from the opening that leads on to the bridge.

XLII

A pilgrim? Perhaps, but pilgrims travel towards a destination. Her feet travel only for the joy of travelling; they do not ever want to stop. Escaping from the silence of her own house to other houses, other silences. A nomad wrestling with fleas, heat, dust. But never really tired, never satiated with seeing new places, new people.

Fila at her side, her small bald head always covered by a bonnet of immaculately clean cotton that is washed every evening and put to dry at the window. Sometimes they do not find a window, and between Naples and Benevento they slept on straw next to a cow who sniffed them with curiosity.

They stopped by the recent excavations at Stabia and Herculaneum. They have eaten water-melon cut in slices by a little boy, on a portable table like the one Marianna uses to write on. They have drunk honey and water sitting in wonder before a large Roman wall-painting in which red and pink mix deliciously together. They have rested in the shade of a gigantic maritime pine after having walked for five hours in the heat. They have ridden mules along the slopes of Vesuvius, their noses peeling in the sun in spite of wearing the straw hats they had bought from a haberdasher in Naples. They have slept in stinking rooms with rotting windows, with a candle end on the floor beside the mattress, on which fleas hopped as if they were on a merry-go-round.

Every now and then, a peasant, a shopkeeper or a squire would follow them, full of curiosity that they were travelling all by themselves. But Marianna's silence and Fila's angry looks soon put them to flight. Once they were robbed on the road to Caserta. They had to abandon to the brigands two heavy bags with brass locks, a silver-mesh chain purse of money, and fifty escudos. But they were not too distressed; the bags had been an encumbrance, and contained dresses they would never wear. The escudos were only part of their money. Fila had hidden the rest of it so well, sewn underneath her petticoat, that the bandits had not found it; and then they had taken pity on the dumb woman and had not even searched her, although she also had money in a pocket of her mantle.

At Capua they made friends with a company of actors travelling to Rome. A comedienne, a young actor, a stage manager, two castrati singers, four servants with a mountain of luggage, and two mongrel dogs. Easy-going and friendly, they spent a great deal of their time eating and playing cards. They were not in the least disconcerted by the Duchess's deafness, and immediately began to talk to her with their hands and their bodies, easily making her understand them and raising peals of laughter from Fila. Naturally it fell to Marianna to pay for supper for everybody, but the actors knew how to return the favour, making everyone laugh by miming their thoughts, whether at the supper table or the card table, in the stage-coaches, or the inns where they stopped the night.

At Gaeta there was a rumour that the road was infested with brigands; a mischievous note warned them that 'for every one hanged a hundred would spring out to replace him, that they had a hide-out in the Ciociaria mountains and were particularly looking for duchesses'. So they decided to embark on a felucca, which took them for only a few escudos. On the boat they played the card games *faraone* and *biribissi* all day long. The manager of the company, Giuseppe Gallo, was the dealer and always lost. To balance this, the two castrati always won. And the comedienne Gilberta Amadio never wanted to go to bed.

In Rome they stayed at the same inn in the Via del Grillo, a small steep street which carriages refused to go up so that they had to make their way on foot from the Piazza del Grillo. One evening Marianna and Fila were invited to the Valle theatre, the only one where the group could play outside the carnival season. They saw an operetta half-sung and half-spoken, in which the comedienne

Gilberta Amadio changed her clothes ten times, running into the wings and reappearing as a shepherdess, a countess, Aphrodite or Juno, while one of the castrati sang in a soft sweet voice and the other, dressed as a shepherd boy, danced. After the play Marianna and Fila were invited to the Fig Tree inn in the Vicolo del Paniere, where they gobbled down huge plates of tripe and put back glass after glass of red wine to celebrate the company's success. Then they all started to dance under the paper lanterns while one of the servants played the mandolin and the other struggled with the flute.

Marianna was tasting her freedom. The past was a tail that she curled up under her skirt, and only made itself felt at rare moments. The future was a nebulous cloud in which could be glimpsed the bright lights of a merry-go-round. And there she stayed, half-fox and half-siren, for once without a ponderous weight inside her head, in the company of people who did not worry about her deafness and talked happily with her, twisting and turning with uninhibited mimicry.

Fila has fallen in love with one of the castrati. This happened at the party after the play, during the dance. Marianna had surprised them kissing behind a pillar and had passed them with a friendly smile. He was a handsome lad, slightly plump, his hair blond and curly. Fila had to stand on tiptoe to embrace him, arching her back in a way that reminded Marianna of Saro.

A jerk, a jump, and the tail uncoils. One does not truly escape by always escaping. Like that character in *The Thousand and One Nights*, who lived in Samarkand. She cannot remember whether it was Nur el Din or Mustafà. He was told, 'Soon you will die in Samarkand', so he galloped full speed to another city. But right in that unknown city, while he was walking peacefully along, he was assassinated, and as he died he saw that the square in which he was attacked was called Samarkand.

Next day the company left for Florence. Fila remained so grief-stricken that she refused all food for a week.

Ciccio Massa, the proprietor of the Grillo inn, himself carries up to Fila's room chicken broth that sends its savoury aroma throughout the house. Since they have been lodging with him he has done nothing but chase after the girl, who, however, really dislikes him. He is a corpulent man with short legs, a boar's eyes, a handsome mouth and an infectious laugh. Quick to use his fists with the scullery boys, he then apologises and treats those he has victimised with generosity. Towards the guests he is affable and nervous, anxious to cut a good figure but at the same time to fleece them of as much money as he can.

Only with Fila is he defenceless. Ever since he first saw her he has stood dazed with admiration every time he meets her. Towards Marianna he often puts on an air of roguish self-conceit and, as far as he can, squeezes a bit more money out of her. Fila has just had her thirty-fifth birthday and has recaptured the beauty she had at eighteen, with an additional sensuality she never possessed before, in spite of her bald head, her scars and her broken teeth. Her skin has become so clear and bright that passers-by turn round in the street to look at her. Her fine grey eyes rest softly on things and people as if she wanted to caress them.

And suppose she were to get married? She would give her a good dowry, Marianna decides, but the prospect of being separated from her is daunting. Then there is the castrato she's in love with. He left for Florence in tears, but he didn't invite her to accompany him. And this caused her so much pain that, either out of spite or to console herself, she has begun to accept the courtship of the boar-like innkeeper.

XLIII

Dear Marianna,

Every human being and every epoch is constantly being threatened by 'an imminent hidden barbarity', as our friend Gian Battista Vico puts it. Your absence has induced a certain negligence in my thoughts, between which weeds have flourished. I am threatened, seriously threatened, by the most perverse indolence, an abandonment of myself, by boredom.

For the rest, the island is in the grip of a new barbarism; while Victor Amadeus of Savoy maintained a certain level of administrative rigour and severity, half-heartedly continued by

227

the Hapsburgs, we now have Charles III re-creating the atmosphere of sloppiness and laxity that so delights our connoisseurs
of ice-cream and sweetmeats.

Here reigns the most judicious injustice. So judicious and so
deep-seated as to be regarded as perfectly 'natural'. And nature
is not to be dictated to, as you well know. Who would think
of changing the colour of their hair or skin? Can a state of
divine authority be transformed into a state of diabolical will?
According to Montesquieu a king has the power to make his
subjects believe that one escudo is equal to two escudos: 'Give
a pension to him who evades two laws, and the government to
him who evades four.'

We are perhaps at the end of a cycle: initially, man's nature
is raw, next it becomes austere, and then benign, then refined,
and finally dissolute. The ultimate stage, if it is not contained,
degenerates into vice, and 'the new barbarity leads men to
destroy everything'. Since your ancestors built the tower at
Scannatura and the lodge at Bagheria much water has passed
under the bridge. Your grandfather tended his vines and olive
trees himself, your father did it through an intermediary. Your
husband from time to time poked his nose into his wine vats.
Your son belongs to a generation that considers the cultivation
of the land to be vulgar and unbecoming. Consequently he has
dedicated his energies solely to himself – and you should see
with what elegant rapacity he does it! Since when, I hear, your
lands at Scannatura are being ruined from lack of attention,
ransacked by the *gabelloti* and deserted by the peasants, the
majority of whom emigrate elsewhere. We are descending with
dancing footsteps towards a happy-go-lucky ebullience that is
much enjoyed by the Palermitans of our time, or rather the
time of our sons: an ebullience that has all the appearance of
action since it contains within it what I dare to call perpetual
motion. These young people rush around from morning till night,
busying themselves with visits, balls, dinners, love affairs and
gossip to such an extent that they are left without a moment's
boredom.

Your son Mariano, who has inherited your beautiful forehead
and your melting, sparkling eyes, has become famous for his
prodigality, which is worthy of our king Charles III, and for
his suppers to which friends, relations, all are invited. You say

he likes to dream and there is no doubt that when he does it is on a grandiose scale. And while he dreams he is setting the table for a banquet. Probably he stuns his guests with food and wine to make sure they don't wake him up. It seems that he had a carriage made for himself equal to that of the Viceroy Fogliani, Marquis of Pellegrino, with wheels of gilded wood and thirty statuettes of silver on the roof, not to speak of coats of arms, and golden tassels hanging from every corner. The Viceroy Fogliani Aragone got to know of it and sent for him to tell him not to be such a show-off, but your sublime son and heir has refused to take any notice.

Other news of your dear ones you will have already had, I imagine. Your daughter Felice has become famous in Palermo for her cures of erysipelas and scabies and all the different varieties of eczema. She charges the rich huge sums and the poor nothing. For this she is much loved, even if many people criticise her for the way she goes about all on her own, a nun like she is, taking the reins of a large Arab horse, sitting on the box of a small gig and always going like the wind. Her project to help the derelicts of the Leprosi swallows up so much money that she has had to seek a loan from a moneylender in the Badia Nuova. To pay off these debts it seems that she has been involved in clandestine abortions. But this is inside information, professional integrity ought to prevent my giving it to you; but you know how my love overcomes all my scruples, all my responsibility.

Your second daughter Giuseppa allowed herself to be found in her husband's bed with her cousin Olivo. The two men challenged each other to a duel. They fought, but neither of them was killed: two cowards who abandoned their weapons at the first drop of blood. Now the beautiful Giuseppa is expecting a child and no one knows whether it is her husband's or her cousin's. But it will be accepted by her husband as his, because otherwise he would have to kill her and he certainly has no wish to do that. Olivo has been sent to France by his father Signoretto, who, it seems, threatened to disinherit him even though he is the eldest son.

As for Manina, she has just given birth to yet another son, whom she has called Mariano after her great-grandfather. At the baptism all the family were there, including Abbot Carlo, who has recently adopted the severe mien of a great scholar.

Actually people come from universities all over Europe to ask him to decipher ancient manuscripts. He is considered a celebrity in Palermo and the Senate has proposed to give him an award of merit. In that case it will be I who deliver it to him in a velvet case.

Your protégé Saro: it seems that he was so upset by your departure that he refused all food for weeks. But then he got over it. And now it appears that he and his wife are having the time of their lives in your villa at Bagheria, where he receives visitors as if he were a baron. He gives orders and spends money like water, at your expense.

For the rest, the person who should be setting a good example could not care less. Charles III, our king, and his delicious consort Donna Amalia force the courtiers to kneel for hours while they are dining. The Queen, they say, amuses herself by dipping biscuits into a goblet full of Canary wine, which her ladies-in-waiting have to hold up to her while they remain on their knees. Good theatre, don't you think? But maybe this is all gossip, I personally have never been present at such scenes. On the other hand the great Princess of Savoy has lost all her prestige since the baby she gave birth to, with the help of a surgeon, turned out to be a girl.

I have to admit that I have become transformed into a third-rate moralist. I can already see your face darken, your lips press together, as only you know how to do, with all the subtle ferocity of your dumbness. But you must know that it is the impairment of half your senses that has brought me into the orbit of your thoughts: they have become luxuriant and flourishing precisely because of the withdrawal from the world which has driven you into the recesses of your library with your books and notebooks. Your intelligence has taken such a strange and unusual course that it has induced in me a delicious longing for love. Something I felt to be impossible at my age and that I value as a miracle of the imagination.

I am writing to you to ask you once more with all the solemnity of the written word: will you marry me? I am not asking you for anything, not even to share my bed, if you prefer not to do so. I would like to take you as you are now, without villas and estates, without possessions, children, houses, carriages or servants. My feeling is born out of a need for companionship that consumes me like butter melting in the sun. The companionship of a woman devoted to the use of her intelligence, something so very rare in our women, who are kept in a state of gallinaceous ignorance.

The more I become involved in my work, the more people I see, the more noblemen I visit, the more deeply I sink into the solitude of a hermit. Is it only the dazzling light of the *esprit de finesse* of Pascal that brings me to you, or is it something else? A movement of currents strong enough to warm the ocean? It is your disability that makes you unique, deprived of the privileges that you are nevertheless entitled to through your birthright, outside the stereotypes of your social position, in spite of it being part of your very flesh.

I come from a family of honest notaries and honest lawyers, or perhaps dishonest, who knows? The rapid achievement of social advancement and financial success cannot be entirely honest. My grandfather (but I confess it to you alone) bought the title of baron for his modest and vain bourgeois family, who wanted to improve their status. All this counts for very little, I know. My eyes have learned to see beyond the robes and redingotes, let alone the full-skirted dresses and pastel-coloured hoop petticoats.

You know too how to see beyond the damasks and the pearls, your impairment has brought you to writing, and writing has brought you to me. Both of us use our eyes to survive and we nourish ourselves like moths greedy for rice paper, lime-flower paper, sugar paper, so long as it is written on in ink.

'The heart has its reasons that reason does not know', as my friend Pascal liked to say, and they are dark reasons that sink their roots into the buried parts of ourselves, where old age is not transformed into loss but into a fullness of purpose. I know my defects, which are many. To start with, a certain perversity acquired as a result of so many years of stupid censure directed against the ideas which I value. Not to speak of the hypocrisy that has devoured me alive. However, I owe it a great deal at times, I think it is my greatest virtue, since it has rewarded me with the patience of a hermit. And it is not entirely separate from a wholly mundane ability to 'understand the other'; yes, hypocrisy is the mother of tolerance . . . or is it the daughter? In any case they are close relations.

I often let myself be overwhelmed by gossip in spite of the horror I have of it. But if one looks into it deeply one discovers that it is gossip that really lies at the roots of literature. Is not Monsieur Montesquieu with his Persian letters a gossip? And what about those missives that drip with humour and malice? Is not our own Signor Dante Alighieri a gossip? Who more than he amuses himself relating all the secret vices and weaknesses of friends and acquaintances? . . . Humour, on which writers slake their thirst with such grace, somehow emerges second-hand from the capacity of writers to throw light on the defects of others and make them seem gross and unredeemable, while they themselves nonchalantly overlook the beam that sails in their own dreamy eyes. Do you not agree, even you?

Here I am as usual trying to justify myself. Is it that I am trying to stir you by using my own self-deprecation as a bait to pull you from the still waters of your silence? I am even more perverse than you think. Of a selfishness that is at times repellent. But the fact that I exhibit my selfishness may mean that it is not the whole truth. I am a deliberate liar. But, as you know, Solon said that at Agira they were all liars – and he himself was from Agira! So was what he said the truth or was it a lie? Or was it a trick to keep you in suspense? Turn over the page, my dear dumb one, and you will find something else to chew on. Perhaps another request for love, perhaps some precious information, or perhaps only another exhibition of vanity. My sensibilities are too crippled, suffocated by the commonplaceness of the world. And yet the world is the only place I would agree to be in. I do not believe I would willingly go to paradise even if the streets were clean, with no intolerable stinks, no stabbings, hangings, extortions, rapes, thieving, adultery or prostitution. What on earth would one do all day? Only go for walks and play *faraone* and *biribissi*.

Know that I await you with a calm mind, trusting your head with its long-sighted vision. I do not say trusting your body because it is as obstinate as a mule, but I turn towards those open spaces in your head where the sea air glides, where you are the most communicative, the most inclined to curiosity, to love; or so I flatter myself to believe. . . . You know, it is often the love of others that causes us to fall in love with them: we see a person only when they invite us to see them.

With all my most tender devotion and the wish that you may return soon. I am lost without you.

Giacomo Camalèo

Marianna gazes down at the sheets of paper that lie untidily on her striped skirt. The letter aroused in her a feeling of weariness, but now makes her smile. Her gaze dims as her nostalgia for Palermo overcomes her. Those smells of seaweed dried by the sun, of capers, of ripe figs, she will never find them anywhere else; those burnt and scented shores, those waves slowly breaking, jasmine petals flaking in the sun. So many rides with Saro towards the Aspra promontory, where intoxicating smells and tastes would overcome them with delight. Dismounting, they would sit down on domes of seaweed out of which swarmed crowds of sea-lice, and would let themselves be brushed by a gentle breeze from Africa. Their hands, groping backwards like crabs, would search blindly, holding each other until their wrists hurt. There would be a long interweaving of arms, of fingers . . . and then, then, where to put her tongue in a kiss that knocks her in the face with the thrill and daring of its novelty? What to do with her teeth that crave to bite? Eyes dissolving into eyes, heart turning somersaults, hours stopping in mid-air . . . and the intense smell of salt seaweed. The hard round pebbles against her back became feather cushions while they held each other in the shelter of an acacia tree, its branches swaying over the water. How has she been able to survive since the moment those embraces were forbidden by her cruel and indomitable will? But she cannot prevent them rising up again like restless corpses that refuse to sink out of sight.

Since Fila has got married to Ciccio Massa, she is finding it difficult to remain at the inn. In spite of Fila saying how she wants to continue serving her, in spite of the way both of them fill her up with food and look after her as if she were a child, she wakes up every morning with the idea of leaving. To return to her children, to the villa, to Saro, to the chimeras? Or to stay? To escape from all those so familiar habits that make up the routine of her life or to take heed of those wings that have sprouted from both sides of her ankles?

Marianna crumples the ten small pages into her skirt pocket and looks round her, seeking some reply to her mute question. There is the sun. There is the river Tiber flowing at her feet, viscous, streaked with yellow. A tuft of reeds of the clearest pale green is bent by the current towards the shore, flattened by the water until it is submerged. Then it lifts itself up again in all its brightness. A myriad of tiny silver fish dart upstream to where the water is almost still, forming a lake between tufts of nettles and spikes of thistles. A succulent smell rises from the water, wet earth, mint, elder. A little further up, the prow of a flat-bottomed boat slips along a taut rope that holds it moored to the bank. Still further away, washerwomen kneel on the stones and rinse their washing in the water. Another boat, or rather a raft, with two oarsmen standing up, moves slowly from one side of the river to the other, transporting cinnamon-coloured sacks and cartwheels.

Higher up, the port of Ripetta opens like a fan with its stone steps, its iron bollards, its low walls of unplastered brick, its seats of white marble, its bustle of longshoremen. In that tranquil noonday Marianna asks herself if she could ever possess this landscape, make a home for herself, a refuge. Now everything is strange to her and therefore valued. But for how long can she expect things around her to remain foreign, perfectly intelligible, yet far away and impossible to decipher?

This withdrawal from the future that is sealing her fate, will it be too great a challenge for her strength? This wish to wander, to meet different kinds of people, is there something arrogant about it, something a little frivolous and perverse? Where will she go to make a home for herself when every home seems too sunk in its roots, too predictable? She would like to be able to carry her home on her back like a snail and go off into the unknown. To suppress the remembrance of those ardent embraces that she so longs for will not be easy. The sluice-gate is there to intercept every drop of memory, every crumb of happiness. But there must also be something else, something that belongs to the world of wisdom and contemplation, something that deflects the mind from its foolish preoccupation with the senses.

It is disgraceful for a well-born woman to drift restlessly, aimlessly from one inn to another, from one city to another, her son Mariano would say, and perhaps he would be right. This rushing from here to there, setting off, stopping, waiting, wandering, is it not a premonition of her end? To walk straight into the waters of the river, first the tips of her shoes, then up to

234

her ankles, then gradually up to her knees, her chest, her throat. The water is not cold. It would not be difficult to let herself be swallowed by those eddying currents with their smell of decaying leaves.

But the will to resume her journey is stronger. Marianna fixes her gaze on the gurgling yellow water. She questions her silences. But the only answer she receives is another question. And it is mute.